TWO DAZZLING SISTERS—
THEY CRAVED ALL THAT
LIFE AND LOVE COULD GIVE

They were two sisters who hungered for the world beyond their Italian-American family and the Pittsburgh slums. Angie's gorgeous voice and looks were her passport to the great stages of Europe—and to protection from men powerful enough to make and break their own rules. Nickie's brains and beauty took her to the top of the banking world. But both would pay the price: Angie, in her affair with a man she loved but could not marry; Nickie, in her marriage to a man she could not love . . . and both in a battle against Mafia evil, and a final showdown with past passions.

BOUND BY
BLOOD

BOUND
BY
BLOOD

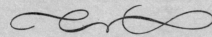

June Triglia

AN ONYX BOOK

NEW AMERICAN LIBRARY

A DIVISION OF PENGUIN BOOKS USA INC.

PUBLISHER'S NOTE

This book is a work of fiction. Names, characters, places, and incidents either are the product of the author's imagination or are used fictitiously, and any resemblance to actual persons, living or dead, events, or locales is entirely coincidental.

NAL BOOKS ARE AVAILABLE AT QUANTITY DISCOUNTS WHEN USED TO PROMOTE PRODUCTS OR SERVICES. FOR INFORMATION PLEASE WRITE TO PREMIUM MARKETING DIVISION, NEW AMERICAN LIBRARY, 1633 BROADWAY, NEW YORK, NEW YORK 10019.

ONYX TRADEMARK REG. U.S. PAT. OFF. AND FOREIGN COUNTRIES
REGISTERED TRADEMARK—MARCA REGISTRADA
HECHO EN DRESDEN, TN, U.S.A.

SIGNET, SIGNET CLASSIC, MENTOR, ONYX, PLUME, MERIDIAN and NAL BOOKS are published by New American Library, a division of Penguin Books USA Inc., 1633 Broadway, New York, New York 10019

First Printing, March, 1989

1 2 3 4 5 6 7 8 9

PRINTED IN THE UNITED STATES OF AMERICA

For Uncle Joe
whose warmth, vitality and eagerness
to embrace life were an inspiration

ACKNOWLEDGMENTS

Much gratitude and love to parents, sisters, aunts, uncles, cousins, and friends, and to past generations of Triglias, who provided the rich mosaic of memories from which this story and these characters emerged.

"And ever has it been that love knows not its own depth until the hour of separation."
—KAHLIL GIBRAN

Prelude

Angie dragged the last cardboard box from the barn into the yard. Where patches of snow remained, the box slid easily. Otherwise, she had to jerk and rock it back and forth across the packed dirt.

At last she reached the creek bank. She dumped the full carton over the edge and watched the unlabeled bottles crack and shatter as they rolled down the embankment. The ditch reeked of liquor—the light sweetish odor of bootleg Canadian whiskey.

Angie surveyed her afternoon's labor with grim satisfaction. Two hundred broken bottles lay strewn along the muddy, half-frozen creekbed: housekeeping with a vengeance. The empty cardboard boxes littered the flat landscape like a child's wooden blocks.

A sharp wind rose, whipping around the farmhouse and catching the endless rows of dead cornstalks. The eerie, chafing sound reminded Angie of a razor honed against a strop.

She returned to the wreckage of the house. Broken records lay scattered across the parlor rug like shards of black glass. The only ones she had spared were the old opera records. She put Puccini's *Turandot* on the turntable and guided the needle till she found "In questa reggia." Then she turned the volume up full blast until the soprano's wildly passionate vendetta against men filled the house.

Driven by the music, Angie climbed the stairs to the bedroom, where a fire burned in the old-fashioned grate. Yet for all the warmth of the room, she felt cold. She opened the closet and methodically stripped her husband's clothing from the hangers, tossing the handmade Italian suits and shoes, the silk ties and expensive fedoras into a jumbled heap next to the fireplace. Then she picked up a poker and started to jab each piece of clothing into the fire, as if each vicious shove could counter the memory of his brand of lovemaking, thrusting and tearing her.

A car door slammed out in the yard. Angie jumped up and ran to the window. Watching Tony's squat, bullet-shaped body emerge from behind the wheel, she felt a shiver of foreboding. She had meant to be gone before he returned. Now it was too late. . . .

She jerked open a drawer in the bedside table, where Tony kept a loaded pistol within easy reach. The weapon gleamed dully, full of menace. She had always been afraid of his guns, sickened by the sight of them. Now, without hesitation, she pulled out the .38 automatic and ran her fingers caressingly along the barrel, familiarizing herself with the feel of it. The weapon was no longer a threat but an ally.

She sat on the bed, staring at her reflection in the wardrobe mirror. The face that stared back at her was that of a stranger's. The music had ended, and the only noise filling the house was the rapid clicks of Tony's heels on the stairs.

"Bastard," she whispered, cocking the hammer of the pistol, "we're going to settle this once and for all."

Act One

1

A heady scent of perfume lingered in the foyer of the rectory. Angie Branzino hurried down the wide hall, eager for a glimpse of the rich committee ladies who had come from the archdiocese downtown. She observed them through the French doors that opened onto Father Lucatta's parlor: elegant and assured in their afternoon frocks as they made themselves comfortable. They may have ventured to the south hills of Pittsburgh on a mission of charity, but somehow Angie knew that the stench of burning coal and the mean poverty beyond the churchyard wall would never touch them.

As Father Lucatta sat beneath the painting of the Last Supper that graced the fireplace mantel, he looked a little like a long-suffering saint himself. He frowned when he saw Angie peeping into the room and gestured her away. She turned and saw her younger sister Nickie coming toward her.

Angie pulled her back to the kitchen. "We've got to get to work."

"Can I help you serve?"

"No."

"Why not?"

"Because it's my job." Angie stopped before the hall mirror, smoothing the collar of her blouse that she had turned and restitched as soon as she had heard about the society ladies' visit. If they meant to pity the raggedy mill families, they had another thought coming. "Go on, Nickie. You're not even supposed to be out here."

"I just want to sneak a look at them. Swells don't

come to Coalport every day." Her husky voice dropped an octave lower. "No one will even see me, I swear."

"Fat chance. Come on, you have a sinkful of dishes to do."

"The story of my life. I slave in the back like Cinderella while you get to hobnob with the Johnny Bulls."

As Nickie held up an imaginary teacup with her pinkie extended, Angie caught her arm and gave her a little push toward the kitchen. "Poor little *poverita*," she needled her.

"Don't touch me!" Nickie flounced away. At fifteen, she was all angles and slants, like a half-starved cat.

Angie followed her back into the kitchen, guiltily remembering her own fascination with Father Lucatta's visitors. "Listen, Nick," she said, picking up the heavily laden tea tray, "maybe it wouldn't hurt if you came and took a quick peek, so long as no one saw you."

Nickie acted like she hadn't heard.

"Okay, forget it, then," Angie said in her soft, musical voice, despairing of ever seeing eye to eye with her tomboy sister. They had always been as different as breadsticks and sugar buns. Where Nickie was brittle and quick to take umbrage, Angie was more yielding and roundly feminine. They didn't even look like sisters. The curly black hair that framed Angie's pale olive skin was more striking than Nickie's tawny Buster Brown mop. Yet for all their differences, they maintained a combative closeness.

"Wait!" Nickie called out as Angie picked up the tea tray. Grabbing a can of olive oil from the pantry shelf, she poured a little out onto a dishcloth. Then she hurried over, knelt down, and rubbed it across the scuffed toes of Angie's shoes.

"Thanks." As Nickie straightened up, Angie gave her a conspiratorial smile. "Come on. Just stay out of sight."

Outside the glass parlor door, Angie paused to rebalance the tray in her arms. Her eyes swept the room. The women were seated on a pair of worn sofas that flanked the fireplace. How stylish they looked as they nodded to each other, their feathered hats bobbing like birds on a telephone wire. There was no use kidding herself. The restitched collar and Nickie's last-minute shoeshine couldn't change the facts. Self-consciously she pushed open the door.

"But there must be something more we can do," one woman was saying. The sharp, metallic ring of her voice seemed at odds with her almost girlish features. Angie guessed she was her mother's age, but the woman seemed twenty years younger. Not a thread of gray showed in her carefully coiffed strawberry-blond waves. "Distribution of clothing hardly seems enough."

"You're right, Mrs. Donahue," another woman said, taking a cup from Angie's tray. "But what more can be done?"

As Angie circled the room, her eyes moved surreptitiously toward Mrs. Donahue, fascinated by the svelte matron's air of assurance.

"I should think what these immigrants need to be taught is some self-restraint," Mrs. Donahue said to the room at large, fastidiously selecting a single sandwich from the proffered tray. "The creatures breed like rabbits. Unconscionable behavior, with so many mouths to feed in these terrible times."

Father Lucatta tut-tutted anxiously. "Now, Mrs. Donahue, we believe the Lord will provide—"

"Yes, indeed, he will. With a helping hand from the Ladies Auxiliary for the Poor."

The priest didn't reply, evidently too timid to confront such arrogance.

"Fiona," called a cultured but rather strained voice from the other side of the room, "do you honestly think it's our place to judge?" Angie turned to look at the woman with the fair features who had spoken up. Though she was the picture of elegance in her tailored green suit and stylish hat, her face looked terribly drawn. "Wasn't it Beethoven who was the seventh child in a desperately poor family? Your philosophy would have denied the world his genius."

Rather than replying, Fiona Donahue gave Angie an accusing stare, as if searching for signs of genius and finding her wanting.

A third woman said, "Perhaps we should consider some sort of nutritional program in the schools." She directed a pitying look at Angie. "How they subsist on their macaroni is beyond me."

Stung by their condescension, Angie ignored Father Lucatta's frantic head shaking and said, "I guess someone should have had a word with Marco Polo."

The woman looked confused. "What?"

"You know," Angie said, trying to look innocent. "Before he carted it all that way from China."

"Ahem, Angelina," Father Luc intervened. "Perhaps more hot water from the kitchen?"

"Yes, Father."

"Mollycoddling isn't the answer. Don't you agree, Father Lucatta?" Mrs. Donahue said as Angie moved toward the door. "Why, this city's been overrun as it is with these immigrant Johnny-come-latelys."

When Angie turned to glare at her, Mrs. Donahue took the opportunity to press her point home. "May I ask, young woman, when your family arrived in America?"

"I think it was '92," Angie said, her dark eyes flashing, "1492."

The fair-haired woman who had mentioned Beethoven started to cough behind her handkerchief, but the sound was suspiciously like muffled laughter.

A loud clatter from the foyer made everyone jump. Startled, the group of women leaned forward. Angie turned to see Nickie hastily righting the hall tree and picking up the coats and purses that had fallen.

"I left my pocketbook out there." Mrs. Donahue hurried out into the hall. "That's all I would need, to have it stolen."

Angie and the woman with the hanky hurriedly followed her. "My sister is not a thief," Angie protested.

"We'll see about that." Mrs. Donahue collared Nickie and pinched her arm. "Young lady, what do you have to say for yourself?"

"You're hurting me!"

Father Lucatta intervened, his neck jutting like a crane's out of his collar. "I can assure you, Nicoletta is not a thief. These girls come from a good family—desperately poor but honorable."

"Very touching, Father," Mrs. Donahue said, her expression still accusatory. "But whatever their background, it doesn't excuse cheek."

"Fiona, please," the other woman interceded. "I'm certain it was just an accident. You know what a clumsy stage girls go through—all arms and legs."

"I'll thank you to stay out of this, Josephine."

The women returned to the parlor, leaving Angie to smile apologetically at Father Lucatta over her empty tray. "Should I get that hot water for tea?"

"I think you girls have done, ahem, quite enough. Mrs. Connell will be back soon."

"Yes, Father."

Nickie was perched on a stool in the kitchen, buttering a slice of bread, when Angie walked in, shaking her head. "We embarrassed poor Father Luc."

"He'll get over it," Nickie said, biting into the bread. "Boy, this store-bought stuff tastes like mush. Know what I could go for? A real 'sangwich' with Pap's tomatoes."

"Now you're dreaming. Summer's over," Angie said, her own mouth watering at the thought of the round loaves their father would bake every Saturday out in the yard, the outsides crusty brown and the insides softly fermented. After Pap had pulled out the last hot pans with his wooden *pala*, they would make sandwiches with the tomatoes too bruised for the boys to sell door to door. If he was in a good mood, they got a drizzle of olive oil with a dusting of fresh *basilico* on top. But Pap's good moods were rare. Once he had caught Vic bruising the tomatoes on purpose and had beaten the hell out of him.

"Well, guess I better make some more of those little tea sandwiches, just in case. And you better get those dishes done. Now."

As Angie worked, music from Rossini's *La Cenerentola* drifted through her mind. The snobbish Fiona Donahue reminded her of Cinderella's stepmother. She hummed and then started to sing her favorite aria from the romantic opera, "Una volta c'era un re."

Nickie, as familiar as Angie with the old opera records Pap played on their battered Victrola, chimed in. "Long ago there lived a king. . . ." Her off-key singing dwindled off as her sister's clear, strong soprano rippled effortlessly over the joyous runs.

When Angie at last turned around, she stared in shock at Nickie, who stood preening in an ermine-trimmed, white silk bedjacket. "For Pete's sake!" she exclaimed, "where'd you find that thing?"

"It just attacked me, Ange." Nickie grinned, gesturing toward the box of donated clothing in the corner. "I swear, it jumped right up onto my body."

"Well, take it off right now. How many times in a day do you want to be accused of stealing?"

"The box says 'clothes for the poor,' " Nickie said defensively, running her hands in a slow, luxuriant movement along the soft fur. "Or did we get rich when I wasn't looking?" She batted her eyelashes and took a deep drag on an imaginary cigarette. "Yes, Clark dahling, I'd love another glass of champagne."

"Very funny," Angie said, pulling the jacket off Nickie's shoulders. "Now put it back."

"Come on, Ange, let me keep it." Nickie's fingers dug into the slippery silk. "I want to wear it home."

"Are you nuts? Pap'd kill you if he saw you in that thing."

"Wait! We could use the fur to make a collar for Mama," Nickie wheedled. "It would keep her neck warm all winter."

"What a generous soul you are, always thinking about everyone else. And what about me?" Angie teased her. "What do I get out of it?"

"We'll share." Nickie slipped out of the bedjacket and held it out for her to try on.

Angie couldn't resist. "La donn' e mobile . . ." She sang another bit of Italian opera, mugging before an imaginary audience as she slipped into the froufrou bedjacket.

"*Bravissima*," said a soft, well-bred voice from the hall.

The girls whirled around, staring horrified at the woman who had been watching them for God knew how long. Angie realized it was the fair-haired woman who had come to Nickie's defense. What could she possibly want in Father Luc's kitchen?

Feeling ridiculous, Angie squirmed out of the bedjacket and tossed it back to Nickie.

"You must forgive me for eavesdropping," the woman said, "but I couldn't help hearing you singing a few moments ago as I came out of the powder room. Your voice is wonderful."

Angie stared at her warily.

The woman persisted. "Have you had voice lessons?"

"I learned from my father's records. We have lots by Caruso. He's Italian, you know," Angie said, then hastened to clarify: "I mean, Caruso's Italian, too."

"Yes, I'm familiar with opera." Her voice caught, and she blinked quickly. "My daughter played many of the overtures on the piano."

Just then Father Lucatta's housekeeper bustled into the kitchen, her bosom puffed up with self-importance. "Mrs. Urbano! Is there some—" Her unctuous greeting gave way to a squawk of dismay when she saw Nickie pulling on the silk bedjacket. "Where in the name of the sweet Virgin did you get that? Miss Nicoletta Branzino, you should have a switch taken to you. Going around like a tart."

"Can't blame me," Nickie said, her eyes sliding toward the elegant woman. "We just found it in the box these ladies brought."

"You know how sick our mother is," Angie chimed in, even though she wanted to strangle Nickie. "We thought she'd like the warm fur."

"And your sister wouldn't have been wanting it for herself, now, would she?"

"No, ma'am."

"Hmph." Mrs. Connell glared at the girls, before turning an ingratiating smile on Mrs. Urbano. "Now, would there be anything you're needing, ma'am?"

"Not really," the woman said with a faint smile, and she headed back into the meeting.

"You deserved to have your ears boxed," Angie said as they left the church rectory. "You better just hope that's as far as it goes."

Nickie stopped rubbing her ears and reached underneath her baggy blouse. Triumphantly she pulled out the bedjacket. "That old Irish witch didn't get the best of me."

"You little *pistad!* Don't you ever learn?"

"I had to have it, Ange." She skipped out of her sister's reach. "I bet you a nickel it belonged to that Mrs. Urbano. Who ever heard of a dago with money? Think she lives with those other 'mericans out in Highland Park?"

Angie replied wistfully, "Didn't you love her green suit?"

Nickie smoothed the wrinkled silk bedjacket and put it on, along with the rich lady's persona. "Your voice is wonderful," she murmured in exaggerated mimicry of the woman's cultured tone. "Have you had formal lessons?"

"But of course, dahling. You've heard of Papa Branzino's pasta-drainer method? When he zings it past your head, you're guaranteed to screech a perfect high C."

Nickie suddenly looked worried. "You aren't going to tell Pap about my taking the jacket, are you, Ange?"

"Not a chance, Nickolodeon." Angie ruffled her sister's fly-away bangs. "Come on, we better hurry."

"For what, Pap's Roman beans and rice?" Nickie grimaced. "I want, just once, champagne and caviar."

"You don't even know what caviar is."

"Sure I do. It's a Russian steak or something." Affronted by Angie's laughter, she snapped, "Well, what is it, smartass?"

"Fish eggs."

"How disgusting! You're lying just to make me sick."

The girls started the steep climb up Millbridge Street, past the Slovak church with its onion-domed spire and the old women in babuskas peeling potatoes outside their doors. Midway up the street Rome and Warsaw met, a national boundary as distinct as any on a map.

Italian immigrant families claimed the top of the hill. Their narrow wooden houses clung to the edge of a river valley congested with the sprawl of the steel mills. On most days, row upon row of Bessemer furnaces belched the sulphuric fumes of burning coke, that left a gritty mantle on white collars and curtains. Angie barely noticed the stench that clung to the hills. It was as familiar as the scent of her own body.

That day the mills were down. Though she knew that

the work slowdowns of the Depression meant more hardship for them all, she couldn't help savoring the clean air and warmth of the October afternoon. A trailing edge of pink tinged the clouds over the far hills, their outlines luminous in the clear light.

The girls' steps quickened as they crossed onto Mitchell Avenue, dodging the purple-stained crates stacked helter-skelter along the sidewalk. Winemaking was an autumn ritual for the Italians on the hill. Crushed and fermenting in basement handpresses, grapes gave off their pungent essence until the air itself seemed to breathe and glow like a rich claret.

Even Prohibition hadn't stopped their vital cultural tradition. The neighborhood had immediately set to work, gouging crude tunnels through the soft limestone that lay under their hill. The tunnels still connected basements along Mitchell Avenue, although they had been boarded up for two years now. Their Uncle Lorenzo had dreamed up the tunnel system to secretly move his wine to Cheech Ignacio's speakeasy on the corner. Angie had vivid memories of Z'Lrenzo's wry jokes, comparing the snooping Prohibition officials to the ancient Romans harassing the early Christians.

Every family had its favorite winemaking method. But year in and year out, their aunt's recipe was generally, if reluctantly, acknowledged the best. A bitter pill indeed for the men of the neighborhood. Widowed seven years since the death of Z'Lorenzo, their Aunt Maria made a nice living selling her delicious wine. Only the family knew her jealously guarded secret: a bottle of whiskey in each barrel to smooth out the harsh "dago red."

Today the whole neighborhood vibrated with life. Cheech, sweeping the sidewalk outside his tiny bar, hailed the Branzino girls cheerfully. So did Elvira Battaglia, shaking her head in wonderment at Nickie's get-up. Next door Signora Trumbo stepped out to shake a rug and stayed to gossip with her neighbor. The women spoke in quick rat-a-tat bursts, eyes darting between Nickie and their open kitchen doors, where chopped garlic could be seen frying on the stovetops.

The girls linked arms, giggling to themselves. At last they saw their mother sitting in a chair on the sidewalk, her cane propped against her knee. She snapped green beans into a pot while Z'Maria stood beside her, arms crossed over her wine-stained apron as she talked. She raised an arm in greeting, and Angie returned her aunt's wave. How different her aunt was from her mother. Unlike Rosa's wispy white hair, Z'Maria's was a thick iron-gray and gathered up into a knot, its position high or low on the back of her head according to her mood. She brooked no nonsense from anyone, least of all from Pap. Angie was crazy about her.

Z'Maria's compact bungalow adjoined theirs on the hill, much to her brother-in-law's everlasting dismay. The Branzinos' own ramshackle house was perched precariously below street level on the ravine edge. The design was so haphazard it looked as if it might crash down at any second. The back parlor and porch sloped crazily and were cantilevered over the ravine. Pap had built the place himself; sometimes Angie wondered if its narrow meanness and skewed angles were a self-portrait in clapboard and shingles.

Rushing ahead to show off her treasure to the two women, Nickie collided with her six-year-old sister, Gina, who had just dashed up the steps from the house. Unfazed, the tiny girl hoisted herself up onto the street-level fence, and straddled it.

"Hi, Ange!" she squeaked.

"Give me a kiss, *carina*."

"Can't! Phil's doin' his 'speriment down under the porch and he gave me a job," she said importantly. "Soon's I see Papa, I'm s'posed to do this." Before Angie could stop her, Gina had put her thumb and forefinger to her mouth and emitted a piercing whistle.

Twelve-year-old Vic came vaulting up the stairs three at a time, his brown eyes enormous in his skinny face. "You seen him? Is he coming?"

"Never mind," Angie said quickly. "It's okay."

Vic slumped against the fence. "Aw, Gina, you scared the crap outta us. We told you not to whistle unless you really seen him."

"He's right," Angie said, waving Vic back down the stairs. "It's no game, honey."

Gina looked solemn. "Pap ain't gonna hit us, is he?"

"No, honey, I won't let him. Here, let me wipe those smudges off your cheeks," she said to her squirming sister. "You look like a *tootzun* in a minstrel show."

Then Angie sidled toward the women, her smile constricting as she bent to kiss her mother. How fragile Mama seems, she thought. Her legs were swollen with dropsy and her prematurely white hair was pulled back from sharp, high cheekbones that retained a pale echo of rosiness. The birth of seven healthy children, the loss of two more as infants, and the trauma of three miscarriages had robbed her of her health. Yet her eyes were soft and full of loving laughter as she greeted her first-born.

"Hey, Ange, tell Mama," Nickie said, preening in the bedjacket. "She doesn't believe someone wears this to bed."

"Angelina, is true?" Rosa murmured. Her voice rasped with the constant battle to get enough air.

Angie nodded, laughing. "She found it in the poor box. And you know Nickie, Mama."

"Struttin' like a *putan'*," Z'Maria groused, swaying her bony hips in comically lewd mimicry of a whore. "Why you no give her a good backhand?"

Sensing which way the wind was blowing, Nickie retreated out of range and grinned at Angie. "Hey, Ange, tell them what the lady said to you."

Rosa's eyes sparkled. "*Che*, Angelina?"

"Oh, it was silly. Nothing."

"The lady thought she had voice lessons."

"No!" Mama smiled.

"Yes." Nickie lowered her naturally husky voice. "And here she is, straight from her triumph in New York, Angelina Branzino."

Taking the cue, Angie clasped her hands rigidly in front of her, puffed up her cheeks like a hefty soprano, and belted out "Yes, Sir, That's My Baby" in a tinny falsetto until Mama and Z'Maria were both convulsed with laughter.

Across the street, Gumbari Niello stuck her head out the door. She shuffled across the street to join them. "I'm glad you can laugh," the woman muttered, her deepset eyes lugubrious with gloom. "My Giuseppe, he say trouble come again. The plant, she gonna cut back some more. Hard enough for me with six mouths. But you, Rosa"—she shook her head accusingly, as if Rosa's laughter had invited the tragedies—"my Giuseppe, he say—"

"Your sauce is as sour as your tongue," Z'Maria answered her tartly in Italian. "I'm not surprised your Giuseppe farts and thinks he's a fortune-teller."

"You're one to talk," the woman fired back, "you who couldn't give your Lorenzo one child before he died."

"Any animal can breed."

"Pah!" The two women glared at each other.

Before they could launch into battle anew, Angie put in quickly, "Mama, look what I brought for you." She handed her mother a small parcel wrapped in butcher's paper. "They call it a tea sandwich."

"Sangwich? No!" Rosa examined the cream cheese and cucumber tidbit. "It's a communion wafer." She divided it and gave bites to the other two women, helping them forget their squabble.

As she chomped on the delicate morsel, Z'Maria focused again on Nickie's outlandish jacket. "What da hell this world come to?"

"Hey, where's Phil?" Nickie said quickly.

Z'Maria grunted. "Leonardo da Vinci's under the porch."

"My Giuseppe, he say that boy gonna blow us all to kingdom come one day." As she spoke, her out-of-work husband opened the window and called gruffly to her.

What a pair those Niellos were, Angie thought as she went down the steps to the house. The old timers' bleak peasant fatalism drove her nuts. But her own father was the worst of all. His pessimism lay like a pall over all of his children.

Angie joined Nickie on the wobbly back porch, her eyes fixed on Phil as he raced around the dirt yard. Like the rest of the kids, he had a scrawny, underfed look, but his nose had grown into manhood ahead of the rest of him and jutted out of his skinny face. Angie smiled as she watched him hover like an anxious mother over his experiment. The weird contraption consisted of a funnel-shaped pipe, a pump to spray in kerosene, and an old car battery—all of which he had mounted onto a little wagon. According to him, if he could get the gas fumes to ignite inside the pipe, the whole thing should push forward.

Phil motioned for the younger boys to take cover. "Come on, you guys, hurry up!" he shouted, as jittery as a sparrow.

Freddie ducked behind the corner of the house while Vic crouched next to one of the porch pillars, getting as close as Phil would allow. As usual, dreamy-eyed Pete was more interested in the crabapple he was eating.

Vic, dancing with excitement, ran to Phil's side. "Are you really going to make it explode again? Remember last time, huh? It was better'n Flash Gordon! Funzi Labrino got so scared he almost crapped his pants."

"I told you to go take cover. You too, Pete."

Pete shambled over to join Freddie, whose foxlike face barely showed around the edge of the wall.

"Okay, guys!" Phil said, elated. "This is it!"

He pulled the string. At first Angie thought nothing was going to happen. Then the crazy pipe engine started to tremble and cough. An instant later, a series of loud blasts shattered the air and the wagon launched forward, screaming across the packed dirt. The girls' cheering ended abruptly when they heard a sickening crash beneath the porch. Leaning far over the rail, they saw the smoking wagon buried in Pap's woodpile.

"Hey, genius!" Freddie shouted in a panic. "You're gonna set the house on fire."

The announcement galvanized Angie into action. "Grab the hose!" she shouted down at them, as the boys stomped and beat at the flames.

"Oh, geez, he's going to kill us," Freddie chattered nervously. "I knew it. We're all dead. How come we let you talk us into these things? We should've been up at the garden. He'll beat the living daylights out of us now."

"Shut up, Freddie!" Phil turned on the water full blast.

"Is it out?" Angie shouted through the thick smoke wafting up. "O God, it stinks up here. You damn kids—"

Her tirade was cut short by Gina's piercing whistle.

Angie and Nickie exchanged horrified glances. "Phil, take the boys and get out of here," Angie shouted. "Go on! We'll stall Pap." She grabbed Nickie's arm and pulled her through the parlor into the kitchen.

"You run up and distract Pap," Angie said frantically, bending over to light the pilot on the stovetop. "But give me that stupid bedjacket first."

"No!"

"I said, give it to me." As Nickie tried to dash out of reach, Angie caught the ermine ruff. A loud rip punctuated their struggle.

Nickie pulled off the torn silk and hurled it at Angie. "I hate you—always sticking up for Phil. What about me?"

"Shut up and stop being so selfish." Angie threw the jacket into a big pot on the stove. She poured a touch of kerosene over it and lit a match to the flimsy silk. Flames and smoke soared upward, creating an awful stink. Angie doused the whole mess with a cup of flour. When she turned and saw Nickie still standing there, she shouted, "Go on, Nick!"

"I'd have taken his beating," Nickie said, staring mournfully at the burning mess.

"Yeah, well, he would've beat all of us. Now, go!" Angie waved agitatedly at the smoke, feeling guilty as hell but not knowing what else she could have done.

By the time Pap had stomped into the kitchen, the whole place reeked. "What is this?" he demanded, his dark eyes wrathful.

She turned from the stove. "I was cooking something," she said, her expression calm, "and forgot about it."

"Stupid slut!" His mustache leapt as he reviled her, its thick salt-and-pepper fullness not quite masking the thin bitter mouth beneath. "I work like a dog to put food on the table." He slapped her hard across the cheek. "And all you're good for is to ruin it."

Angie tasted warm blood but held her ground. She stared back into his eyes, spider lined in their web of hard despair. He slapped her again, harder. Still, she didn't flinch. As he raised his hand to strike a third time, the screen door crashed open.

They both turned.

In the doorway Z'Maria and Nickie flanked Rosa. Her expression was mild, but her hands betrayed her. White knuckled and shaking, they clutched the top of her cane. "Angelina," she whispered, *"cara mia."*

"What are you waiting for?" Z'Maria called to Angie. "Come help your poor mama up to bed."

Together the girls got her up the stairs. "What happen?" Rosa gasped, reaching up to touch her daughter's face.

"Nothing, Mama." Angie tried to smile. "It's okay."

Hearing raised voices from downstairs, Angie crept to the top of the staircase.

"Such a gentleman is my dead husband's brother," Z'Maria harangued Pap. "To beat his own flesh and blood like a dog."

"What the hell you know about a family?" he growled. "You who are as barren as the moon."

"*This* is my family."

Cursing under his breath, he stomped out.

As soon as Pap had disappeared, Angie and Nickie hurried back downstairs. Z'Maria pulled them into the kitchen. "What da hell happen?"

All three of them jumped when the screen door banged open again. But it was only Phil. Z'Maria tore into him, her voice low and raspy. "Who do you think you are with your head always up in the clouds—God Himself?"

"But Z'—"

"Shuddup! I have it up to here with you, too. Every time I turn around, it's something else. You tie a wire between our houses to make a telephone, and you almost strangle that poor Polack who came to buy wine. You try to make steam power with the pressure cooker. *Ecco!* I have tortellini splattered all over my kitchen."

Nickie smiled meanly. "Hey, Z', you forgot the time he—"

"Nickie, shut up," Phil snapped, then turned back to his aunt. "Come on, Z'—"

"Enough! Get back up the garden!"

Phil looked so downcast Angie started to follow him outside, but Z'Maria called her back. "And you," she railed, "make it worse by always defend him. Here, let me see that face—*madonna', che famiglia!* Nickie, bring ice for this other *stupido* who thinks she's Saint Angelina the Martyr."

There was a festive air at the dinner table that night. The day's disasters had been forgotten when one of their *gumbaris*—a kinswoman from the old country—had dropped off a half pound of homemade sausage for "poor Rosa to enjoy."

Angie winked at Phil as she forked the meat on top of his dry rice. He quickly shoveled the rice down his throat while he stared at the fat slice of sausage that he was saving for last.

When heavy footsteps creaked on the stairs down into the yard, everyone looked up from their plates.

"Hey, Frank," Giuseppe Niello called out to Pap from the doorway, "we gonna play *cartelin'* tonight?"

Angie tensed, remembering that the man had been home when Phil's experiment had gone awry. Were they going to get in trouble after all? The guy was so unpredictable—sometimes he just liked to torment them, like a cat waiting outside a mousehole. Niello gave Phil a nudge and squeezed a kitchen stool in beside him at the crowded table.

"See, what'd I tell you? You wouldn't get that coal-slinging job out at Braddock today," he said, sipping the wine Angie immediately served him. "Too many Hunkeys ahead a you, Franguch'." He rubbed in his I-told-you-so by using the patronizing nickname.

Pap only grunted.

Angie forced herself to sit down, wondering frantically if Niello had gotten wind of the day's fire under the porch.

"You miss a nice day on the hill, Franguch'," Niello went on, the shadow of his arm falling across Phil's plate as he gestured expansively.

Pap grunted again.

"It was some day, eh, Filippo?" Niello ruffled Phil's hair with mock affection, all the while eyeing his plate. "Sausage, eh? That's good for a boy like you, always working. Always busy with his big projects."

Pap's eyes narrowed. "What—"

"Here," Phil said quickly, spearing the meat and holding it out on the end of his fork to the wily extortionist. "Have it."

Niello popped the sausage into his mouth, chewing noisily. *"Tante buono."* He licked his lips, grinning as

Phil shot him a look of impotent rage. "Well, what do you say, Frank? Ready?"

More footsteps clumped down the outside stairs at a slow, measured pace. Standing hesitantly on the threshold, his black hat in hand, was Father Lucatta.

Angie felt Nickie tense beside her. Before she could bolt, Angie had clamped a hand on her shoulder and gestured for her to calm down.

"You!" Pap stood up, staring in irritation at the priest. "Nobody has died in this house. Or has the Church created yet another sacrament to torment us with?"

Angie knew her father had little use for priests; he had regaled his family long and often with tales of their hand-in-glove union with the rich. Pap's message was always the same—the Branzinos, like all the poor, were destined to be crushed, whether in Italy by oppressive landowners or here by Scotch-Irish mill owners. Father Lucatta was further suspect by having been born half-Irish. Pap barely tolerated the fact that his daughters occasionally found work in his kitchen.

"Forgive the intrusion, Signor Branzino," the priest said mildly in his lettered Italian, ignoring the insult, "but I need to speak with you and your wife about a matter of some importance concerning one of your daughters."

Pap turned fiercely, his questioning eyes on first Angie and then Nickie, who had begun shaking like a rabbit on the chopping block. It took all of Angie's strength to keep her from squirming out from beneath her hand and darting away.

Niello sat quietly, no doubt hoping the family would forget he was there. But Pap was no fool. Irritatedly, he waved the nosey neighbor out, promising to meet him later.

Rosa, eager to make amends for her husband's rudeness, smiled kindly at Father Lucatta and gestured for him to come inside. "Angelina," she said softly. "Bring wine for our guest."

A few minutes later, after serving the wine, Angie lingered in the parlor doorway until Pap told her angrily to leave and shut the door. She did as she was told, then bent down to listen at the keyhole. Nickie crowded next to her, demanding urgently to know what they were saying.

"Shut up," Angie whispered.

As Phil sat down behind them on the back stairs and the younger kids clustered around him, Angie pressed her ear closer and could just make out the priest's reedy voice: "As you can imagine, she is quite lonely, what with her son and her husband working long hours at the bank. The daughter died only last year of the rheumatic fever. She was your Angelina's age."

Angie tensed when she heard her own name. Like Nickie, she couldn't quite shake the feeling that she was somehow going to have to pay for smartmouthing the women at the rectory. Yet Father Lucatta was talking about a dead girl. The whole conversation, even the priest's presence in the house, seemed mysterious and improbable.

Pap's answering growl was a cold return to reality. "Why did you come here? No daughter of mine will ever leave this house." Mama murmured something in return, and he started to shout. "And it is my job to uphold her honor and chastity—impossible if she is not under this roof."

"Signor Branzino, they are an honorable Italian family."

"And now I'm supposed to believe the word of a priest? Bullshit!"

"Frank, I beg you," Mama said, raising her voice. "At least invite these Urbanos to our home to hear their intentions. What harm can there be in that?"

Father Lucatta cleared his throat nervously. "Signor Branzino, there is also the matter of a—a salary. Given these hard times, it—"

Pap exploded. "You push my back up against the wall, is that it? I'm expected to barter one of my children like a slave in order to feed these eight other hungry mouths? Is that what this goddamned life has reduced me to? Get out of my house!"

"Frank!"

Angie gave the frantic signal to scatter.

She and Nickie were tackling the pile of dirty dishes in the kitchen when they heard the door to the street quietly closing. A moment later, Rosa appeared in the doorway. The girls flew to her.

"Mama!" Nickie cried. "I'd take that jacket back, but Ange burned it. Is Pap going to kill me?"

"Hush, Nicoletta, this is not your business. Go up to bed."

Nickie's relief was almost palpable as she ran out of the kitchen.

"Mama," Angie said, feeling confused and frightened, "what's happening? What did Father Lucatta want? Why was Papa screaming?"

"He's a proud man, Angelina. Too proud, maybe. It has made him bitter, blinded him to goodness." Her voice quavered and she stopped. For a long moment she regarded her eldest daughter.

"What is it, Mama? Tell me."

Rosa reached up to brush the girl's bruised lip. "My beautiful Angelina, you deserve so much more than this," she whispered, her eyes unnaturally bright. "And I will see that you get it, no matter what Papa says."

2

Angie sat on the edge of the bed she shared with Nickie and Gina, staring down at her shoes. Lightly she licked her fingertips and bent down to rub them across the tops. The fugitive gleam evaporated, leaving the leather worn and cracked as ever.

As she straightened up, a cramp twisted her stomach. Everything was happening far too quickly. She wasn't ready to leave yet.

She squeezed her eyes shut, remembering the barely concealed dismay on the Urbanos' faces when they had come to visit the Sunday before. Angie had tried to picture the house through their eyes—the warped lino-leum floor, worn through in places to bare wood, the scuffed walls cheaply stencilled to simulate wallpaper, the succession of dark rooms opening one off another—and for the first time she had been ashamed of her poverty.

Mr. Urbano had addressed Pap in a perfectly enunciated Florentine Italian that sounded almost as alien as Russian. Because the visitor was of northern Italian stock rather than a southern Calabrian *paisano*, Pap had found him automatically suspect. Angie had been almost glad when her father was curt with their well-to-do guests, secretly hoping that his rudeness would drive them away. Yet, bit by bit, he had been won over, forced to respect Louis Urbano's gravity in the tragic loss of his daughter, to admire his manners and his position in the world.

And so, over glasses of the silky anisette liqueur that the guests had brought as a pledge of friendship, Angie's fate had been decided. She was to live in these strangers' home, not as a servant but as a companion to Mrs. Urbano. She would spend the holidays with her own family; otherwise her place would be with the Urbanos, who vowed to protect and cherish her as if she were their own.

The matter of money had been skirted delicately. After all, what was a daughter worth? The two fathers had decided at last: The amount was enough to compensate for the filial loss without being so much that it could in any way be construed as charity. Angie smiled regretfully. The Urbanos, consummate diplomats, had pretended not to see how vital even this meager amount of money would be to the Branzinos.

Angie drove the memory of that evening from her mind as she heard Mama's cane slowly tapping toward her through the connected bedrooms. Composing her features into a semblance of calm, she got up and picked up the shopping bag into which she had packed her few possessions. "Mama, I'm ready," she said, going out to meet her.

Rosa began to fret over the frayed collar of her dress as Angie bent to hug her. "What will the Urbanos think?"

"They know we're poor, Mama."

"Go call one of the boys for me," Rosa said suddenly. "I need something from the attic."

Angie went to the top of the stairs and hollered down. Vic, eager for any excuse not to do homework, came up at a gallop. Mama murmured her instructions and he climbed up into the attic, returning with a worn cardboard suitcase and an old-fashioned detachable collar that men hadn't worn in thirty years.

"Here, Mama," he said, thrusting the bag at her. Then he put the collar on backward and stuck his neck out like an ostrich. "Don't I look like Father Lucatta now?"

"Vittorio, shame," Rosa reprimanded him, but he had already dashed away. Sighing, she laid the little suitcase on the bed.

Angie stared at it. "What's this, Mama?"

"You must put your things in this, like a proper traveler. I won't have you going off like a peasant. When I came to America, poor and humble as I was," she said, turning the tarnished brass key, "I had this little *valigia*."

Mama lifted the lid. A lace-edged nightgown lay neatly folded inside: saved for tomorrow and tomorrow, until the snowy linen had yellowed with age, forgotten. Mama touched the stitches, as if her fingertips could conjure up the memory of the girl she had been, the girl who had so lovingly hand tatted the lace for her trousseau.

"This was all I brought with me, Angelina," she murmured softly. "This and the olivewood crucifix that belonged to your grandmother. I hadn't intended to leave so soon, but the *terramot'* changed everything. Never will I forget that night, huddled up underneath the attic like a terrified mouse while the earth shook and the ceiling groaned above my head." She paused. "In one short minute my whole family was dead."

Angie had heard the story so many times she felt as though she had lived through the earthquake herself. She could almost taste the chalky white dust from the fallen masonry walls. She saw it eddying like mist through the ruined village, clinging ghostlike to the survivors. She imagined the young Rosa emerging, shocked and terrified, from the attic.

"Oh, Mama," Angie murmured, ashamed now of her own paltry fears.

"I want you to take care of yourself," Rosa whispered. "Don't worry about us. You're not afraid, are you?"

Angie grabbed her mother's hand and kissed it. "No, Mama," she lied. "It's—it's going to be a big adventure."

"Yes. Such a dream." Rosa breathed the words so softly they were almost inaudible. "But Angelina, listen carefully to me. Don't be afraid to come back to us if you find you are not happy. That is what truly matters. Remember."

Angie kissed her again, trying hard not to cry. "I'll remember, Mama."

"Good." Rosa turned quickly and strode away.

Angie repacked her things, listening to Mama's cane as it tapped away from her. It was the loneliest sound she had ever heard.

"Ange?" She turned to see Phil in the doorway, his hands behind his back.

"I'm almost ready."

He swallowed. "Geez, Ange," he whispered, "we're gonna miss you."

Not wanting him to see her cry, she bent over the suitcase, pretending to fumble with the lock.

"Ange, you okay?" When she wouldn't look at him, he persisted. "Come on, what is it?"

She put the bag on the floor, then moved toward the window. "I don't know," she said, staring outside. "I keep thinking about that afternoon when Mrs. Urbano came to talk to me in Father Lucatta's kitchen. She had this peacock feather in her hat; you know, it's got that circle on the end of the feather. When she talked, the circle moved up and down. I got this funny feeling it was another eye watching, making fun of me."

"You're talking crazy."

"No, I'm not. You weren't there with those ladies. The rich are different, I'm telling you. It's like they live by different rules. I felt it as soon as I saw them. Even when they do their charity work, I get the feeling it's sort of a game for them, the way Pap's cards are for him. Whatever their real lives are about, it doesn't have anything to do with us . . . with me." She turned and caught the briefest flicker in his eyes. "God, Phil! What I just said doesn't scare you, does it? I wish you were the one going instead of me! You're the smart one. You're so bright, you and Nickie both. You're the ones who deserve all the chances."

"Stop talking stupid."

"I'm not, I tell you. This is where I belong—right here. What's going to happen to you and Mama and the kids? You know what Pap's like." Her eyes searched his. "He'll try to beat you down, Phil."

"I'm not afraid." His gaze slid away uneasily. "It's just—I don't want you to go."

She nodded, not trusting herself to speak.

"Ange, wait," he said as she bent to pick up her bag. "Stick this in, too."

She unrolled the paper he had pulled from behind his back. Phil's portrait of their mother, drawn in sepia tones, was as warm and evocative as a cherished memory. The deft, sure lines had somehow managed to capture the essence of her gentle humor and nurturing, protective love that had bound her children so inextricably to her.

"Oh, Phil," she breathed, touched.

"I just didn't want you to forget us, Ange."

"Idiot!" she said, hugging him. "You're my blood. How do you forget the blood running through your veins?"

She stared into the face that in so many ways was a mirror of her own. The attractiveness of his features was in their strength—in the clear, high brow and the prominent Roman nose over firmly etched lips, in the wide, deep-set dark eyes that were almost a family signet. Only Pap and Nickie's eyes—narrow and slightly canted—were different, a capricious throwback to some ancient invader who had left his mark in the mongrel bloodlines of southern Italy.

Gently Angie traced the line of Phil's cheek. The only way she could bear the thought of leaving was to believe that she was going as much for them as for herself.

When she came downstairs the dining room was in its usual state of uproar. Rosa sat in a rocker with Gina in her lap, and the two of them were laughing as Rosa struggled to pronounce the "th" in "the cow jumped over the moon." Freddie and Vic sat at the table, throwing spitballs instead of grilling each other on their multiplication tables, as they had been told to. As soon as they saw Angie with her bag, they high-tailed it up to the street to look for the Urbanos' automobile.

From the kitchen came the delicious smell of food frying. Angie poked her head in the doorway. "Already taking over my job, I see," she teased Pete, who stood at the stove, one of Mama's big aprons wrapped around his waist.

He grinned and stuck a fork into the pan. "I'll make you a fried-pepper sandwich."

"I don't have time." She leaned over to kiss his cheek.

"Hey, Ange, there's this *Polack* kid at school, George Walinsky," Pete said, oblivious to the need for hurrying anywhere. "He gave me this book on picking wild mushrooms. Want to see it?"

"Pete, I have to leave."

"Aw hell, Ange, why?"

She pulled him close to give him a hug, then hurried out to look for Nickie.

But Mama called to her. "Angelina!"

"Mama, where did Nickie disappear to? I can't leave yet. I haven't said good-bye."

"Never mind. It's almost time." Mama's face contorted with the effort not to cry as she pushed her daughter away from her. "Go kiss you papa."

Angie stood in the parlor doorway, imagining as she always did when she stepped into the sloping room that it was the cabin of a ship frozen forever on the downward side of a wave. She felt dizzy. "Papa?" she said uncertainly, her tone almost childlike. "I'm leaving."

He stood up, his deep chest puffing like a pigeon's. "You will behave yourself," he said sternly. "And no make trouble."

"Yes, Papa."

"And no bring shame to the family."

"No, Papa, I won't."

"You are eighteen. Not a child anymore." Awkwardly he touched her shoulder. "I know the world, you don't. It can be dangerous, evil. . . ."

She waited for him to go on, thinking for an instant that he might stop her from going. She was torn, desperately wanting to experience all the wonderful things the Urbanos had promised and yet terrified of abandoning her family. "Papa," she said at last, "I have to go."

For an instant she sensed a confused fragment of emotion behind the fierce gleam of his eyes: remorse, perhaps, or fear. Fear of losing one of the few things in his beaten-down world that was in his power to control. She wanted to believe there was love in his eyes, too—did he love her?

The uncomfortable moment of communion was broken when Freddie burst into the house, Vic close on his tail. "That big car's coming!" he shouted excitedly. "It's as big as a boat."

They all hurried out to see Angie off in a flurry of hugs and tears. The car idled in the street as Mrs. Urbano descended the steps into the yard, her white gloves barely touching the rickety rail. At Pap's brusque prodding, Angie advanced to meet her.

"You haven't changed your mind, have you, Angelina?" the woman said, her eyes anxious.

Angie swallowed and shook her head.

Mrs. Urbano's smile lighted her whole face, but it had been that instant of uncertainty beforehand that made Angie warm to her a little.

Mrs. Urbano turned to Rosa and Pap. "Your daughter will be happy with us," she said in her elegant Italian.

Pap stared at her stonily. "It is not her happiness that concerns me."

The woman's fingers tightened on the leather bag tucked under her arm. Rosa reached out to touch her clenched hand. "I know you will treat my Angelina as if she were your own daughter."

Mrs. Urbano looked at her gratefully. "Yes."

"Mama, I'll write," Angie whispered, bending to hug her one last time. "I'll send you the money."

Rosa stroked her hair. "Go. Be happy."

Mrs. Urbano touched Angie's shoulder. "It's getting late, my dear. We really must go."

Angie climbed the steps to the street, staring in surprise at the uniformed driver who held open the rear car door. She looked from him to the automobile's dim interior, all deep gleaming leather and thick carpet, and she shrank back a little. Leave it to the rich, she thought, to surround themselves with the plush comfort that the poor enjoyed only in their coffins.

"Go on, dear," Mrs. Urbano urged, her gloved hands gently pushing the girl forward.

Angie turned one last time to stare down at her family

standing in the ramshackle yard. Already they seemed small and distant, as if a great gap separated them.

They waved and shouted good-bye, Pap frowning and Mama's face radiant. Swallowing her tears, she lifted her hand and waved back.

Nickie, concealed behind the bedroom-window curtain, watched her sister jauntily wave good-bye like a movie star in a newsreel. Then the long black car disappeared around the corner, and Nickie's world became instantly bleaker. She had been too angry at Angie's abandonment to say good-bye, knowing that would hurt her sister more than anything. Now she regretted what she had done, realizing too late it had hurt herself more. Yet even as she mourned, an ache of envy squeezed her heart. In her mind's eye she saw Josephine Urbano descending the steps into the yard. She had memorized everything about her: the red feather in the upturned brim of her hat, the darker red pumps, and the snakeskin handbag. Nickie moved away from the window, struggling to imitate the woman's graceful carriage as she walked, her gravely elegant way of speaking to Mama and Pap. Nickie wished desperately that she had been the one singing in Father Lucatta's kitchen the previous week, the one who had reminded Mrs. Urbano of her daughter.

Life stunk. Even if she had been singing, it wouldn't have done any good. Who'd want a girl who couldn't carry a tune in a bucket?

Still, the escape hatch had miraculously opened for one of them. For now she had to be satisfied with the knowledge that such an escape existed.

The muted, powerful thrum of the Cadillac's V-16 engine reminded Angie of a cat's purring. As the crisscrossing train tracks and belching furnaces of the Coalport Works slid away behind her, she tried to calm her heartbeat to the same steady purr. Instead, her stomach clenched in another spasm. She held her breath, too embarrassed to lean forward to try to ease the pain. Finally it went away, and she breathed a tiny sigh of relief. She stared out the window, withdrawing more and more into herself with each passing mile.

As they sped across Liberty Bridge toward the city, Pittsburgh's grimy skyline rose above the sluggish Monongahela River. As they inched along through city traffic, Angie craned her neck to stare up at the top of the Gulf Building, its red-neon tube lights glowing dimly through the murky air. How remote and vast the city was. She had never felt so lonely or vulnerable.

Mrs. Urbano was chattering companionably in her ear, pointing out Duquesne University on the bluff. Even though Angie was only half listening, it struck her that the woman was talking not to relieve Angie's loneliness but her own.

Angie steeled herself not to pull her hand away as Mrs. Urbano laid her gloved hand on her wrist. "We're going to be friends, you and I."

Angie nodded mutely, knowing she should be smiling her gratitude and chatting back in the lilting voice that had drawn the woman to her in the first place.

"Everything's going to be just wonderful," Mrs. Urbano said into the silence. "You'll see."

Highland Park on Pittsburgh's swank east side was an hour from the Branzino home in Coalport. Yet Angie felt as if she might as well have crossed an ocean, so distant were these sweeping emerald lawns and spacious houses from the familiar world she knew.

At last the Cadillac turned into one of the curving gravel driveways and drew to a stop. Ivy softened the two-story, gray stone facade of the Urbano house, lending an air of gracious permanence that Angie found somehow comforting. Maybe Mrs. Urbano was right after all: everything would be wonderful.

The blue-eyed chauffeur, his curly blond hair just visible beneath the rim of his cap, held the door open. As Angie stepped out onto the sidewalk, she smiled her thanks. He stared back at her with the same furtive curiosity he had exhibited enroute, when she had caught him staring at her from time to time in the rearview mirror. Angie sensed nothing flirtatious in his manner; he just seemed wary.

He tried to take the cardboard suitcase from her hand, but she stubbornly refused to relinquish this last tie to her old life.

Mrs. Urbano intervened. "Let her carry it, Harry, if that's what she wants. And you might as well put the car in the garage. I don't think it will be needed again this evening."

Angie was only dimly aware of the woman issuing orders to the young driver. Her own curiosity getting the better of her, she started up the sidewalk. She was halfway to the front door when a small gray dog appeared suddenly around the corner of the house and launched itself in her direction, barking up a frenzy.

For the first time that day she felt like laughing. With its square face and muttonchop whiskers, the dog was a ridiculous sight. But when he started making nipping feints at her ankles, she realized he was all business.

"Kaiser, no!" Mrs. Urbano cried at Angie's back. She lowered her bag like a shield, but the dog, undaunted, hurtled himself against it. Startled by his quick ferocity, she dropped the suitcase.

As it hit the ground, the worn hinges gave way and the bag gaped open, burying the dog in a small avalanche of clothing. He shook himself free and grabbed a pair of flour-sack bloomers in his teeth, dashing back and forth across the wide lawn with them as if they were a battle trophy. Mortified, Angie watched her homemade underthings being paraded before the world. She was debating whether to give chase when more outraged shouts came simultaneously from Mrs. Urbano and a young man in gray slacks and trim blue blazer who had stepped out the front door.

"Kaiser, no! Bad dog."

Although the animal stopped dead in his tracks, his nubby tail continued to wag vigorously. Angie marched over to him and tried to retrieve the bloomers. He backed up, growling, delighted at the prospect of a tug-of-war.

Refusing to take any more guff, Angie bent down and snatched the bloomers from his teeth. The dog must have recognized the game was over, too, because he sat back on his haunches and offered his paw. Reluctantly she took it, wishing she could have bopped him one on the head.

As she straightened, she came face to face with the young man who had appeared. "Sorry about the welcoming committee," he said, too well-bred to laugh at her predicament, though his eyes hinted otherwise. "I'm afraid he's your typical male. Has to show off for a pretty face." Blushing, Angie shoved the bloomers behind her back. "I'm Louis Junior. You must be Angelina."

She nodded.

"So you're to be my mother's new companion."

She studied him covertly, trying to read his tone. He had spoken the words with the same light insouciance another man might have said "So you're to be my partner for this dance." She didn't know whether to feel insulted or relieved by his detachment.

Mrs. Urbano joined them, holding the broken suitcase in her gloved hands. "My dear, I'm so sorry about Kaiser."

Before Angie could reply, Louis leaned down to kiss his mother's cheek. "I'm going out, Mother. Mind if Harry drives me?"

"But I was hoping you would help Angelina feel welcome her first evening home."

"How about if I promise to be back for dinner?"

"But Harry's just put the car away."

"I'll talk to him," he said, directing his gaze at Angie again. "Glad you've come, Angelina. Mother needs someone around. High-spirited and amusing though Kaiser can be, he's rather trying to converse with. German, you know—quite opinionated and stubborn. Well, see you at dinner. We dine fashionably late, I'm afraid."

"So do the Branzinos," Angie replied, getting up the courage to speak. "At least in the summer, when Pap and my brothers are up in the garden. Nine o'clock supper's the rule."

"So I see Mother didn't lie, after all." Louis grinned amiably. "You do have a voice."

"Don't mind Louis," Mrs. Urbano said. "He loves to tease."

"Oh!" Angie jumped, startled, as the dog's cold nose snuffled at her leg.

"What a little pest you are today, Kaiser," Mrs. Urbano scolded. "Dogs don't frighten you, do they, Angelina?"

"Only if they're foaming at the mouth."

Louis Urbano smiled. "Charming sense of humor." Angie stared at him, mystified, thinking he must never have seen a rabid dog. "Well, Mother," he said, chuckling, "we had better remember that before we take our houseguest down to the club. She'll see a few old dogs there who tend to foam."

"You know your father doesn't like you talking about his friends that way," she chided her son affectionately.

Angie observed the interaction between them with interest. How alike they seemed: the same sandy hair and light brown eyes, the high-bridged noses and long elegant faces that she had seen before only in the art books Phil brought home from the library—the faces of northern Italian nobility. Elegant but somewhat jaded and bored, at least in the son's case. Angie had the impression of a young man constantly in need of some new diversion. She was relieved when he finally sauntered in the direction of the garage.

Mrs. Urbano took Angie's arm. "Shall we go inside? I'm sure you're anxious to see your new home."

As she opened the door, they were greeted in the foyer by a housekeeper, who whisked Angie's bag away and disappeared with it up a wide staircase that curved gracefully toward the second story. For the first time Angie caught a glimpse of her new world. A round marble-topped table stood in the center of the black-and-white tiled floor. Gracing it was an enormous crystal vase filled with pink roses, their aroma almost intoxicating.

Doors opened to either side of the entryway, and she glimpsed a grand piano and high shelves filled with books, more flower-filled vases, porcelain figurines and sumptuously patterned rugs.

A telephone rang in the library, to the left. "Make yourself at home, my dear," Mrs. Urbano said, moving to answer it.

Angie wandered into the drawing room, drawn by the large oil painting that hung above a rose quartz fireplace. She stood before the portrait, transfixed. Was this Julia? She could feel the girl's vivacity and humor radiating out into the room.

"She was so lovely, wasn't she?"

Angie whirled guiltily to face Mrs. Urbano, who stood in the doorway. "I—I never saw a painting like that except in a museum. She seems so alive." As soon as the words were out, Angie knew that she had said the wrong thing. The woman flinched as if she had been slapped.

"I try to remember her that way," she said finally, "but it's difficult. So difficult."

Something in her wistful manner reminded Angie of her mother. Then she realized why the two had hit it off at once: Both women lived through their children, wanting nothing for themselves. Angie turned back to the portrait. Staring at the blonde, blue-eyed girl, like a princess out of a fairy tale, Angie felt as if her own personality had begun to seep away, subsumed in something she could not understand or fathom. She backed away from it, then jumped a little as Mrs. Urbano touched her arm.

"Come along, dear. I hope you like pink," she said, linking her arm companionably through Angie's as they moved toward the staircase. "It was Julia's favorite color."

The spacious bedroom was like a bower. Wallpaper with a pattern of pink rosebuds covered the walls and ceiling, and the curtains and bedspread were in a matching fabric. The furniture was French provincial and pristine white, trimmed with gold.

Angie felt as though she had fallen into the crystal vase downstairs. Almost fearfully, she opened a closet door and was relieved to find it empty but for her own bag. It looked so small and pathetic in the opulent surroundings.

"I don't expect you to replace Julia."

Angie turned swiftly. Mrs. Urbano had not entered the room but remained in the doorway, eyes no longer smiling but haunted.

"I couldn't replace her," Angie said. "I'm a different person."

"You remind me of her, though. That afternoon at the church rectory, you made me smile. I hadn't laughed since she died, or been anything other than numb with misery. This room, this house, have felt so empty. All I ask of you, Angie, is that"—she hesitated—"is that you help me get through the days."

Touched by the woman's pain, Angie went over to her.

"Julia had aspirations to be a concert pianist. She loved music, just as you do. Angie," Mrs. Urbano said suddenly, "I want you to have voice lessons. Would you like that?"

"I . . . sure."

"And we'll go shopping tomorrow for a few things. We'll lunch at the William Penn. They have a pianist in the lobby. Julia loved . . . Well, anyway, I should let you get settled." Mrs. Urbano gave her a quick peck on the cheek and was gone.

Angie closed the door and leaned back against it, rubbing her arms. She still had the same Alice in Wonderland feeling, as if this new world were a dream and everything in it were slightly off-kilter. She ran her hand lightly along the silk-embossed wallpaper and the curving edges of the furniture. Her heels sank into the deep plush of the pale pink rug. And she wondered what she was doing here, what was going to happen to her. Usually once you dreamed, you woke up.

She opened her·suitcase and took out Phil's portrait of their mother. She propped it up on the bureau top, taking heart from Mama's eyes smiling back at her, full of love.

Carefully, she folded back the coverlet on the bed. The faint scent of attar of roses emanated from the crisp linen pillowcase. She was just about to lie down when she heard a funny scratching at the door.

She opened it to find Kaiser there, his mischievous black eyes staring up at her expectantly. Without waiting for an invitation, the dog trotted in. He moved about the room, sniffing at her bag and at her shoes. When Angie bent down to pet him, he backed away. It seemed that even the dog expected her to be someone she was not. He raced out of the room and she closed the door again, relieved to be alone. Still, Kaiser's presence lingered. The indifferent, pampered dog somehow epitomized this alien world she had been thrust into.

As she lay down, a long-buried memory surfaced. She had been four or five. The Branzinos had a dog named Fanny, a dainty feminine creature with a white fluffy tail. Though Fanny was gentle and dignified, she was profligate with her love.

Then one day the cops shot her. The family had been careful to keep Fanny in the yard that summer of the bad rabies epidemic because they had been shooting dogs on sight in the streets. Angie remembered standing with her nose pressed to the screen door, laughing as she watched Fanny chasing a butterfly, her feathery plume of tail waving behind her. Then without warning the shots had rung out, two of them in rapid succession, and an instant later Fanny lay dying in a pool of her own blood—killed in her own yard, where she should have been safe.

Deep down Angie felt like Fanny. Her protected world had been an illusion. She started to tremble. She thought again of the unknown Julia whom she could not replace and wondered: What am I doing here?

3

The square-heeled black shoes marched past Angie's head with drill-like precision—five steps forward, swivel and five steps back.

"Again, Angelina."

Lying on the floor as she was, the ceiling seemed miles away. Her back was hurting like hell, but Angie was not about to let on that she was in pain. For the twentieth time she went through the exercise: "Do-mi-so-do-so-mi-do."

"Again."

As her voice ran up and down the scales, Angie's eyes slid sideways to watch the almost hypnotic progression of Madame Francini's rugbys on the studio's wooden floor. With each passage, her long skirt fanned a curtain of air faintly fragrant with eau mauve.

At long last the woman said, "Enough. You may get up." Angie scrambled to her feet. She dusted off her behind and twisted her head over her shoulder, worried that she might have gotten the new black skirt dirty. "Are you quite through with your primping?"

Angie froze, intimidated by the voice teacher's militant attitude.

"If you continue to be more concerned with the state of your appearance than the quality of your voice, we will not get anywhere."

The piano accompanist, an Englishwoman with an anvil-shaped face, gave Angie a superior little look.

Madame went on. "Now, did you feel the difference when you were lying down? Newborn babies use those muscles naturally when they scream. You must work on developing that same supporting cushion. The sound must come deep from the diaphragm if your high notes are to be free and open. Now, sing the scale again, using those muscles."

"Do-mi—"

"Open your throa . . . t. Concentrate on breathing correctly," the woman insisted. "Drink in the air as if you were drawing it in through your eyes."

Angie sang the monotonous notes again and again.

"And once more."

Fifteen minutes later, she was still singing them.

"Adequate. Merely adequate," Madame said at last, taking a sheet of music from the piano and handing it to Angie. "I will permit you to sing now, on one condition—that you concentrate on the vowels. 'Cello' does not rhyme with 'Jell-o.' The 'ay' is a long, clear vowel, like wind whispering across a chime. And none of your sloppy dental consonants, either. It's not just bel canto singing that is our goal. I want to hear the same quality in your speaking voice. Your lazy small-town slang has grated on me for two weeks now. Enough is enough. You are not stupid by any means, Angelina. You will be transformed."

Aware of the accompanist's critical gaze, Angie said with injured dignity, "I don't want to be transformed. I just want to sing."

Madame Francini gave her a long, assessing look. Turning to the pianist, she said, "Sarah, you may leave now." When the woman had left, Madame turned back to her pupil. "You must understand something, Angelina. I am not being paid merely to teach you to sing. You are Josephine Urbano's Galatea."

"Who's Galatea?"

Madame sighed, as if she regretted having spoken. "In Greek mythology there was a sculptor named Pygmalion.

He created a statue of a woman so beautiful that he begged the gods to make it come alive."

Angie stared at her, mystified, wondering what this had to do with her.

"The gods answered his prayer, Angelina." The woman's eyes flicked over her in their probing way. "They gave him Galatea—a woman fashioned down to the last detail by his imagination, by his will." Madame took the sheet music from her with a decisive motion. "But I have said enough. The lesson is over, Angelina. I think you have learned more than enough for one day. You must not keep Mrs. Urbano waiting."

Angie refused to be dismissed so easily. "The story has something to do with me and Mrs. Urbano, doesn't it? But she already told me she doesn't expect me to replace Julia. I'm nothing like her daughter. I never will be."

"You're young, Angelina. You haven't had time yet to determine who or what you really are. I have seen it happen time and again—young women molded into what someone else decides they should be."

"But maybe I want to be the same thing."

"I see." Madame Francini's eyes moved restlessly to the rows of framed photographs arrayed on the wall behind the grand pianos: autographed portraits of Caruso and other operatic greats, photos of Madame herself on stage in costume.

Angie's eyes followed hers. "Your life must have been exciting," she murmured wistfully. "Do you ever miss the stage?"

Madame looked at her. "The human voice is fragile, its life sadly limited. My own talent is nothing now but a remembered dream. So I teach. Through my students— through you—I am able to recapture that dream." Her eyes moved longingly back to the wall of photographs. "Even my beloved Milano is like a dream to me now. But one day I'll go back. The city is my spiritual home; it is the true heart of the operatic world." She shook her head briskly. "But I've said too much. That is all, Angelina. You may go."

Angie was almost at the door when Madame called after her. "You may think I've been rather harsh with you these first few weeks. If I have, it's not because I'm an ogress—though I may be that too—but because I recognize talent. I want you to make just as harsh demands on yourself. There's a freshness and originality about you that is quite lovely."

"Oh." The compliment left Angie thunderstruck.

"Now, I'm not telling you this to give you a swollen head, Angelina." Her lips tightened. "I'm saying it as a . . . sort of warning. I would hate to see those lovely qualities of yours squelched."

"I don't under—"

"I've already said the lesson is over. You'd better go," Madame Francini cut her off, glancing down at the jeweled watch pinned on her bodice. "You'll be late otherwise."

"Yes, Madame Francini. I—"

"That's all for today, Angelina."

Angie stepped out into the small reception area, so enthralled by Madame's praise that she barely noticed Sarah behind her desk. Angie was halfway out the door when she remembered something and turned back. "I almost forgot, Miss Langston: Mrs. Urbano would like us to reschedule my Thursday lesson, if possible. We've been invited to a recital."

Frowning, the woman flipped through the engagement book. "The impertinence of some people," she muttered, erasing so hard that she gouged the paper. She looked up at Angie. "Madame is too generous by far— wasting her precious time and energy on a rich woman's silly whim."

Angie flushed hotly. "Madame believes I have talent."

Sarah sniffed. "Friday at one o'clock sharp. Good day," she said coldly, dismissing her.

Angie walked out of the studio, nonplussed by the Englishwoman's resentment. She shook her head, unable to fathom either of them. She had thought that Madame despised her. Now all of a sudden, it seemed as though the voice teacher somehow wanted to protect her. But from what—the Urbanos?

Reymer's, on the ground floor of the Clark Building, was a sleek tea room decorated in the distinctive art moderne style of the late twenties. As Angie stopped in the entryway and slipped out of her coat, the maitre'd looked up from his podium. "Yes, madame?"

She half turned to look over her shoulder before she realized the man was speaking to her. "Yes," she said, reaching up to pat the soft black beret perched on the side of her head. "I'm supposed to meet Mrs. Urbano?"

"She's already been seated. This way, please."

As they threaded their way among the tables, Angie's reflection leaped back at her a dozen times from the large circular mirrors gracing the restaurant's silver-leafed walls. She reached up to fluff the white organdy and lace at her throat and gave a nervous tug at the boleto tabs that formed a little half-jacket over the frothy gilet. The sleeves of the white crepe blouse were fashionably long and tight, the skirt beautifully fan-pleated. She couldn't believe the changes that had occurred in so few weeks. Her appearance, elegant and modish as the surrounding decor, buoyed her spirits. Everything she possessed, everything she was becoming, had been a gift from the Urbanos. Now she began to understand the unsettling questions Madame Francini had raised. Oddly, Angie felt as if she and Madame had somehow betrayed the rather lonely woman who had brought them together.

Mrs. Urbano looked up eagerly. "Angie, dear, how did your lesson go?"

"Madame Francini says I don't breathe right." Angie smiled overbrightly as she sat down. "She made me sing scales lying flat on my back on the floor."

"You have to trust her." Angie looked away, relieved that the woman's attention was focused on pouring tea. "Giulia Francini is the finest vocal coach in Pittsburgh. The Opera Guild managed to lure her from New York," Mrs. Urbano confided, handing her a cup. "We're determined to build an opera company of our own one day."

Staring down into the watery brew, Angie had a sudden intense craving for Pap's black coffee, thick and strong as espresso from simmering on the stove all day.

Mrs. Urbano shot her a quizzical look. "You seem so quiet. Is something wrong? Don't you care for the tea?"

"It's fine." Angie dutifully lifted the cup to her lips. For all its transparency, the tea tasted surprisingly bitter.

She reached for the small silver tongs and dropped a cube of sugar into the cup, watching it slowly dissolve.

"Now, I must hear every detail about your lesson. Madame Francini thinks you have wonderful potential. You know, I've been thinking. You should have language lessons. French would be helpful, and it shouldn't be difficult for you—oh," she interrupted herself as the waiter materialized at their table with two plates.

"Angie, I hope you don't mind. I took the liberty of ordering tea sandwiches—curried chicken and smoked salmon with cream cheese. We need to hurry just a bit. I'd like to stop by the bank before we go to the seamstress's for your fitting. And that reminds me—I've been thinking that red gown simply won't be enough. You'll need at least four evening dresses for the winter season. We'll sit down this evening and go through *Vogue*. Oh, it's going to be so lovely having you here for the holidays." She broke off her hurried monologue and flashed a brilliant smile. "As soon as Madame thinks you're ready, I'd love for you to sing at one of our little parties."

Angie listened, so overwhelmed by the fairy-tale splendor of Mrs. Urbano's plans that her misgivings were brushed aside.

After tea they walked uptown, threading their way through the throngs on Smithfield Street. Angie stared around her. The well-dressed shoppers seemed totally buffered from the grinding poverty of the outlying milltowns. The only reminder of that other life was a shabbily dressed woman on the corner with her few tired-looking heads of cabbage for sale. Her bleak expression reminded Angie of Pap.

The Urbano Bank was an imposing building guarded by a pair of immense bronze lions. Mrs. Urbano steered Angie through the revolving doors, and as they entered a marble-covered hall, the building gave Angie an impression of dignity and quiet power, not unlike that of Father Lucatta's church. Her impulse was to walk on tiptoe as they crossed the polished floor. The long row of grilled teller cages reminded her of confessionals. Observing the customers lined up patiently, she imagined them whispering secret sins to the rather bored-looking clerks. At last they reached a spacious carpeted alcove at the rear of the bank and were greeted by an efficient-looking woman seated behind a desk.

"Good afternoon, Mrs. Urbano. Shall I tell Mr. Urbano you're here?"

"Yes, Madge. We'll just go right back. I'm sure he won't mind the intrusion."

Mrs. Urbano led Angie toward one of the heavy carved doors and pushed it open. "Hello, darling," she trilled.

Angie followed her inside and was shocked when she saw Louis Junior seated behind the massive, gleaming desk. She had somehow assumed the office would be his father's.

"Isn't this a lovely surprise." He rose and came around to greet them. Despite his angular build, he moved with a lazy, fluid grace that reminded Angie of Fred Astaire. He kissed his mother's cheek, then turned to her. "Hullo there. So how's the future mezzo-soprano?"

"More mezzo than soprano," she said from the doorway. "The voice teacher has sunk to forcing the notes out of me. I felt like a set of bellows today."

His eyebrows lifted a fraction. "How intriguing. By the way, I don't have a reputation for biting. You can come and sit down if you like."

Angie was relieved when he turned back to chat with his mother. She felt daunted by his air of bored insouciance —as if the world and everything in it had been expressly created for his amusement. Even his office, with its oil paintings and tastefully arranged objects d'art, seemed more like a man's private library than a place of business. She couldn't help admiring how he moved through his elegant setting with such effortless grace. Angie was reminded of something Madame had said about a certain quality that was "bred in the bone." No doubt about it—Louis had class.

"Oh, by the way, darling," Mrs. Urbano was saying, "I spoke to Fiona Donahue today. She said Maura will be coming down from Vassar."

"Kicked out, was she?" His grin was faintly mocking as he reached for the sherry decanter on the table.

"Louis, dear, must you always be such a tease? It's her winter break. She's eager to see you, you know."

"Eager to have me put in a good word with David, you

mean." He smiled as he poured out the sherry into three tiny cut-crystal glasses. "She's been after him for two years."

"But I had the impression she was quite fond of you."

"Ancient history, Mother. She found me too agreeable by far." He handed the glasses around. "Maura needs a harder nut to crack. David's indifference suits her hunter's instinct to a tee."

"Louis dear, how you talk. What will Angie think of our set?"

"The worst, as she should." He smiled lazily. "I'll never forget the time Maura, David and I went speeding through Schenley Park at three in the morning in old man Donahue's new roadster, and she wound up wrapping it around an elm tree that inconsiderately jumped in front of her."

"Louis, really. Maura has grown up."

"Amazing what a year off the sauce can do for a girl."

"I hope you don't remind her father of that incident when you see him."

Louis's grin widened.

Angie had the impression that he was expert at keeping his mother off balance, using equal parts of mockery and charm. She had the distinct impression, too, that he did what he damn well pleased, regardless of his mother's efforts to control him.

"At any rate, darling, your father and I have extra tickets to the opera Saturday evening. Modarelli's conducting. I was thinking—"

"You were thinking I might give old Maura a call."

"Actually," his mother said, her smile soft and persuasive, "I was thinking you might escort Angie."

Angie was so surprised she spilled some sherry down the front of her jabot. Nervously she fluffed the lace, aware that Louis had turned his attractive hazel eyes on her. He regarded her thoughtfully, and, to her mortification, Angie felt herself blushing.

"Capital idea, Mother. We could make it a foursome— Angie and I, David and Maura." He chuckled. "A cozy evening all around, wouldn't you say?"

The long slip swished faintly beneath her robe as Angie

sat down at the small writing desk. Light glowed from beneath the shirred lampshade, enveloping the bedroom with cozy warmth. The rose-patterned walls and ceiling no longer made her feel closed in; she felt cosseted and safe—almost as if she truly belonged. Louis's attentions had more than a little to do with the change in her.

Still, doubt niggled at her. With his looks and social standing, he had to have women falling all over him. She couldn't help wondering if he were taking her to the opera to please his mother or to please himself.

Pushing aside her doubts, Angie pulled out her sheaf of letters from home and reread Nickie's last letter, describing the architectural model Phil had begun for his class project. "The design is bizarre," Nickie had written, "typical Phil." Angie smiled. Leave it to him to envision a cantilevered glass house perched on a rocky promontory—as if he wanted to lift Pap's ramshackle hovel into an imaginary realm of light and beauty.

Angie drew out a sheet of her own scented notepaper and wrote a long, loving letter to Mama, omitting any mention of Louis. God only knew what Pap would say if he heard that the Urbanos' son had begun paying her attention, for whatever reason.

With the letter she enclosed not only the money Mr. Urbano gave her without fail every Friday afternoon but most of what remained of the weekly allowance Mrs. Urbano insisted she have. She looked forward to this little end-of-the-week ritual, envisioning Mama's pleasure as she opened the envelope and Pap's relief. The knowledge that she was contributing to her family's well-being did make the pain of separation easier to bear.

After sealing and stamping the envelope, Angie rose and went to the bed where Berthe, the housekeeper, had laid out her evening gown. As she slipped it on, Angie had the odd feeling that when her head reemerged she would be back in the drab, drafty bedroom she had shared with her sisters. She knew she did not belong here, and yet, guiltily, she wanted to stay, to make the dream last forever.

The red velvet gown, cut on the bias, was the essence of simplicity. Despite its high neck, Angie felt half naked and vulnerable as she swirled and felt the air cool her bare back. Swiftly she finished her toilette, spraying a fine mist of Charbert's Drumbeat at her wrists and throat. She fastened on the strand of pearls that Mrs. Urbano had loaned her and patted her hair. Set in a permanent wave, the silky natural looseness of the topwaves framed her eyes, while the tight short curls at the sides set off the strong oval of her face like a cameo. She felt curiously light, as if a stranger inhabited her skin and she were watching the performance from a distance.

Shaking off the funny feeling, Angie slipped into her new red pumps and hurried downstairs. The foyer was empty, but from the book-lined library to her right she could hear Mr. Urbano's deep voice murmuring rapidly into the telephone. Even when the man was home, he spent long hours in his study talking of liquidations and capitalization and other terms that were Greek to Angie. She hesitated in the doorway, observing him. If it hadn't been for her children, Josephine Urbano would have been a lonely woman all her life.

As she was deciding whether to enter the study, a slight sound made her turn. Louis Junior emerged from the shadowy darkness of the drawing room, holding an empty cocktail glass in one hand and a cigarette in the other. Wordlessly he stared at her, stunned by her transformation. His silence unnerved her.

"I feel like Little Orphan Annie," she joked finally, "dressed up in somebody else's duds." Even as she spoke, she knew she had said the right thing. She could sense him relaxing.

"Daddy Warbucks at your service." As he smiled in his droll, mocking way, his momentary unease was so swiftly banished she thought she must have imagined it.

An instant later they heard a door opening upstairs, and Mrs. Urbano appeared at the top of the stairs with a fur in her arms. "Angie, dear, I want you to wear this," she called, hurrying down.

The heavy warmth of the rippled marten cape felt heavenly against Angie's bare back as Mrs. Urbano draped it around her shoulders. "There, my dear," she said, satisfied, "you look wonderful. And I won't have to worry about you catching cold."

Drawn by the voices in the hall, Mr. Urbano came out

to join them. "I see we're all ready. Shall I have Harry bring the car up?"

Louis stood before the hall mirror, engrossed in tying an ascot knot in his silk muffler. "Actually," he said, not bothering to look at his father, "I've decided to take Angie in the Auburn."

The older man shrugged indifferently. "As you wish."

Louis plucked his hat from the hall table, kissed his mother on the cheek and then smiled at Angie. "Meet you out front." He left without a glance at his father.

Angie's gaze moved uneasily to the elder Urbano. "See you there," he said, his pale blue eyes revealing nothing. "Now, if you'll excuse me, I have a few more calls to make." Without waiting for a reply, he disappeared back into the study.

Mrs. Urbano touched Angie's arm. "He doesn't mean to be abrupt. That's just his way. Louis and his father understand each other, they truly do." Outside a car honked, and Mrs. Urbano gave her a gentle push. "Go on now. We'll see you there."

Angie hurried out, crossing the lawn toward the long cream-colored roadster. From the corner of her eye she glimpsed Harry's silhouette in the open garage. The chauffeur lounged against the Cadillac, idly smoking a cigarette as he watched them.

"He's a strange guy," she said as they backed out of the drive.

"Estranged, don't you mean?" Louis said curtly. "Don't bother trying to live up to his expectations; you'll do no better than I did."

"What? I—I was talking about Harry."

"Harry!" Louis looked startled for an instant and then laughed. "Now, don't tell me you don't think he's attractive. Women are always throwing themselves at the poor devil."

"He's not very friendly."

"Ah ha, you *do* like him!"

"He's always watching me."

"How can you hold that against him?" Louis grinned. "You're a lovely creature."

Angie blushed and fell silent. She couldn't get over how differently Louis acted when his father wasn't around.

Accustomed as she was to a family that forever brawled, the Urbanos had seemed perfect at first—civil, considerate and kind. Only gradually had she become aware of the coldness between father and son. She couldn't help but feel sorry for Mrs. Urbano, caught in the middle.

Angie stared out into the night, discomfited by the roller-coaster feel of the low-slung automobile as it climbed and descended the hills with gathering speed.

"Why so quiet, Orphan A?"

"To tell you the truth, I feel more like Cinderella now," she said, trying to keep her tone light. "I'll bet her coach to the ball wasn't this fancy."

"I doubt if fairy godmothers knew much about supercharged speedsters." As they came into a straight stretch of road, Louis shifted to high gear. "This machine can hit a hundred miles per hour."

Angie clung to the seat, her eyes wide. "Slow down, please! I'd like a chance at hitting a hundred myself."

Instantly he eased up on the accelerator and looked over at her with a grin. "Not only beautiful but witty, too. How lucky can a fellow get?"

She gave him a sideways look, uncertain whether he was serious or mocking. Pittsburgh's Carnegie Hall loomed ahead, and Angie was saved from having to reply. She stared in fascination at the ornate structure built through the philanthropy of Andrew Carnegie. The son of an impoverished Scottish weaver, Carnegie had emigrated to Pittsburgh in 1848 and within twenty-five years built up a steel-making industry that made him one of the richest men in the world.

Louis drew to a stop beyond the huge seated statues of Bach and Shakespeare. As Angie swung a leg out the door, the red-jacketed parking attendant gave a long, appreciative whistle. Then she noticed his eyes riveted on the sleek rounded curves of the Auburn. He dashed around, practically hauling Louis out of the driver's seat.

"She's a beaut, sir," he said reverently as he slid behind the wheel. "Straight-eight 150 horsepower. Dual-ratio rear axle. I read all about this here model."

"Yes, but nothing's perfect," Louis told him with a straight face. "Turns into a pumpkin at midnight."

The attendant laughed and so did Angie, watching from the steps.

"I'm afraid that in some men's hearts a woman takes second place," Louis joked as he came around to take her arm. "Aren't I lucky you're not the vain, jealous type?"

"How do you know I'm not?"

He touched her lightly under the chin. "I know women."

Feeling secure on his arm, Angie hurried up the steps beside him. Beautifully dressed people thronged the opulent Grand Foyer with its dark rose marble walls.

"Ah, there are the Donahues," he said. "Let's go say hello."

As they approached, Angie nodded at the couple, blanching at the look of ill-disguised disapproval on Fiona Donahue's face. "Actually, Louis, Mrs. Donahue and I have already met."

"I can see that Josephine has worked wonders—at least on the surface," the woman condescended to reply before turning to Louis. "Have you seen Maura yet?"

Before he could reply, a lively voice full of laughter called out, "Louis!"

Louis grinned. "If it isn't Mr. Princeton himself. You're looking spiffy, O'Rourke."

From the way they greeted each other, it was obvious the two were the best of friends. O'Rourke certainly looked Irish, for his strong, angular face with its cleft chin was enlivened by the most mischievous green eyes Angie had ever seen. He pretended to take her aside and said in a loud stage whisper, "I warn you, Louis is a rakehell, a regular devil on wheels. No woman's been able to slow him down yet."

"Angelina Branzino, may I present David O'Rourke?" Louis grinned. "My worthless childhood friend."

"Ignore him and maybe he'll go away," David joked, his eyes never leaving Angie's face. "So, where did you find this exotic beauty, Louis—Majorca, Madrid, Buenos Aires?"

"Actually, David," a bored feminine voice drawled from behind them, "she's one of Mummy's Coalport canaries."

Angie turned to stare at a delicate redhead in a stunning green gown. No need to guess who she was. Maura Donahue was a cookie-cutter replica of her mother.

As her parents drifted off through the milling crowd, Maura flicked a disdainful glance in Angie's direction. "I think it's positively droll, don't you, Louis, the way our mothers have taken up slumming in their dotage."

David's left brow lifted. "Not jealous, are you, Maura?"

"You're a scream, David. Say, can I cadge a cigarette? Mummy's so damn stuffy," she drawled. "When I'm home, I have to sneak them as though I were twelve."

He lit one for her and another for himself. "Don't look now," he murmured, "but your old man's on to us."

"Don't worry." Exhaling a cloud of smoke, she grinned and held up her forefinger. "I've got Daddy wrapped."

"Like mother, like daughter."

She laughed gaily, looking from David to Louis. "Listen, a bunch of us are going dancing down at the William Penn later. Come along if you like, unless you're worried your houseguest will turn back into an ash puddle if you don't get her home before the witching hour."

Stung by the girl's cruel jibes, Angie bit her lip. Before Louis could say anything, David took her arm and led her toward the auditorium entrance. "Ignore her. She's envious of any woman more beautiful than she is. Listen, are you familiar with *The Tales of Hoffmann*?"

She swallowed. "No."

"You're in for a treat, then. It's Offenbach's masterpiece, a wonderful fantasy. The character of Hoffmann is incredibly fascinating. When he finds out Olympia isn't a woman but a mechanical puppet, your heart bleeds for the poor guy. . . ."

Angie envisioned the opera as he described the story, imagining the beauty of the singers' intertwining voices. How wonderful it would be to hold an audience enthralled through sheer emotive power. If she had that, Angie thought, she'd be impervious to the hateful Mauras of the world.

4

Nickie burst into the kitchen, her ragtag jacket wide open despite the cold. She dropped her books on the table and raced over to Rosa, who was dozing by the stove.

"Mama! Another letter from Ange!"

"Go call Filippo."

Nickie raced to the top of the cellar stairs. "Hey Phil, another letter from Ange!" Without waiting for a reply, she hurried back into the kitchen.

Rosa tore open the envelope, and dollar bills fluttered down into her lap like confetti. "God bless my Angelina," she murmured, tucking the money carefully into her bodice. "Here, Nicoletta, you read."

Nickie's fingertips traced the raised pattern of twined flowers and leaves around the borders. A faint scent of roses emanated from the pale pink sheet. She lifted it to her nose and breathed in deeply.

Phil rushed up, dropping his clay-sculpting tool on the table. "What's she say?"

" 'Dear Mama,' " Nickie read aloud, " 'I send you a thousand kisses. How are you feeling? Does Nickie make the poultice for your chest like I showed her? I think of you and pray for you every day. I miss you all so much, even though the Urbanos treat me just like one of their own family. I am happy here, but I can't wait to see you all at Christmas. Tell Phil I think Frank Lloyd Wright is going to be jealous. . . .' " Nickie stopped and looked over at her brother, who grinned.

The letter went on, describing her voice lessons and afternoon teas with Mrs. Urbano, the paintings in their home and the woman's lovely furs—all the myriad details that Angie knew would entrance and delight her family.

When she finished, Phil took the letter from her hands to reread it for himself. When he left, it was Nickie's turn again, her eyes flying avidly down the neatly penned lines.

"Nicoletta," Rosa interrupted, smiling, "read me where our Angelina say she happy, they treat her like *famiglia* . . . she come home soon to see us."

Nickie turned the page over to find the desired lines. By the next day the letter would have the crinkled, limp feel of old paper—so many times would it have been passed from hand to hand, read and exclaimed over, folded and then reopened to be read again. Within its rose-scented boundaries the family shared Angie's new world; they could forget for a few minutes the torn linoleum underfoot, the drafty rooms that funneled every cold November wind whipping around the Hill.

Nickie sighed. "Boy, this Mrs. Urbano with her fancy clothes, and I couldn't even keep one lousy hand-me-down."

"Enough, Nicoletta," her mother said. "Your turn will come."

A knock on the door interrupted Rosa's mild rebuke. Gumbari Niello shuffled in, not waiting to be invited. "I gotta talk to you, Rosa."

"Nicoletta, bring coffee," Rosa said and then turned to their guest. "Come sit, Clara. We just hear from our Angelina. Nickie, show her the letter."

"I no have time for foolishness," the woman said, ignoring the chipped mug Nickie plopped down before her. "We got to talk."

Nickie began to read the letter anyway.

Their neighbor began to shake her head as if Nickie had been reading the obituary column aloud. "I no like the sound of it," she interrupted, blessing herself. "Too much good *fortuna*, my Giuseppe, he always say, and you call down the *maloch'*. It has begun already."

"Pah!" For all her softly voiced scorn, Mama glanced over her shoulder, as if the evil eye might indeed be seeking out her family, to strike in the hour of their happiness. "I no believe in the *maloch'*."

"No? Look at your sister-in-law. She sells her wine, makes good money." Gumbari Niello lowered her voice to a bare whisper. "The Black Hands, they take notice. My Giuseppe, he say they already make her pay."

"Shh," Mama warned her.

"Truth is truth," the woman answered darkly, drawing her shawl tighter against her body. "You rise above yourself, you stand out—they find you."

"Hsst!" Mama turned to Nickie. "Go upstairs, do your homework."

She made it as far as the bottom steps.

Gumbari Niello muttered in Italian, "Your sister-in-law's been shooting off her mouth as usual. . . ." She started to whisper.

Though Nickie strained as hard as she could, she could only catch bits of their troubled whisperings. As soon as the neighbor had left, Mama called out to Nickie. Her raspy voice was agitated.

"What's wrong, Mama? What's going to happen to Z'Maria?"

"Nothing. Go tell her we have to talk," Mama said, unable to mask the worry in her voice.

Nickie ran along the side of her aunt's house and slipped in through the kitchen door. The air was heavy with the smell of olive oil. "Hey, Z', Mama needs to see you right away."

"Later. Can you no see I'm busy?"

"What're you making?"

"A little surprise."

"Surprise for who?"

"You talk too much. Go home," she said, sounding as agitated as her sister-in-law had been. "Tell Rosa I be there in a little while."

Nickie glanced at the skillet of oil heating on the stove, then around the room. There was no pasta, no garlic, nothing. "That looks like a lot of oil. What's it for?"

"So, you pick today to learn how to cook," Z'Maria muttered, glaring. "Go like I told you."

"Hey Z', how about if I go get Ange's letter to read to you?" she said, determined to hang around until she found out what was going on. She had never seen her aunt so worked up.

"Little stupido, you blind?" she railed, turning her

sharp black eyes on Nickie. They were full of wrath. "I said, go home. Tell you mama I'll be down when I finish cooking."

"Cooking what?"

Z'Maria cuffed Nickie's head soundly, then grabbed her by the scruff of her neck and pushed her toward the door. "What I do is no you business. Go home."

At that moment someone pounded forcefully on the kitchen door. Z's iron grip tightened on the back of Nickie's neck as she wheeled her around and pushed her toward the hall. "Go out the front."

"No." Nickie dug in her heels. "Let me stay. I want to know what's going on."

The knocking grew louder and more insistent. "*Gesu Cristu Maria*," she swore under her breath, giving Nickie one last desperate shove toward the hall before hurrying toward the kitchen.

Pretending to leave, Nickie slammed the front door loudly, then crept back down the hall.

"I tell you no come back here!" Nickie froze, thinking her aunt had eyes in the back of her head, until she realized she was talking to someone outside her kitchen door.

"Where's my money?" The cocky voice, speaking a slurred Calabrian dialect, was annoyed. "I don't got time to listen to you."

"Miserable little leech," she accused. "Trying to suck the lifeblood of your own *paisan'*. What right do you have to steal from a poor widow like me?"

In reply he kicked the door so hard the hinges started to buckle. She unlatched it, then moved quickly to the stove.

As the man stepped over the threshold, Nickie caught a glimpse of black hair slicked back in a series of waves, the slickness a weird contrast to his acne-scarred cheeks. "You know the rules, eh, *gumbari*?" he said. The traditional term of kinship sounded condescending on his lips. "You pay, you get protection. You should be grateful."

"And is the dying mule grateful to the vultures as they pick over his bones?" She spat at his feet.

The man lifted his hand to hit her. Nickie sprang from her hiding place in the hall, but Z'Maria motioned her angrily to stay out of it.

"I warn you, *asino*." The man froze as Z'Maria picked

up the skillet of hot oil. "Take another step and you're gonna wish you were in hell after I'm done with you."

"I could kill you for this." His right hand darted inside his jacket.

"You try and they'll be scraping off your skin like melted wax." She grinned. "Maybe that's what you want, eh? The hot oil treatment would be an improvement for that *faccia brut'* of yours."

Every nerve in Nickie's body was taut, waiting for one of them to make a move. Her mind was working feverishly. If Z'Maria burned him, Nickie figured that they would have no choice but to kill the flunky. Sweat broke out on her forehead as she imagined plunging Z's knife between the man's ribs, hiding his body in the basement until it was dark enough to dig a hole in the ravine, burying the evidence of their defiance.

With infinite delicacy, the man pulled his hand out of his jacket and started to back toward the door. "Don't think you can get away with this," he blustered from the safety of the sidewalk. "It's not me you answer to, old lady. I'm just the messenger."

Z'Maria followed him out. "Then take this message, you piece of goat dung." She dashed the oil to the pavement in front of him, splattering his shoes. Dark droplets beaded up like moles on the expensive calf suede. "I got nothing to lose. You hear me? Nothing!"

"You'll pay for this."

She brushed her joined fingers under her chin in contempt as he retreated toward the street. "Worm!"

Nickie stared at her aunt in proud disbelief. She looked both angry and exultant, as if the confrontation had somehow purged her blood. "Z', are you crazy?"

"You say nothing to nobody. *Capish?*" Her eyes snapped as she turned on Nickie. "Not you pap', not nobody."

"That creep could've killed you."

"Him?" she scoffed. "Not unless his boss give the order."

"That's what I mean," Nickie said, her heart still pounding. "What are you going to do when he comes back?"

"Listen," she said, clamping a bony hand on Nickie's shoulder. "Four weeks I pay and shuddup. Then I ask myself, what da hell for? When your Z' Lorenzo was

alive and the mills were strong, those filthy *mani neri*
slunk around like dogs, holding out their hands every
payday. My Lorenzo, you pap', all the *italiani* they pay
because they fear for their families. But me, I'm alone
now. They no scare me."

"But they'll kill you."

"*Sì*, and when I go, I take my wine with me." She
grinned, making a slashing motion across her neck with
the side of her hand. *"Finito."*

"Z', you can't get away with this."

Her hand tightened on Nickie's shoulder until she
winced. "I'm warn you, stay outta my business. Keep
your mouth shut. Now, go home and tell you mama I be
right over."

Pittsburgh's strip district crowded the narrow bank of
the Allegheny River at the base of Polish Hill. The
bulbous dome of the Immaculate Heart of Mary Church
loomed over the wholesale-food market like a reluctant
patron saint. From early dawn until noon, the district
hummed with life. A train off the Baltimore & Ohio line
disgorged shellfish from Maryland, sides of beef from
Omaha and winter oranges from distant California. Butch-
ers, bakers and vendors of all kinds plied their trade,
loading up the old Model T trucks that converged on the
marketplace, enroute to and from Delilo's Market in
Coalport, Stein's Deli in Squirrel Hill and scores of other
neighborhood groceries. By night the large warehouse
doors were locked up tight and the narrow alleyways
were empty.

The last warehouse on the north end of the strip district was a decrepit place with a sign that read "Carlo's
Wholesale Beer Distribution" in faded letters. Behind
the padlocked steel doors, however, the cavernous interior boasted rows upon rows of stacked crates of unlabeled liquor bottles and gleaming new pinball machines
ready for delivery.

Carlo DiPiano sat in his office at the back of the
warehouse, methodically recounting the bills sorted on
his desk in neat stacks according to denomination. He
was a small-boned man with finicky manners, the kind
who might have made an excellent florist.

At last his eyes flicked up from the money. "I'm going to ask you one more time, Bruno," he said to the pock-marked man standing nervously by the door. "Where is the rest of my money?"

"Boss, I swear I'm telling the truth. It kills me to admit it, but it's true," Bruno whined. "The old bitch threatened to douse me with boiling oil, and she would a done it, boss. I seen her eyes. She said she had nothing to lose."

"Nothing?" He cocked his head like an inquisitive bird. "Nobody has nothing to lose. Sit down, Bruno, and pay attention to how I do business." He picked up the telephone and asked the operator for a Coalport number. He smiled at Bruno while he waited for the call to be put through. "I'm curious about an old *gumbari* who's got such balls. Tomorrow you and me and Jimmy, we're going to pay a little visit to this Maria Branzino. And no mistakes this time, eh? Hey, Cheech!" he interrupted himself as he spoke into the telephone. "Yeah, it's Carlo. I need some information. . . ."

5

Saturday dawned bright and crisp, one last illusory taste of Indian summer before the Hill hunkered down for the cold gray reality of December.

Nickie slopped a rag from the bucket of water and ammonia. I hate washing windows, she thought as her thin arms moved like angry pistons up and down on the glass. At least if Angie had been here they could have laughed and talked, and the time would have gone fast.

Out of the corner of her eye, she watched Pap climb the outside steps and head down Mitchell to his bocci-ball game. As soon as the coast was clear, Vic and Freddie raced out to play stickball with their friends. She grew so used to their shouting and arguing that when they suddenly fell silent she got suspicious. She dried her hands on her skirt and opened the window.

The kids scattered before the shiny grille of a black Dodge Deluxe nosing up Mitchell Avenue. The pulse in Nickie's temple started to throb when the big sedan drew to a stop across the street from Z'Maria's house. The pockmarked man had returned with his boss. "Freddie, Vic!" she shouted. "Get in here."

She was about to shut the window when suddenly the door to Z'Maria's small second-story balcony opened. Nickie ducked back as her aunt stepped out to drape her prized "Turkey carpet" over the wrought-iron railing.

Concealed behind the curtain, Nickie saw the pockfaced man and one other emerge from the car. Their eyes methodically swept the street, now empty. Nickie stared at the balding, slightly built man whom they ushered out of the back seat. She guessed he was about Pap's age, but there was an air of youth about him, maybe because he was so small. He didn't look like much of a boss man.

Her eyes darted back to Z'Maria, who was acting as if she hadn't seen a thing. She rolled up her sleeves and pushed her thick gray bun up higher on her head. Then she took up the rug beater and began to thwack it rhythmically against the faded carpet, sending columns of dust dancing upward in the morning light.

Nickie saw the flunky jerk his head toward the balcony. The rhythm of the rug beater quickened until dust rained down on the street. At last she straightened and locked gazes with him.

"Signora, you got a couple a minutes?" The man addressed her in a cool, unruffled way. "Can you come down here?"

Affecting not to have heard him, Z'Maria turned her contemptuous gaze on the pockmarked flunky. "You think just because you bring your *capo* to the house, now I'm going to pay?" She looked back at the boss. "I tell your *mulo* the other day, not another cent."

Smooth as silk came his reply in Italian: "My dear signora, I didn't come here for any money. I just want to have a talk with you. Come downstairs."

"Your kind is clever with the lies."

"Such vinegary words from one whose wine is said to be so sweet." Nickie heard the cold amusement in his voice. "I swear on the grave of my dear mother, I have only come to taste this wine for myself."

Seconds passed. Then Nickie heard Z'Maria opening her door to admit the three men. As soon as they had disappeared inside, Nickie bolted from the window.

Crouching, she ran along the narrow walk that led back to Z'Maria's kitchen, following the sound of her gravelly, complaining voice through the open windows. She edged up to the sill and peeked in. The man stood in the doorway to the hall, flanked by his guards. Staring at him, Nickie saw that the air of youth was deceiving. There was strength and a subtle focus of will in his narrow face.

"Ah, no boiling oil today," the man said, sniffing the air delicately. "Only the incomparable bouquet of good country wine."

"Say what you came to say," she commanded. "I am a busy woman."

"Your neighbors talk, signora. I have heard nothing but praise for the wine you make. How about a sample for a *paisan'*?"

Z'Maria pulled out a bottle and slapped a glass down on the table. Then she gestured him rudely toward a chair.

He made no move to sit. "You realize, signora, I am sure, that you have unpardonably flouted long-standing rules of, shall we say, etiquette." His voice was soft, the graceful gesture of his soft manicured hands almost lulling. But what unnerved Nickie was the way his deep-set eyes emanated latent cruelty.

"Etiquette! Is that what you call your game now? You expect me to pay 'protection' money to you? To protect me from what? I can take care of myself. Go ahead and hurt me—what do I care?"

"Signora, you don't want to make enemies for yourself or for your family."

"Leave them out of this!"

"You and me, signora, we are not so different. We both care about our families. You care about the safety of yours, and I care about the honor of mine. I have to tell you this, dear lady: Injured honor demands restitution."

Nickie didn't hang around to hear more.

She crept away and slid down the steep embankment that marked the border between the Branzinos' two lots and raced toward Phil, who sat with his sketchpad beneath the porch. "Z's in trouble," she said, her breath coming in quick gasps. "The mafiasos are twisting her arm to pay up."

"You sure?"

"They're with her now."

Phil jumped up and started to pace. His eyes moved speculatively to the wagon with his experimental engine, which had lain innocently under a tarp since the last fiasco. "I could drag this up into her yard."

"Yeah, and then what?"

He grinned. "I'll scare the hell out of those goons."

It sounded dicey, but since she couldn't think of anything better, she didn't argue. She scrambled back up the embankment and peered cautiously into the kitchen, only to find her nose inches from a broad, nail-bitten hand leaning on the sill. Her heart pounding, she eased to a sitting position beneath the window and prayed they wouldn't come out.

She heard Z'Maria say, "So what did your Bruno expect? A woman alone must protect her honor."

A whisper of laughter breathed through the faked soft voice, giving Nickie the creeps. "Such a small woman to have held you at bay, eh, Bruno?"

The man at the window shifted uneasily, as if remembering his humiliation.

"You mentioned a deal. . . ." Z'Maria said, tension making her voice harsher than usual.

Nickie heard the scrape of chair legs across the linoleum and ventured another quick peek inside. The boss had sat down and was gesturing to one of his men to pour from the bottle on the table. He drank deeply from the small tumbler. "I see the tales of your wine were not exaggerated."

"I don't share my recipe."

"I am a man of business," he said, sponging his lips fastidiously with his handkerchief. "Not a vintner."

Z'Maria answered bluntly, "I see that at least I am not dealing with a fool."

"The men of Naviti have never been fools, dear lady."

"Naviti?" Z'Maria echoed, surprised. "Then you are *paisan'* of my cousins, the Tellarios."

"I was named for Carlo Tellario. He stood for me at my baptism, God rest his soul."

Z'Maria clucked. "Shame on you then to wish ill on *me*, the man's favorite."

"You still misunderstand, signora. I came here today in the spirit of friendship. I wish to propose a partnership. If you will permit me to assist you in augmenting your production, I will become your exclusive distributor around town. My private operations will save us the expense and, shall we say, the inconvenience of dealing with the state liquor board."

Z'Maria grunted noncommittally.

The man went on. "Naturally, I would expect our partnership to benefit us both. You could, for example, present me with a certain percentage of your production. As a gift . . . between friends."

There it was—the shakedown—couched in a way that would let them both save face. Nickie wondered what was going through Z'Maria's head. She knew her aunt was a realist. These people were a fact of life. They were *paisan'*; in a twisted sense, they were almost family. And families stuck together. On the other hand, she could be as stubborn and irascible as Pap.

Nickie strained to hear her answer, while out of the corner of her eye she watched Phil. He had tied the wagon to the big elm tree in Z'Maria's backyard and was pouring kerosene down the pipe. Frantically she motioned him to wait a second, but he took her signal as the go-ahead. Backing away toward the shelter of the old root-cellar door, Nickie watched him flick the battery switch. A series of rapid explosions rent the air as the unpredictable pipe engine blew itself apart, sending pieces of metal flying like shrapnel.

The mafioso's men burst out into the yard with their pistols drawn. Z'Maria was hot on their heels. "Don't shoot—he's my nephew!" She screamed like a mad woman. "Rotten *fragiada* kid, I'll kill him myself!"

Her heart sinking, Nickie watched the pockmarked flunky catch Phil by his hair just as he started to slide down the embankment. "**All right, you little asshole, what's goin' on?**"

"Nothing!"

Nickie could see that Phil's ear was bleeding. Z'Maria's yard looked like a war zone: Ragged shards of metal were scattered everywhere. Z'Maria and the flunky dragged Phil into the kitchen. As soon as the coast was clear, Nickie ran back to the window. Her aunt's important visitor was just emerging from beneath the table. She watched Z'Maria hurry over to the man, dusting off his suit and straightening his white-carnation boutonniere.

"A practical joke on my nephew's part. He invents things—foolish things," she said sharply, grabbing a big floursack towel from the sink and binding it around Phil's head like a turban.

The man eyed Phil calmly. "What is the boy's name?"

"Filippo, my godson." She pushed Phil forward. "Go on, you apologize to Signor DiPiano."

Phil stubbornly kept silent. The man gestured with a snap of his fingers for Bruno to pour more wine.

Z'Maria prodded Phil with her thumb. "Tell him."

"It wasn't anything," Phil mumbled, giving his aunt a dirty look. "It was just a game."

"Such an elaborate game," DiPiano said expressionlessly.

"We didn't know Z' had company."

"But of course you didn't." The man's irony was stinging. "I have just one warning for you, Filippo. When clever boys play clever games, they better be careful. Their cleverness can backfire on them—with dangerous consequences. Now get out." To Z' he said in the same soft, unruffled voice, "The boy is smart, signora," DiPiano said. "But smart boys can be an expensive complication. His little stunt will cost you."

Nickie slunk off down the street like a wet cat, mulling over possible alibis until she settled on one that seemed airtight. But she should have known better than to think she could fool her aunt. Z'Maria knew her too well.

When she caught up with Nickie later, she railed, "I should break you neck. Did I no tell you to stay out of my—"

"But I thought they were going to kill you."

"Kill me?" Z'Maria cuffed Nickie's head. "*Stupida.*

The man just wants to do business. You know what they say—better to talk with the devil than lay silent in a casket with your rosary. *Ha capito*?"

Nickie nodded. She understood all right. Her aunt had done the only thing she could. Coalport wasn't Highland Park. Survival in these mean streets invariably meant compromising with the devil.

6

Angie stood with Mrs. Urbano in the foyer of the Highland Park house, smoothing down the skirt of her raspberry-colored wool suit. She was eager to be off.

Berthe emerged from the kitchen, bearing a shopping basket overflowing with tangerines and apples, a canned ham and an enormous wheel of cheese, and set it on the marble table. Mrs. Urbano beamed. "Angie, we wanted to select something that your whole family could enjoy. I hope we did the right thing."

"The basket's lovely." Angie fought to hide her dismay. "But maybe it'd be better if you brought it yourself tomorrow when you come."

After a moment's hesitation the woman nodded. "Your father must understand it's a simple holiday gift. Not charity."

"Of course," Angie said too quickly. "Besides, I've got a lot to carry already."

"Of course you do. How silly of me." The woman's smile returned. "I'll go ring Harry."

The front door opened and Louis breezed in, his sandy hair tousled. Angie turned from the mirror, where she was fiddling with the lamb's-wool collar of her coat. "Louis!"

"I hope that's pleased surprise I hear in your voice," he said, lounging casually against the marble table.

Angie turned back to the mirror, acutely aware of his eyes on her. She had noticed a subtle but distinct change in his attitude toward her since the night of the opera. His air of sardonic amusement had vanished, leaving in its place a disarming attentiveness. Although she felt attracted to him, she hardly dared admit it to herself.

He came to stand behind her, resting his hands lightly on her shoulders. "I'm glad to see you're bundling up. It's cold out."

Her eyes met his in the mirror. To cover the nervous flutter of her pulse, she teased him: "Judging by that red nose, it must be."

"I ordered it specially for Christmas."

"You should have got one for me, too. It would match my suit."

Louis turned her around to face him. "I've never seen you quite this radiant and bubbly before. It makes me rather jealous of the family you're so eager to see."

Angie blushed, not knowing what to say.

"We'll miss you very much," he went on in the same intimate, faintly teasing way. "You know that, don't you?" He brushed her cheek with his forefinger. "Look, I'd like to drive you home."

Thrilled and flattered, Angie said, "Oh, I'd love—"

"Louis." Startled, they both looked up to see his father standing at the top of the stairs. Mr. Urbano's voice was raspy and congested from the effects of a cold. "What were you intending—to dash off with her in the Auburn? That would make a fine impression on her parents, wouldn't it?"

"I intended to ask to use your car," Louis answered tightly. "And surely there'd have been nothing improper in just seeing her home."

Just then Mrs. Urbano came out into the hall again. "Louis darling, how nice of you to come home early to see Angie off." She looked up as her son's eyes flicked to the second-story landing. "I thought you were resting, dear," she called to her husband. "Feeling any better?"

"I was." He straightened the lapels of his bathrobe. "Have a nice Christmas with your family, Angelina, and give them our regards." She nodded, but he had already redirected his gaze toward his son. "Louis, I'd like to see you upstairs."

"Come along, Angie," Mrs. Urbano said, pushing her with gentle firmness toward the door.

Disappointed, Angie allowed herself to be walked out to the car. She longed to ask Mrs. Urbano what went on between father and son, yet she didn't dare. Angie realized she was still an outsider, no closer to understanding the source of tension between them than when she had first arrived.

Angie leaned back against the soft leather upholstery and tried to relax, to put everything out of her mind but thoughts of home. As they got closer to Coalport, she grew ever more excited. Familiar landmarks swept past one after another in the swiftly falling dusk. She was startled by a pair of deer that leaped high amid the tombstones in St. Mary's Cemetery before disappearing into the woods at the far edge. As the Cadillac sped across the bridge toward town, vibrations from the metal-slatted trestles made her whole body tingle. The gray December mist had lifted enough to reveal the muzzy outline of coke furnaces rising from the floor of the river valley. Angie's heart leaped as her eyes swept a distant wooded ridge, its bare-limbed trees forming a frieze of stark and desolate beauty. She was almost home.

At last they turned onto Mitchell Avenue. She was shocked at how narrow and dingy it seemed. The houses hunched close together like animals seeking warmth.

The automobile eased to a stop. She and Harry had not exchanged a word during the whole trip. Still without acknowledging her presence, he got out and opened the trunk. When Angie saw he wasn't going to open her door, she climbed out herself.

"Thanks a lot," she cracked as he dumped her suitcase and shopping bag of brightly wrapped parcels on the sidewalk. "You're such a swell guy, I bet Santa'll bring everything on your list."

"You're the expert on that, aren't you?"

"What's that supposed to mean?"

"I mean, you're the expert on getting everything on your list. I've never seen such a slick gold digger—little miss sweet innocence, living high off the hog. Bet you think you're real sly the way you insinuated yourself into the big house, making sure they couldn't do without you."

"Look," she retorted, stunned by his hostility, "I didn't insinuate myself anywhere. I was invited into their home."

"Yeah, yeah." He slid back behind the wheel of the Cadillac. "Must be nice to be able to play the bigshot slumming in the old neighborhood."

He slammed the door shut and gunned the motor.

Upset by the attack, Angie turned and stared down into the Branzinos' cobbled yard. Her eye was drawn to the castor-bean plants she and Phil had planted to hide the unsightly girth of the brick bread oven. The tall plants had long since shriveled to ugly brown stalks. How pathetic their efforts had been!

What if her family felt as Harry did, that she was just a bigshot coming back to show off? Her uneasiness grew as she imagined Pap's reaction. To him the little gifts she had brought might be a slap in the face.

Her fears were momentarily allayed when the screen door shot open and Freddie and Vic burst up the steps, shouting with excitement. Angie clung to them, drinking in their familiar scents. Impatiently they pulled free, their eyes drawn to the mysterious parcels in the shopping bag.

"Listen, you two," she said hurriedly, "I want you to take all this stuff and put it up under your beds, okay? It's a surprise. I—I don't want Pap to know yet."

Vic looked disappointed. "But when can we open 'em?"

"Tomorrow morning."

Gina came running out of the house. "Ange, Ange!" she squeaked.

Angie swung her little sister up in her arms. "Oh God, you're getting so big! Pretty soon I'm not going to be able to lift you at all."

Gina wrapped her legs monkey-style around Angie's waist. "Ange, guess what! Z'Maria and Pete cooked all kinds a fishes."

Angie nuzzled Gina's neck until she giggled. "And did you help?"

"Naw, I was helpin' the boys with the Christmas tree."

"Tree!"

"Yeah. Vic found it."

"Oh, my."

"An' guess what else!" she rushed on. "Phil drew stars and I cut 'em out. And I was an angel at school in a play. We learned all about Santy Claus. You think he'll find our house, Ange? He ain't never been here before." She spoke with such wistful earnestness it tore Angie's heart.

"Of course he'll come, *carina*," she said, thinking of the pretty doll she had chosen with such care in Kaufmann's toy department. "He's going to bring you something really special."

As Angie carried her up the steps, Gina smiled radiantly.

Warmth and noise and life surged around Angie in a wave. Everyone was laughing and talking and touching her, all except Nickie, who barely looked at her. Angie's eyes sought her mother. She rushed over toward the rocking chair by the coal stove and knelt down beside her. "Mama!" Tenderly she cupped her mother's face between her hands. "I missed you so much!"

"So beautiful," the woman crooned. "My Angelina is growing into a beautiful woman."

For all her mother's joy at seeing her, Angie could see that she was wan and tired, that even talking cost her an effort now. Angie smiled despite the tears that threatened to well up. God, how wonderful it felt to be home.

The tumult died when Papa appeared in the doorway of the parlor. Angie stood up and looked at him uncertainly. His expression was shuttered, as if he were confronting a stranger.

"Hello, Papa." She went forward to kiss him. His bristly mustache grated her cheek, and she caught the acrid scent of steel shavings and coke that clung to him always.

Phil called to her again. "Hey, Ange, dinner's not for a little while yet. I want you to come down the cellar and see my model."

She turned away from Pap with relief. "Let me get a cup of coffee first."

The kitchen was steamy and redolent with the pungent, sharp aromas of an Italian Christmas Eve. Pete wiped his hands and gave her a big bear hug. "Hey Ange, we made a feast to celebrate your coming home."

"Smells like Atlantic City in here," she teased him. "What did you do—cook up every fish in the ocean?"

He grinned sheepishly. "Mama told me to go all out. Here, taste my sauce."

"Mm, delicious," she said, licking the spoon. "Now, how about some of that good strong coffee to warm me up?" She reached for a mug and scooped out a ladleful of milk-laced coffee from the big pot simmering on a back burner.

Cup in hand, Angie went down the steep cellar steps. Phil had switched on the dim overhead bulb and stood waiting impatiently by his model. Angie drew in her breath as she stared at the delicate construction of glass and wood geometric shapes cantilevered out from a carved clay base. "Nickie's letter didn't do it justice. It's fabulous!!"

"You mean it?"

"They've never seen anything like it at Coalport High. You'll take first prize."

"I have to confess something, Ange." He leaned back against the workbench littered with tools and wood and clay. "It's not the teachers at school I'm worried about impressing. I—I applied for a scholarship to Carnegie Tech."

"That's wonderful!"

"You're the first person I've told. I didn't want to say anything because I'm afraid I won't get it."

"What do you mean you won't get it? If anyone deserves a scholarship, it's you."

"Pap says I'm wasting my time. He says I can make models and do experiments until I'm blue in the face, but it won't do any good." He turned away and started to punch a mound of clay on the workbench. "You know how it is when he starts in about how he had dreams when he came to this country, how he worked for twenty years and it only got him deeper in a hole. He says nothing's ever going to change for people like us."

"Why do you even listen to him? I warned you once, you can't let Pap drag you down to his level." Out of the corner of her eye, she saw Nickie sit down on the top cellar step, but she pretended not to notice, afraid of driving her away.

Phil spoke again, his voice tight. "Let's face it, Ange, I wouldn't exactly fit in with the other Tech students. How many of them do you think have a mill laborer for a father and an aunt who makes bootleg wine for the neighborhood mafioso?"

"Want me to finish it for you, Phil?" Anger tinged Nickie's husky voice. "And an older sister who's a glorified servant downtown. Yeah, she gets to dress nice and live like a queen, but that doesn't make her any less a servant—ready to jump at the least command."

Angie looked up at her reproachfully, knowing what she said was true but hurt anyway.

"Shut up, Nickie," Phil growled. "That's crap and you know it."

"Leave her alone," Angie said. "God, I wish there was a way you and I could trade places. You don't know how it kills me to come back and hear you talking like this. And to see Mama so frail! She's worse, Phil. You can't deny it. I should be the one at home, helping her."

"Mama wants you to stay in the city, Ange."

Shakily, she set her coffee mug on the step. "You don't know how guilty I feel sometimes," she confessed, sighing. "I used to think the whole world drank coffee out of a big pot, so no one would get any more sugar or milk than anyone else. Then that first morning at the Urbanos I saw a whole pitcher of cream on the table. I—"

"*Veni, mangia!*" Z'Maria shouted down at them. "Or you want us to throw down scraps?"

"We're coming," Phil called, pulling the cord of the naked overhead bulb.

They got to the table just as Pete and the younger boys emerged from the kitchen carrying serving bowls heaped high with fried smelts and spaghetti with calamari sauce. Under Z'Maria's direction, Pete had also baked a mullet —as close a replica to the Mediterranean *triglia* as could be found—and stuffed the fish with bread crumbs and rosemary. But occupying the place of honor on the table was a whole coiled eel, roasted in a casserole with oil, wine, garlic and bay leaves. A hush fell over the family as they gathered around the rare abundance that graced their table. The holiday feast was a sacrament, in its way as miraculous and sacred as Church ritual.

"Angelina," Mama said as they all sat down, "you lead the grace for us."

Angie nodded. "Bless us, O Lord, and these thy gifts. . . ." She uttered the familiar words with such lilting, resonant clarity that everyone stopped praying aloud with her to listen. "And thank you, God," she concluded, faltering before their stares, "for our family, for the closeness and the love that we share. Amen."

"Someone bring the knife," Pap barked as he stood. "Quick, before it gets cold." Unceremoniously he cut into the rich, oily flesh of the eel. The sumptuous repast and the return of his daughter left him outwardly unmoved. "Eat," he commanded.

Between mouthfuls of food, everyone shouted back and forth—a dozen conversational threads splitting, intertwining and unraveling again.

"Angelina, you no touch your spaghett'," Rosa admonished during a momentary lull in the cheerful bedlam. "And it's your favorite."

"I've had quite enough, thank you, Mama. I'm too excited to be hungry, really."

Again everyone stared. Angie laughed nervously as her eyes darted around the table. "What is the matter with all of you?"

Finally Phil spoke up. "It's just—you sound different, Ange. You don't sound like someone from the Hill anymore. If I closed my eyes, I'd think I was listening to a stranger talking."

"But I'm not a stranger. You know that. I'm the same old Ange." The more she insisted, the more she realized they didn't quite believe her. "Come on," she pleaded. As she opened her arms in appeal, she knocked over her wine glass. She jumped up to get a damp cloth to sponge the red stain from the tablecloth.

"Can we no eat in peace?" Pap roared, his eyes baleful. "You come home with your fancy clothes and talk— turn my whole house upside down. Sit and be quiet!"

"No, I won't be quiet," she retorted angrily. She glanced at Phil, so tainted by Papa's pessimism that he had begun to doubt himself, and went on recklessly, "Maybe it's time this family sees a person can change her life and be given a little respect."

A tense silence fell over the table as Pap stared at her. When he spoke at last, his tone was uncharacteristically soft, a malicious softness that sent a warning prickle of fear down Angie's spine. "You think all of a sudden you got to be treated like a queen because you look like one?"

"Not like a queen," she said, making peace. "Like a decent human being. Why should that be too much to ask?" Her anger surged anew as she leaned forward and rested her hands on either side of her plate. "Why do you never have a nice word for your own family? The Johnny Bulls call us rude peasants—well, maybe you deserve to be called that, but not the rest of us."

In a fury Pap shoved his chair back. "Not another word, understand me, or I'll ram your teeth down your throat!" He jumped to his feet, his narrow mean eyes moving slowly around the table. "You want to hear about nice words, eh? I tell you. I save them—I save them to beg for work so my family won't starve. I save them to say something nice to the sonofabitch foreman down the mill who calls me a dirty lazy dago when I'm shoveling coal into a furnace hotter than hell itself. I save them for that lickspittle pig at the pay window."

"So you have to treat us the way they treat you—like dirt?"

"Shut up. You don't know nothing. You come back here, try to tell me how I should speak within my own family." His voice quavered with suppressed fury. "The outside world I cannot control. My own family I can and will control, you understand me, Angelina?"

"You won't control me. I won't let you. I live my own life now."

Pap looked toward Mama with supreme contempt. "Is this why I allow her to go live with the 'merican? A daughter must live as her father decrees. Any other is no better than a whore."

Rosa went white. "Frank!"

"Oh, you try to put a pretty face on it—voice lessons, companion to a lonely woman. But it's all the same bullshit. In the old days the rich priests and landowners took women as they pleased. It's no different in this country. She's nothing but a rotten *bagascia*, a whore to the rich."

Angie shouted, "You make me sick! I don't have to listen to this!"

"Bullshit, you will listen!"

Tears of anger and humiliation streaked her face. "I hate you!"

Before anyone could intervene, she picked up her plate of spaghetti and heaved it full force down the length of the table toward him. Pap lifted his arm and ducked. The plate missed him by a hair and crashed into the wall behind him. Broken shards of china clattered to the floor, but the pasta and calamari adhered to the wall as if it were a bizarre decoration. The family stared in horrified fascination at the red smear of sauce oozing down the wall.

No one dared to budge as Pap started around the table toward her. Despite the dread that twisted her stomach, Angie stubbornly stood her ground.

"The food I provide, the life I gave you is not good enough, is that it?" He dragged the big ceramic bowl filled with spaghetti across the table, then without warning he caught her head and shoved her face down into it. "Eat, greedy piglet that wants everything. Eat!"

Sauce filled her nose and mouth. She started to choke, unable to breathe. Flailing, she clawed in desperation at his shirt. After what seemed like an eternity later, she was aware of someone pulling Pap off her.

"Get away!" He struck out wildly, fighting and cursing. *"Che te posina sufocat' sangue tue,"* he cursed. "May you choke in your own blood."

Angie dimly heard Mama crying as she wiped the girl's face with a dishtowel. Angie fought to catch her breath, more terrified of suffocation than of Pap. The sauce stung her eyes and weighed down her lashes, and she felt as if she were looking through a smeared window.

"Get away!" Pap tried to swing at Phil and Z'Maria, who clung to him like ticks on a dog's neck.

Z'Maria screamed, "Angelina, run! Go over to my place. *Franguch'*, enough now!"

Angie stumbled out the door. She ran up the steps,

hearing Pap still raging like a maniac down in the house, and stood gasping on the sidewalk. It looked as if she had bled all over the jacket of her new suit. It would have to be burned, she thought dully. She could never let the Urbanos or anyone else find out what had occurred in this house that night.

She began to shiver, as much from shock as from the cold. She barely noticed when Z'Maria joined her, putting a protective arm around her shoulder as she guided Angie down the sidewalk toward the lighted warmth of her own kitchen.

Z'Maria set her down at the table. She filled a basin with warm water, then washed Angie's hair and face as if she were a little child. Not a word passed between them. Then her aunt put her to bed and closed the door softly after her.

Angie huddled in the narrow bed, faintly comforted by the faint scent of rosemary that lingered on the flannel shift Z'Maria had given her. She stared sightlessly at the shadows on the wall cast by the streetlight, remembering past Christmases.

She envisioned her aunt winding up the old Victrola and playing her favorite record. As the tinny strains of "The Merry Widow Waltz" filled the small, sloping parlor, Z'Maria would execute a jaunty three-step. In retaliation Pap would fetch his concertina and begin to play, singing over the recording in his loud, rusty baritone. Drawn by the music, the neighbors would drift in, bearing gifts of food—deep-fried *cannariculi* soaked in sweet wine, or the roasted almond-stuffed figs they called *crocette*. At midnight the distant church bells would herald midnight mass, and the women would draw up their shawls over their heads as they left the house.

Angie drew scant comfort from the memories. They only served to remind her how much of an outsider she had become.

If she no longer belonged here, where did she belong? Despite her attraction to Louis, she couldn't shake the notion that her presence in the Urbano home would always be a lovely, unreal game. She was a toy for Mrs. Urbano, a smiling, singing wind-up doll that performed on cue, easing momentarily the pain of her loss. Angie was a poor substitute. She shivered, wondering what would happen to her. Suddenly, even her feelings for Louis seemed like a will-o'-the-wisp.

Angie sat all during the cold and gray Christmas morning at Z'Maria's kitchen table, sipping coffee. Her stained jacket was soaking in the sink, and the whole kitchen reeked of calamari. The smell made her sick, and she realized she probably looked as bad as she felt. Her eyelids were puffy and heavy from crying.

Nickie came over at noon, carrying her sister's overnight bag. Angie noticed that Nickie was wearing the new skirt and sweater she had brought for her. "Oh, no. Don't tell me you guys opened those presents."

"How could we disappoint Gina? You know she was expecting Santa Clause. We opened our presents upstairs. Pap didn't see us."

"But he will. You're wearing yours, for Pete's sake."

Nickie bent down to open her sister's bag. Crammed on top of Angie's neatly folded belongings was one of Dolly Labrino's hand-me-down dresses that had been passed along to the Branzino girls. Nickie pulled it out with a grin. "I just put this on over it whenever Pap's around."

"You're too sly for your own good."

Nickie ignored her. "Better hurry and change before the Urbanos come. If you're stupid enough to stick around here, I'll go to Pittsburgh in your place—maybe their dog will make room in his doghouse for me. I'll bet that dog's treated better than Pap treats us."

"Don't talk that way."

"Why not? It's true."

Angie sighed. "I wish I could've just kept my mouth shut last night. I feel like a louse. I get all of you worked up; I ruin everyone's Christmas, and now I'm leaving again."

Nickie shot her a narrow, mocking look. "Yeah, come to think of it, you should feel like a louse."

"I'm going to apologize to Pap."

"Hey, don't get carried away." Nickie grinned. "I'll never forget the way you zinged that plate at him."

*   *   *

The Branzino house was deathly still when the two girls came in. Angie went immediately to the parlor, but Pap wasn't there. Instead she saw the Christmas tree Gina had been so thrilled about.

Vic had "found" it, she thought, imagining the denuded top of some poor neighbor's juniper bush. The dark green fronds hung almost flat against the wall, like a painting. She recognized Phil's handiwork in the clever design of the construction-paper stars, misshapen though they were because of Gina's clumsy snipping. Knowing all this effort had been for her sake, Angie felt at once touched and saddened. She had ruined the holiday for everyone. The room's festive air seemed a mockery.

Angie turned sharply as she heard Pap's heavy tread. "Pap," she began, her hands clenching the sides of her skirt. "I'm sorry."

He stopped, his eyes burning into her. "What are you doing here? I no want to see your face again."

"Papa, please—"

"I don't know you," he said with stony disdain. "You are not my daughter."

"Pap, what are you saying?"

"Frank," Mama appealed softly from the top of the stairs, clutching Phil's arm for support. Angie stared up at them, mute with misery, as Mama began to beg. "Listen to her, she's your daughter. Frank—"

"Shut up!" Pap roared, almost drowning the sound of someone knocking on the front door.

Nickie flew out of the kitchen. "Gesu! Isn't anyone going to let the Urbanos in?"

"Merry Christmas!" Josephine Urbano called cheerfully, nearly bumping into Nickie, who hovered around her, greedily taking note of her sapphire necklace and earrings. "I hope we're not too ear . . ." She stopped, looking from Nickie to Angie and their father. Unaware of the tension, Louis Junior bustled in behind his mother, carrying the enormous basket of food.

Angie stepped forward to greet them. "Merry Christmas," she said stiffly. "Thanks so much for coming, but I hate to think of Mr. Urbano being left alone and ill on Christmas Day. We should go."

Mrs. Urbano, who had begun unwinding the cashmere

muffler from around her neck, gave Angie a guarded look. "Of course, dear, if that's what you—"

"Signora Urbano," Mama interceded warmly, despite her obvious exhaustion from descending the stairs. "Please come in, sit."

Instantly Nickie and Phil took their cue from their mother, doing their best to smooth over the situation and make their guests feel welcome. Louis won the admiration of the Branzino children by shaking hands with them all around. Only Angie and Papa stood isolated and remote from the cheerful tableau.

Rosa broke off her conversation with Mrs. Urbano to address her husband in a softly rebuking voice. "Frank, we have guests. How about the anisette, some wine . . ."

Angie watched her father warily, feeling sick at heart. Pap had made it clear he had washed his hands of her; why did Mama have to pretend last night's ugly scene hadn't occurred?

As the Urbanos chatted, graciously accepting the coffee and biscotti Rosa offered them, Angie stood by the parlor door, refusing to sit down. Pap sat in his armchair by the Victrola, puffing on his pipe as if the smoke could shield him from the unwelcome guests.

"I must tell you both," Mrs. Urbano said, turning to encompass Pap in the conversation, "that I am so grateful to you for letting Angie come to stay with us."

Louis added, "Mother hasn't been this cheerful in a long time. Last year she was too blue to even think about the holidays. Angie's presence has brightened all our lives."

Angie's gaze slid uneasily to Pap, wondering how he would take this praise of her. But he sat stonily, his expression revealing nothing.

Louis turned to Pap with his most charming smile. "With your permission, sir, I would like to escort your daughter to a few of the parties this season . . . under my parents' chaperonage, of course."

Pap stared at him, his eyes now glittering with malice. "Be my guest," he rasped. "Parties are all she is good for now." With that he stood and stomped out of the room.

Mrs. Urbano and Louis stared after him, their excellent manners a shield for their embarrassed shock. Angie turned to them, her face clouded with humiliation. "You'll have to forgive my father. Things—things haven't been going well."

"I'm so sorry, my dear," Mrs. Urbano said at once, standing up. "Perhaps we shouldn't have intruded on your Christmas." She turned to Rosa. "You do understand, don't you, that our actions are motivated solely out of affection for your daughter? I hope we haven't offended . . ."

Rosa held out her hand to the woman. "I am so grateful for everything you're doing for her. My husband . . ." She broke off, shaking her head.

When Angie left with the Urbanos, her head was pounding. What a mess she had made of everything. She had meant to set an example for the other kids; instead she had lowered herself to Pap's level—brawling with him like an animal. God, how she hated him. But he wouldn't have the last say. She vowed that her own life would refute his narrow, bleak vision of the world.

7

May 1936

Nickie settled into the Cadillac's front seat next to Z'Maria, smoothing her hands over the pink taffeta dress Angie had sent.

"Nicoletta," Z' Maria warned her before the others got into the car, "I no want you forget what you mama, she tell you. We want to make Angelina proud tonight. Besides, she's only engaged, not married yet. I no want to see you mess things up for her. No funny business."

"Relax, Z'. I got an etiquette book out of the library. I know all about how to impress rich people." And what Nickie didn't know, she was sure she could fake.

"You listen to me, not to a book. I tell you how to act."

Nickie shifted position, enjoying the papery rustle of the taffeta and its slippery coolness against her skin. The interior of the big car smelled wonderfully of tobacco and leather. At long last she was getting her chance to sample the dream that Angie had been living for the past eight months. What more could she ask for?

She sneaked a glance sideways as the blond driver slid in beside her, but his attention was riveted on the rearview mirror as he waited for Pap and Louis and Phil to get settled in the back.

Phil, with his usual intensity, was talking about the preliminary notification he had gotten from Carnegie Tech. As he peppered Louis with questions, Nickie sensed that their future brother-in-law got a kick out of playing the big man. Funny thing was, Louis always seemed to be playacting—charming Mama, deferring to Pap, being nice to the younger kids. Nickie couldn't help but like him.

She twisted around and saw Pap sitting rigidly by the window. He pulled out his pocket watch as if checking it against an imaginary time schedule. He had been ugly and sullen since April, when the Urbanos had begun to plan this formal engagement party. Poor Mama defended him like she always did. She said it was hard for a man to let one of his children go. Nickie knew better—it was eating at him that Angie had proved him wrong.

As the car pulled away from the curb, Nickie watched the driver out of the corner of her eye, admiring the smooth way he shifted through the gears and the movement of his muscles beneath his green gabardine slacks when he depressed the clutch. Then she noticed that out of the corner of his eye he was still watching the rearview mirror. A regular neb-nose. She wished he'd glance her way just once so she could practice her Jean Harlow smile.

The foyer of the Urbano home had been transformed into a garden bower with white chrysanthemums, snapdragons and smilax massed against a backdrop of feathery green cibotium ferns. Angie was still overwhelmed at the thought of all the effort and expense that had gone into the evening. Even Mrs. Urbano's selection of Angie's gown—sheer white tulle over a slip of cloth-of-silver—coordinated with the overall effect.

Angie knew she was meant to sparkle amid this atmosphere of floral radiance, yet as she stood at Louis's side, greeting the guests, she couldn't shake the feeling that she was an inexperienced actress in a play she did not understand. Suddenly she heard Pap's damning voice: You want to be treated like a queen, just because you look like one? She shook off the memory and smiled more prettily than before, murmuring pleasantries to each new arrival, determined to charm and dazzle them into forgetting where she had come from. But the guests' faces began to merge indistinguishably—the men stiff as penguins in their black dinner jackets and the women vivid and fluttery in their tropical plumage. Although she had met most of these people before, they remained strangers, holding her at arm's length. To them she was a curiosity to be indulged for her guardians' sake.

Although Angie despised their condescension, she was smart enough to recognize her limitations. Sometimes she felt as if one little misstep would destroy it all. And so she clung to Louis, attuned to every nuance of his behavior. She nodded and smiled, outwardly serene. Seeing all the rich beautiful women in Louis's life, she was more mystified than ever. Why had he chosen her over them? The gap between them was so vast she knew it would be a constant struggle for her to attempt to bridge it.

Now she couldn't help worrying about how the Urbanos' circle would react to her family. She wanted at all costs to buffer Phil and Nickie from the barbed innuendos and snide remarks she had been subjected to since the engagement had been announced. Only David O'Rourke treated her as a friend and an equal. She prayed he'd be here tonight. She knew she could count on him to treat her family civilly.

Her eyes searched the crowded room. For all her inner turmoil, Angie had to smile at the sight of Nickie. That gawky pink flamingo had managed to insinuate herself right into the center of things, leaning nonchalantly against

the grand piano as if she owned it and the room, too.
Angie only prayed that she would not do anything too
outrageous. Phil was nowhere to be seen.

Z'Maria and Pap were perched as gingerly as eggshells
on the edge of the white velvet sofa in the drawing room.
Angie stared at her father, both irritated and pleased by
the puffed-up dignity of his torso. Finally she caught his
eye. Look at me, she telegraphed, smiling with a confident smugness she did not feel. Look at how far I've
come. He merely frowned and stared down into the glass
of expensive whiskey he was nursing.

If only Mama was well enough to be here, Angie
thought. How she would have basked in her daughter's
moment of glory. Mama—patient and forgiving and so
sweetly self-deprecating that she wouldn't even have noticed the snubs and snide looks. Mama's whole universe
was her children; her dreams reposed in them.

Angie's thoughts were interrupted when she realized
Louis had been trying to introduce her to someone. "I'm
sorry," she apologized. "My mind was somewhere else."

Louis seemed to read at once the worry and concern
behind her eyes. He leaned down and whispered, "Just a
little while longer, darling, and we'll go join your family.
Stop worrying. Everything's going to be just fine."

When they were finally able to find a moment to
themselves, she asked him, "Have you seen my brother?"

"You mean Boy Wonder? He's probably up in the
attic redesigning the wiring or something."

"Please, don't tease." She rubbed her fingers across
her forehead. "I just want to find him and make sure he's
all right."

Louis pulled her into the alcove beneath the stairs.
"Phil is fine. They'll all get through this evening with no
lasting scars. Look, I know the past month's been hell.
But darling, I promise you, once we're married all the
sniping will stop." He gave her shoulders a reassuring
squeeze. "We'll be old news then, you and I. You do
believe that, don't you?"

She smiled uncertainly.

"I promise you, Angie, we'll be untouchable." His
expression was indulgent, soothing the fears of a child.

"Just keep thinking of how wonderful it's all going to be."

She nodded, wanting so much to believe in the lovely future he sketched for them.

"Good girl." He was about to kiss her when the sound of men's voices in the foyer made them step back.

"Rum old thing, that aunt of hers," one of them said. "Did you see the way she tossed back that drink like one of the boys? I hear she's got some sort of Mob connection."

This was answered with a disapproving grunt. "I thought the Urbanos were beyond all this ethnic claptrap. They've regressed a hundred years in allowing this match. Josephine's state of mind has been none too strong since Julia's death. But to have father and son join in the madness . . . incomprehensible."

The voices trailed off as they wandered into another room.

"Bastards," Louis swore under his breath. "Why can't they mind their own business? Come on, let's go into the library. I think a touch of brandy would do us both good."

Shakily Angie agreed.

They found Phil in the middle of the library, intently examining every detail of the elegantly proportioned room—from its mahogany-beamed ceiling and book-lined walls to the marble Corinthian columns that framed the two fireplaces. Typical Phil, Angie thought with mingled relief and amusement, so absorbed by the ambience of the room that he had tuned out everything else. The knot of men cloistered nearby with their Havanas and brandies might have been cigar-store Indians for all he cared. Then Angie noticed David O'Rourke in one of the club chairs by the fire. He was watching Phil with a look of amused curiosity.

Her spirits lifted as David came over to join them. "Hello," she greeted him warmly. "I was hoping you'd be here. Have you had a chance to meet my brother?"

David grinned. "No. I was afraid to break his concentration."

Then Nickie wandered into the library, a glass of champagne in hand, and waved gaily at them. Louis said with a wry laugh, "The family's wasting no time getting acclimatized. See? All your worrying has been for nothing."

Phil turned at the sound of their voices and came over to the laughing group. "Geez, this place is like a museum. The paintings and the books . . ." he enthused. "I could stay here forever."

David teased him. "Isn't this a little conservative for your taste?"

"I could jazz it up easy."

Louis laughed richly. "Do me a favor, will you, and spring that one on my father."

"Forget your old man, Louis," David said. "I think we should take him over and introduce him to George Donahue." David turned to Phil, his eyes glinting with mischief. "Donahue's the tall guy waving the cigar. He's on the scholarship committee at Tech. Don't be daunted by that bulldog face. Underneath he's a lovable puppy."

Louis grinned. "Just ask his daughter, right?"

As the two men guided Phil over to Donahue, Nickie came up to Angie. "That Louis sure is smooth."

For all Nickie's admiration, Angie felt a little unsettled at hearing her fiancé described in those terms. But before she could say something, Nickie went on. "Hey, I almost forgot: Mrs. Urbano sent me to find you."

"She probably just got tired of looking at you draped over her piano like a Woolworth's scarf."

Nickie preened in her taffeta. "Woolworth's doesn't have anything this swell."

"Did she say what she wanted?"

"Something about you singing," Nickie said, her gaze following Phil as he was introduced to the men around the fireplace. "Say, will you get a load of those old moneybags."

"They're bankers, goof."

Nickie shrugged. "Same difference, right?"

As Angie made her way gracefully through the groups of seated guests in the drawing room, Nickie sat in one of the rows of chairs that had been set up in the back. She sighed with sheer contentment, feeling that this was just where she belonged. She deserved to live like these people. After all, what made them so special? Mentally she subtracted the jeweled brooches and fashionable silk gowns, the ivory fans and beaded evening bags. Without them the women seemed no different from Z'Maria, who looked as proud as a peacock in the shiny black rayon dress she had bought for her husband's funeral years before. All it took was money, Nickie concluded. That was the only thing that made the rich special.

Two young women brushed past, not paying her the slightest heed, and sat in front of her. Annoyed, she gave them the once-over. The pouty strawberry blonde wasn't much older than Nickie, but she looked like a sultry temptress in her sequined sheath. Her companion seemed like a fairy-tale princess—all pale gold from her blond hair down to the hem of her billowy chiffon gown.

The girls huddled close together, their eyes focused on Angie as she stood at the piano. The pouty one whispered, "Honestly, what can Louis see in her? Mummy says it's all Josephine's fault. She says the poor dear went a little crazy when Julia died."

As Angie began to sing, the other girl sniggered, "I'd rather watch a performing pig in a circus."

Nickie steamed, thinking, I wish I could fix her ass. Glancing down at the frothy chiffon, its billowing panels so full they nearly touched her shoes, she had a brainstorm. With a quick check around to make sure no one was watching, she caught an edge of the chiffon with her toe and pulled it back with infinite delicacy. Then she stood up and nudged the edge of the frothy fabric under her chair leg. Grinning, she crept out into the hall.

In the foyer the intimate rumble of men's voices from across the hall made her forget momentarily about the two women. She followed the sound toward the library and peeked around the doorway. The moneybags had pulled up several club chairs, looking as if they were settling in for the evening. Mr. Urbano held a pipe between his teeth as he moved among his seated guests, pouring brandy from a crystal decanter that glinted like amber in the firelight.

"My secretary got another of those chain letters, too," one of the men was saying, stretching out his gleamingly shod feet toward the fire that had been made against the crispness of the early May night. "Excited as a silly shop-girl by the damn thing. The whole country's gone mad with them."

"Poor buggers need some sort of diversion from their grim lives," another put in. "A dime's not all that much to send out for the promise of a thousand more. Harmless fun, I say."

"Harmless? Is that what you said about the Ponzi scheme back in the twenties—a little harmless fun for the poor buggers who lost their shirts because they didn't understand fundamental logarithmic mathematics?"

"Now, if the letter writer had said to send a pint of whiskey to the person at the top of the list, and be guaranteed of one hundred more on your doorstep," another man put in, "I might have bitten at the bait."

His remark elicited several appreciative chuckles. Nickie had no idea what they were talking about nor what the joke was; still she listened and watched, enthralled. She felt as if she had stumbled onto a club whose rules and secret bywords were known only by an exclusive few.

"We might all be reduced to soliciting dimes through the mails if that madman in the White House has his way," a fourth voice rumbled. "Damned traitor to his class."

"You truly believe such gloom and doom, George?" Mr. Urbano put in smoothly. "Admit it, investment banking was in sore need of some controls. And as for the rest of Roosevelt's 'new deal' ideas, I don't think we need worry too much. The Supreme Court has already proven that. In the end we'll have the basic system we've always had—clients who can invest or not as they please, produce more or less, be content with a five-percent gain on their money or wait out a major debacle in hopes of getting six percent. The money and the power will be where it has always been, take my word for it."

His words sank into Nickie's mind. She had sensed the men's contempt for the shopgirl and her coveted dimes; now she vaguely began to understand that money wasn't simply the stuff Pap sweated for day after day down at the mill to put food on the table. Money was potentially power, something to be used and controlled. These men in the library knew the secret; that's why they were rich.

As the men grumbled on about the T.V.A., the W.P.A. and a whole indecipherable alphabet soup of terms, she moved away. The foyer was empty. From the drawing room she heard a scattering of polite applause. She hurried back, just in time to watch the girl stand up. As she did, the dramatically sharp, jagged sound of ripping fabric made heads turn along the whole length of the room. "Oh, no!" she wailed. "My dress is ruined—I don't see how it could have happened!"

Nickie backed away, her expression blandly innocent, and moved up the curving hall staircase. At the top, she stared down the long gallery. All the doors were closed but one. Someone had left a lamp on inside, and a pool of soft light spilled out onto the carpet running the length of the gallery. Nickie stopped in the doorway.

Twin crystal-based lamps glowed atop the walnut bedside tables, shimmering off the deep blue brocade of the bedspread, which was half hidden under a pile of fur coats. Drawn like a hummingbird to nectar, Nickie went over to the bed. Here was what the power of money provided—this incredible wealth of soft, luxurious splendor. She ran her hands over the furs, her fingertips reveling in the diverse textures of long fluffy fox and the sleekly pelted heaviness of mink, the buttery smoothness of suede. She lifted one of the coats and drew it on, marveling at the elegant way the lapel fell back to form a rippled revers of curly black lamb.

Nickie preened before the beveled triple mirrors on the dressing table, mourning the burned bedjacket that had so briefly been her link to this otherwise unreachable world. Amid the feminine array of silver-backed brushes and crystal scent bottles on the table, she picked out a gold lipstick case and twirled the base until the creamy scarlet tip emerged. She was about to press it to her bottom lip when a slight movement in the mirror caused her to whirl around in fright.

"Well, if it isn't the sister of the bride."

Nickie stared at the redhead who swayed toward her, looking for all the world like a slithery snake in her black-sequined gown. The other one, looking frazzled, followed her friend into the room. "Oh, never mind about her, Maura. Just look at my dress. Where is that Berthe? Maybe she can restitch this."

Maura ignored her friend. Her attention was focused on Nickie. "Just what are you doing up here?" she demanded. "Too busy filching to toast your sister and her future husband?"

"I didn't filch anything!"

"No?" The girl's laughter tinkled maliciously as she turned back to her friend. "Babs, wouldn't it be giddy fun to raise a stink and see the expression on everyone's faces when I tell them we caught Angie's sister up here redhanded, leaving in your mother's coat?"

"Maura Donahue, you leave my sister alone." Angie stood in the doorway, her dark eyes fierce above the soft flush of her cheeks.

The other girls' heads swiveled in surprise to face her.

"Babs," Maura said, ignoring Angie completely, "haven't you always heard how these ginzo guttersnipes stick up for one another? It's just too impossibly quaint."

Now that Louis wasn't around, Angie felt no need to hide behind a ladylike facade. She grabbed Maura by the arm and forced the girl to face her.

"You ever hear of stinkbugs, Maura?" Angie said, her voice deceptively soft. "Well, we've got them in Coalport. Their backs are oily and shiny like that gown of yours—sort of pretty in a way, until you flip them over and see how ugly they are underneath. If you smash them, they stink worse than a dunghill. After a while, you realize it's better just to let them crawl back into whatever hole they came out of."

Maura stared back at her in astonishment. "You sly, insulting bitch. So you do have a mind of your own, after all. Poor Louis," she said suddenly, startling them with her sharp burst of laughter. "Thinks he's getting a simpering Shirley Temple doll he can keep on the shelf. Wait 'til he finds out he's got a sharp-tongued dago fishwife."

Nickie lunged at her with her fists raised, but Angie caught her around the waist and pulled her back. Babs backed toward the door, looking at the two Branzino girls with distaste. "We'd better get out of here," she said, "before we're the innocent victims of one of their infamous brawls."

"What a joke. You haven't been innocent since the day you were born." As soon as they were gone, Angie turned on Nickie. "Get that coat off, and let's get back downstairs."

A ghost of a smile lightened Nickie's narrow face. "I'm glad to see you're the same old Ange underneath."

"You better believe it." Angie gave her a fierce hug. "That snobbish witch was right about one thing—we do look out for each other."

8

Angie sat at the desk in her bedroom. The evening air wafting in through the open window was fragrant with the scent of the trumpet-shaped honeysuckle blossoms on the vine that climbed up the pergola in the Urbanos' back garden. She reached for another envelope, addressed it, and slipped an engraved wedding invitation inside.

At the last minute she had decided against going to the symphony concert with her future mother-in-law's coterie of friends. Mrs. Urbano had pressed her, knowing that Louis intended to work late, but Angie was secretly grateful for the respite. Since the announcement of their engagement two weeks before, she and Louis had been caught up in an endless round of dinners and parties— one more traumatic for her than the next, though she somehow got through them without anyone realizing how badly she was floundering. If only she and Louis had more time alone, perhaps she'd be able to relax and pull herself together.

Angie looked up from the envelope she was addressing and cocked her head at the distant thrum of a car engine. Rounding the corner onto Maplewood Drive, it grew steadily louder. She smiled in delighted surprise, recognizing the characteristic roar of Louis's Auburn. His meeting must have ended earlier than he had expected. Hearing the automobile slow and turn into the Urbanos' drive, she jumped up and went to the mirror. After pulling a brush through her hair, she dug through the lipsticks on her make-up table until she found the new shade of mauve rose that Louis had complimented her on the night before at the Donahues' dinner dance.

"You look lovely," he had said as he led her onto the dance floor. Then he had lightly caressed her white shoulders, which the long halter-necked black sheath left bare. "The loveliest woman in the room."

She had stepped meltingly into his arms, yearning to feel his closeness, but he had held her at a proper distance, his eyes teasingly regretful.

For once we'll be alone, Angie thought as she ran down to greet him, without fifty pairs of eyes watching our every move.

She stepped outside into the soft June night. Venus shone brightly against the midnight-blue sky, and she caught the faint glimmer of stars emerging from the gauzy curtain of dusk. All her senses seemed vibrantly alive. Beneath the heavy sweetness of the honeysuckle, she smelled the rich loamy musk of newly turned earth. The fullness of approaching summer made her blood quicken. How she longed for more than the chaste, gentle kisses Louis bestowed. He was always the gentleman, chary of his passion and protective of her honor. But after all, they were engaged now. She blushed guiltily, shocked by the depth of her own hungry impatience.

Angie struck out across the expanse of lawn that led around to the converted carriage house. She opened the side door and looked past the Cadillac to Louis's Auburn. Where had he disappeared to so quickly? Then at the back of the garage her eyes picked out two figures at the bottom of the steps that led to Harry's apartment.

She was about to call Louis's name when she realized they were arguing. Although she heard both men with crystal clarity—one voice strident and angry, the other low and conciliatory—Angie could make no sense of what they were saying.

"That's an unfair accusation, and you know it."

"Is it? You keep telling me to be patient. How long do I have to wait?"

Angie crept closer. Harry stood on the bottom step, his back turned to Louis, who reached up to touch his shoulder. "Look, I know I've been neglectful these past months, but what do you think this has all been for?"

"Not for us. I don't believe that anymore. It's been for you, Louis. All for you."

"That's simply not true." Louis turned Harry around to face him.

"It makes me sick the way you court her."

"Be fair, damn it. You know I couldn't risk losing her. She's perfect—young and naive, malleable. She'll never suspect a thing, and dear Mother's already keeping her occupied with a million social things. Don't you understand? For every hour she's away, that's another hour we'll have together."

Angie heard the teasing caress in Louis's voice, the tender insinuating cajolery of a lover patching up a quarrel. Although she did not want to believe it, the air of long-established intimacy between the two men was too clear to be mistaken.

She had known vaguely that such abomination existed. She had overheard Z'Maria and the other women's whispered reminiscences about the *frosc'* on the streets of Reggio and Naples, simpering men who aped feminine mannerisms and copulated in unspeakable ways. But those were fables, told with archly ribald scorn to while away a summer's evening on the sidewalk. They had nothing to do with Louis and his masculine, attentive nature; they could not. He was adoring; they had never even quarreled. He had done and been everything she wanted, hadn't he?

She heard Harry say, "I've seen you kiss her."

"But you know I've been faithful in my heart to you," Louis murmured. Angie watched in horror as he touched Harry's face, caressing the line of his chin and outlining his lips with a featherlight fingertip, and she felt that she was staring into a vicious funhouse mirror that distorted everything she had believed in. Louis had caressed her face in just that way.

She watched him pull Harry close and kiss him with all

the fire and passion she herself had longed to feel from him. Suddenly she could hardly breathe, suffocated by the weight of his betrayal.

In a state of disbelieving shock, she watched Louis seduce his lover. Slowly he unbuttoned Harry's shirt, bending to place slow kisses across his muscular chest. He sank to his knees and fumbled with the buttons of Harry's trousers. She caught a glimpse of white tumescent flesh before Louis took it into his mouth. Harry cried aloud, a low, passionate cry that touched off a wellspring of anguish and disgust within her.

"No," she whimpered. "No! No! No!"

Panic stricken, Louis pushed Harry from him, his lips still red and moist as he turned toward her with blank horror. "Angie!"

She turned and ran blindly from the garage. She was halfway across the lawn when he caught up with her and grabbed her arm. "Angie, please, you've got to listen to me."

"You're a goddamn animal!" she cried, continuing to run, trying to yank her arm free. "Leave me alone."

"Get hold of yourself, for God's sake," he cried, his breath coming in shallow, rapid gasps. "We've—we've got to discuss this calmly, rationally."

She jerked to a stop and spun to face him. "We have nothing to say to each other, Louis. Nothing."

"Please," he said, releasing his rigid grip on her arm, "I beg of you."

She stumbled through the back porch door and fell against the laundry tub. Leaning over it, she started to retch.

"Dear God! Here, Angie, let me help you."

But she waved him furiously back. "Keep away!" She turned on the cold water full blast, splashing it over her face and rinsing her mouth. For a long time she stood there, her heart pounding, as alternating waves of heat and cold washed through her. With an effort of will, she forced down another wave of nausea.

"Angie, we have to talk," Louis said, his voice taut as he followed her into the kitchen.

The homey warmth of the room seemed to mock them both, its wholesomeness only serving to underline the obscenity she had just witnessed. Although it was dark, neither made a move to turn on the light. "Angie," he said with growing desperation. "I am truly, deeply sorry."

"You disgust me."

"Please, just listen to me. What happened doesn't have to change things between us. You and I, we were friends. We got along so beautifully. We could still be happy together."

"What are you saying?"

"Why throw everything over just because your pride's hurt?"

"Something worth so little."

He looked at her quickly. "There—there are marriages in name only, Angie. Why not for us? A civilized arrangement. I need a wife, and you—why, you could help your family so awfully much through me. Would it be too unreasonable to ask that, in exchange, you overlook the rest?"

"You're asking me to live a lie?"

"A comfortable lie." As he said the words, she looked up and met his gaze. His eyes were unnaturally bright with mingled fear and hope.

"Louis, stop," she said dully.

"Listen, Angie. We can start over, I promise you. We can pretend this awful night never happened." Desperation edged the glib persuasiveness of his tone. "I'll send Harry away—back to Harrisburg."

"So much for your vow of being faithful to poor Harry in your heart." Angie's contempt was withering.

Louis went on as though she hadn't spoken. "You know I can give you a good life, that your family will be taken care of. Why, look at how I've already helped Phil with the Carnegie scholarship," he pushed on inexorably. "And think of your mother. Our marriage would mean she would have the attentions of the best physicians in the city."

"Stop, I said!" She covered her ears. "You're a goddamn monster. Leave my mother out of this."

Louis caught her hands and pulled them down to her sides. "Please," he babbled, "I can change for you . . . turn over a new leaf."

She shook her head, sickened by his desperate pleading. For the first time she saw him with relentless clarity. He had the gift of making himself into a blank canvas onto which she had created the image she wanted to see. Intuitively she understood that he was prepared to do the same now: to be whatever it was she required of him. But it would be a lie, it would always be a lie. She wondered if this was the source of the conflict between Louis and his father. Perhaps the man had long since recognized his son's weakness of character.

Angie's turbulent feelings coalesced into a cold, hard core of anger. She had been betrayed, used in such a calculated way. Their courtship had been nothing but a sham to give Louis a facade of respectability and normalcy. He had misjudged her innocence for stupidity.

"Take your hands off me, Louis. I'm going home. I'm calling a cab and getting out of here."

"But what am I supposed to tell my parents?"

"Tell them anything." She trudged wearily down the hall that led to the library. "Make up whatever lies you need to. Tell them Mama's taken a turn for the worse, that my family needs me."

He stopped in the doorway, nervously running his hands through his hair. "Maybe that's a good idea. You go home for a while. You'll have a chance to calm down and see things in a more rational light."

She picked up the phone and called the taxi company. After murmuring her address into the phone, she hung up and turned to look at him. "I meant what I said: It's over." She pulled off her diamond solitaire engagement ring, and with icy calm she set it on the desk. "I never want to see you again."

The finality of her tone got through at last. He began to look frightened. "What are you going to do?"

"I'm not vindictive, Louis. I don't want to hurt your parents. They've been very good to me," she said with quiet emphasis. "If you stay away, I'll say nothing to them. You understand me?"

"You're making a mistake, Angie."

"Just stay away from me and my family. That's all I want."

She went out into the street to wait for the cab. She

took nothing with her, nothing but the miserable coldness in her heart.

The ride seemed to last forever. At last the cab reached the outskirts of Coalport. It labored slowly up Millbridge Avenue and turned onto Mitchell.

"This it?" the cabby asked, his eyes flickering curiously between her and the dump she had pointed out to him. Without replying, she handed him a bill and stepped out into the dark street.

She took a deep breath, seeking comfort from the familiar surroundings. But the comfort was spurious. Fear twisted her stomach at the thought of having to confront Pap.

She descended the steps into the yard. She hesitated at the door, wondering whether to knock. Finally she just walked in. The family sat around the dining-room table, finishing a late supper. Pap must have kept the boys up at the garden until dark because they all looked beat. But their exhaustion vanished as their heads swiveled in surprise toward the door. Pap was the last to turn his head. He too simply stared.

"I've broken off with Louis Urbano," she announced without preamble, standing rigidly just inside the door. "We're through."

Pap threw his spoon down. "What happen?"

"It's a private matter between Louis and me."

"What the hell you mean, 'private'?" Pap barked, his expression truculent. "The two families, they have an agreement."

"I said it's over." Her voice started to rise, and she fought vainly to get it under control. "Can't you all just accept that?"

"Frank, leave her alone," Rosa said weakly, her eyes fixed on her eldest daughter. "Angelina, you look sick, afraid. Come here, let me hold you."

Angie ran across the room and knelt beside her mother, burying her head in her lap like a child. "It's all right," Rosa crooned, stroking her head gently. "Whatever it is, it's all right. You're home again."

Nickie stared at Angie as she started to cry. She didn't understand what could have happened. Had she and

Louis fought? They'd make up, she told herself uneasily. They would have to.

Angie's sobs filled the room like cold gushing rain, washing away in rivulets of despair the gaiety and adventure, the sense of promise that they had all fed on the past year. Nickie exchanged a helpless glance with Phil. Pete, Freddie and Vic sat cowed, as if afraid of somehow being blamed.

Pap moved restlessly about the room, kicking a chair out of the way. Nickie tracked him with her eyes, recognizing all the signs of one of his black, violent moods.

"Cry, cry, cry!" Pap thundered, towering above the two women. "I hear enough a this bullshit! Angelina, go up to bed. Tomorrow you go back."

"I'm never going back there. Never."

"You no going to shame me." He twisted his hand in her hair and pulled her head up. "The two families, they have an agreement now. You go back, I tell you."

"No!"

He yanked hard on her hair, making her wince.

"Frank!" Rosa cried faintly. "*Ni fa mala.* Can't you see she's hurt enough already?"

"Shuddup! This is my business," he shouted, never lifting his malevolent gaze from Angie's face. "So this is what the city teach—to disobey your own father? I tell you now, you no gonna forget who I am."

As he raised his hand, Phil rushed over and grabbed his arm. "Leave her alone!"

Pap shook him off with one jerk of his broad powerful shoulder, sending Phil flying into the sideboard. Then Pap balled his hand up into a fist and came at Angie again.

"Yeah, go ahead and beat her," Nickie screamed. "Then how you going to explain to the Urbanos when they come looking for her!"

Pap reversed his hand in midswing and caught Nickie across the nose hard. Blood spattered over her white blouse.

"Frank, no!"

He turned on his wife. "You no could listen to me. You had to let our daughter get above her station, go live like a bigshot. Now look what happen. She too good for us, too good for them."

"Frank, listen . . ."

He lifted his hand to slap his wife. Phil rushed over as Angie grabbed Pap's arm. It was all the catalyst he needed. With his free hand he punched Angie's shoulders and back mercilessly, shoving Phil out of the way each time he tried to intervene.

A wave of hatred washed over Nickie. "Why?" she screamed at her father. "Why do we have to live like animals?"

Pap threw Angie back down so hard in Rosa's lap that the force nearly knocked both women over. Mama, Angie and Nickie were all crying now, but it was as if Pap didn't hear them. His eyes, red with fury, were fixed on Phil. "You too, eh? You all learn from your smartmouth sister?" he said between gasps for breath. "Bigshot number two, I show you."

Phil ducked. But instead of striking out at him, Pap turned and strode toward the parlor. Phil ran after him. Nickie, holding her bloody nose, followed. Pap paused for an instant, his compact, work-hardened body seeming to fill the tiny parlor. Then he moved toward the low table, where Mama had insisted on displaying the house model Phil had designed.

"No!" Phil screamed, launching himself against his father as Pap brought his muscular forearms down across the table, sweeping it clean with one ferocious gesture. The wood and glass construction crashed to the floor like a frail house of cards. Pap then grabbed Phil and shoved him down on top of the destroyed model.

"Damn you!" Phil shouted. "Can't you see anything beautiful without having to destroy it?"

"A beautiful toy, useless as you are." Pap stared down at him in contempt. "*Sciocci*, you and your sister both—fools meddling in a world where you never belonged. If I have to beat it into you, you will learn there is nothing but to eat, survive and be satisfied with that. When I was your age, I was already slaving like a man, for man's wages. Backbreaking work, hauling stone for the landowner's mansion. That is the real world, a man's world. You better all learn that now, once and for all." He pushed past Nickie and stormed out of the house.

Angie pulled herself up and went to Phil. As he stared numbly down at the shattered fragments, she felt sick.

He had worked on it for months, constructing it bit by bit out of the fabric of his imagination and dreams. Now, in one moment of vengeful fury, it lay destroyed.

"I'm so sorry, Phil," she murmured, her voice strained. "I should have known Pap would take it out on all of you."

His hurt eyes searched hers. "Why did you come back, Ange?"

She turned away without another word.

Nickie stared after her. Angie had been surrounded by incredible wealth that made her own existence look so shabby by comparison. For a little while they all had glimpsed the wonderful possibilities that the world held. As Angie climbed the stairs, Nickie swore to herself that no price could be too high to possess those things.

9

Nickie stood at the kitchen table, her gaze fixed dreamily on the morning sunlight slanting into the dingy room. As if from a distance she heard Pap shouting in the yard and Angie bustling around her. But they didn't intrude on her daydreams: She was sitting at the marble counter in Lapik's Drugstore, dressed in a white linen suit with a black straw hat and pumps, as Louis Urbano walked in. As they spoke and sipped their tall strawberry sodas with double scoops of vanilla ice cream, he smiled at her adoringly, realizing it was she whom he loved and not Angie.

She frowned, remembering what Angie had confided to her late one night after Nickie had woken up and heard her crying. She had whispered in a shamed voice that Louis was queer. Nickie tried to tell herself Angie had made up the story. She refused to believe it, because she still wanted to blame Angie for ruining everything.

"Come on, Nickie, quit dawdling," Angie snapped, returning with a cloth-covered bowl of dough. "There'll be hell to pay if we aren't finished."

" 'There'll be hell to pay,' " Nickie mimicked her. "Where were you every other baking day for the last year?"

"Go ahead, rub it in. As if I'm not miserable enough."

Their words flew back and forth across the sheet-draped table littered with salt, yeast, oil and flour—enormous drifts of it, which they had scooped out of the hundred-pound sack in the pantry.

The Saturday ritual of turning flour into their daily bread was more sacred to Pap than Sunday's transformation of bread and wine into the body and blood of Christ. The baking required a split-second precision, which he presided over like a drill sergeant of the carabinieri.

Now they ignored Pap's martinet shouts out in the yard, too engrossed in their own bickering.

"I still can't understand why you won't make up with Louis."

"It's over." Angie punched down a lump of dough viciously.

"But he sent you flowers. Whatever he did, he must be sorry."

"He's a phony."

"You didn't know that before? I thought you always knew that."

"What are you talking about now?"

"I used to watch him, the way he did things to make everyone like him. When he was around Mama he acted one way, when he was around Phil he acted a different way—you know."

Forgetting the dough she was working, Angie straightened and gave her sister a strange look.

"What did I say now?" Nickie looked aggrieved. "What's the matter with wanting to make everyone happy?"

"You can't make everyone happy without being a liar."

"There are worse things than lying, aren't there?"

"Be quiet, you don't know anything." Her fist rammed the dough again. "You're just like I was—too young, too blinded by all the nice things."

"Oh yeah, 'nice things,' " she mocked just as Phil came into the house, sweaty and grimy from being in the garden all morning. "You're the one who doesn't know anything."

"Back off, Nick," Phil warned her as he went over to

the sink and dropped his armload of tomatoes and a few misshapen eggplants that Pap insisted on planting year after year though they never thrived like they had in their native Calabrian soil.

"Ange thinks she's such a know-it-all, I can't stand it. Instead of sticking up for her, why don't you tell her how Vic got so sick with arthritis last winter he couldn't even stand a sheet on him, and all the while Angie was living her hunky-dory life downtown. Tell her how her high-and-mighty money came just in time because Pap couldn't even scrounge twenty-five lousy cents to get grape juice like the doctor ordered. Now what's going to happen to us—ow!" She yelped when Phil pinched her arm hard.

"I told you to back off, didn't I?" he muttered.

"You big phony—how come you're on her side now?"

Pap appeared in the doorway, his shirtsleeves rolled up and his cheeks ruddy above the bristly coarseness of his mustache. "Where are those loaves?" he shouted, scooping up a handful of flour on his way back out to attend his oven. "My fire is ready."

Hastily the girls divided and shaped the risen dough into smooth circles. As soon as they had filled one tray, Angie handed it to Nickie. "Get out there with this, quick. I'll bring the other one in a second."

As soon as Angie had pushed open the screen door, Pap started in. "What's the matter, you forget what real work is? Your hands too soft to hurry up when I tell you? Get t'hell over here."

Nickie stood beside Pap, waiting. A blast of heat hit them full in the face when he opened the small metal-lined door. He threw in his handful of flour, and it burst instantly into flame. Working quickly so as not to lose any precious heat, Nickie transferred the raw loaves onto his wooden *pala,* then watched Pap slide them into the recesses of the brick hearth. Angie twisted her tray around just as Pap reached toward it. His long-handled board caught the edge, sending it cartwheeling into the ground. Nickie moved out of his way in a hurry.

He swore viciously as Angie bent to retrieve the dirt-spattered loaves. "Is this what the city has made of you?"

He punctuated his curses with a sharp kick that caught

Angie on her back, sending her sprawling. "Can't you leave me alone?" she screamed.

Nickie felt torn, despising Pap and yet secretly glad to see Angie getting her comeuppance.

Before the brawl could escalate, Z'Maria's raspy voice called down from the street into the mayhem. "A happy group I see. Maybe the pope will want to put the whole bunch of you on the church calendar to celebrate Catholic Family Month." She marched down the stairs, her own tray of loaves balanced easily on one shoulder. "So much screeching. Since when did baboons move in, eh?"

Pap didn't bother to look up from the rags he was stuffing around the perimeter of the oven door. "A baboon would be of more use than that one."

Angie, rubbing her sore arm, took a step forward, but Z'Maria intervened. "Angelina, look at you. Go clean up, take a walk, get outta his hair. Go on, Filippo, take her. . . ."

Phil and Angie stood together over the rusted cast-iron basin in the bathroom, throwing cold water over their faces. "I'll take a walk, all right," she said, grabbing a coarse towel and rubbing her face until it was raw. "For two cents I'd just keep on walking forever. I hate him." She threw the towel to Phil. "You're on his side, aren't you? You all are. You think I'm being selfish."

"That's bullshit."

"Is it?"

The past week since her homecoming had been lonely and full of anguish. Her obstinate silence had alienated her from everyone but her mother, until she could no longer meet their eyes, so tired was she of their questions and disappointment, the ill-concealed accusations she read in them. Nickie had been the worst of all, her knifelike little thrusts cutting deeper and deeper, throwing her into an agony of doubt.

"None of you understand," Angie said, her voice breaking. "You can't. Christ, Phil, what's going to happen to me? I can't go back there. Pap won't let me live here in peace. He's never going to stop punishing me. I feel like everyone's against me. Even you."

Phil couldn't meet her eyes. "Come on, let's go up the park, forget all this crap for a while. You're making yourself crazy, Ange."

They came out into the yard just as Vic started shouting up on the sidewalk. "Hey, I see the Urbanos' big car. They must be coming to see us!"

Angie stared up at the street. As soon as she saw the long black hood of the Urbanos' Cadillac, she panicked, turning to Phil. "O God, no! What are they doing here? Look at me."

Phil squeezed her arm tightly. "Take it easy."

"I . . . you just don't understand, Phil. None of you do." Tears started in her eyes. "Can't you ask them to leave?"

"Ange, it's too late," he whispered frantically. "They're coming down the steps."

"Is Louis with them?"

"I don't know. No, I don't see him."

She nodded, then closed her eyes and took a deep breath. When she turned to face her former benefactors, her features were pale but composed. Mechanically she went forward to greet them.

Mr. Urbano's expression was grim, remote. He nodded stiffly at Angie. His coolness was balanced by the compassionate warmth and hope in his wife's eyes. "Oh Angie, darling," she whispered, "how have you been?"

"Fine," Angie said stiffly.

"I've missed you, dear. Our shopping expeditions, your lessons—which reminds me." She reached into her purse and retrieved a folded piece of notepaper. "Our Madame Francini is returning to Italy. She hopes you'll write."

Angie took the address without a word.

Mrs. Urbano went on brightly. "She was a wonderful teacher, but I'm sure we'll find another for you who is just as good."

"Mrs. Urbano, I'm not coming back."

The woman put an arm around Angie's shoulders. "Do you think we two might have a word alone, in private?" Her expression was anxious, confiding. "Woman to woman?"

Not knowing what else to do, Angie led her inside the house to the parlor and closed the door. How little time had passed since she had stood on the other side of that door, an innocent girl eager to be privy to life's secrets. Somewhere in the past week she had crossed the invisible barrier into womanhood. She only wished someone might have warned her how hurtful and lonely the passage would be.

"My dear, I'm not quite sure how to begin. I know that nowadays we're all expected to be modern and up to date on the subject of men's and women's . . . relations," Mrs. Urbano said as she sat down on the worn horsehair sofa and patted the spot beside her. "Louis's behavior was inexcusable. But I'm sure this terrible misunderstanding can be corrected."

Angie ignored the invitation to join her on the sofa. She failed to see how Louis's depravity could be dismissed as a misunderstanding, or how his parents could deal with the situation so casually.

Mrs. Urbano hurried on: "You simply must try to understand, Angie darling. Men are built differently. They have stronger needs. Women are naturally less inclined . . ."

Angie could only stare, mystified. She needed no primer on men and women. In her head she heard the *gumbaris* whispering together with their earthy directness, alternately complaining and laughing about men's urges, about their ill-usage. Yet the complaints had been undercut by the peppery spice of anticipation and desire. She had long sensed the passion, magical intimacy and pleasure that swirled about the marriage bed. She had never felt any of that from Louis.

"What I'm saying, my dear, is that you must make allowances."

Angie felt her face flood with color. "Allowances!"

"You see, a man's needs are powerful," Mrs. Urbano explained with grave earnestness, "so powerful that he sometimes doesn't think of the consequences. He may let those uncontrollable feelings carry him away."

"Sure," Angie retorted, scandalized, "and what if next time it's an animal? I've heard of that, too."

The woman's mouth dropped. "What do you mean?"

"Oh, dear," Angie said quickly. "May I ask how . . . how much Louis told you?"

"He confessed everything to his father and assumed full blame, of course. He said that the two of you had gotten amorous—which is perfectly understandable, mind you—and that he mistook your ardor for acquiescence. Of course he's inexperienced, too. He just didn't understand."

"Mrs. Urbano, please don't say anymore." Angie stood up. "I think I understand now."

"You do?" she said hopefully.

"It won't change anything."

"But why?"

"This past week I've had some time to think. I never belonged there in Pittsburgh with you. Everyone else saw it—even me, I suppose—but I tried to pretend I could fit in. I know now that if I stayed I would be living a lie."

"Dear, don't be hasty." Mrs. Urbano stood up, fighting back tears. "Please reconsider, I beg of you."

"I'm sorry," Angie said, pity and disgust warring in her heart. The woman was as blinded by love as Angie had been, eager to believe any lie Louis offered. Anything to prevent having to face the truth. Angie was disgusted as much with herself for having allowed herself to be duped. "I—I think you should just go now. It'll be easier on all of us that way."

"Please, just take a little more time," Mrs. Urbano said, her voice quavering.

"I'm sorry," Angie said again, shaking her head.

To forestall any further conversation, she turned and climbed the stairs to her bedroom. From the window she watched the couple leave. Her heart lurched when she saw the chauffeur emerge from the car to open the rear door for them. Then she realized it wasn't Harry. Louis must have wasted no time in erasing his mistakes. Clever man, she thought, a charming manipulator who thought only of himself first and foremost. Angie was fortunate to be rid of him. And yet, as she watched the Cadillac disappear around the corner, she felt a fleeting sense of loss.

She heard Mama stirring in the next room, softly calling to her, and the feeling vanished. Although a secret corner of her heart might pine for what might have been, Angie knew that this was home. This was where her heart bound her.

Act Two

10

The brassbound trunk that Mrs. Urbano had sent to Coalport sat in a corner of the girls' cramped bedroom. Angie insisted on avoiding that reminder of her "dream" life, but to Nickie it was a marvelous treasure box. She couldn't keep away from it.

Kneeling down, she threw back the curved lid and pawed through the filmy silk and satin underwear to reach the dresses. "Angie just has to let me wear one of them to Phil's graduation party tonight." She pulled out a blue cotton halter frock and held it up before the scratched dresser mirror, imagining herself at some swell affair. When she heard footsteps on the stairs, she threw the dress in the trunk, slammed the lid and fell back on the bed as if she'd been lying there for hours.

Angie came in, a towel draped over her damp hair. "I left a pot of hot water on the stove if you want to go wash up."

"Okay." Nickie watched her walk over to the rickety wardrobe and pull out a faded dress. "Oh, brother, don't tell me you're going to wear that old thing. It's Phil's big night. He's going to think you don't even care."

Ignoring her sister's needling, Angie draped the cheap dress over her arm as if it were the epitome of elegance. "Would you care to try it, mademoiselle? This is the latest in afternoon wear from Madame Schiaparelli."

"Who the hell—"

"A big-time fashion designer in Paris. Now, are you sure you wouldn't care to try this wonderfully giddy garden-party frock of hers?"

"Oh, for the garden. Why didn't you say so in the first place? It's just the thing for spreading chickenshit around Pap's rhubarb, wouldn't you say?"

"I'm sure Gumbari Schiaparelli had that precisely in mind—designed to go straight from the garden to tea at the William Penn."

Nickie laughed, relieved that her sister was back to her old self. "Come on, Ange, seriously, how can you put that old rag on when you got all that swell stuff just going to waste?"

Angie's eyes went to the trunk. "Snooping again, huh?"

Too late Nickie saw she'd left a bit of fabric exposed when she slammed the lid shut. "So what? Don't the priests always say it's a sin to waste things?"

"Then I'll give those clothes to Father Lucatta for the poor."

"No! Here, I've got something that's just right for you." Nickie slid off the bed and ran to the trunk. She found what she was looking for in a flash. With its rope halter and full pants, the white jersey evening pajama was simple but stunning. She held it up to check the effect on her sister. "Come on, wear this tonight. For Phil."

"Don't!" Angie grabbed it away from her sister and flung it down. "That was part of my trousseau. I was going to take it on my honeymoon. You think I want to parade around in it here?"

"You'd have worn it for Louis, but it's too good for us dagos on the hill, is that what you're trying to say?"

"You talk so stupid sometimes, I could scream. You just don't understand, Nickie."

"Don't I? You say Louis was such a monster, but I think you're still sorry you left." She rushed on when she saw the look on Angie's face. "If it really is over, you'd doll up instead of wearing an old rag tonight."

"Quit exaggerating," Angie said, eyeing the tumbled heap of white jersey on the bed. "Besides," she said lamely, "it's cruisewear."

"So why not cruise over to Z'Maria's in it?"

"You're not going to let up, are you?" Frowning, Angie picked up the evening outfit and shook the wrinkles out. She stared at it for a long moment. "I suppose you're probably right, Nickie. It's time I started picking up the pieces of my life. When I was in downtown Coalport this morning, I saw a sign in Belle's Dress Shoppe. They're looking for a sales clerk.'' She sighed. ''Maybe I'll apply.''

''The way you presented that gown by Madame Shabby-Belly, I'd say you're a natural.''

''Schiaparelli, you goof,'' Angie said, almost smiling. ''Okay, kid, you win. Let's get so dolled up we'll outfalute the highfalutin.''

Nickie executed a fancy foxtrot step she'd picked up from the latest Fred Astaire-Ginger Rogers movie. ''Now you're talking, Ange.''

Z'Maria's kitchen was bustling with life. Once the neighborhood had gotten wind of her plans to throw a party for her godson, who was graduating a year early from high school, all the old *gumbaris* on the Hill had agreed to help. The women worked quickly, arranging meats and cheeses on platters, gossiping among themselves.

Z'Maria gave her nieces the once-over when they appeared at the back door. ''Who are you two trying to impress?''

''You want us to hold our heads up, don't you?'' Nickie said, preening in her borrowed finery.

''But not so high you draw the *maloch'*.''

''That evil-eye stuff is garbage.''

''Never mind. Go down the basement and bring up a couple jars of my hot peppers.''

''It's dusty down there! And I'm all dressed up.''

''You think you're the queen of Italy? Go! I want to talk to your sister.'' When Nickie had reluctantly disappeared, Z'Maria looked at Angie. ''Your mama, she okay, she come?''

''For a little while maybe. You know how tired she gets.''

A tiny old woman, covered with a black shawl despite the warm evening, looked up from the crumbs she'd been pecking at like a scavenging crow. ''Poor Rosa,'' she muttered, blessing herself. ''God-a bless.''

Z'Maria pulled her niece out of earshot. ''And you, Angelina, you okay?''

''Don't I look okay?''

''I tell you one thing,'' Z'Maria grunted, ''the outfit may be a little flashy, but that soft fabric becomes you more than a hairshirt. Two weeks to cry and mope over a fool is enough."

"I'm through crying."

"Good girl." Z'Maria's sharp eyes searched her. "You may be sweet like you mama on the outside, but inside you're tough like me."

Angie laughed. "You make me sound like one of those pastel candies the 'mericans set out in little covered glass jars."

"*Menagg'*," Z' barked, "I'm sick of hearing about the 'mericans."

Her old cronies looked up and chuckled. Angie could see that Z'Maria was in her glory. She reveled being at the center of things, giving orders and making things happen. The traditional sphere of power relegated to the Italian woman had been denied to Z'Maria, a fact that Pap never failed to remind her of. Invariably, in moments of fury he would needle Z'Maria about her barrenness; it was a source of bitter satisfaction for him. In their narrow society, the Italian matriarch exercised her power subtly but powerfully through the bonds of attachment she forged with her children. They became her faithful army that she wielded and influenced. The father might nominally be the head of the family, but emotionally, the children belonged to her.

Z'Maria's only offspring were her barrels of wine. And all she got for her efforts was attention from the local Mafia chieftain. Even then Z'Maria had made the best of a bad situation, winning him over with her crusty, straightforward charm.

Taking heart from her aunt's unerring ability to land on her feet, Angie wandered off down the hall. Z'Maria's front parlor had already been transformed into a ballroom of sorts. The carpet had been rolled up against the wall, and an impromptu band was tuning up in a corner. Freddie did a practice run of chords on a beat-up accordion almost as big as he was, while Pete plucked away on his guitar.

"Ange!" She turned as Phil strode across the room toward her. His face was drawn, and she could imagine his disappointment at having lost the Carnegie Tech scholarship. Secretly she feared that he thought her break with the Urbanos had made him suffer, too. But he had never said a word, acting as though he had wanted to go to Pitt all along. "You look like a million bucks."

"One class act deserves another, right?" She reached up to smooth the lapels of his suit. "Only the best for my kid brother."

"Hey, watch the 'kid' stuff," he joked. "I'm almost a college man now. Think I should start to smoke a pipe so I'll look older? I can practice on Pap's when he's not around."

"Try that and your growth'll be stunted in more ways than one."

He grinned. "It sure is good to have you back, Ange."

"It's you and me and Nickie again," she replied. "Just like in the song."

"What song?"

"You know—'Fwee widdle fishes in a iddy biddy pool.' " She sang the nonsense ditty that had been number one on the radio hit parade for weeks. " 'Fwim, said the Mama Fish, fwim if you can, and they fwam and fwam right over the dam.' "

"Geez, I love that highbrow stuff."

"Like I said, only the best for you."

"Ange, seriously, how about singing a song or two tonight? It'd mean a lot to me."

"Not yet, Phil. Give me a little time."

"Yeah, sure, okay," he said, turning away.

Angie saw the look of disappointment in his eyes and she suddenly realized that they were all depending on her. They needed her liveliness and encouragement as a counterbalance to Pap's bitterness. Mama was too ill now. And Z'Maria stood on the periphery as she always had, doing what she could only when Pap's back was turned. Angie had to be the strong one.

"Phil!" she called after him. "How about if I sing a little Rossini?" He turned, and she began to gesture like an overacting tenor. " 'I am the barber of Seville . . . Figaro, Figaro, Figaro!' "

Phil started to laugh. "Sing it, Mr. Caruso!"

Nickie stood close to the food table against the wall. She bit into the enormous sandwich that she had heaped high with salami and provolone cheese. As she ate, she took in the room. A bunch of people had crowded onto the middle of the floor, bouncing to some crazy Spanish rhythm that Pete was picking out on the guitar. Kids darted in and out among the dancers like minnows, playing tag. The older women were clustered against the wall. Angie sat with them, like a white swan in the company of a flock of bedraggled black geese. Inconspicuous though she tried to make herself, Nickie saw that every eye in the room eventually found her. The men stared with open admiration, and the women darted more complex glances that mirrored both envy and pity.

Nickie scowled, knowing she had felt much the same way, and turned to sample the array of peppers on the relish tray. She savored the blisteringly hot assault on her tongue that she assuaged with a hunk of bread. She smiled and waved when she saw Tootsie Calandro come in. At thirty, the milkman was painfully shy and still a bachelor. The Branzino girls loved to tease him. "Hi, Tootsie," Nickie trilled, imitating the worldlier girls she knew in high school.

He flushed to the roots of his thinning hair. "How you doin'?" he muttered, his eyes skating past her toward the corner of the parlor. Nickie knew without turning around that he had his eye on her sister. He'd had a crush on Angie ever since the girls had started leaving poems in the milkbox as a joke and serenading him from their window in the early-morning dark. Nickie had always liked the sound of his truck coming around the corner of Mitchell Avenue, the trays of milk jingling against one another like loose coins.

"You going to ask my sister to dance?"

"Aw, Nickie, you know I can't dance. I just wanted to stop by tonight to congratulate your brother."

She winked at him. "At least hang around to hear her sing."

Tootsie's face turned a deeper shade of red.

The front door opened. Nickie forgot all about teasing the shy milkman when she saw Carlo DiPiano walk in, accompanied by a guy she had never seen before. Nickie still got nervous whenever the mafioso came around.

And he seemed to be around a lot more since he had bought his fancy house near Coalport Park. The man with him threw back his shoulders and tugged on the lapels of his suit. He was short like DiPiano, but there the resemblance ended. He had a bull neck and powerful shoulders, with short arms that swung easy and free like a fighter's. He looked like the type who enjoyed throwing his weight around.

"Know who he is, Toots?" Nickie asked as Angie walked over to the band and started to sing an old Italian ballad.

"I heard he runs a bootleg racket up in Ohio. A real tough guy."

"What's he doing here?"

"Business, I guess," Tootsie said distractedly, his eye on Angie. "But with them, who knows?"

Nickie watched DiPiano and the newcomer stop next to Phil, who hadn't even noticed them come in. She sidled over to check the situation out.

"Who's the looker?" she heard the guy mutter as he gestured with his chin toward Angie.

DiPiano touched Phil's arm. "*Como stai*, kid? I brought a friend tonight. Antonio Malfatti, meet the oldest Branzino boy, Filippo." Nickie watched Phil's eyes fix themselves on the newcomer. "I think Tony here would like an introduction to your lovely sister Angelina."

Malfatti didn't even glance Phil's way. His eyes were fixed on Angie.

"My sister's busy," Nickie piped up, instinctively disliking the guy.

DiPiano's purring voice went on as if Nickie hadn't spoken. "I heard about Angelina's bad luck. Such a pity." He shook his head, full of false sympathy.

Nickie watched Malfatti drift off in Angie's direction. The man moved with the slow, confident stride of an animal that knows everything else will get out of his way. Angie turned smilingly from the band and bumped into the man she had noticed coming in while she was singing. He caught her by the elbow to steady her. His eyes, the dark bluish-purple of a new bruise, stared her up and down.

"Excuse me," she said, lightly trying to pull free from his iron grip.

"You wanna dance?"

She quickly shook her head. "Thanks, but I have to check on my mother."

Angie sensed his obvious reluctance to release her. Even after he did so, she felt his eyes on her back as she threaded her way through the maze of seated women, grateful now for the lilting flow of gossip and closed ranks of chairs that would buffer her. One of the *gumbaris* had taken Angie's seat, drawing it closer to Rosa. She in turn nodded at the other woman's voluble words, struggling to appear interested, although Angie could tell she was exhausted. Then she saw her mother's eyes flicker in her direction, full of questions, and Angie knew that she had also taken note of the newcomer.

Angie knelt down beside the two women, taking Rosa's cold hand between hers. "Are you okay, Mama?" Angie asked when she could squeeze a word in amid the neighbor's colorful recital of her daughter's argument with the Slovak grocer.

"I'm-a fine." But the words seemed to catch in her throat. "Maybe a glass of water . . ."

Angie went to the empty kitchen and filled a glass. She turned to find DiPiano's friend blocking the doorway, watching her. The sounds of laughter and music from the rest of the house seemed suddenly muted, as if his powerful torso were a shield that cut them off. Although he dressed expensively, the well-cut silk suit did not mask the rough peasant underneath. He had a long nose, slightly flattened at the tip, and a small, tight mouth.

"Did you get lost or something?" she said lightly. "The party's in the other room."

"Not for me." The harsh, guttural drawl of his voice was an echo of Pap's.

Annoyed by his attitude, she snapped, "Look, I'm not interested."

She started to brush past him, but he put his hand against the door jamb, blocking her way. "What, I ain't good enough for you?"

Angie laughed in disbelief. "Look, mister—"

"Call me Tony."

"I don't even know you."

She watched the tip of his tongue touch the corner of his lips. "So, that's why I'm here."

"Maybe I don't ever want to know you." Although she tried to keep the put-down light, Angie saw that she had angered him.

"Think you're hot shit, don't you?" His lips stretched back over his teeth in a parody of a smile. "You remind me of a filly I saw at the track once. I watched her in the paddock before the race. When the jockey hit her, she'd turn and try to bite him. He'd whip her, and she'd snap. They went through that routine a dozen times, until she finally got the message who was boss. She went off a twenty-to-one long shot. I won on that filly and never forgot the lesson. Horses or women, they're all the same— only as good as the man with the whip."

"You ever worry the whip might crack both ways?" She tried to stare him down but too late realized the trap. Almost leisurely, those eyes began to rape her, untying the rope halter of her lounging pajama and tugging the fabric down inch by inch in a slow but thorough perusal of her body. His psychological assault repulsed her.

Angie ducked beneath his arm and stumbled out into the hall, so upset that for a moment she was disoriented. A noise from Z'Maria's bedroom startled her. But it was only Nickie, lurking in the shadows. Angie stumbled into the bathroom and splashed cold water on her face. What was it with men? First Louis, so deceitful and weak. Now this one, an animal who thought he could grab whatever he wanted.

Angie hurried back to her mother, who was anxiously waiting for her. "That man, I see him follow you. You okay?"

Angie smoothed back her mother's hair with trembling fingers. "Mama, I'm a big girl now," she said, trying to smile. "I can take care of myself."

"Not with that kind. All you've known are gentlemen, like the Urbanos."

Angie didn't know whether to weep or laugh with bitterness. While she and Mama whispered together, she tracked Malfatti out of the corner of her eye. He moved restlessly around the room, as if the space were too small to contain him. Then he seemed to make a decision. He swaggered toward the group of older women and stopped before them, his legs spread wide. The corner of his mouth twitched. Angie held her breath, waiting.

"What kind of hospitality is this?" he said, flashy and loud as a crooked politician. "Here I am, a *paisan'* visiting from Ohio, and no one to dance with. What's happened to good old Calabrian hospitality, eh?"

The bouncy accordion music died away and, like Angie, the whole room seemed to be waiting. She felt her mother's hand tighten on her arm as Malfatti's gaze came to rest on her. For Angie herself, there was almost a sense of inevitability to the moment. She did not look away. The bastard was going to force her hand in front of the whole neighborhood.

She stood up and threaded her way through the cluster of chairs, feeling everyone's eyes on her. She paused as if she were going to stop in front of him, then at the last instant she turned and headed across the room toward the musicians. "I'll sing some—"

Before she could finish, Malfatti's arm whipped out and pulled her to him. "Play!" he shouted. "Something pretty for the lady here to dance to."

Angie nodded okay, and tentatively Pete plucked out the opening chords of "O Sole Mio." The notes rose and fell, slightly offkey like a tinny merry-go-round air.

"Louder!" Malfatti barked, swirling Angie around the floor as the other dancers edged away from them.

She resisted the viselike pressure of his hands, but her efforts were futile. He pulled her so tightly against him, she felt the pressure of his groin. The smell of his strong cologne made her sick to her stomach. She stared past his shoulder, her neutral expression shifting only an instant when she caught Phil's eye. Almost imperceptibly, she shook her head in warning. Just let it go, she telegraphed. Don't give the jerk any more ammunition to play with.

At last the song ended, and he released her with exaggeratedly slow reluctance. Then he turned and walked toward DiPiano and Pap, who stood near the table. As

Malfatti joined them, they smiled and toasted each other's health with shots of whiskey.

"Angelina!" Rosa called to her daughter sharply. "Let's go. I am tired."

Rosa leaned heavily on her arm as they made their slow way home. The wild strains of a tarantella spilled out into the street, beckoning everyone young and old to dance. "Don't go back," Mama whispered, each word an effort. "I don't want that man near you."

11

Angie worked like a demon all morning, trying to forget what had happened at the party. On her knees, she dipped the stiff brush in the bucket of lye soap, then scrubbed the worn linoleum in a vigorous circular movement. Even the astringent smell of the soap and the monotonous work could not purge the memory of Malfatti's obscenely intimate embrace on the dance floor.

The screen door creaked open behind her. "Hey!" she warned. "Stay off the wet floor 'til it dries."

"Get up!"

Her head snapped around in surprise at the sound of Pap's voice. She had thought he was working in the garden.

"Get up, I said. You have a visitor."

Tony Malfatti stepped into the dining room behind Pap. He smirked when he saw her down on her hands and knees. The bandana covering her hair had slipped so far down her forehead she realized she must have looked like an immigrant just off the boat.

Self-consciously she pushed back the bandana and stood up. She noticed under Tony's arm a candy box with a pink satin lid decorated by an enormous red ribbon bow. It reminded her of the showy funeral arrangements that Z'Maria was so contemptuous of. The bigger the bou-quiet, Z' always said, the lousier they treated the dead one in life.

"Signorina," Tony addressed her in coarse peasant Italian, "your father has given me permission to call. I brought you this gift as a token of my esteem."

Angie's gaze moved from the fancy box to his face. His exaggerated show of respect toward her, his alliance with Pap—underscored by the bond of their shared Calabrian dialect—angered her.

"Take it," Pap barked.

She took the box, holding it away from her like a rotten fish. Her disgust almost seemed to please Tony, as if he were secretly keeping score.

"What do you say to him, eh?"

Her muttered thanks was barely audible.

"That's better," Pap said, nodding toward Tony. "Now, bring caffè and anisette. And be quick about it."

In the kitchen, Angie threw the candy box on the table. Let the kids enjoy Malfatti's flashy largess; she wanted no part of it. She turned up the flame under the coffee and searched for the liqueur in the back of the cupboard. No one had touched the anisette since the Urbanos had drunk a toast with the Branzinos ten months before. She swirled the clear liquid, watching it coalesce into slow, fat droplets on the inside of the bottle. She imagined a fly trapped in the sticky sweetness, its wings fluttering feebly.

Pap gestured angrily at her when she appeared in the parlor with the bottle and two cups of coffee on a tray. "Are you deaf? I said you have a visitor. Go get a cup for yourself."

Her fists tightened on the tray. "I have work to do."

"Stupido, I said, go get another cup."

Angie slammed the tray down so hard the hot coffee splashed over her hand.

She raced upstairs, sucking on her reddened fingers while inside she burned with hatred for her father. It galled her to be humiliated like this in front of someone like Malfatti. She stopped outside her mother's bedroom and peeked in, wondering how much she might have overheard. Rosa lay propped up against the pillows, her eyes closed. Sometimes she seemed so still Angie was terrified she might have slipped away without anyone noticing.

"Angelina?" she murmured, her eyes still shut. Like an animal, she seemed to sense her young.

Angie crossed the room to her. "Yes, Mama."

"Who was talking?"

"Papa."

"And who else?"

Angie said nothing. She sat beside her mother, listening to the drone of the men's voices downstairs. The bedroom was stiflingly hot despite the ancient fan Phil had managed to keep going with bits of wire. Angie stared down at her mother's drawn features, weary even in repose, and wondered if she had made a horrible mistake in refusing to marry Louis. She would never forget the way he had pleaded with her that night, promising that her mother would have the finest of medical care. As it was, the Branzinos could not even afford the occasional visit of Dr. Sawicki, an overworked but kindly Polack who would gravely shake his head after each call and state there was nothing more to be done for her except bedrest.

Mama stirred, pushing at the light sheet that covered her. Angie forced herself to smile as she opened her eyes. "Why don't you sleep a little more?"

"Sometimes I'm afraid to close my eyes, Angelina." She sighed as she looked toward the door Angie had closed. "Afraid I won't open them again."

It dawned on Angie that the noisy, tumultuous flow of life in the Branzino household infused her mother with the courage to go on, rather than tiring her.

"Mama," Angie said, smoothing back Rosa's white hair from her forehead, "would you like me to sing to you?"

A smile worked its way behind the weariness in the woman's eyes. "Nothing sad, eh? Something from *Le Nozze di Figaro*; that, I always love. When me and your papa were first married," she murmured in her soft, melodious Italian, "he would take me in a trolleycar downtown to the symphony house. Such a long, long time ago—how beautiful the women were, their hair poufed up around their faces like halos."

"You were one of them, Mama," Angie said, thinking of the beautiful dark-haired Rosa in her parents' wedding photograph. As Rosa shook her head in denial, Angie insisted, "Oh yes, yes you were, Mama!"

The teasing light in Angie's eyes was quenched by the heavy sound of footsteps on the stairs.

"What is it, Angelina! *Che fata*?"

Pap flung open the door, his whole body tense with festering anger.

Rosa turned. "Frank! What—"

"Shut up." Pap's eyes were fixed on his daughter. "I make one warning: You try to make me look small before another man again, I beat the shit out of you."

"*Per piacere*," Rosa pleaded, "tell me what's the matter?"

"I'll tell you what's the matter." The weight of his disgust shifted toward his wife. "You wanted her to go live in the city, to have a life above what I, her own father, could provide for her. And look at what returned to us—this disrespectful piece of trash."

Rosa lifted her arm placatingly. "Frank, she's our daughter."

"A daughter obeys. She shows proper respect for the *paisan'* of her father."

Angie stood as Pap came around the bed toward her and said to him, "Is that who you call *paisan'* now? An ignorant bull who tries to hide his animal scent with cheap cologne?"

Pap's hand connected with her face like a whip cracking. Angie flinched from the pain. Neither of them heard Rosa's feeble cry of protest.

"You've shamed me enough. Now, go change." Pap held his upraised hand inches from Angie's mouth. "Tony is taking us out."

"Frank, listen to me," Rosa said, reaching up to tug weakly at her husband's arm. "That man's no good. I don't want him around our Angelina."

He jerked his arm away. "I made a mistake once when I listened to you and that sniveling little priest. But no more. Angelina will do as I say." He turned his focus wholly on Angie. "You turn your back on what the Urbanos would give. Now you will live in this world—my world—as it always should have been. I tell you one last time—go, get ready. Tony's waiting."

"If that son of a bitch wants me, he can take me as I am."

As she brushed past him, he yanked off her bandana so viciously that some of her hair came out with it. Holding her head, she flew out of the room and down the steps. At the bottom, she nearly collided with Malfatti. His blue eyes glittered with anticipation, and she realized he had overheard everything.

Up in the street, she gulped in the humid summer air that was thick with the smell of dust and coke—honest smells that had nothing to hide. The neighborhood kids were swarming over the shiny green Hudson parked in the street, investigating the vertical louvers on the sides of the hood and the chrome-wire hubcaps. Little Funzi Labrino showed up with his dog Amos, a swaybacked black mutt. Amos sniffed at a tire, then lifted a leg.

Nice work, Amos. Angie smiled to herself.

An angry shout behind her evaporated her bitter amusement. "Hey!" Malfatti shouted, his coarse voice rubbing her nerves raw. "Get away from that car."

The group of kids scattered like buckshot, all except for Funzi, who frantically dragged at Amos's neck. But the dog refused to budge before he had finished baptizing the tire.

Tony shot past Angie. "Keep your goddamn dog away from the car!" He scooped a stone out of the gutter and flung it, hitting Amos squarely on his skinny back. The dog yelped with pain. "I catch that kid and his dog again, he'll be lickin' the piss off."

"The dog won't be back," Angie said with a straight face. "You and he speak the same language."

Tony slowly turned to face her. "You got a mouth on you, Angelina. Maybe somebody ought to shut it."

As he talked, his face was constantly in motion with nervous tics and grimaces, revealing yellowing, widely spaced teeth—a sign of good luck, the old Italians said. Angie stared at him with undisguised loathing.

He leaned possessively against his car. To Angie the flashy car reeked of venality and greed. For a moment she felt bitterness towards her aunt. It was Z'Maria's friendship with Carlo DiPiano that had brought Malfatti into their lives.

He pulled a tiny leatherette case from a pocket and retrieved the slender gold toothpick inside. As if it were a cigar, he rolled it between his broad fingers before sticking it in the corner of his mouth. "I been hearing all kinds of stories about you, Angelina. All kinds." The toothpick jumped as he talked. It caught the sunlight, a glittering fang full of venom. "You can turn your nose up at some uptown *ginzo*, but you ain't gonna get away with that crap with me."

"You heard stories about me, did you? So maybe you heard this one: I'm used to high-class Italians, Malfatti. Men with manners and finesse. That word probably isn't even in your vocabulary. I won't try to explain it; you'd never understand in a million years. Those 'uptown *ginzos*' treated me like gold."

"You spread your legs for a rich man, so you think it's made of gold now, eh?"

"Foul-mouthed pig!" Angie's arm swung up, but he caught it. "Yeah, you're stronger than me, but so's a brute animal." She taunted him despite the pain he was inflicting. "You're nothing, Malfatti. You're like that dog who doesn't know any better. I feel sorry for you."

"They say you sang at fancy parties and the uppity bastards, they applauded real nice and polite. Gave you a big head. I think maybe it's time you were knocked down to size," he said, pulling her closer. "Now that we're gonna be going out, you better learn how to talk to me. You're gonna open your mouth only when I say so."

Angie tried to pull away. "If you think for one minute I'd turn down a gentleman only to wind up with a lout like you, you're nuts." She laughed in his face. "Your tough talk doesn't faze me. I'm not afraid of you."

"No?" He twisted her arm painfully. "Then you just don't know me well enough yet."

Angie crept into the dark bedroom. Gina slept in a tight little ball in the middle of the bed, accustomed as she was to being crowded between her two big sisters. Nickie lay facedown next to her, one arm hanging off the edge. Candy wrappers were strewn everywhere. Greedy little pigs, Angie thought tiredly, pulling off her dress. Still wearing her slip, she eased down onto the bed, trying to keep the springs from squeaking. She heard Pap down in the kitchen, moving around like a bear patrolling his territory. At last he clumped upstairs. Angie squeezed her eyes shut, waiting for him to flash the overhead light in their room. She felt Gina stir beside her and moan softly when the light hit her. A moment later it went off, and he closed their door.

"Ssst. Ange." Startled, Angie turned to see Nickie up on her elbows, wide awake and staring at her. "Where'd you guys go?"

"Up the Italian Club."

Nickie snickered. "Some date."

"It's not funny. That low-class jerk acted like he owned me. I wanted to die. He and Pap are two of a kind. *Paisan*'," she muttered bitterly, staring up at the ceiling. "They make me sick, both of them."

"I betcha Pap's a little scared of him."

Angie's head jerked around on the pillow so fast that Gina stirred again. Angie waited for her to settle back into sleep, then snapped at Nickie, "What are you talking about?"

"Word's out he isn't just a bootlegger, Ange. They say he's killed people."

"Where'd you hear that?"

"Tootsie's brother drives a truck out of DiPiano's warehouse. You know how word gets around. Everyone's heard it now."

"I wish to God he'd go back where he came from."

"You should've heard the *gumbaris* talking about him in the street today. Their fat mouths were going like machine guns. They say the guy wants you, Ange. They say that's what you deserve after playing the 'big-a shot.' "

Angie's mouth twisted in hatred. God, how the neighborhood must have relished that sordid scene on the dance floor. It was as though Pap and all the rest of them wanted to see her punished for having dared aspire to more. They wanted to see her cut down to size by scum like Malfatti.

She thought of his big-man act at the club—dropping fives and tens down on the bar as if they were small change, buying round after round of drinks, bragging about how he "took care" of guys who crossed him, until she'd sensed that even Pap was shamed by his display. So much for his sense of brotherhood with this "man's man," she thought contemptuously. Pap had opened the door to a monster that he was powerless against.

She sat up on the edge of the bed and clutched her hands over her stomach, vainly trying to hold back the nausea and growing fear.

"Ange, you okay?"

"Yes," she lied.

"Ange, if I were you," Nickie whispered, "I'd hide. I'd run away!"

Right, Angie thought in despair. Where the hell am I supposed to run to?

Nickie drowsed beneath the big maple tree in Z'Maria's yard, deliciously lethargic after their Sunday feast of fried chicken livers and yellow peppers. An old *Vogue* magazine lay open in her lap; her head swam with images of elegant women in wonderful clothes. Hearing the raised voices of the kids up in the street, she glanced around lazily to see what the excitement was all about. She jerked wide awake as soon as she saw Tony Malfatti's car. He climbed out onto the sidewalk and was immediately surrounded by a bunch of kids. The guy had all the crude charisma of a neighborhood bully.

She watched him make a big show of pulling a coin out from behind Vic's ear. The other kids went nuts at its magical appearance. Tony presented the coin to Vic with a flourish, then cuffed him on the side of the head as if to remind him where his good fortune came from.

Nickie glanced toward Pap and her aunt, perched on the weathered garden bench like unmatched bookends. Z'Maria frowned at Pap as Tony started down the steps into the yard, and Pap glared back at her—each blaming the other for the man's disruption of their fragile Sunday afternoon peace.

You're both to blame, damn it, she thought angrily, looking around for Angie. She and Phil must have gone to check on Mama again. Nickie hoped to God Angie stayed out of sight until the creep got tired of waiting.

Tony was about to cross the yard when he caught a glimpse of Gina playing beneath the grape arbor. He turned toward her with a swaggering flourish, like a bad actor mugging it up for the audience. "Hey, little Gina!" he said in his bluff way, reaching toward her. "Lemme see what old Tony's got for ya."

She shrank from his hand, spoiling the effect of his magic coin trick.

"Hey, come on," he cajoled, his voice tense beneath its bluff cover of lighthearted fun. "Whatcha afraid of, huh?" Gina kept backing away from him until she was scrunched against the trellis.

Nickie jumped up, poised to rush to Gina's aid and yet curious, too, to see how far the guy would go. She had seen his type before, guys almost pathetically eager to win over a reluctant child or indifferent dog. Maybe they couldn't stand the risk that a child's ingenuous honesty might pierce their shell to reveal things they desperately kept hidden. Nickie sensed the danger inherent in a man like that. He would go to extremes to prove otherwise about himself. Fear quivered along her spine. Before she could decide what to do, Angie and Phil appeared at the side of the house.

"Leave her alone, Tony." Angie's voice shook with anger.

"Butt out. I'm just trying to make friends with the little *gumbari* here."

"You blind? Can't you see you've got her scared?" Angie held out her hand toward Gina. "Come here, honey."

Gina started to run, but Tony's hand shot out, holding her back. "Wait a minute. Here," he barked, forcing the nickel into her hand. "Take it. Buy yourself an ice cream."

"Angelina!" Z'Maria called out with spurious gaiety. "How about some of my good wine for our guest?"

Angie went over to the cloth-covered table under the tree, and with shaking fingers she poured out the last of the wine. As Tony started toward her, Nickie called to him. "You been here three days in a row now. What are you going to do, move in?"

"Nickie!" Z' snapped. "Shuddup."

"Nice manners your daughters got," Tony growled at Pap, who in turn looked angrily at Nickie.

"Sit down, Angelina," Pap growled between clenched teeth as he joined Tony at the table.

"How's your wife, *Franguch*?" Tony asked, addressing Pap familiarly, flexing his muscular shoulders. "You need some money for doctors, medicine for the poor woman? You need anything, you just tell me."

Pap stiffened as if he had been slapped. "I take care of my own."

"You take care of your own, eh, *Franguch*?"

Pap stared at him sourly.

Tony smiled. "The *italiani*, we got our pride. Look at Il Duce. He's gonna make Italy like it was with the Romans."

Infuriated by her father's impotence in the face of Tony's mockery, Nickie hit back. "You admire that windbag Mussolini, huh?"

Tony's eyes took on the flat sheen of metal. "What do you know, little girl? No one stands above Mussolini. No one. You compare him to that pansy Johnny Bull in the wheelchair who's running this country. Il Duce is God." Tony's eyes moved slowly around the group, stopping to rest on Angie. "People respect him. They fear him."

Angie stood up. "Excuse me."

"Where you think you're goin'?" He flashed a couple of concert tickets. "I came to take you downtown."

She stared at him. "I told you, I'm not interested."

Tony looked at Pap. "*Franguch*, I thought you and me, we had an agreement. Is this how you control your family?"

Pap flushed brick red. Slowly he stood up, his eyes murderous as he approached Angie. Without warning, his arm flew up and he backhanded her so hard her neck snapped back. "You heard the man."

A tense silence fell over the table, broken only by the homey clatter of pots banging up in the kitchen.

Finally Angie said in a subdued voice, "How about a little more wine before we go?"

Tony smiled maliciously. "That's more like it."

But Angie's apparent submissiveness didn't fool Nickie. She jumped up to follow her sister. "I'll come help you, Ange."

Once they had gotten around the corner of the house,

Angie started to cry. "Christ, I hate men!" she breathed, dabbing at her bleeding mouth.

"What are you gonna do?"

"I don't know. But I'll be damned if I let that son of a bitch win." Angie stopped in front of Z'Maria's old root cellar. She reached down and pulled open the slanting door.

Nickie stared at her in disbelief as she started down the mossy steps. "Where the hell you going?"

Angie didn't reply.

A dank, musty smell filled the cellar. Angie stared at the crude wooden wall along the back. The day Prohibition ended, every winemaker on the Hill had boarded up his tunnel entrance and went on about his business like a model citizen, as if the passages had never existed. Without hesitating, Angie pulled down a couple of the rough boards. As she crawled through the small opening, a jagged edge of wood caught her stocking and tore it. She stumbled across a cache of bottles and other debris.

Fighting down the fear rising in her throat, she moved as quickly as she dared in the blackness. Ever since Pap had punished her when she was five by forcing her down the cellar stairs and closing the big trapdoor over her, she had been terrified of enclosed dark places. Yet for all the claustrophobic fear weighing her down, Angie had to smile when she thought of Tony Malfatti waiting in vain at the table for her to return with his wine.

As she crept along in the direction of Cheech's bar, Angie sensed the tunnel growing steadily more narrow. It was little wider now than the circumference of a barrel, and she had to stoop to keep from brushing her head on the ceiling. Panic began to constrict her throat. Her lungs and brain cried out for open space and fresh air.

Angie was about to crack when a faint half tone of light glimmered in the distance. That had to be Cheech's cobwebbed old basement window. Eagerly she crept forward.

As her eyes readjusted, Angie realized the light shone unimpeded down the length of the rough stone corridor. Cheech had never boarded his end up. Then it dawned on her that the old packrat was using the tunnel as a convenient storage dump. Gingerly Angie picked her way among the clutter of empty bottles and broken-down wine presses.

She crept cautiously out of the tunnel into the dark cellar and peered up the stone stairs toward the door. Through it came raucous laughter. Angie knew that from the outside Cheech's place would appear closed up, tight and sober as a judge.

As she stood there debating what to do, the cellar door swung open and a man staggered out onto the landing. Angie shrank back into the shadows when she realized he was fumbling with the buttons on his fly. An instant later, a streaming arc of piss rained down the steps.

Embarrassed and disgusted, Angie turned away. As she did so, something brushed against her foot. She let out a stifled scream and kicked at a rat the size of a football. It scuttled away deeper into the darkness.

"Hey, who's down there?" the guy yelled, buttoning up his pants as he moved down the stairs. "Cheech!" he bellowed, grabbing Angie by the arm. "You thought it was rats down here, but all the time it's Minnie Mouse."

"Will you let me go?" Angie said in irritation, trying to pry his hand off her arm.

By this time the revelers had crowded onto the cellar landing.

"Angelina," Cheech said in bewilderment. "What the hell you doin' in my basement? I thought . . ." He turned around slowly. The other men were jostled and shoved by someone behind them.

Angie followed Cheech's gaze. She stared in shock at the squat, powerful body silhouetted in the doorway, his hand wrapped around a beer bottle.

"Hey, Tony," Cheech said, "I thought you said Angelina had to take care of her sick mother."

The man holding onto Angie laughed. "Mebbe her sick mother just wanted a beer."

"Shuddup!" Tony roared angrily over the laughter. "All a you, get out. This ain't none of your business." He called down the steps, "You too, Bruno. Get your fuckin' ass up here."

The man beside Angie shuffled up the stairs and disappeared back inside the bar. Tony slammed the door after him.

Angie stared as Tony moved down the steps toward her. He tossed away the bottle in his hand. The sharp sound of the breaking glass splintered the air between them. He shoved her so hard against the wall she felt the wind knocked out of her.

Gasping, she said, "What do you want from me?"

He smiled. "Everyone's gonna say Malfatti got what that son of a bitch Urbano couldn't hold onto." His hand closed around her throat, and she marveled at the coldness of it, the ugly brute strength in his fingers. The mix of hatred and desire in his eyes terrified her. "I want to taste your sweet, rich, uptown cunt."

"Disgusting pig!" she spat. "Go roll in the slop where you belong."

His hand tightened on her throat and forced her to her knees. He pulled her face against his crotch, its tumescent heat pulsing through the thin fabric. "You're going to worship the ground I walk on, *signorina* high and mighty. You're gonna make me look like a big, big man."

Angie struggled and squirmed. "Never! You'll have to kill me first."

"Angelina, Angelina." He reached down to squeeze her cheeks together, forcing her lips into a parody of a smile. "You don't know how weak you really are."

12

She stood on the stage of Carnegie Music Hall. Its baroque gold and red plush decor felt oppressive, threatening to crush her. As she opened her mouth to sing, she was drowned out by the sound of contemptuous laughter. She realized that the audience was pointing and laughing at her. Looking down, she saw with horror that she was in the filthy dress and torn stockings she had ruined hiding from Tony in the tunnel. She tried to run, but it was as if her feet were glued to the stage. The laughter crescendoed, pounding in her head.

Angie woke with a start. With maddening slowness the pealing laughter receded into her subconscious. She took a deep breath, desperate to erase the memory of the Urbanos in the front row of her dream. Their elegant faces had been contorted with vengeful hilarity.

She pushed away the sheet. She was drenched in sweat. As she sat up on the edge of the bed, her eyes were drawn by a strange flickering light from outside. She jumped up and went to the window.

Flames licked around the foundation of the empty house next door, a brilliant necklace of fire that held her transfixed. Then the flames whooshed skyward with a tremendous sighing gasp.

A dog started barking somewhere, but Angie's screams drowned it out. "Get up! Hurry! Fire!" she cried frantically as she went to shake Nickie and Gina. Nickie woke instantly. She stared at Angie in fear, her narrow face glowing from the reflected heat of the burning house.

"Come on, Nickie! Get Mama and the boys up. I'll take Gina."

Angie dragged the sleeping child from the center of the bed. "Gina!" She slapped her face lightly. The girl's sleep-swollen eyes opened at last. "Come on, carina, we have to go outside."

"How come?"

"Just get up, honey," Angie urged, doing her utmost to keep the panic out of her voice as she pulled Gina to her feet and brushed her hair back from her face.

She led her out into the hall. "Nickie! Take Gina out!"

Pap and Phil appeared in the doorway with Rosa between them, her arms hanging limply over their shoulders. Angie's heart constricted when she saw the terror in her mother's face.

As quickly as they could, Pap and Phil moved through the succession of rooms, half dragging and half carrying their burden. Heat pulsated through the open windows; the night sky glowed unnaturally bright, like a lurid painting. From below they heard the neighbors shouting frantically, intermixed with Amos's barking. "Frank, fire!" they shouted over and over again. "Get your family out before it spreads!"

Mama was prostrate from exertion and fear by the

time they had reached the safety of the street. "Mama!" Angie cried as Rosa's head lolled forward onto her chest.

Old Niello ran up barefoot, his hairy chest exposed above his suspendered trousers. "Everyone out? Thank God there's no wind!"

Z'Maria rushed along the sidewalk toward them, her bony arms protruding from her shift. Even she looked vulnerable, like a newly plucked hen.

The street was chaos. Angie tried to stay out of the way as Pap and the other men rushed back and forth, their faces grimy with sweat and soot. Using buckets and hoses, they wet down the side of the Branzinos' place, all the while keeping a watchful eye on the flames that licked at the edge of the yard. Someone gave a shout an instant before the shingled roof of the burning house collapsed with a muffled roar, rocketing a column of shooting flames and smoke high into the sky. The men shrank back, momentarily daunted by the destructive fury of the conflagration.

Angie stared, unable to turn away from its terrible, hypnotic beauty.

From a distance came the ringing clamor of a fire truck. She turned with relief toward the sound. Just when she had begun to think that the family would be safe after all, she saw Tony Malfatti standing beyond the circle of light cast by the streetlamp. The sight of him sent a chill through her.

Tony casually flicked a match and put it to the cigarette between his lips. In the reflected glow of the tiny flame, she saw his face contort in a feral smile. With purposeful deliberation he extinguished the match between his thumb and finger. Still smiling, he nodded at her—a nod of complicity. No words were said; none were needed. Angie alone bore the burden of the simple, terrible truth. Satisfied, he tossed the match to the ground with a flick of his hand and strolled away.

As his slow, measured footsteps echoed down the sidewalk, she started to shiver uncontrollably.

13

Angie paced outside her mother's bedroom door. The stifling heat of the summer afternoon pressed down on her like another dimension of her fear. Z'Maria stood grimly nearby, while Nickie and Phil sat huddled at the top of the stairs.

The door opened and Dr. Sawicki came out, his compassionate eyes full of sadness. "I am sorry." He shook his head as Angie rushed over to him. "You had better send for your papa right away," he said quietly. "And the priest."

As Z'Maria clumped down the stairs after the doctor, she called sharply to Freddy and Vic to run down to the mill.

Gently Angie opened the door. A shadowy half light bathed the room. Through the open window came the acrid stench of the smoking ruins next door, an ugly reminder of what had brought about this tragedy. Angie stared at the still figure on the bed. How frail and tiny Mama looks, she thought. Her delicate hands were almost translucent against the patched sheet that covered her. Angie approached her, barely aware of Phil and Nickie creeping into the room.

Angie dipped her fingers into the pitcher of water on the bedside table and gently moistened the woman's dry, cracked lips. Rosa stirred and opened her eyes, already filmy with death, and yet the corners of her mouth lifted in an attempt to smile. An ache of tenderness welled up in her eldest daughter. "Oh, Mama," she whispered.

Rosa moved her fingers, gesturing with a fluttering tremble to Nickie and Phil. "Must . . ." she whispered, her voice faint as a breath of wind. "Must understand Papa."

"Sshh," Angie begged. "Mama, save your strength."

"Deep down he loves you," she breathed, her fore-head creasing with the tremendous effort to speak. "Like you once—young, loved laughter . . . music." Her weary, pain-filled eyes came to rest on Angie. "Night . . . you born, threw open the window and shouted to the whole neighborhood. Woke them all." Angie watched the tears well up on her mother's lower eyelashes and felt her own grief rising like an uncontrollable flood. "He wanted to give you all so much. Wound up giving . . . nothing. The pain for him!"

"Mama, please," Angie cried.

Rosa shook her head. "He looks at you now, he sees only his own failure. But I see the future. You must get what Papa never had. Let my love give you that courage. I'm glad I live this long to see you almost grown. . . ." Her voice trailed off, and she held out her trembling arms to them. "You made my life worth something."

Angie clutched her mother's hand, willing her strength to flow into the dying woman. But Angie sensed her spirit slowly receding, as if the life force were being drawn by something beyond her. The only sound in the room was Phil's muffled sobs as he buried his head in the covers at the foot of the bed. As Rosa sighed her last breath, Angie felt a sweet, fleeting peace before the jagged pain engulfed her.

They buried her in the parish cemetery. Amid the grass and worn tombstones, her grave was an open wound. Angie lingered there long after everyone else had left. The hot sun beat down on her, but still she stayed on, overwhelmed by desolation. "Mama's death in a sense is my death, too. My pride has destroyed us both. In spurn-ing Louis, I opened the door to Tony Malfatti." Now she would have to pay: The sin of pride commanded a terri-ble penance.

As Angie headed down Mitchell Avenue later, she heard the bluesy sound of Vic's harmonica. He had been playing it incessantly since his mother died. She knew she would forever connect that wavering, mournful sound with Mama's death. Phil had tried to take the harmonica away from Vic until Z'Maria intervened. Let him grieve in his own way, Z' had said. And so each of them had: Pap in his chair at the edge of the ravine, staring out over

the smokey horizon that had swallowed up his dreams;
Freddie bouncing a ball endlessly against the side of the
house; Gina clinging to her rumpled doll as she sobbed, a
low despairing whimper that tore at Angie's heart. Rosa's
death had wrenched out the heart of the family, leaving a
gaping black emptiness.

Much later, Angie went into the house, moving like a
sleepwalker through the dark rooms. She had just taken
down Phil's portrait of Mama in the parlor when Nickie
appeared in the doorway. "Put that back," she whispered, her voice swollen with misery. "You can't take
that away, too."

"Nickie, it's all I'm going to have," Angie said, clutching the picture frame. "You still have each other."

Nickie rushed forward in a fury, flailing at Angie's
arms as she tried to wrest the picture from her. In the
struggle it slipped from Angie's hands and crashed to the
floor. "Now look what you've done!" Nickie cried, staring down in horror at the shattered glass. She went for
Angie again, clawing and swinging with renewed ferocity.

Despite the bruising rain of her fists, Angie managed
to pin Nickie's arms and they crashed backward onto the
sofa. Angie clung to the girl's writhing body. Panting, she
gritted her teeth and held on for dear life. Angie feared
the raging bitterness that flowed out of her sister. More
than any of them, Nickie was Pap's child—the child of his
twisted, impoverished spirit. Now that Mama and Angie
were being torn away, who would protect Nickie from
herself?

"Don't go away with him, Angie, please," Nickie
sobbed, her voice muffled against Angie's chest. "Don't
go!"

"I have to," Angie murmured brokenly, rocking Nickie
as if she were a child again. "I love you all so much. I
can't allow him to hurt the rest of you."

"Do you, Angelina, take this man, Antonio Malfatti,
to be your lawful wedded husband . . . to love and cherish, to honor and obey . . ."

As the justice of the peace read the words in a perfunctory monotone, Angie stared at the top of his head. Dust
motes danced in the late-afternoon light slanting through

the Venetian blinds at his back, wreathing his mottled scalp in a tarnished, wavering halo.

The words droned on. Angie felt their crushing weight piling up until panic gripped her throat in a choke hold.

The man's pale eyes blinked. "Miss Branzino?"

She swallowed painfully. "Yes?"

"The response?"

"I . . ." Her response was barely audible. "I do."

The justice sighed with obvious relief. "I now pronounce you man and wife."

A wave of hatred for the colorless minister swept over her. He did not bother to question why the bride was dressed in mourning black, why her face was haggard and swollen from crying, nor why she flinched as the groom leaned forward to kiss her.

They went out into the still summer afternoon. Heat rose in shimmering waves from the steps of the small Ohio courthouse. Beyond the edge of town, Angie glimpsed cornfields stretching endlessly into the distance. Tony settled his new bride into the front seat of his Hudson, while the elderly justice chirped a bright farewell from the door. Staring straight ahead, Angie pretended not to see him.

A deep-red glow rimmed the sunset sky as they drove into the industrial outskirts of Youngstown. Tony turned down a brick street lined with rows of grimy mansions that had been converted into rooming houses and drew to a stop at the last one on the right. Angie's eyes swept up the peeling gray facade. A radio blared from one of the upstairs windows, broadcasting the repartee of Gracie Allen and George Burns. Angie suddenly remembered Mama and Z'Maria sitting side by side in the parlor, chortling in disbelief at the daffy couple on the radio. The vision filled her with a piercing homesickness.

She climbed the cracked concrete steps behind Tony. Inside, he set her bag down in the dimly lit foyer. As he flipped through the pile of mail on the entry table, a door opened off the hall and a slatternly creature in curlers and robe scuffled out. "I told you—no women."

"Hey, this broad ain't no jailbait." Tony grinned as he pushed Angie toward the stairs. "She's my old lady, all nice and legal-like."

The landlady's despising glare impaled Angie. "You dagos are all liars."

Infuriated by the insult, Tony rounded on her. "You want proof, is that it?" He pulled the marriage license out of his pocket and shoved it under her nose. "Here it is, you fucking neb-shit."

"Two people living in that room," the woman whined. "It's gonna cost you two dollars a week more."

Angie climbed the steps like a robot, her cheeks stained dull red from humiliation.

The third-story room had mildew-stained walls and a sagging, unmade bed that smelled of tobacco and whiskey. Looking around distastefully, Angie broke her self-imposed silence. "So this is home sweet home."

"It's temporary," he growled, the corner of his mouth twitching spasmodically. "I got big plans, Angelina, big plans."

"Little men always do."

Tony pushed her roughly inside. "I ain't in no mood for your smartmouthing." He grabbed her arm and twisted it. "Understand me?"

His eyes bored into her. Their electric depths emanated a darkly malevolent beauty that froze her like a doe caught helplessly in the beam of a hunter's spotlight.

"You're mine now, Angelina," he growled. "You're all mine—every juicy inch of you." Still holding her pinned with one hand, he jerked up her dress and thrust his hand into her panties. His fingers probing obscenely, he shoved her down onto the bed. . . .

When he had finished with her, Tony fell into a heavy, snoring sleep. Angie lay curled up at the edge of the bed, staring out into the darkness. Terrified of waking him, she inched out of bed and crept down the hall to the bathroom.

Shakily she sat down on the edge of the tub and examined herself. Pain rasped through her as if she'd been all cut up inside. But his brutal assault had hurt her more than physically. She felt defiled, transformed into something filthy and worthless. She sunk to the floor and laid her burning cheek against the cold tiles, wishing that she were dead.

14

Angie winced as her bruised hipbone touched the edge of the sink. Peering into the bathroom mirror, she daubed the yellowing bruise beneath her eye with a powder puff and pinched her cheeks to put color into them, but the defeated eyes staring back at her reflected the futility of her efforts. She wouldn't fool Z'Maria or Nickie for a second. As deeply as she longed to see them, she dreaded having them see how low she had fallen.

The mass of bruises she bore this week had resulted from a poorly ironed shirt. "Try to make me look bad, I'll kill you!" Tony had screamed, ripping the monogrammed shirt apart and then slamming her against the closet door. When she picked up the hot iron to defend herself, he had knocked it out of her hands and started to pummel her with his fists. She had torn away, but he'd tripped her and sent her sprawling to the floor. Like a whimpering dog, she had tried to crawl beneath the bed. But he had come after her relentlessly, beating her head against the floor as she clung to the frame. "Fucking bitch," he had raged, "I'll show you who's got the upper hand."

Angie cocked her head, listening. At first she thought it was the wind whipping around the drafty old farmhouse. Then the faint thrum grew louder. She went to the window, expecting the taxi that would bring Nickie and Z'Maria from the train station. When she saw the truck careening down the dirt lane, her stomach tightened with fear. Please don't let there be trouble, she prayed. Not today. Mud and melting snow flew up from beneath the speeding truck's wheels, splattering the side of the house, before it screeched to a stop beside the ramshackle barn out back.

Tony stood on the running board, barking out orders to the two young toughs who sloshed through the mud to the barn. Like a little general, Angie thought hatefully as she walked toward him, a two-bit dictator in a cashmere overcoat and handmade shoes.

"Tony—"

"Get back in the house."

"Joey!" she called to one of the boys rushing past, his wiry arms laden with two cases of whiskey. "What's going on?"

"Feds nosin' around." He grinned. "But we're gonna outsmart 'em."

Angie turned fearfully to Tony. "What if they show up here?"

"So? They ain't gonna find nothing."

"I'll be here."

Tony laughed. "T'hell they want with a piece of shit like you?"

Angie turned and crept back to the house.

The almost casual abuse that had begun on her wedding night had escalated to a full-scale psychological and physical assault: He threatened and insulted, taking sadistic pleasure in demeaning her before others; he attacked her with a random violence that left her constantly terrified and uncertain when the next blow would fall. Her life with Pap had well accustomed her to such ugliness, but at least at home the kids had been able to band together to buffer each other from his rages. Here Angie was totally alone.

What she had come to dread most was her growing sense of isolation. She felt overwhelmed and completely powerless. At times she felt like ending it all, but she would never give the son of a bitch that satisfaction. Instead, she built a wall inside herself.

She stood on the narrow porch as the taxi drove up.

Z'Maria climbed out of the rear seat almost before the cab had braked to a stop. "Angelina, what are you doing standing out in the cold?" she rasped. "Get back inside."

Ignoring the brusque order, Angie came down the

steps from the porch and kissed her aunt on both cheeks. Nickie got out and looked around warily. Finally her gaze came to rest on her sister. "Hi, Ange." Her voice was clipped, sharp, like the angles of her body.

"I've missed you, Nick," Angie said, going to kiss her. Nickie's gaze didn't lift farther than the bruise under Angie's eye.

Inside the house, Z'Maria impatiently waved away Angie's invitation to sit in the parlor and marched straight toward the kitchen. In one motion she lifted off the hat lodged against her bun of iron-gray hair, shrugged out of her coat and sat down at the table. Her unflinching eyes swept Angie up and down. "I always thought you were the most beautiful of Rosa's children. Like a queen. Now look at you." When Angie didn't reply, she said with sharp contempt, "So, where is he, eh, that charming example of a husband?"

"Out." Angie moved around the kitchen with nervous, awkward motions, turning the flame up under the coffee pot, pouring milk from the icebox, arranging biscotti on a plate. She noticed Nickie hovering in the doorway, looking angry and frightened at the same time.

"Nicoletta!" Z'Maria barked. "Come talk to your sister. Tell her how the teachers, they want you to go to college."

Nickie shrugged, pretending it was of no importance.

"I'm glad," Angie said dully, setting the cups on the table. "That's wonderful."

"What does a girl need with college?" Z' complained.

"You want to see her stuck in Coalport for the rest of her life?"

"Why not? It's her home. She's got a nice boyfriend."

"Does Pap know that?"

"Will you two stop talking about me like I'm not even here?" Nickie pulled a chair out and sat down.

"So, who is it?"

Nickie gave her a defiant look. "Rocco DiPiano."

"Carlo's son?" Angie's voice rose in disbelief. "You must be out of your mind, associating with scum like that."

"He's not scum. Rocco's going to law school."

"You think that makes a difference?" Angie asked,

sinking wearily onto the chair opposite her. "Don't you understand? These mafiosos are all alike—it's in their blood." She looked accusingly at Z'Maria. "Why do you encourage her? The DiPianos' power doesn't rub off. It only makes you smaller."

"Angelina, these are not easy times. You know the old saying: One hand washes the other and they both wash the face." Z'Maria shrugged. "Whatever you think of Carlo, he's been a good friend to me. You cannot blame him for your situation. Your papa is as much to blame as anyone."

Angie made as if to spit.

"So why are we here?" Z' rasped. "So that we all can fight?"

"No!" Angie reached across the table and grasped their hands, willing their warmth to fill the cold places inside of her. "O God, no! I can't tell you how much I've missed—" Her voice broke.

Nickie squeezed her hand tightly. "Ange, why don't you come home with us for a while? Please."

Angie bowed her head. "As if Tony would allow it."

"Maybe if Z' talked to him . . ."

Angie shook her head despairingly.

"Listen to me, Angelina," Z'Maria said with rare gentleness, "we'll invite the two of you for Easter, eh? Spring's not so far away now. Remember how you and Nickie would pick dandelions for me and your mama and we'd wheeze?"

"I remember, Z'," she said, envisioning the fuzzy golden suns massed on a hill.

Z'Maria continued to reminisce, talking about the old country and the lives of the peasant women who knew nothing but to endure. Angie tried to lose herself in the comforting, raspy drone of her aunt's words. Z'Maria's voice—scolding, laughing, caressing—was as familiar and dear to her as her own mother's. Now they sat together as equals in this warm kitchen, woman to woman.

The fragile peace of the afternoon was shattered by the sound of Tony's footsteps on the porch. Angie's stomach tightened instinctively with fear. How well he had trained her! Angie was filled with loathing for both him and herself. Once again she felt the cold despair seeping through her, eating at her like a cancer.

15

Angie sat in the back of the bus, her head bowed. She stared down at a loose coat button hanging by a thread, like her own life, unraveling bit by bit. She crossed her arms disbelievingly over her belly. The doctor had to be wrong. How could she be carrying the seed of a new life when she felt so empty?

She cleared a spot in the misted window and stared out over the flat Ohio landscape. Her future with Tony was like the road stretched out before her—a bleak, terrifying wasteland. She had dreamed of running once. The empty road had beckoned to her. But it had been only that—a dream. She knew him too well now; she understood his capacity for vengeance. Never could she risk exposing her family to that kind of hatred. Her own life didn't matter. She was already lost. This pregnancy was another link in the chain of his brutalizing domination.

The bus driver switched on the interior lights against the wintry gloom. Angie turned away from the despairing eyes reflected back in the glass, fighting to imagine the luminously beautiful girl who'd had the world at her feet and the whole future stretched enticingly ahead. Inevitably the vision faded. She could not allow herself the luxury of regret, the painful futility of imagining what might have been.

The bus came to a stop. Wrapping her coat tightly against the frigid wind, Angie walked down the rutted lane toward the lonely farmhouse. To her surprise, she saw a stranger waiting on the front porch. As Angie climbed the steps, her misery gave way to faint curiosity. Her eyes fixed on the pair of dainty gold earrings that seemed incongruous against the young woman's broad, sturdy features. "Who are you?"

"Domenica Malfatti." Her bright eyes studied Angie covertly. "*La moglie d'Antonio.*"

"I don't understand," Angie muttered in shock. "What do you mean—his wife?"

For answer the woman dug into her pocketbook and pulled out an ornately stamped document interwoven with ribbons. *"La licenza,"* she said simply.

A few minutes later, Domenica sat at the oilcloth-covered table in the kitchen, dipping the hard biscotti into her milky coffee to soften them. Although it was obvious she was ravenous, Angie's presence must have made her shy, because she took tentative, mincing bites. *"Mangia!"* Angie said impatiently. "Go on, eat!"

Angie had to prod her the same way to get her to talk, which the young peasant woman did haltingly, in her southern Italian dialect. From her Angie learned that Tony had returned to his native village six years before and married Domenica when she was fifteen. Every few months he had written, promising that he would send for her soon. This year the letters had stopped coming. So she had embarked alone on a five-thousand-mile journey with a few lire in her pocket and little more than the clothes on her back. She had come to America in search of her husband. As Angie listened to the poor woman's story, she felt a long-suppressed rage pounding inside her skull like a kettledrum. Tony was nothing but an unscrupulous swine. He had made Angie not his wife but his whore. And her child, the tiny seed containing her only dreams of the future, was nothing but a bastard without a name. Yet her rage was mixed with exultation. The path to freedom that she had dreamed of with such longing had opened miraculously.

"E chi e voi?" the woman asked Angie with wary politeness.

Angie stood up, fighting to control her feverish excitement. "It doesn't matter who I am." She grabbed the flour canister and poured out the few dollars in change that it had taken her weeks to scrounge from her meager household funds. While Tony carried great wads of cash to squander on show, he begrudged her pennies. "I've called a taxi. It will take you to a hotel in the city." Hurriedly Angie wrapped the rest of the biscotti in a dishcloth, pressing them into Domenica's hands along with the money.

When the taxi arrived, Angie bundled the bemused woman outside. "Antonio will come for you at the hotel. He is your husband. I will not allow him to desert you." Angie tucked her into the cab, whispering, "I am your friend, not your enemy." The woman nodded uncertainly, her eyes fearful and questioning.

Angie paced slowly through the quiet house, as if she were just awakening from a bad dream. She saw the furniture, the curtains, the cheap knickknacks as through the eyes of a stranger—all part of the false nightmare world that Tony had carefully constructed to ensnare her. Everything within these four walls was his except Angie herself. She lifted a vase and hurled it against the wall. Then she moved from room to room, driven by a wild fury. . . .

Tony slammed to a stop in front of the house and jumped out of the car, staring in disbelief at the boxes strewn in wild abandonment across the empty fields. The air reeked of whiskey. What the hell had happened—the feds again? As swiftly as the thought arose, he dismissed it. This wasn't how they operated. His heart hammering, Tony ran toward the open door. A soprano's powerful wail blared from the record player, the flowing sounds at once eerie and ominous. He rushed inside and stared in shock at the destruction.

"Angelina!" His voice echoed through the ravaged house. He raced up the stairs two at a time, shouting her name until he was hoarse. Christ Almighty, his enemies wouldn't have dared touch her—his most prized possession —not if they weren't prepared for all-out war.

He froze in the bedroom doorway. She sat calmly on the edge of the bed, her eyes quenched and dark. Then he saw the pistol cradled in her lap, and his relief gave way to a kind of confused dread. "What happened—what the hell you doing!"

"You made me your whore, Tony," she said, her voice eerily soft. "But I'll survive that."

"What the fuck are you talking about?"

As he started toward her, she lifted the .38 and pointed it at him. "You come through that door, I swear to God I'll kill you. Poor Domenica will be a widow before she's even been a wife."

His eyes narrowed. "So's that's what this is all about," he said coolly. "She don't mean nothing to me."

"You bastard."

"Angelina, put the gun down," he said, fighting to keep his voice steady and quiet, his eyes fixed on the gun wavering in her hand. "You ain't no murderer."

"Stop!"

He kept moving toward her. "Gimme the gun, Angelina." The pistol exploded.

Tony staggered back against the door frame. As he stared down in shock at his groin, blood oozed out in a slowly spreading stain across his pale gray slacks. With a strangled cry, he pressed his hand over the wound. Then he lifted his eyes to Angie's face, and his look of blank shock gave way to a murderous rage. "You bitch, I'll kill you for this!"

Trembling uncontrollably, Angie stared back at him. He tottered toward her. She fired again wildly. The second bullet hit his temple, jerking his head. He stumbled forward and crashed to the floor at her feet. She stared down in horror at his motionless body, at the blood flowing into viscous scarlet pools beneath him.

"O God, dear God," she murmured, crazy with fear and dread. Maybe she had meant to kill him all along. Heaven help them both, he deserved to die! She dropped the pistol as if it had scalded her hands.

She dragged her cardboard suitcase from beneath the bed and threw clothes into it heedlessly. When she had finished, she eyed the portrait of her mother above the bureau. "It's over, Mama," she whispered, snatching the picture off the wall and cradling it to her. "He can't hurt us anymore."

She steeled herself to approach Tony's body. Gagging, she bent down and rifled his pockets. She slipped his key ring over her finger and then counted through the thick wad of bills folded in his money clip, feverishly calculating how far it would take her. Home was forever barred to her. She was a murderess now, a fugitive. She had no choice but to run.

16

Wakefulness pounced on her like a cat and her eyes flew open. She lay in a bunk, staring into the unfamiliar darkness that smelled faintly of diesel fuel and dampness. Then she grew conscious of the slow, sickening rise and fall that left her stomach somewhere in midair.

"O God," she groaned. "Not again."

She got up, bracing herself against the wall that curved in toward her. The windowless cabin deep in the bowels of the vast ocean liner had been all that she could afford. From the moment the ship left the calmness of the Hudson River, she had felt too ill to do anything but sleep.

The past week since she had fled Ohio was a blur—the clackety train ride to New York, the cheap Bowery hotel with its odor of defeat, the bright poster of a ship in a travel agent's window that had held her spellbound on a rainswept street. The woman sipping champagne at the ship's rail had seemed as carefree as the breeze that lifted her platinum-waved curls. For all her misery, Angie could not help but smile in wry self-contempt at her own naiveté. What carefree future could lie ahead for a pregnant woman on the run?

Unable to bear the dank, close air of the cabin, she pulled her coat on over her nightgown and went out onto the deck, moving with the unsteady lurch of a drunkard as she tried to match her steps to the rolling pitch of the ship. The sea air enveloped her, cold and clingy as a damp scarf. She drank it in with great gulps. As the ship plowed steadily eastward, Angie tried to envision the port of Le Havre six days distant, but she could see no farther than the next rising, sickeningly hypnotic, wave. She clung to the rail, retching until her throat and mouth burned from the bile. Her eyes closed tightly, and she retched again, purging the poison of fear and degradation that had eaten away at her life the past year: a painful cleansing that left her exhausted and empty.

"Here, let me help you."

Angie started as a man's snowy linen handkerchief materialized beneath her nose. She took it with trembling fingers and dabbed at her lips, murmuring her thanks, too humiliated to face her benefactor.

He persisted. "Can I get something for you—ginger ale, soda crackers? They say it works. . . ."

The attractive baritone, full of concern, struck a familiar chord in Angie's memory: An upper-crust voice saved from stuffiness because it had always been so alive with mischievous, teasing undercurrents. And she envisioned the man that went with the voice: his long, angular face with its strong cleft chin; his slitted green eyes watchful and quick as a cat's but infinitely warmer.

"David O'Rourke," she whispered, lifting her head in numb surprise.

"Who the . . ." He blinked rapidly, confusion giving way to the shock of recognition. "Angie? Angie Branzino, or what is it now, Mrs.—?"

"It's Branzino," she said, her voice cracking. "Just Branzino."

He shot her another look from beneath his dark brows, a questioning look, mixed with pity. For an instant Angie saw herself with his eyes—a worn-down woman in a drab coat, anxiety furrowing her face. She began to back away, eager for him to be gone, to forget that he had ever seen her. He caught her by the elbows, but she shrank from his touch. "No! Please."

"Look, Angie, I don't want to leave you like this. Is there someone in your cabin I can get to help you?"

"No," she whispered, shaking her head. "I'm alone. There's—there's no one."

The words had such a quiet ring of finality that they filled her with despair. There was no turning back. She had left everyone and everything she had ever known to embark on this wild flight toward—what? She felt the unfamiliar sting of tears in her eyes. How long had it been since she had cried? During her sham of a marriage she had donned an icy shell. Instinctively, she had protected her inner core. Now without warning, the ice began to thaw. Hot tears welled up in her eyes and spilled down her cheeks. Her shoulders began to tremble, yet she made no sound.

Astonished and oddly moved by this strange, silent outpouring of grief, David put his arm around her shoulder and this time she did not resist him. "Come on," he urged, "let me walk you back inside. You're in no state to be alone."

He was appalled by the cramped bleakness of her steerage cabin, but he said nothing. He went in search of soda and crackers, which Angie gamely tried before she lay back against the pillows and closed her eyes. He couldn't help staring at her. What in Christ's name had become of her? He remembered envying Louis his lithe, charming fiancée. With her dark, brilliant coloring, she had reminded him of a Spanish painting—so sensual and full of life. Suddenly he realized that she was staring up at him from the narrow bunk. The corners of her mouth lifted in a pathetic attempt at a smile.

"You're a duck out of water, aren't you?" she said. "Slumming down here with us galley slaves. Won't your friends be missing you?"

"Somehow, I don't think Maura will be." In response to her questioning look, he added in a tight voice, "Hell of a way to start off a marriage, isn't it?"

"Oh, David, I'm sorry, I didn't mean . . . I didn't know . . ."

"Forget it." He touched her hand. "Listen, would you mind if I sat here with you a bit?"

"I'd like that very much," she whispered. "I've been so lonely, I can't tell you."

They talked—or, rather, Angie talked. Her fingers plucked nervously at the thin blanket, and her eyes occasionally searched his to see if they were condemning her. Each time she was reassured, and with a deep breath she reluctantly resumed the sordid tale of her life with Malfatti. He did his best to hide his shock at the ugly denouement. Murder? he thought. Her litany of tragedies made his situation with Maura seem trivial by comparison.

"So, now you see why I'm running," she said, her eyes huge against the pallor of her cheeks. "Why I had to run."

"You did what you had to do, Angie," he said, grazing her cheek with a fingertip. "Don't ever blame yourself, you understand me?"

"O God . . ." Her voice started to break, but she brought it under control. "I'm so glad someone understands."

"You'd better rest now."

She nodded. "David," she called out as he opened the door to leave. "Thank you. Thanks for being here tonight."

Angie paced the deck, the collar of her coat drawn up tightly against the cold March wind. She felt much better today. It may have been David's seasick remedy; more likely it was the comfort of his presence that had given her strength. She leaned against the rail, lulled by the rhythmic swoosh of the waves as the ship's bow sliced through them. A shout of laughter floated down from the reaches of the upper-class decks, and Angie craned her neck upward. She thought about David's flippant reference to his honeymoon. How clearly she remembered Maura Donahue. For all her ethereal, strawberry-blond prettiness, the girl had been a cruel, self-absorbed snob.

On impulse, Angie turned from the rail and made her way to one of the stairways that linked the various decks. As she climbed upward, she stopped at each level to peek inside. Bare wood gave way to plush carpets and sleekly geometric brass sconces that filtered light over oil paintings gracing pastel-papered walls. The luxurious surroundings elicited a sharp pang of loss in her. For all her disillusionment with Louis, she realized she craved a return to that life. Standing in the doorway, she made a vow to herself. She would regain all that she had lost, but this time she would do it in her own way and on her own terms.

Angie continued her explorations but with steadily mounting caution. Shipboard rules were strict—third-class passengers were forbidden to venture elsewhere. Nevertheless, curiosity drove her on. Eventually she emerged on a glass-walled deck open to clouds scudding high overhead. Potted palms formed a feathery green curtain between the bar and the gaming areas, where women in flowered dresses and men in white flannels played croquet and shuffleboard. The sunshine filtering down through the early-spring sky was watery and pale, yet to Angie's eye the deck fairly dazzled, as if the elegant crowd provided its own radiance.

She spotted David reading on a deck chair. Although he seemed absorbed in his book, she backed up until she was well hidden behind a decorative pillar. The last thing she wanted was to embarrass him by her presence. A light peal of coquettish laughter caught her attention, and she turned. Maura, in an ivory Chanel jersey dress that set off her fair coloring beautifully, had sent her disk skittering wildly off the shuffleboard court toward a burly young deck attendant, who raced back with it and placed it on the end line for her.

"How silly of me," she trilled to her opponent, a silver-haired man with an erect bearing. Then Maura turned to David, who had not appeared to notice his wife's little show. "Come on, darling, you really must give me some pointers if I'm not to go all out of control."

David barely glanced up. "You're doing fine without me."

Maura tossed her head. "Well, what do you think of that, Mr. Jensen?" she said to her playing companion. "What do you think of a man who won't satisfy his bride on her honeymoon?"

The old gentleman replied with a gallant air, "Believe me, my dear, if you were mine, I would certainly strive to please you."

A frail woman with a cane pulled herself up out of her cushioned lounger. "I think you've had quite enough exercise for one day, Harold Jensen," she said to her husband, ignoring Maura. "We'd better go and dress for luncheon."

Maura watched them move off together, idly tossing one of the game disks in her hands. "What a bore," she murmured.

As Maura glanced around for another distraction, Angie backed farther behind her pillar. She watched in fascination the way Maura's eyes fastened on the good-looking deckhand, who had come over to collect the gaming pieces. On the pretext of helping him, Maura stooped down and then touched him for support as they both stood up. Her pale hand lingered caressingly on his tanned muscular forearm.

"Maura!"

Both Angie and Maura jumped as David's low voice, vibrating with barely controlled anger, rang out. He threw his book down and went over to take his wife's arm. Their argument, whispered in bitter undertones, lasted until Maura pulled away from him and flounced away. With a grimace of disgust David returned to his chair.

Angie was so engrossed in the scene that she wasn't aware of the ship's officer until he towered over her, resplendent in his white uniform and colorful epaulets. "Excuse me, miss," he said in a well-bred voice edged with disdain, "but I think it's rather obvious you do not belong up here with our first-class passengers."

Stung, Angie nevertheless refused to show remorse. "Silly man," she said in a perfectly mimicked la-di-da tone as he hustled her back to the netherworld. "Of course I belong. You just don't realize it."

Angie wrung out a cloth in the tiny washbasin, then held it to her forehead as she lay on the bunk. The cabin was sweltering and claustrophobic. Once the ship docked in the morning and she stepped ashore, she would gladly kneel to kiss solid ground. The Old World—land of culture and history. The irony never failed to stun her: She was reversing the journey that her parents had made a generation earlier, leaving behind everything they had known to risk a new life in America. "God, how I wish Mama were here now," she said aloud. Had she felt as terrified and alone as Angie did? At least Mama had had Pap. Angie had nothing but an address in Milan, a year out of date, and the memory of a stiff, unsmiling woman who had always demanded more than Angie thought she could give. "Dear God," she prayed silently, "don't let Madame Francini spurn me. I've got no one else. No one."

A knock at the door interrupted her fervent prayer. She tossed the cool cloth into the basin and jumped up to answer it.

"David!" He stood there in the corridor, laughter in his eyes and traces of five-o'clock shadow on his lean, pale face. His formal white tie hung askew like a crooked painting. "I thought you wouldn't come down here anymore. What if Maura—"

"Damn Maura," he said breezily. "It struck me that pregnant women are supposed to have whimsical food cravings, so I grabbed some of the strangest things I could find from the midnight buffet in the grand salon, and here I am." Grinning, he held up a bottle of champagne and opened his fist to reveal what looked like a handful of squashed mushrooms. "Marzipan—spun sugar and almond paste." He bit into one experimentally.

"Well?" she asked, laughing.

"Not bad, actually."

They sat crosslegged on her bunk and toasted each other's health. He poured her champagne into a tooth mug while he drank straight from the bottle.

"Oh, David, you've really been wonderful to me. I'll never forget all your kindness. But for Pete's sake, it's your last night on ship. I wish you'd go up and enjoy yourself. You don't have to worry about me. I'll be fine, honestly."

"Well, since we're speaking honestly, I have to say I'd rather stay right where I am, thank you." He held out the bottle to top off her mug. "Shall we make another toast?"

Angie touched her mug to the bottle. "To the future?" She spoke the toast in such a hushed, uncertain way that she regretted it immediately. Why spoil this moment of carefree fun? Though he'd said little about Maura or himself on their late-evening rambles over the lower deck, she had sensed his growing disappointment, not simply with his new wife but with the whole direction of his life.

"To the future," he echoed quietly. "May it be everything you hoped for."

"And for you, too."

His answering laugh was short and bitter. "Right."

An awkward silence fell between them. "So—so what are your plans for the rest of your honey—the rest of the trip?"

"Well, I think Maura and I have basically agreed to disagree. In Paris she'll refuse to visit Notre Dame and the Louvre, and I'll refuse to visit the big fashion houses and watch her flirt with mustached Romeos. In Vienna she'll refuse to—"

"David, stop," she said, giving him a troubled look.

"I know what you're thinking, Angie: Why in God's name did I ever marry her?"

She shook her head. "I'm the last person to pass judgment on anyone."

He acted as though he hadn't heard her. "The rich marry the rich. You know, that's the plan." His fingers tensed on the neck of the champagne bottle as he twisted it upward. "They marry and have perfect children to carry on the grand tradition."

"Believe me, I know all about other people manipulating your life. It nearly destroyed me," she said with sudden fierceness. "You only have to look at me to see that." She reached over to grip his hand. "David, you have to do what's right for you. If you don't, you pay in the long run, and sometimes the price—"

"Thanks for the advice," he cut her off, "but it's too late for me."

"Don't give in so easily. David, really, I just can't see you as some fat plutocrat chomping on a cigar."

He laughed sharply again. "How do you see me?"

"I don't know . . ." She turned over the hand she still held between hers and lightly rubbed his palm. His hands were beautiful, strong, uncallused—hands unaccustomed to manual labor. She lifted her eyes to meet his; they were quizzical and bright, expectant. She read, too, a glimmer of something else that made her blush. Glancing down again, she said softly, "All I know, David, is that you seemed most alive the times you were talking about art with Phil, or about music with me. I always got the feeling your true passions had very little to do with following in your father's footsteps at G. & O. Steel."

"Did you?" He stood up, shoving his hands into his pockets, and began to pace restlessly in the narrow space beside her bunk.

"David, all I meant to say is . . . don't sell yourself short."

"Listen, Angie," he said abruptly, "I came down here tonight to talk about you. We'll be docking in the morning. Look, I know you must be short of cash." He reached for his billfold. "I'd like to help—"

"I'll be fine, I told you." She stood up swiftly beside him. "David, I don't want money. What I value is your friendship. I don't know what I'd have done without you this week. But there is one thing I must ask of you—one small, vital thing." She hesitated. "You have to promise me you'll tell no one we've met."

"Angie—"

"Will you promise?"

Her intensity was so compelling that he could not take his eyes from her face. "Yes," he said at last. "Is that all? Isn't there anything else I can do for you?"

"There is one thing." She smiled as she reached up to straighten his tie, her eyes brimming with an affectionate warmth. "Just . . . I want you to remember what we talked about tonight and . . ." She broke off huskily, trying not to cry.

As he brushed his lips against her cheek, she had to steel herself not to throw her arms around him and cling to his strong, comforting presence.

'If you ever need me, Angie, I'll come. I promise you."

Then he was gone.

From the sea the Normandy coast seemed a wild, rugged land of high cliffs. Its aloofness daunted Angie. But as the ship nosed into the wide mouth of the Seine River, her eyes swept the wooded hills that rose above the busy port of Le Havre, and she wasn't quite so afraid. The hills reminded her a little of home. She tried to imagine her family back in Coalport and what they were doing, but all that her mind conjured up was a frozen snapshot like the one she carried in her purse. She felt ephemeral and unreal as a ghost, as if she had somehow died to them. In a sudden fit of panic she wondered if Z'Maria had received the cryptic telegram she had sent from New York. She didn't dare write again. She assumed the police would be watching the mail. Fearfully she touched her stomach. If they were to track her down and arrest her, they would take her baby away.

A blast of whistles and foghorns jolted her as the

magnificent white liner was warped to its berth at the pier. Angie clutched the conversational French book in her pocket. How would she ever find the train station? How would she make them understand that Milan was her destination? She fingered the dwindling roll of bills she had grabbed in desperation from Tony's still-warm body. How long would the money last?

17

Angie stepped down from the train, clinging to her suitcase. She rubbed the back of her neck, stiff from having slept sitting up all night, and stared around at the noisy, cavernous Milan station. People bustled past her, their voices bursting to life as they greeted friends and family. Angie realized with somewhat of a shock that she understood them, and that realization alone bolstered her waning self-confidence.

"*Mi scusi, signore,*" she said to a porter piling luggage on an already overloaded cart, "but where would I find—"

He turned. "*Mi scusi, signore,*" he mumbled, mimicking the southern Italian dialect she had spoken all her life. "Stupid, woolly-mouthed peasants every one of you," he groused as Angie backed away, horrified by his stinging contempt. "Coming north to steal our jobs. Why don't you go back where you belong, eh? Back to your goats and your mountain villages."

Angie ran out of the station, her suitcase banging painfully against her leg. She stopped and raised a shaking hand to shield her eyes against the fierce Lombardy sun reflecting up from the dark pavement of the piazza. "Peasants." The word echoed like a curse in her head as she crossed to the newsstand in the middle of the square.

"Please," she said to the vendor, this time enunciating with the exaggerated long vowels Madame Francini had once drilled into her. She showed him the slip of paper. "Can you tell me where this address is?"

"Of course, signorina," the old man replied with courtly dignity and proceeded to give her intricate directions that she knew she could never follow. Still, she smiled and nodded, her sharp ear picking up every nuance of his Milanese accent as he spoke. Never again would the epithet "peasant" be spat at her.

She walked for what seemed like miles. Traffic hummed along the busy Via Manzoni. Occasionally a taxi would slow and honk inquiringly. Much as she longed to rest, she would shake her head no and continue walking, shifting her heavy suitcase from hand to hand. She had not eaten anything since her spartan coffee-and-roll dinner at the Gare du Nord in Paris. Even so, her money was evaporating at an alarming rate.

The narrow thoroughfare opened up at last onto a wide, graceful square set off by massive stone buildings that looked centuries old. She snagged the arm of a passerby and asked him where she was.

"Piazza della Scala," he informed her, gesturing toward a faded ocher and white building whose deep portico opened onto the square.

She stared up in wonderment at the famous opera house. Here was Madame Francini's world; she lived in the shadow of her beloved La Scala. At that moment Angie's heart beat fearfully. It seemed another lifetime since the voice teacher had coached her. Angie recognized her shameless audacity in showing up like this with no warning, but it was too late to turn back.

Across the square she marched toward an olive-drab palazzo with brown shutters and iron-railed balconies that overlooked the opera house and the fountain in the piazza. An enormous pair of iron-studded doors stood open, giving access to the inner courtyard of an eighteenth-century palace that had long ago been converted into apartments. The neatly raked gravel of the driveway crunched beneath Angie's shoes as she passed through. A tiny old man bent over a rake looked up at her approach and smiled. "La, la, la," he sang in croaking fashion, pointing knowingly up toward the gallery that ran along the second story. He reminded her of a fairy-tale creature, a wizened gnome mockingly announcing her arrival at the queen's court. She climbed the worn marble stairway, her suitcase banging against her knee. Exhausted, she dropped it next to the apartment door and pressed the buzzer. She heard a piano playing and, fainter still, an aspiring soprano reaching for high notes. Angie rang again.

After an interval, the door opened a crack. A pair of close-set eyes set in an anvil-shaped face peered through the narrow opening. Angie smiled uncertainly at Madame's devoted watchdog secretary. "Hello, Miss Langton."

"Angelina!" she said sharply.

A voice in the background made a trilling run up the chromatic scale and down again. As it trailed off, Madame's no-nonsense voice called out, "Sarah! For heaven's sake, what is keeping you?"

The door opened wide. Madame stood in the foyer, looking just as Angie remembered: Her sharp-boned face was unsoftened by the tight chignon of graying brown hair, and her slender body was clothed in a black dress and shoes of puritan severity. Madame's clear gray eyes widened. "Angelina, what a pleasant surprise." Madame turned to her assistant. "Sarah, you may finish drilling Signorina Vinelli with her scales. As for you, Angelina, come in, come in."

Sarah shot Angie a questioning glance before turning away. Leaving her suitcase by the door, Angie followed Madame Francini down the hall.

"Clara!" Madame called into the white-tiled kitchen at the end of the hall. "Bring coffee into the *sala,* please. We have a guest." Madame gestured for Angie to precede her through a pair of French doors that opened into a large, high-ceilinged drawing room. A pair of wine-colored sofas flanked a carved wood fireplace inset with veined black marble. An olivewood sideboard adjoined a multipaned door that opened onto a balcony. A painting of a ship at sea hung above the mantel, its dominant colors the brooding green-grays of a stormy sky. The room was every bit as severe and elegant as its owner. Madame went to stand before the mantel. "Well, sit down, child." The woman's English was crisp and perfectly enunciated.

Angie eased onto the sofa edge, not daring to lean back for fear she would be too exhausted to get up again.

"Now, why didn't you write and tell us you'd be visiting?"

"I—" Angie's reply was cut short by the arrival of Madame's cook, Clara, a plump, fair girl who stared at Angie as she set the tray with its single espresso cup on the delicate table of inlaid wood adjacent to the sofa.

Madame gestured for Angie to take the cup. "So tell me, are you with a group? Is this a tour of the Continent?" Angie gulped the hot coffee. "I hope you're at the Grand Hotel. It was Verdi's fav—"

"Madame Francini," Angie interrupted her. "I came alone. I—I intend to stay in Milan permanently."

The woman stared at her in disbelief. "You what?"

Taking a deep breath, Angie launched passionately into the speech she had been rehearsing for two days: "I wish to continue my voice lessons. You told me once that I had talent. Now I have decided, I want the opera to be my future. You also said that Milan is its spiritual center." Noticing Madame's frown, Angie's voice rose anxiously. "So, you see, I—I took your advice to heart—"

"Indeed."

Angie clung to the empty cup, as if the trace of warmth lingering in the thin porcelain might protect her from the woman's decided coolness.

Madame marched across the room and held open one of the glass doors. "Come. There is soup in the kitchen. You will eat. Then you will rest. As for this other nonsense, we will discuss it later."

Before Angie could say anything more, Madame had moved off down the hall with her long, gliding stride. From the music room Angie could hear the singer's young voice rising over Sarah's piano chords. Angie recognized the aria from Donizetti's *Lucia di Lammermoor*. The soprano in Madame's study did not understand the character of Lucia at all, Angie thought wearily. The lines should have been infinitely more feminine, more vulnerable, more heartbreaking.

Angie awoke to the low murmur of voices. The dark room was as simple and spare as a convent cell. She had no idea how long she had slept. Throwing back the covers onto the iron bedstead, she got up and crept barefoot across the cold marble floor. She opened the door a crack. The parlor was directly across the hall, its glass doors ajar. From her vantage point, she could see Sarah sitting in a warm pool of light before the fire, her head bent over a piece of sewing in her lap. She drove the needle in and out furiously, looking up from time to time toward the tall balcony door, where Madame was apparently standing in the shadows.

"But how do we know what's happened to her?" Sarah said, her voice querulous and full of suspicion. "The effrontery of her behavior, showing up on our doorstep like a ragamuffin. She is obviously deluded. Why, it's laughable, unthinkable."

"Sarah." Angie caught the subtle warning note in Madame's voice.

Sarah dropped her needlework on the sofa and stood up. "Madame Giulia, I speak only out of feeling for you," she went on in a rather offended tone. "Your energies are limited. You would be wasting your time with that—that creature."

Terrified that Sarah would convince Madame to send her away, Angie grabbed her coat and draped it over her bare shoulders, then shoved her swollen feet into her shoes and hurried across the hall. Both women looked up in surprise.

"Angelina!" Madame's tone was sharp but not without kindness. "I thought you would sleep longer."

"I'm fine," Angie said. Feeling Sarah's eyes on her, she straightened her shoulders. "I'm accustomed to little sleep. I know the meaning of work and more work. You, of all people, I think know that."

"Hm," Madame answered, her expression hidden by the shadowy darkness. "Angelina, sit down, please."

"No thank you. I prefer to stand."

"As you wish." Madame Francini moved into the soft light emanating from the fire and the parchment-covered sconces to either side of the mantel. "Angelina, I am afraid that you have placed Sarah and me in a very difficult position."

"Please, Madame," Angie said urgently, "if you'll take me as your pupil again, I promise I'll be committed. You yourself told me I have great natural ability, that I learn quickly and have a facility for language. My Italian is adequate, I know I can learn French and German. I have a good ear. I—"

"Angelina," Madame interrupted her sharply, "you must return to America, to your family and your life there."

"I can't do that." Angie had to struggle to speak through the tears swelling her throat. "I no longer have a life in America."

Sarah interposed: "What idiotic nonsense."

Madame silenced Sarah with a curt gesture. "Angelina, whatever your life has become, I presume it has not allowed the luxury of singing. Your instrument becomes rusty with disuse. It is foolish to think you can resume training on a whim. You have no idea what is involved— the years of work, struggle. Angelina, you are an innocent. A child."

Angie shook her head. "No, I am not the child you remember. My decision to come to you wasn't made on a whim. Nor was my decision to leave America. I will not go back." In control of her emotions now, Angie spoke with quiet conviction, determined at all costs to preserve her dignity. "There are other teachers in Milan. If you'll excuse me, I'll leave now. Thank you both for your hospitality."

Fighting the urge to get down on her knees and beg, Angie summoned a confident look as she turned from them. She was out in the hall when Madame's voice rang out: "Wait." Angie turned back, her heart pounding wildly. For what seemed like an eternity, Madame stared into the fire burning in the grate. At last she looked around. As soon as Angie saw her eyes, she understood that she had won the woman over. Madame's expression was no longer shuttered and forbidding but darkly luminescent, as if she had somehow read the young American's future in the leaping flames and been moved by the vision. However, when she spoke, it was with her usual brisk, businesslike air.

"First things first. You will need to find work," she said, pacing before the hearth. "Sarah, you will go to Signora Vessi in the wardrobe department at the opera tomorrow morning. They always need assistants."

Sarah dropped her sewing in agitation and stood up. "Has she bewitched you? This is madness. Where is she to live? How will—"

Madame's authoritative voice overrode her. "Sarah, put away your sewing. I'll need you in the music room. Angelina, you will not audition for me dressed like Lucia in her mad scene. Dress and run a comb through that unruly tangle of hair."

"Yes, Madame."

Sarah glared as Angie flashed her a smile of triumph. Madame Francini did not miss the exchange. "Angelina," she said, her tone biting. "One thing must be clear from the start: My decision to allow you to stay is strictly provisional. If I find you lacking in any way—talent, discipline, character—you will be sent home. Understood?"

Angie nodded, nervously smoothing her hands down over her stomach. She could not tell Madame that she was pregnant, not while her foothold here was still so precarious. Perhaps after she had proven her worth . . .

18

The early April wind buffeted Nickie Branzino as she walked down Mitchell Avenue. It always seemed to blow longer, harder, and colder along the unprotected ridge of Dago Hill; everyone sat hunkered close to their coal stoves. Only the yellow dazzle of blooming forsythia bushes challenged winter's hold. Nickie shifted her books to her left hand, while with her right she held the collar of her hand-me-down coat up close under her chin. The coat had been missing its top button ever since she had inherited it, and rather than advertising her Raggedy Ann status with a mismatched button, mickie wore the collar folded open like the lapels on a man's suit. Into it she had tucked the green silk scarf that had been a gift from the long-vanished Urbanos. The touch of luxury against her skin never failed to buoy her.

She quickened her step, saying to herself, "Too damned cold to revel in rich-girl daydreams." If she were lucky, she would get a few quiet hours of study in before Pap and the kids came home, demanding dinner, for help finding their socks and arbitrating their squabbles. She resented the mother's role that had been foisted on her. It took too much of her limited time. This afternoon she had ditched gym class: another waste of time. Ever since she had applied for a full scholarship to Duquesne University on the bluffs of downtown, Nickie had become a bookworm. Study was her ticket out. The moment she entered college, she would put the ugly milieu of Coalport behind her forever.

Nickie was so caught up in her plans for the future that she paid scant attention to the long black car nosing along beside her. Only when it drew to a stop at the head of the Branzinos' rickety stairs did she notice it. Christ, she thought, he was still supposed to be in the hospital. Watching Tony Malfatti slowly emerge from the car, she felt her stomach tighten with revulsion. He turned to face her, his teeth clenched as he leaned heavily on a cane. His head was bandaged. He looked gaunt, pain riddled except for his cyanotic eyes, which were vibrant with menace. His rapacious leer followed the sway of her slim hips. Animal, she thought.

She stopped a few feet from him. "What are you looking for—another wife?"

He limped over to her. "Little bitch. Turning out just like your sister, aren't you?"

"Too bad Angie botched the job," she said, continuing to taunt him. "I'd have finished you off instead of leaving you half a man."

Without warning the steel-tipped cane flashed up and whipped across her calf. As she doubled over with pain, her books went flying.

"Enough!" Z'Maria's authoritative voice rang out. "Nicoletta, go downstairs."

Nickie picked up her books, cursing Malfatti under her breath. Behind her she heard her aunt's tone, at once placating and steely. "Tony, Tony, hasn't enough hurt already been done—on both sides? How come you want to come back now? To enjoy our suffering? We don't know where our Angelina is. She is gone from us. You have ruined her life."

Nickie hunched on the steps, rubbing the throbbing welt on her calf. Pig, she thought with fierce hatred as she heard him tell Z'Maria to shut up. But Maria Branzino wasn't a woman to be silenced.

"You had a wife, Tony." Z's rasp was a drill bit grinding away at him. "How could you marry our Angelina—bring this shame on our family? Tony, you done enough. Get away from us. Go home. We no can take anymore."

"*You* been shamed, old lady? What about me, eh?" Tony barely spoke above a whisper, breathing hatred and anguished self-pity. "My life, it's ruined because of that woman. Her bullet, it left a hole that drained away everything from me—sons, family, future."

Nickie held her breath, waiting. When Z'Maria spoke at last, the sound of her words was like a low keening. "Tony, Tony, I'm sorry, but what you want from me? You got a wife. Go home, take care of her. Who knows? Miracles, they can happen. Why you want to go on torturing us, torturing yourself? You know me, Tony. I don't lie. Wherever our Angelina is, she's lost. To all of us."

"No!" he burst out, and Nickie winced involuntarily as his cane whistled through the air and snapped against the pavement. "No, I'll find her, old lady. And when I do, I'm gonna kill her."

He tossed aside the broken cane and limped to his car. The engine screamed as he revved it and tore off, leaving a harsh stink of smoke and scorched rubber in the air.

Nickie crept down the steps and through the empty house to her room. She eased down on the bed and turned toward the grimy stencilled wall that she had covered with pages from fashion magazines. Svelte women in colorful bathing attire reclined on yachts that cruised through turquoise waters with magical names like the Hamptons and St. Croix.

"Nicoletta, get up," Z'Maria said from the doorway. "Let me see what he did to you."

Five minutes later, Nickie was sitting with her leg propped up by the stove, waiting for her aunt to finish making her homemade salve. The woman swore under her breath at the angry welt that would become a mass of black and purplish blue. "*Che bruta bestia*," Z' said, biting down on the side of her forefinger to show her disgust at Malfatti's brutish behavior. "But you asked for this, Nicoletta. You know what he's like."

Nickie wrinkled her nose as Z' started spreading the salve across the welt. "That stuff stinks. How come we can't buy stuff at a drugstore like the 'merican?"

"Shuddup, you. Always mouthing off." Z' lightly buffeted her shoulder, getting some of the smelly mess of animal fat and rancid olive oil in Nickie's hair. "We got bigger problems, eh, than you worrying about smelling like a goat."

"You think Tony knows something, Z'?"

"How would he know?"

"I keep thinking. Maybe he sent the telegram, to make us think it was from Ange. To fool us or something." Nickie winced as she shifted the weight to her sore leg. "Maybe . . . maybe Angie's dead."

"Stupida," Z'Maria barked. "It was from her."

"Z', I want to read the telegram again."

"What, you crazy? I burned it." Z'Maria lowered her voice to a harsh whisper. "The *telegramma* is our secret, yours and mine, eh? And another thing: We no tell your papa, we no tell nobody Tony showed up here. As long as you keep your mouth shut, it's gonna be okay."

An irrational burst of anger flushed Nickie's cheeks. This was all Angie's fault. She should have been there to face the consequences of her act, so the rest of them wouldn't have to suffer in her stead. Whether alive or dead, Angie had once again escaped the sordid life Nickie felt trapped in.

19

"*Buon giorno*, Angelina!"

The cheerful greetings rang out amid the clattering hum of thirty sewing machines as Angie made her way down the rows of seamstresses, her arms lifted high to keep the pale pink confection of floating tulle she carried from snagging. The women stitched away, crowded together beneath a large, grimy skylight. Angie never tired of the friendly chaos that reigned in the wardrobe department of La Scala—bolts of fabric piled helter skelter, baskets of sequins, diamanté and stage jewels spilling out around the seamstresses' feet as they busily pumped away at their ancient machines, repairing last year's costumes and sewing new ones for the coming season. Marking the periphery of the huge wardrobe room were yards of open closets jampacked with vibrantly colored costumes. Kingly robes of richly figured brocade, ball gowns of shimmering silks and soft velvets, ragged gypsy skirts and brilliant blue army tunics all awaited that moment of being swirled and strutted across a stage.

Angie spread the tulle gown across the enormous table that was the domain of the wardrobe mistress. Signora Vessi turned from the dressmaker's form over which she had experimentally draped yards of stiff white linen. Vessi was a big woman whose body almost seemed an extension of her trade. Lengths of fabric trim spilled out of her pockets, and a cloth tape measure hung down the front of her gray smock; tailor's chalk and seam rippers were lodged within easy reach behind each ear. She leaned over the gown Angie had brought, her broad fingers amazingly delicate as they traced the filigree embroidery edging the boat neckline.

"Well done," she said through the mouthful of pins held tightly between her teeth. Her lips moved so slightly, she might have been a ventriloquist. "Now start ageing that green velvet I laid out. There are wire brushes in the storage room; use the stiffest you can find."

The long, narrow room tucked behind Vessi's work area never ceased to intrigue Angie. High boots and dainty slippers, hats of every shape and size, scarves, gloves and petticoats, riding crops and carved ivory fans, wigs and false mustaches filled the ceiling-high shelves. Angie loved to poke around, experimenting one time with Carmen's fringed gypsy shawl and castanets, another time slowly fluttering the fan of the scheming Chinese princess Turandot. She would pose before a cheval mirror so old that half its silvered surface had worn away and imagine herself on stage. But today there was no time for daydreaming. She grabbed a wire brush from the toolbox and hurried back out to the wide-skirted gown spread out on the end of Vessi's work table.

Angie energetically dragged the stiff brush down the length of the skirt, ripping at the finely woven warp of the velvet, until Vessi's big hand clamped down on hers.

"Angelina, give me that brush," the woman said around her mouthful of pins. "We don't want this costume torn to shreds. We just want to make it look a little bit old . . . here." Vessi took the brush and snaggled the fabric with quick, gentle strokes. "See? Technique, technique. We brush lightly, lightly to bring out the threads. That's all we want to do. Rossini's Cinderella is an impoverished gentlewoman, not a castaway from a shipwreck. You see the difference?" Vessi handed the brush back to Angie and looked on approvingly as she imitated her light-handed snagging technique. "That's it, good. When you're done, take this other gown to Signorina Baldini's dressing room. Then go report to old Leppo. No doubt he's already got your day plotted out in that big book of his."

Angie hurried along the maze of dim corridors and steep staircases that linked the various departments of the elegant old opera house. She paused to catch her breath outside the door of Renata Baldini's dressing room. Hearing voices raised in heated argument, she debated whether to knock. Then the door was flung open from inside, and Angie found herself staring at Tito Massarro,

La Scala's artistic director. "You will wear it, and that is final!" he shouted. An instant later, a dainty bonnet adorned with ribbons and flowers came flying out into the corridor past his head. Angie bent to pick it up as the irate director stormed off. *The lady's got a throwing arm like Pap's,* she thought in admiration.

Angie cautiously approached the door and peered inside. The singer was pacing and swearing. "*Menaggia!* That man is a fool." She stormed to the piano against the wall and forcefully struck the keys. Angie recognized the tragic notes leading up to Violetta's death scene in *La Traviata*. While playing with one hand, the woman reached up with the other and mimed pulling off a hat and throwing it to the floor the instant before she launched into the first note of Violetta's aria. Angie stared at the soprano, entranced. Finally the woman looked up, noticing Angie. "I will wear his damned hat. But I will wear it my way." She laughed, her eyes flashing as she took the bonnet from Angie. "Who are you?"

"I am Angelina," she said quickly. "I've been studying here since April."

The soprano's gaze shifted to the bulky costume draped over Angie's right shoulder. "And working in wardrobe, I see. Help me into this heavy thing, will you?"

"I'd love to, but you know Signore Leppo with his scheduling book," Angie said as she draped the gown over the chaise. "He's a tyrant. I'm already late for my diction class."

The woman laughed again. "Leppino has been like that for centuries. I too was terrified of him when I was your age. But you will learn. He's a curmudgeon only on the surface. He has to be. Discipline is the mother of our art." She tossed off her dressing gown and stepped into the cumbersome costume that Angie had laid out for her. "Hurry now with those buttons. Then you may go."

While Angie quickly buttoned up the gown, the woman threw out questions and odd tidbits of advice over her shoulder. "You are Italian, of course? Milanese, I can tell by your accent." Angie said nothing, but the singer didn't notice; she was already off on another tangent. "You should know, of course, that the only way to achieve a rich coloratura sound is to stiffen the muscles of the buttocks; try it and see." Angie listened in fascination, darting looks at the woman's profile. Fine lines wreathed her wide, seemingly guileless blue eyes, and Angie noticed the strands of gray mixed in the curling blond tendrils at the nape of her neck. The soprano was probably in her early forties, yet she exuded the vitality and ingenuous charm of a girl. The magic of theatrical illusion, Angie thought. She saw it in the very essence of the shabby dressing room. Angie barely noticed the peeling gray walls and grubby window, but rather the mauve and pink challis shawl tossed with seemingly artless abandon across the stained couch, the painted screen in the corner, and the still life of silver-topped scent bottles and photographs on her dressing table. A thoroughly entrancing illusion of luxury and warmth, all of it arranged to show off the jewel at its center—the woman herself. The prima donna at her zenith.

Angie left Renata Baldini's dressing room, her senses drenched in the soprano's magic. She might or might not heed her iconoclastic theories about singing, but what Angie would never forget was the sensual power of her personality, the fluid elegance of her smallest movements that Angie sensed had been honed until they had become second nature. It was these qualities as much as the soaring power of her coloratura that projected her womanly essence up to the highest balcony in the theater; it was these qualities that had made her a star.

Angie raced down the corridors, one eye on where she was going and one on the German pocket grammar she studied in snatched moments here and there. *"Ich bin, du bist . . ."* she murmured over and over to herself, committing the conjugations to memory. She hoped she didn't run into old Leppo in the hall. He would read her off soundly, legitimate excuse or not.

"Ich bin . . . oh!" Angie doubled over in startled surprise. There it came again, another swift kick from inside her belly. Trembling with fear and shock, Angie leaned back against the wall for support. For the first time the enormity of her deception hit her. She had thought herself so clever: The tightly laced whalebone corset filched months before from Vessi's storage room compressed her burgeoning six-month belly, keeping her secret safe. But

to what end? This child she carried was real. She had meant to confess to Madame Francini, but somehow the weeks and months had passed. Now she saw no way out but to persist with the lies. She would wake up suddenly in the night, rigid with fear, and begin to plot elaborate, impossible schemes: She would sneak off to Switzerland, give birth and hand the baby over to strangers. . . . By day she coped by half convincing herself that this life within her was a chimera, that it didn't really exist. The self-deception had worked—until now.

Rapid, sharp footfalls at the end of the corridor signaled Signore Leppo's approach. God, more trouble, she thought. She shrank into the shadows of a recessed doorway, praying that he would pass by without spotting her. But he had a sixth sense where errant students were concerned. He stopped before the doorway, a small man enlarged by a white nimbus of hair circling his head and the enormous, gold-embossed journal that seemed an extension of his arms. Mussolini himself couldn't have looked more forbidding, she thought.

"Villains skulk in dark corners, Signorina Branzino," he enunciated in a dramatic stage whisper, his reedy tenor still vibrant for all his seventy years. "Wolves and other unpleasant creatures of the night skulk. What is your excuse?"

"I . . ." Knowing apologies would do her no good, she ventured a tentative smile. "Who knows, Signore Leppo? Perhaps I'll be the first woman to sing Iago's role in *Otello*. The art of skulking will come in han—"

"*Silenzio!*" he thundered. "I find your humor impertinent, your inattention to duty reprehensible." Ostentatiously he flung open his book and scratched a flourishing black X adjacent to her name. "I have marked you absent from Maestro Conti's class. Once more and you will be sent away. Understood?"

"Yes, sir," Angie whispered, her smile vanishing.

Late that evening, Angie sat at the small table in Madame's white-tiled kitchen, gulping down the tomato salad and bread that Clara had set in front of her. Her German grammar was propped open against the sugar bowl so that she could study while she ate. From time to time she wriggled her feet beneath the table, sloshing them around in the basin of warm water and Epsom salts that helped ease the painful swelling.

A soft breeze wafted through the open window, cooling her cheeks, and she looked up. The dark-blue sky, barely illuminated by the last pale blush of sunset on the horizon, reminded her of late summer evenings up on the sidewalk on Mitchell Avenue. Nostalgia swept through her in an unexpected flood.

Clara turned from the sink. "Would you like some— Angelina, are you all right?"

"I . . . yes." Angie swallowed. "Clara, will you make me a double espresso, please? I must be alert for my lesson with Madame."

The windowless music room was suffocatingly hot, and sweat trickled down Angie's neck. From the pleased side-long glances Sarah darted up at her from the piano, Angie knew that she was singing badly. Madame listened expressionlessly, her eyes fixed on the score spread open on the music stand. But Angie recognized the subtle warning signs—the gradual tightening of Madame's lips, the forefinger bouncing impatiently against her crossed arms. In desperation Angie tried to compensate by drawing air deeper into her lungs to provide that reservoir of extra power she so desperately needed. She wound up sputtering like a badly tuned car engine.

Madame slammed the music score shut. "This is disgusting. High C is meant to be floated on the air, not croaked like the last gasp of a tubercular frog." She marched over to where Angie stood rigidly by the piano. "Have you forgotten every single thing I have taught you? Here, let me feel your diaphragm." Angie tensed as Madame placed one hand high on her stomach and rested the other against her back. The moment seemed to spin out interminably, marked by the sharp ticking of the metronome atop the piano. Then Madame's sharply questioning eyes met hers. "What in the name of heaven is this?" Swiftly she yanked Angie's blouse front from her skirt and hiked it up. She stared at the old-fashioned corset in disbelief. "What have you done?" she said, jerking at the lacings tightly crisscrossed over her stomach. "No wonder you can't breathe. My God, you've got this ridiculous contraption—"

Sarah smirked. "Vessi was just complaining to me about thefts from her department."

Angie clung to Madame's hands, trying to stop her from loosening the corset any more. The woman shook her off irritably and finished untying the last few knots. Freed from its stiff ribbing of bone, Angie's squashed belly poured out over the top of her skirt. Madame and Sarah simply stared at the huge blue-veined mass of flesh.

Sarah spoke first, moving swiftly to the attack. "Didn't I warn you she was not to be trusted?" Her long English nose quivered with moral indignation. "I knew we should have sent the little strumpet packing. She must have known she was pregnant when she appeared on our doorstep."

Madame's eyes bored into Angie. "You have deceived me."

"I . . . yes, but—"

"Silence!"

"Madame, please . . ." Suddenly the room felt hotter to Angie, the ticking of the metronome louder. "You don't understand."

"I have seen all that is necessary to understand. You will go and pack. Immediately."

As Angie moved toward the door, it was as if the mingled pressure of the room's heat and the inexorable ticking of the metronome suddenly united to overwhelm her. She felt herself drifting in slow motion toward the floor. Through her diminishing consciousness she heard Sarah's sharp voice: "Just another cheap trick to play on your sympathy . . ."

Madame Francini had drawn a chair close to the narrow bed. Angie sat propped up, a pillow cushioning the iron bars behind her back. The woman noticed Angie's hands as she reached for the teacup on the nightstand. They had the pallor of white roses. Watching her lift the cup to her lips, Madame realized the tea must have long since grown cold. The girl had been spilling out her heart for an hour.

Angie looked at her, her eyes gleaming darkly. "So I abandoned his car in Philadelphia and took the train to New York. When I got there I realized it wasn't far enough, and I bought passage on the first ship. . . ." Her voice trailed off.

Madame sighed. "Why did you not tell me all this when you first came to me?"

"Because I was terrified that you would send me away," Angie said in a quenched tone that, Madame noticed, didn't mask the incredible vitality of her voice. "And I couldn't risk that." Her voice dropped to a whisper, and still it breathed warmth and drama. "You understand that, don't you, Madame?"

Against her will, the woman was moved by Angelina's story. She felt almost guilty that while the child poured out her soul, she herself could only marvel at the extraordinary emotional depth that breathed through Angelina's voice. If she could project that same quality upon the stage, there was no doubt Angelina would someday be a star. Still, the girl's passionate nature was as much her weakness as her strength. Such compulsive, driving ambition alarmed her. Angelina's voice was powerful and occasionally beautiful; yet it could be wild and wayward, too. Madame had to rein her in somehow, to force calm growth upon this avid, tempestuous child who was so ravenous for another chance at life.

She realized Angie was watching her alertly. "Madame, what are you thinking?"

"Only that you should have confided everything from the start," she said with acerbic coolness. "We would have known then better how to proceed."

"What will happen to me?"

"Now that we know what the situation is, we shall deal with it in a rational manner." Madame Francini stood up. "Once you have this child, we will pick up and proceed."

"Thank God!" Angie flashed her a smile of such warmth and brilliance that Madame could not help but smile back. It was the merest quirk at the corners of her mouth, but a smile nonetheless.

20

October in Milan. The brittle night air smelled like winter, a wonderfully sharp odor of hoarfrost and smoke that almost hurt her lungs as she inhaled it. This kind of night calls for fast-paced walking if you aren't to be chilled to the marrow, Angie thought as she waddled at a duck's pace across the palazzo's graveled courtyard. Her belly was immense, a heavy, spinnaker-shaped protuberance that made every sharp step, every breath she took, an effort. Doctor Lungarno had confined her to bed days before after a series of false labors, but how many chances would she have in a lifetime to hear the famed German soprano Helga Mueller?

Martini, the palazzo's ancient caretaker, turned from the small fire in the middle of the courtyard, where he was burning leaves. "Almost time, eh?" the shadowy gnome with perpetually winey breath greeted her in his childlike voice when she stopped to catch her breath. "Your son will arrive soon."

Angie smiled. "And how are you so sure it's a boy?"

"Martini knows these things." His rheumy eyes sparkled briefly in the firelight, and his laughter was as soft and light as the smoke curling up from the pile of burning leaves. "Martini knows."

Angie went out through the arched driveway. Across the dark piazza the lamplit facade of La Scala beckoned. Laboriously she made her way over the cobblestones and after what seemed an eternity reached the stagedoor entrance. An unusually sharp contraction twisted her insides, but she had been through these false alarms so often that she ignored it as she pushed the door open.

Old Leppo of the big book prowled the corridors even on performance nights. Spying Angie, he gave her a severe look, although she knew that that night he was teasing. "What are you doing here?" he demanded. "I do not have you down in my book."

"What?" She grinned and patted her stomach that strained against the buttons of her coat. "Don't tell me you forgot to schedule my biggest assignment of all."

Leppo raised his open hand and shook it lightly, miming a spanking. "If la Francini and that English witch see you here tonight, look out."

"Shhh, this will be our secret."

As Angie made her way into the wings, another sharp pain gripped her, and she promised herself she would go back home after Mueller's first aria. As she peered around the edge of the stage curtains, she took in the sumptuous proportions of the horseshoe-shaped auditorium with its magnificent center chandelier and clusters of lights surmounting the six balcony tiers. Her eyes sought the private boxes that displayed the illustrious coats of arms of the great Milanese families: the Borromeos, Torianis, Viscontis. For a brief heady moment, she imagined herself on stage before the packed house of 3600 people, her voice projecting outward to touch each one of them.

"Angelina!"

She turned as two stagehands rushed up with a fake-Louis XV settee borrowed from the third-act set. "Thanks," she whispered, smiling warmly. "Best seat in the house."

"That *bambino* of yours is starting early with his musical education," one of them joked, gesturing with his head to the Munich opera company on stage. "Just cradle your hands over your stomach when the German steam engine cranks up her lungs."

Excitement tingled Angie's spine as Helga Mueller appeared in the opposite wing. The stalwart soprano swept out onto the stage like a ship under sail. Despite the rather lighthearted role of the Feldmarschallin in *Der Rosenkavalier*, her voice rang out with dark Wagnerian intensity. The soprano's incredibly drawn-out high notes enthralled Angie. The powerful rise and fall of her voice seemed almost an echo of the tidal rhythms of pain bursting every few minutes within Angie's womb.

Angie became dimly aware that Renata Baldini had slipped into the wings. Angie turned to smile at her, but the woman's eyes were fixed upon her rival on stage. Milan's resident diva looked resplendent in a decollete black evening gown that set off her ivory shoulders to perfection. Next to her idol, Angie felt as glamorous as a fireplug. Renata glanced down, then smiled conspiratorially and gestured for Angie to make room for her on the settee.

"So, what do you think, you adorable little elephant?" the diva whispered affectionately, taking Angie's hand.

"Of Mueller? A real powerhouse."

"Pah!" Renata bristled. "She's a mechanical wind-up box. Her idea of strong emotion is to crank up her vocal chords fortissimo." She lowered her own warm, rich voice a notch. "You know what they call her? *La voce de vendetta.* The voice of vengeance. Woe to any singer who tries to outdo her—she'll blast him from the stage like a foghorn. . . . Shhh, shh," Renata warned, even though she had been doing most of the talking. "Mighty Mueller's about to upstage the poor tenor again."

Angie squeezed Renata's hand in excitement. She was about to whisper something when she felt a sudden wet gush between her legs. Groaning softly, she pulled herself up. She stood splaylegged, staring down with shocked embarrassment at the spreading stain of wetness.

Renata tore her eyes from the stage. "What is this?" she murmured, her eyes taking in Angie's drenched skirt and odd stance. "Dear God, don't tell me—"

"Oh!" Angie doubled over as another spasm gripped her.

"Angelina?" Renata's voice rose on a panicky note. When Angie didn't reply, she jumped up and ran over to the men lounging against the coils of ropes in the corner. "Quick! Call Doctor Neri from his box. Tell him it's an emergency!"

Through her haze of fear and climaxes of pain, Angie was aware of the soprano directing the men: "Carry her to my dressing room." Angie felt herself being lifted tenderly in the stagehands' arms and laid down on the settee, while Strauss's liltingly romantic score filled the air. She watched the corridor walls rush past dizzyingly. A chorus of assurances followed her, promising that everything would be all right. But the voices seemed faint.

What she heard with compelling clarity was the sound of her own heartbeat, the liquid pulse of her blood that drove up into her head and spilled down through her belly, the pressure building and intensifying until it transformed itself into a powerful urge to push. Just hold on another moment, the cheerful anonymous voices continued to whisper from far away; just hold on.

Someone had thought to grab one of the set artists' tarpaulins and flung it over the chaise in the soprano's dressing room. As Angie threw her head back, panting in quick gasps, the odor of dried paint and varnish filled her nostrils. She blinked at the bright amber bulbs that framed Renata's dressing table, shining like footlights. Angie felt as though she were on stage, the star in a tumultuous, improbable farce. The doctor swept in, supremely elegant in his black tie and tuxedo, followed by Madame Francini, who had been summoned from her seat. "Madonna! What is she doing here?" the voice teacher exclaimed in shocked dismay. "I left her home in bed. . . ."

"Our Angelina simply had to hear the legendary Mueller," Renata said airily. "All that uncouth Teutonic bellowing must have jarred the poor baby."

The doctor gently palpated Angie's abdomen. "When was the first contraction?"

"I . . ." Angie tensed as she felt his hand beneath her skirt. "Maybe . . . thirty minutes."

He looked up in surprise. "This is a precipitous delivery."

"Is something wrong?" Anxiously she tried to sit up, but Madame and Renata coaxed her back down.

"Everything is fine," the doctor reassured her, moving toward the wash basin as he shrugged off his jacket.

Madame asked sharply, "What are you doing, Doctor? Shouldn't we get her to the hospital?"

"No time for that."

Angie stared at the two women in their evening gowns, their faces pale with shock. Then all thought was driven from her mind as another agonized cramp gripped her. She cried sharply in pain.

With quick precision, the doctor removed his cufflinks, handed them to Madame for safekeeping and rolled up

174 • *June Triglia*

his sleeves. "Now then," he said, calmly regarding his improvised team, "shall we get to it, ladies?"

"Huh, huh, huh." Angie's breath escaped in a series of anguished gasps. She clung tightly to Madame's fingers, trying to lose herself in the calm, hypnotic drone of the woman's voice. "Good, good, excellent. Breathe deeply, deeply, draw it down into the diaphragm, control it, measure it out just as if you were singing. Good, good . . ."

Now the urge to push became an overwhelming tidal force that imploded deep within, ripping through her with a swiftness that felt as though she were being rent apart.

Then as if from a great distance, she heard the doctor's cool, patrician voice calling for towels. The tiny dressing room filled with a newborn's high, thin wail. The life she had nurtured and tried to deny had become a squalling baby. A feeling of wonderment mixed with terror engulfed her.

Renata came around the side of the chaise with the towel-swaddled infant cradled in her arms. Blood speckled her throat and shoulders, but she seemed oblivious. "A son, Angelina!" she cried over its lusty wail. "You have a son—*menaggia*, but he's louder than Mueller herself!"

As Renata laid the baby upon her chest and Angie lifted her arms to receive him, an unexpected sensation of peace settled over her. Angie stared down into the tiny, wrinkled face, as if she were a seer who might glimpse the future in that minute network of lines. But the tiny, squashed face was a mystery, a cipher—an inextricable part of herself that was now forever separate and unknowable.

Madame Francini gently touched the infant's face. "Have you thought what you will name him, Angelina?"

Angie flashed a mischievous if exhausted smile. "Marshall, I think. After the Feldmarschallin in the opera. My contractions seemed to come in time with Strauss's music."

Renata threw back her head and laughed richly. *"Grazie a dio!* For an instant I thought you were going to say 'Mueller.' " She moved to the dressing table and threw back the lid of a padded jewelry box.

"Here!" she cried, returning with a tiny gold crucifix on a chain. The ends of each crosspiece were carved in graceful trefoils. "This was a gift from my mother after I sang my first role on stage here at La Scala. I want you to have it, Angelina, as a remembrance of our little marschallin's birth." She clasped the chain around Angie's throat, where the gold cross gleamed against her luminous, perspiration-slicked skin. "May your son be blessed."

Act Three

21

April 1940

Angie sat rigidly on a stool in the music room, her feet in worn loafers tucked behind the stool's front legs. Her dark curly hair was drawn back in symmetric rolls along the sides of her head. The look suited her, showing off her fine cheekbones and the beautifully arched brows that she could move with such subtle expressivity. Madame thought the style made her look too thin and too sophisticated. Angie smiled in disbelief. As if a woman could ever be too much of either.

"Wipe that smile off your face and start again with 'ah.' "

"Ahhhhh," Angie enunciated, her head thrown back to allow the sound to emerge from deep behind her larynx. She might as well have been in a dentist's chair. Madame Francini's new exercise, emphasizing vowel production and enunciation, was torture. After what seemed like hours, Angie lifted her head and gave the woman a beseeching look. "Enough?"

"I will decide when it has been enough," Madame barked. "Now drop your head and proceed with 'e.' I want to see those neck and jaw muscles stretched until you are grimacing at the ceiling. Absolutely grimacing, do you understand me?"

"Why can't I just sing as I was meant to?"

"As you were meant to?" Madame's tone was withering. "This understudy business has gone to your head, Angelina. The good singer who is satisfied with herself may remain a good singer, but she will never be a great one. Do you understand?"

Only slightly chastened, Angie murmured, "Yes, Madame."

"In my judgment you are far too young to be assigned as understudy to Renata. You are what—twenty-three? Your passage notes are not even close to being fully developed yet. Since I cannot override the maestro's decision, I will force you to become a more controlled singer. You will guard the gift you have, not squander it."

Angie's eyes flashed. "Jenny Lind sang at eighteen, Anji Silja at twenty!"

"Silja was finished at twenty-five, her voice utterly destroyed. Do you wish to take the same risk?"

"If I have to." Her hunger for stardom spilled through the simple words, leaving Madame momentarily speechless.

"You frighten me, Angelina." The woman leaned forward, her thin fingers clutching the sides of her music stand. "Sometimes you frighten me."

Angie lowered her eyes. It had taken forever to get this first break, and Madame felt that she was rushing headlong toward disaster. For almost two years she had done nothing but live music and voice, studying and working and pushing herself. Pregnancy and the birth of her son had been but a short detour from her chosen path. Now things were moving forward again, just as she had worked and schemed for. This understudy assignment was her reward. The life she and Marshall had with Madame and Sarah was one of genteel poverty, a life enriched by culture and little else. Angie wanted so much more for her son. Yet for herself, all that she wanted was to be immersed in the music, to master it and make the character come alive.

"I know Floria Tosca better even than Renata because I lived what Tosca lived," Angie said impatiently, her eyes seeking the older woman's. "The character breathes through me. I know what it's like to suffer at the hands of ruthless men. I lived Tosca's terrible helplessness. I know what it is to feel choked and smothered until something snaps inside—and you're driven to violence because you don't see any other way." She stopped as a shiver ran through her. "I relive it every time I sing Puccini's lines. Sometimes I feel like he wrote them just for me."

"Angelina, your intuitive grasp of the character's inner state is not at question here. The power of your dramatic interpretation won over our esteemed artistic director.

Unfortunately," she added dryly, "your superb acting blinded him to the physical limitations of your voice and your lungs."

"I will surmount those limitations."

"You had better. An audience would never put up with that hideous yodeling you subjected Sarah and me to yesterday. If we cannot bridge and strengthen those breaks in your top middle, there will be nothing for it but to export you to Switzerland. You can serenade mountain goats for the rest of your life." Madame stood and walked toward the door. "Sarah!"

Madame's acid jokes had a way of cutting her to the quick. Angie did not want to admit there might be a kernel of truth in them. Leaning forward, she picked up her copy of the score and started to leaf through it eagerly. Puccini's lush symphonic music engulfed her as it played through her head, pulling her effortlessly into the brutal, erotic world of Tosca and the evil Baron Scarpia. Angie looked up in surprise when Sarah struck the opening F-flat chord of the "Vissi d'arte." She hadn't even noticed the woman entering the room and sitting at the piano.

Angie launched into the aria, allowing the slow, passionate sweetness of her remembered sorrow to breathe through every note. Angie never really heard herself sing. She relied on the buzzing vibrato that filled her head and chest, trusting to the veracity of her emotions to carry the flow of her voice. She hesitated fractionally as she climbed to the top of her middle register, worried that her voice would again break and subject her to the women's derision. Just when she thought she had smoothly bridged the difficult passage notes, a shriek pierced the air. Angie froze. Sarah stopped playing in midnote, her disapproving gaze shifting from Angie to Madame Francini. Another squeal, scarcely muffled by the closed door, broke the silence.

"From the sound of things, Angelina, your son has acquired some of your less pleasing vocal qualities," Madame said, her frown deepening. "Go see to him at once."

Angie hurried out into the foyer, just in time to see eighteen-month-old Marshall barreling down the hall toward the kitchen, his high-topped black shoes tapping with a woodpecker's light insistence. Stella, his nanny, stared after him indulgently. She turned to Angie. "Much as I love the little one, I must confess I will be happy to have a few days' peace and quiet at my sister's home."

Angie stared at her in confusion. Then she saw the woman's suitcase by the front door. "Oh no, I totally forgot."

"It's time for our boy's morning walk. That's why he's so wound up." Stella took his tiny red jacket from the hall closet and handed it to her. "Until Sunday evening then, signora."

Marshall turned at the closed kitchen door and came rushing back. As he spied his mother, he screamed with pure, exuberant delight.

Despite her dismay Angie couldn't help but smile. He was such a lovely child, with his dark curls and vivid blue eyes. She caught him and swung him around playfully in her arms. " '*Knusper, knusper, knauschen,*' " she sang to him in German, mimicking the comically grotesque witch from Humperdinck's *Hansel und Gretel*. " 'Nibble, nibble, mousekin, who is bringing the house down?' " Marshall patted her cheeks, his eyes dancing.

"*Ciao*, my Marshallino," the nanny said, blowing a kiss to the baby.

Happily he flapped his chubby fingers against his palm, waving the way the old caretaker Martini had taught him. "*Ciao, bambino*," he said so clearly that Angie had to laugh.

"You're going to be an angel for Mama today, aren't you?" she asked him playfully, distracting his attention as she knelt down and stuffed his arms into his jacket sleeves. "Mama has to sing and work hard; this is her first chance, darling. But you just wait. The audience will be shouting '*brava*' and throwing bouquets to me on the stage. We'll have a big house with a wonderful garden. You'll have a fine rocking horse," she whispered as she pulled his knit hat down over his head, "a whole carrousel!"

Lifting him up again, she hurried back into the music room. "I forgot that Stella had the weekend off," she said in a rush as the two women looked at her questioningly. Sweeping up her copy of the *Tosca* score with her free hand, she added, "I'll have to take Marshall for his walk. I can study while he plays, if that's all right, Madame?"

"I suppose it will have to be." For all the sternness of her response, the woman held out her arms to her god-son and kissed him lightly on the cheek before handing him back to Angie. "Don't dawdle."

"Motherhood is a twenty-four-hour-a-day obligation." Sarah's sharp voice followed Angie out into the hall. "Not a whim to be indulged when one feels like it. Mark my words, that child will suffer one day for the sake of his mother's ambition."

Angie hugged Marshall close as they went outside. "Don't listen. Maybe one day she'll fly off on her broom-stick." Angie crooned another of the witch's tunes in the baby's ear. " 'So hop, hop, hop, gallop, lop, lop!' "

Her head was filled with Madame's ringing criticism of her vocal limitations as Angie pushed Marshall in his stroller toward a side street that angled off the piazza. She looked down its length, trying to gauge the distance to the iron lamppost halfway down the block. Taking a deep breath, she wheeled the baby forward. She was three-quarters of the way to the lamp when she felt herself growing purple; still she forced herself to hold her breath. Marshall cried in delight as the stroller screamed down the bumpy stone sidewalk. They reached the lamp-post and Angie exhaled in an explosion of relief, bending over the metal handles. She would do this every day from now on, she promised herself, until she had doubled her breath capacity.

In this unorthodox fashion, racing from lamppost to lamppost, they completed their walk around the block and came out again at La Scala. Angie pushed Marshall in his stroller across the wide piazza, which bristled with military activity. Huge Fascist banners fluttered in the cool spring wind, their imperial symbols a gaudy counter-point to the elegant lions and banded stone facades of the classical Lombard architecture. Aristocratic *bersaglieri* with tall feathered plumes in their army caps swaggered past, full of self-importance. Marshall chortled excitedly at the handsome soldiers, but his cries were drowned out by the heavy rumble of a truck convoy moving slowly in the direction of the train station. A sense of unease enveloped Angie. Until now the war had been an abstraction. The German invasion of Poland, followed by Britain and France's declaration of war, had been little more than newspaper headlines that did not affect their lives here in Italy. But for how much longer, she wondered; for how much longer?

Angie wheeled Marshall over to the fountain. She sat on the rounded stone edge and opened her music score. Puccini's melodic orchestrations never failed to move her, to involve her totally. The music was her escape not only from a world gone mad, but from her own more personal griefs. How she longed to create a role on stage, to lose her self in some larger-than-life destiny that she could, however briefly, make her own.

While she rehearsed the score in her mind, she absent-mindedly wheeled Marshall's stroller back and forth with her foot. After a while he began to fuss. She turned the stroller around so that he faced her. Bending down, she began to sing tenderly of her love as if she were playing to her on-stage amor. The toddler bounced up and down, crying "Ma, ma, ma!" so enthusiastically that she broke off with a laugh. "You're my best audience, Marshallino," she said, planting a kiss on his forehead.

A flurry of commotion across the square caught her eye, and she stood up. She watched several black-jacketed policemen smash the windows of a small shop with their billy clubs. The owner rushed out, and they began to beat him mercilessly until he lay bloodied and still. Stunned and sickened, Angie turned away. She shoved her music score under her arm and hastily wheeled Marshall across the square toward home. As if aware of the sudden tension in the air, Marshall started to cry. "Shh, shh," she murmured down to him in a tight voice, pushing the stroller faster. Breathless, she didn't stop until they were safe again within the thick walls of the palazzo.

With its shabby elegance, the apartment suddenly seemed a haven of peace and sanity. Angie leaned back against the door, holding Marshall tightly against her breast even though he squirmed to be put down. A faint odor of lemon oil emanated from the slender bow-fronted cabinet of dark walnut in the corner. Her eyes swept up the papered walls. Their once-rich pattern of saffron silk stripes had faded to a mellow topaz gold. Her eye followed the deeply carved ceiling moldings that framed each room like a painting. Here was a beauty born of simplicity and order, of cherished possessions imbued with the spirit of their owner. The apartment had an almost tactile warmth that reached out to envelop her. How strange that she had never so acutely noticed or appreciated it before.

As she set Marshall down, she became aware of the murmur of voices behind the glass doors of the drawing room. Clara emerged from the kitchen, bearing a silver tray set with small crystal glasses and a china plate piled with biscuits. Marshall rushed over to the round-faced cook and hugged her legs. Clara ruffled his hair affectionately and handed him a treat.

"Sherry and biscuits. How veddy, veddy elegant," Angie joked. "Must be special company."

"It's Renata Baldini," Clara whispered, her eyes bright. "She is leaving Milan."

Angie stared at the girl. The soprano leaving? How ridiculous. Clara must have gotten things mixed up.

Madame Francini and Renata looked up smilingly as Marshall burst into the room ahead of Clara and Angie. He ran to kiss each in turn, then sidled up to Sarah, who motioned him away with an impatient wave without even looking up from the needlepoint work in her lap. Marshall never stopped trying to win her over, and she just as stubbornly refused to allow him a place in her heart. Angie hated her for that more than anything. She could understand and even accept Sarah's resentment of her, but why let the bitter feelings between the two of them spill over onto an innocent child?

Angie turned to Renata and instantly her spirits lifted. The soprano, looking dazzling as always, lounged with effortless elegance on one of the sofas. She wore a black moire silk suit set off by a forward-tipping black felt hat, black kid gloves and a silver fox stole. As Angie took in the large gold-burnished buttons on her suit, the gold-and-ruby pin clipped to her hat and the black kidskin-and-alligator pumps, she thought, "This cost more than I make in a month." That didn't stop Renata from pulling

Marshall up into her lap and tickling him until he screeched with delight. Then Clara called to the boy, promising hot chocolate, and he dashed off with her back to the kitchen.

"You're spoiling him rotten, all of you," Angie said, smiling.

Renata gestured with her tiny sherry glass. "But that's why men exist, dearest, so that we women can spoil them rotten."

"A credo you obviously live by," Angie teased.

Renata's low laugh rang out, warm and vital. "Now come sit down beside me. I was just telling Giulia and Sarah my news." She paused for effect. "I'm leaving Italy."

"But your life is here!" Angie burst. "How could you possibly think of leaving it?"

"*Menagg'!*" As Renata shifted to face her, the fur stole fell casually down her back. "I know work has absorbed all your energies these last few years, Angelina, but it hasn't left you blind, has it? Europe is at war."

"I'm well aware of that." In her mind Angie saw again the long convoy of trucks in the street, the shopkeeper beaten senseless for God only knew what offense. "But Italy is neutral," she said without much conviction.

"Not for long." Renata leaned forward and set her glass on the table. She spoke with cool deliberateness. "Our great dictator will declare war before spring is over, before his generals think it wise."

Here was no Cassandra spewing wild prophecies. Angie knew the source of Renata's oracular power was Fabrizio Farleone. She made no secret of her affair with the wealthy industrialist who was a trusted member of Mussolini's inner circle. "Italy will declare war on both France and England." Renata cast an amused look in Sarah's direction. "I suppose, Signorina Langton, that that will make you one of the enemy."

Sarah looked at her coolly. "I may be English," she said, her fingers resting atop the footstool cover she had been laboring over for months, "but my first loyalty always has been and will be to Madame Giulia."

Impatiently Angie watched Renata's chin dip, a subtle bow to Sarah's imperturbable dignity. "Renata," Angie asked pointblank, "when will you leave?"

The soprano burst with warm and spontaneous laughter. "Angelina! You conniving, ambitious little minx. I can see that war and politics and the insanity of these murderous Fascists haven't clouded your vision in the least," she said. "You've got your eye fixed on my roles."

"Why not?" Angie smiled. "There's an old American saying: The show must go on. Someone will have to sing Tosca in your place. I want the chance to be that next rising star."

"But what point is there in investing all this energy into pursuing something that may be in pieces at your feet a year from now? Angelina, war will come and it will be devastating. It will destroy everything." Renata was absolutely serious now. The engaging facade of light charm and elegant gaiety that seemed so central to her nature slipped for an instant to reveal another woman—highly intelligent and eminently practical, with a keen instinct for survival. Her gaze roved slowly over the three women. "I plan to join family in Argentina. Come with me, or at least return to America. Angie can sing there as easily as here."

Angie held her breath, waiting to see how Madame Francini would respond. A note of tension crept into the air. Renata must have sensed the change, because she looked sharply from one to the other.

It was Sarah who broke the silence. "Perhaps we should return to America," she said, her eyes fixed on Angie rather than Madame. For an instant Angie wondered if Madame had divulged to Sarah the secrets she had poured out that night long ago after they had discovered she was pregnant. More likely, Angie had given away her secrets herself. Her categorical refusal to answer even Sarah's most innocent questions about her past must have tipped the woman off long ago.

Sarah was so jealous of the bonds that had deepened between Angie and Madame since Marshall's birth that Angie could not even begin a conversation without Sarah creeping around to make her presence felt, to keep them from excluding her. Maybe she had sensed that the possibility of returning to the States would disturb Angie more than anything else could.

Angie took a biscuit from the plate. She nervously

picked at it until it was nothing but a pile of crumbs. Finally she looked up. "I intend to stay in Italy with my son."

"Angelina—" Renata began, her voice vibrant with concern, but Sarah cut her off, lashing out venomously.

"Ignorant little fool! I am utterly sick of your behaving as if life were a lark. I lived through the Great War; I saw the suffering and the deprivations first hand. How dare you presume to endanger our lives by your foolishly naive bravado?"

"My decision has nothing to do with you, Sarah," Angie said, forcing herself to answer calmly. "I will do what I think is best for me and my son."

Sarah stood up, her fingers twisting the half-finished needlepoint canvas. "I've seen how you try to twist people around to do as you want. You'll never change. You think only of yourself, never of anyone else. You're a selfish, egotistical—"

"Shut up," Angie said, white hot with anger, and Sarah's mouth snapped closed in surprise. Madame's watchful eyes revealed nothing. She stood up, pausing to rest her hands briefly on Sarah's shoulders before going to stand at the French doors that opened onto the balcony. For a long moment she stared at La Scala on the far side of the busy piazza. Afternoon sun slanted through the multipaned glass, which segmented the light into neat squares on the polished floor. Angie wondered if Madame's thoughts were that orderly, or, if like Renata, another woman lurked beneath that austerely practical exterior, a woman of passion and dreams.

At long last she turned back to face the waiting women. "My home is here," she said simply. "War or not, I intend to stay."

Angie nearly slumped with relief. Too late did she realize that both Sarah and Renata were observing her, Sarah with undisguised bitterness and Renata with curiosity. How could she possibly explain that the specter of one man that hung over her was far more powerful than the threat of a lifetime of war?

22

The sidewalks of Duquesne University, shaded by over-arching sycamore trees, were a cool oasis in the gritty Pittsburgh summer. Nickie strolled across campus with three other coeds, matching their languid pace, as though she too were a rich girl possessed of an inborn sense that the world was at her beck and call. Nickie had swiftly mastered the bored persona of the wealthy, finding it a convenient camouflage for her raging ambition.

Never had her friends suspected that she was anything other than what she represented herself to be: Nicole Branson, only daughter of an eccentric Ohio heiress whose whimsy occasionally veered into madness. Nickie had calculatedly created an ambience of mystery for herself. That faint whiff of scandalous, Bronte-esque madness in the attic had given Nickie instant panache and a wholly plausible excuse for keeping the other girls at arm's length. After four years they were accustomed to her weekend disappearances, to the way her mind seemed to drift off in the middle of important gossip, such as the latest predictions from *Vogue* on how War Planning Bureau dictums would affect next season's fashions.

Nickie listened distractedly to their chatter, her eye drawn to the smoggy city on the horizon. The city council had finally passed a smoke-control ordinance the past year after long and stormy debate, only to have its implementation put on hold by America's entry into the war. In this first summer of wartime, the steel mills had begun around-the-clock production, mobilizing to fulfill the whopping defense contracts pouring in. All that month, while up late studying for finals, Nickie had had the fiery night sky for company. She never tired of watching the way it flared in great pulsing streaks of red and yellow as the Bessemers in the distant river valley began to blow—modern alchemist's cauldrons transforming molten iron into steel. The air had possessed a weird tenebrous beauty, at once magical and ominous. By day that beauty receded, leaving nothing but a grimy, stinking reality. Not that Nickie wholly minded it, not when it dovetailed so neatly with her own future plans.

Armed with her business degree, she intended to storm the banking citadels downtown. She had never forgotten the crucial lesson she learned that evening long ago in the Urbanos' home when she had eavesdropped on the wealthy men in the library. Money was power, and more than anything Nickie wanted access to that power.

"As if Nicole would care . . ."

Hearing her name mentioned, Nickie looked around at her friends with a lazy smile. "Which one of you is slandering me now?"

Muffy Caruthers, a lanky brunette, shrugged. "I was just saying that that outfit you're wearing is terribly unpatriotic. With the government cornering dyes for war chemicals, the W.P.B.'s issued an advisory that women should start wearing only natural-colored fabrics."

"The only patriotic thing about me is my lipstick," Nickie said, her voice a low, husky drawl. "Victory red. As for this," she went on, smoothing her hands over the peplum flare of her jonquil jacket, an unexpected counterfoil to her vibrant grape-blue skirt, "you'll just have to direct your complaints to those disloyal French designers. Mummy had this smuggled out of Paris right from under the Germans' noses."

From beneath her lowered lids Nickie watched the other girls doing their best not to look impressed. She laughed to herself, looking forward to telling Bathsheba, her resourceful Negro seamstress downtown, that her talents had just been elevated to haute-couture status.

"Why are you so damned dressed up, anyway?" Muffy asked carelessly.

"Because she has an assignation with Professor Mortimer," laughed Jane Fitzhugh, a snub-nosed redhead who was planning to volunteer with the International Red Cross in order to be closer to her Air Force lieutenant fiancé being shipped overseas.

"Listen to Miss Romance, will you?" Nickie said in mock disgust. "Believe me, all I want from that good-looking weasel is a letter of recommendation."

"Isn't it too much?" Jane laughed again. "Our Nicole actually is serious about getting an honest-to-God job."

"You're both insane," said Muffy grumpily, whose summer plans of yachting in the Hamptons seemed drab compared to her friends' far more quixotic schemes. "I mean, really."

"Nicole, I'd be wary of Mortimer, if I were you," said Cara MacCready, a cool blonde with a knowing air whom Nickie had molded herself after during the past four years.

"But she's been the only one immune to his charms all year," protested Jane.

Nickie stopped outside the administration building, taking leave of her friends with a desultory wave. "Ta-ta, girls."

As she climbed the steps, she once again cursed her shortness next to her tall, elegant cohorts. But what she lacked in height she made up for in bearing. She carried her wide shoulders proudly, giving subtle emphasis to a full bosom, which contrasted with her narrow hips. A figure tailormade for chic clothes, according to Bathsheba, who worked days as a fitter at Kaufmann's Department Store. She loved to regale Nickie about the monied matrons who never stopped trying to cram their heavily girdled bodies into pencil-thin silhouettes.

Nickie entered the building and encountered a stream of secretaries coming out. She hadn't realized how late it was. Nickie stepped off the elevator on the third floor and started down the hall, almost on tiptoe. Funny how places seem to echo once they are emptied of people, she thought.

She hesitated but a second outside Professor Mortimer's door, then resolutely pulled it open. The reception area was deserted, but from the inner office came the sound of industrious typing. Nickie poked her head around the corner. The man sat with his back to her. His office was a mess of books spilling out from shelves onto a well-worn leather sofa, cigarette butts filling the ashtray on the cluttered desktop. "Professor Mortimer?" He finished typing, rolled the sheet out of the machine and turned around to face her. "Nicole," he said in surprise as his light eyes flicked over her.

He was a tall, lean man with an air of boyish charm, though both the boyishness and the charm were spurious. Nickie flashed him a cool smile, meant to keep those she mistrusted at bay. Mortimer reminded her of a Hollywood stereotype: fair hair combed straight back from a high forehead, wide smile revealing teeth that were a little too large and too even. His was a breezy, engaging surface meant to disarm.

"I stopped by to ask if you would write me a letter of recommendation," she said from the doorway, her tone neutral and polite.

He stood up and came around the desk toward her. "There's nothing I would love to do more," he assured her. "Unfortunately, I simply don't feel that I know your work well enough."

She looked at him in disbelief. "That's ridiculous. I've gotten As in every one of your economics classes. And you positively raved about my last term paper—"

"Always so sure of yourself, Nicole, so coolly aloof." He shook his head with mild regret. "Wouldn't your rich chums have a laugh if they knew the truth behind your exotic F. Scott Fitzgerald fantasies—an immigrant's daughter from Dago Hill masquerading as one of them."

"What is this?" she said tightly. "Blackmail?"

"Now, Nicole," he murmured, fingering a strand of her silky straight hair which she had lightened to a rich bamboo blond. "You misunderstood me."

She flinched at his touch. "You don't know what you're doing. You're toying with my future."

"Oh, I know perfectly well what I'm doing. You know, my dear, I could write you a mediocre letter right now, or . . ." He smiled disarmingly. "I could write you a glowing reference after dinner tonight." When she didn't answer right away, he cocked an eyebrow. "Well, my dear? The choice is yours."

"I was just trying to decide," Nickie said, forcing herself to smile, "if I prefer French or Chinese food."

She steeled herself against his touch as he slipped his hand inside her jacket front, his cool fingertips insinuating themselves snakelike along the top of her slip. "I knew you'd see things my way."

So this was to be her price of admission to the real world, Nickie thought bitterly. Now that she understood the rules, she vowed that she wouldn't be caught again.

Nickie stopped outside the enormous bronze doors of the Urbano Bank. Leaning against one of the lions that flanked the entrance, she bent down to rub her aching instep. Throngs of shoppers hurried past her on Smithfield Street. Despite the fact that it was midafternoon on a summer's day, every streetlamp was burning in a futile attempt to cut through the smoky darkness choking the city air. Nickie straightened up and fluffed out her gilet of navy-blue and white handkerchief linen, which coordinated with her navy summer suit and white kidskin scroll belt. She had chosen the outfit with utmost care in order to present a thoroughly professional appearance. Not that it had done much good so far, she thought as she rummaged through her big soft gabardine "investment" bag, on which she'd spent several weekends' pay from her job as a checkout clerk at Perugini's Market. She quickly reapplied her lipstick and checked to see there were no fly-away wisps from her French roll. In preparation for her next interview, she had also donned a pair of oversized reading glasses.

Nickie had been pounding the pavement all day long, making her pilgrimage to every financial institution in the city—classical temples of wealth replete with bronze and marble and living men seemingly carved out of stone. In every interview so far, she had encountered the same undercurrent of suspicion as she discussed with them the effect of Keynesian economics on monetary supply and her specific interest in capital investment. They acted as if she were a witch who had somehow stolen the arcane secrets of their wholly masculine world. In every face she had read the same commingling of contempt and hostility. Despite the fact that her typing was abysmal and her shorthand nonexistent, she had been offered four secretarial positions. Damn all men to hell, she thought in exasperation.

Louis Urbano Junior was last on her list. She had

heard rumors about him, although none of them had to do with his private life, which surprised her. Sometimes she wondered if she and Angie were the only ones privy to that secret. The last time she had seen him, she had been a scrappy, underfed kid with muddy-brown hair. She remembered Louis as elegant, somewhat foppish, a lazily smooth charmer. From what she'd heard, he hadn't changed much: He was still an epicurean inclined to live off the fat of the land and disinclined to pay attention to Papa Urbano's banking empire. That situation had apparently deepened the rift between father and son over the past several years.

Nickie passed through the huge bronze doors into the high-ceilinged bank lobby with its Edwardian profusion of green and white marble. She crossed to the suite of directors' offices, determined to project an air of confidence despite her sudden attack of nerves. Urbano's secretary showed her into his office at once, giving Nickie only scant seconds to pull herself together.

Louis stood up behind his polished oak desk. "Miss Branson, how do you do?" he said, extending his hand. "Please come in and be seated."

"Mr. Urbano." She nodded her thanks and sat down.

He leaned back in his chair and made a tent of his fingers. For a long, thoughtful moment, he studied her. Nickie sat quietly, fighting the urge to smooth back her hair, push up her glasses or display any other gesture of nervousness. If he recognizes me, she thought, it will be damned awkward.

"I must say," he began, "I find your background impressive. Rather surprising for a woman?"

Nickie was nonplussed by the question in his voice. Did he expect her to agree or disagree? She decided to take the bull by the horns. "If you'll forgive my immodesty, I think it's impressive for a woman or man."

Louis chuckled, and Nickie began to relax. Instinctively, she had chosen the right note on which to deal with him—keep him amused, keep him interested. She had no fear now that he might recognize her. She realized that people see only what you mean them to see—the surface polish that has been buffed to such a dazzle of perfection it blinds the eye to anything else.

"May I send out for some iced coffee . . . tea?" he inquired after a moment.

"I . . . yes, thanks." After the dismissive treatment she had been getting all day, this gesture of kindness unexpectedly touched her. "Iced coffee sounds delightful."

Nickie watched him as he depressed the button on his desk intercom. His fingers were long and aristocratic, graced by a small signet ring. Nickie regarded the superb tailoring of his gray suit and the subtle contrast of his wine-colored silk tie. He was elegant, handsome, seemingly thoroughly male. Watching him, she found it hard to believe his sexual preferences ran to muscular young chauffeurs.

He looked up. "Where were we, then?"

She smiled wryly. "You were expressing your considerable astonishment at my achievements."

Smiling as well, he leaned back comfortably in his chair, as if he had all the time in the world to chat. Nickie glanced around the office, at the oil landscapes on the paneled walls, the tray of cut-glass decanters on a sideboard, the collection of carved meerschaum pipes on a shelf. Nowhere did she see papers or contracts, no file folders piled haphazardly or messages tucked beneath the phone—none of the usual clues that this was an office where important decisions were made. The office seemed strictly for show.

Almost as if he had read her mind, Louis asked, "I'm curious about one thing, Miss Branson." He regarded her steadily. "Why did you come to me? Anyone who'd bothered to do the least bit of checking would have found out that my father pretty much runs a one-man show around here."

Although he smiled as he said it, Nickie heard an almost imperceptible tightening in his voice. All the rumors were not exaggerated, then.

She took a deep breath and plunged right in. "But you're the young blood, Mr. Urbano, the up-and-coming generation. I know that as you grow in power and stature, those around you will grow as well. Men like your father have had their people in place for years. There's no room for newcomers." She smiled. "Besides, I get the impression you're not like the rest of the fuddy-duddies in this town who look at a woman and see nothing but a secretary or a sex object." O God, did I actually say that! She was about to fumble past her ironic faux pas when, mercifully, the door opened and a clerk came in, bearing two tall glasses on a small tray. Nickie took the glass of iced coffee gratefully and sipped it. The caffeine jolt revived her at once. Over the past four years of her acculturation into the white Anglo-Saxon upper class, the one thing Nickie had not acquired was their unfathomable preference for tea.

Feeling Louis's eyes on her, Nickie looked up. For one scary second she imagined him a mindreader. Then she realized his probing stare wasn't personal.

"Go on, Miss Branson," he said lazily. "I admit you've piqued my curiosity."

Nickie set her glass down and took another deep breath. "The way I see it, Pittsburgh is on the brink of tremendous change. As long as the war goes on, the city will thrive. But the war's going to end." Nickie pushed her glasses back up onto the bridge of her nose with a gloved finger. "And when it does, we won't be able to go on ignoring the appalling reality. Pittsburgh's become an industrial wasteland of worn-out buildings and polluted air. The city's going to die if it doesn't transform itself completely." She paused and smiled, enthusiasm lighting her eyes. "I'm banking on the latter, if you'll excuse the pun. Commercial banks like yours have traditionally made short-term loans to finance businesses. What I envision is a new emphasis on construction loans. Such a shift would make the bank a partner in the city's growth. I mean, you can just imagine the incredibly vast potential."

Louis leaned forward on the desk and cupped his chin in one hand as he studied her. "You seem to have enough energy and ambition for two people."

"Yes." As Nickie met his look, some sharp, unspoken communication clicked between them. "Yes, I do."

"Miss Branson, I think you may just have talked your way into a job." He smiled. "Can you begin tomorrow at nine?"

She nodded just as the office door opened again.

"Louis, darling—oh, I'm sorry, I didn't realize you had a . . . a client with you." Nickie stiffened at the sound of

Josephine Urbano's familiar cultured voice. Without warning, it catapulted her back in time to Father Lucatta's kitchen when the woman had first entered the Branzinos' lives. From the first moment the woman had adored Angie but merely tolerated her sister. Nickie would never forget the annoyed look she had caught on Mrs. Urbano's face the night of the engagement party, watching Nickie swagger around in her borrowed finery as if she owned the place. No, Angie's complaisant charm had not been Nickie's style, and it never would be.

"Mother, come in," Louis said, standing up. "I'd like you to meet my new assistant, Nicole Branson."

Nickie half turned to the woman and nodded politely. She felt Mrs. Urbano's eyes move speculatively over her, from the upward sweep of her dark-blond chignon down to the toes of her navy pumps.

"Branson," the woman repeated thoughtfully. "You look familiar. Have we met before?"

Nickie stood up, her face still halfway averted. "I don't believe so." She looked at Louis. "See you tomorrow, then. I'm looking forward to being part of your team."

As she left, Nickie heard Mrs. Urbano ask her son anxiously, "Team? Louis, what did she mean? What are you doing? I'm not at all sure your father would approve of your hiring a woman."

Before closing the door softly, Nickie heard Louis's tight answering laugh. "Probably not, Mother. But, then again, when has he approved of anything I've ever done?"

23

Nickie and her brother Phil sat on a blanket, balancing plates of food on their crossed legs. They had spread the blanket on a tree-shaded knoll that overlooked the packed picnic grounds of Kennywood Park. To the right rose the top of the Ferris wheel and the roller coaster, while through the screen of dense foliage they could just glimpse the bright red and yellow fantasy of Noah's Ark rocking slowly on its moorings. The air was filled with a curious melange of cotton candy and cannelloni.

Nickie picked at the heavily sauced food in her lap, while Phil seemed to have inhaled his in three big bites. She felt his eyes on her and looked up. "Now what's wrong?"

He shrugged. "Just wondering why you never come home. Before you always had the excuse that you were studying. Now you've got a regular job and we still never see you."

Nickie put her barely touched plate aside and started to get up. "I'm going to get a hot dog."

He grabbed her arm. "What is it—you ashamed of where you come from?"

"Damn it, Phil, can't you give it a rest? I'm here, aren't I? Italian Day at Kennywood Park," she said with withering contempt. "Mussolini and Hitler are thick as thieves, bombing Europe into smithereens, and we're celebrating the dagos—Christ!" She broke off, her gaze moving restlessly down the hill to the knots of people gathered around the rows of picnic tables. Here and there the red, green and white tricolors of Italian flags fluttered in the wind, raised in defiance of the fact that Italy was America's sworn enemy. Elsewhere people had raised hand-lettered banners proudly proclaiming regional heritages: Basilicata, Napolitano, Siciliano, Calabrese, Abruzzese, Pugliese, Romano.

Phil followed her gaze. "Looks like a medieval fair, doesn't it?"

"Yeah, and there's the king of Dago Hill." Nickie gestured with her chin toward Carlo DiPiano. Fastidious in a pale silk suit, he sat flanked by bodyguards while the locals sidled up to pay their obeisances, thanking him for his patronage or for the job he had gotten them twenty years earlier.

"Come on." Phil tugged her arm. "Let's try some of Z's *pizzelle.*"

Nickie allowed herself to be dragged back down into the noisy, gesticulating milieu. Z'Maria was deep into a tirade, defending Mussolini. "But he's a dictator, Z'," Nickie interrupted in English as she reached for one of her aunt's delicate, anise-scented waffle cookies.

"So what, eh?" The woman turned, her big-knuckled hands flying through the air. "Here in America you got *la democrazia*—you got a thousand thieves in the government. In Italy now you got just one thief. A big thief like that, no matter how big, he always eats less than a thousand little ones, eh? So what's better?"

For the first time that day Nickie laughed. "I can't argue with that kind of logic. Now come on, Z', shut up about politics. Let's go take a spin on the merry-go-round before I have to leave."

"Go tell you pap first, so he no worry."

"Let him worry."

Z'Maria gave her a sharp warning look. "Go, Nicoletta."

Nickie's smile died. She turned toward her father, sitting by himself with a blanket over his knees despite the humid late-summer day—a shrunken, cachectic ghost for whom the prosperity of war had come too late. He had slaved for twenty-five years down in the mills, only to be rewarded with the slow destructive assault of tuberculosis resulting from decades of constant inhalation of metal dust. Reluctantly Nickie touched his forehead, which burned dry and hot. When he looked up at her, it was as if his eyes had distilled that quarter-century of bitterness down into two burning coals of despair.

Nickie resented the pity that began to war with the hatred ever present within her. Why should I go home? she thought. There's nothing left but an empty shell that's been gradually depleted of light and hope. All the younger boys had been drafted overseas, Mama and Gina had long been dead, while Angie . . . where was Angie? The question never ceased to haunt Nickie. For all intents and purposes, the beautiful older sister she had idolized was dead too—dead at least to this life and freed to recreate a wholly new existence for herself. Nickie swallowed her bitterness and bent to whisper to her father, "Pap, we'll be back soon."

He nodded, not caring.

Laughing and staggering a little, Nickie and Phil jumped down off the slowly turning carrousel. Then they each took one of Z'Maria's arms and lifted her down onto the pavement. The woman was cackling with pleasure.

"What next, eh?" Z'Maria cried, circumscribing a big circle in the air. "The *dondolo?*"

"I can't, Z'." Nickie shook her head regretfully. "I've really got to go. I brought home a lot of paperwork."

"I no see you for weeks. A fancy lunch in the city, then nothing," Z'Maria railed, her voice rising. "Now you no can take a nice little Sunday walk through the park. What, you too good for us now?"

"Z', shhh . . ."

"You no tell me shuddup," Z'Maria snapped, glaring at her. "I give you one piece of my mind, eh? Maybe I no work at a bank, but I know this: You try to eat the sheep whole, you vomit up wool. I'm tell you, you better watch. You push too fast, you want too much, it gonna get you in trouble."

They stood toe to toe, their noses inches apart. Z'Maria wore her dowdy black and Nickie a purple pique beach skirt slit stylishly up the front to reveal green linen shorts that matched her sleeveless top. A vast generational and cultural chasm separated them, yet for all that they understood each another. At heart they spoke the same language—two strong-willed women who looked at the world through the same unblinkered eyes to accept it as it was and somehow turn it to their advantage.

"You win, Z'." Nickie grinned. "How about some cotton candy?"

" 'Merican crap." The woman made as if to spit, although her eyes brightened with a glimmer of answering amusement. "Ah, *sì,* why not. When in *Roma* . . ."

A minute later, as Nickie turned away from the concession stand with a huge blob of spun-pink candy on a stick, she bumped squarely into Rocco DiPiano, Carlo's good-looking son.

"Rocco!"she greeted him. "I thought you were already up at Columbia."

"Uncle Sam got me first." He grinned. "I ship out next week."

"Too bad."

His eyes held hers for a delicious moment before she looked away. She'd had a crush on him since high school. Delightful as the flirtation was, she wanted no part of a serious relationship with any Italian man. She knew all too well that once they married, their wives were relegated to second-class status.

Rocco accepted her standoffishness with no hard feelings. "So, how about Phil—he's the last one home, isn't he?"

"Yes. He wanted to join up," she said quickly, "but they gave him a deferment because of his broken eardrum. He wasn't too happy about that."

"Yeah, tough luck. How'd it happen?"

She laughed. "Don't you remember when we tried to scare your dad off with Phil's rocket experiment? The stupid thing backfired right next to his ear."

Rocco grinned. "Our families have been through some times together, huh?"

They walked toward the Ferris wheel, where the elder DiPiano was talking to Z'Maria and Phil. The Mafia chieftain's wife, a well-dressed and once-pretty woman whose features had long since filled out with matronly fat, stood silent and smiling at her husband's side.

"So what you think of our kids, eh, Carlo?" Z'Maria asked with a short laugh after the greetings had been made. "Your son off to be a lawyer. These here, we got the banker, the architect."

DiPiano's hazel eyes sharply regarded the younger generation. "Enough to control the whole city someday, eh?"

Nickie exchanged an uneasy smile with her brother. DiPiano's subtle overtures never stopped. The Branzinos wanted no part of Mafia life, yet it was a reality that they had to face.

DiPiano looked at Phil. "So I hear you're gonna start up your own office downtown. With some Johnny Bull."

"O'Rourke's a big name in this city," Phil said. "I think it'll work to my advantage."

"But I hear your partner, he had a falling out with his *famiglia*, no?"

Nickie stared at DiPiano in astonishment. His touch on the pulsebeat of the Italian community never faltered for an instant. But his access to private information about a wealthy figure like David O'Rourke was daunting, even frightening. Despite the heat of the day, she shivered a little. These were not people to cross, ever.

The man's quiet, probing interrogation was interrupted by a rough voice hailing him. "Hey, Carlo!"

They all turned as Tony Malfatti approached the group. His left leg dragged slightly, and he leaned for support on an ebony walking stick. Nickie's gaze moved slowly from the cane up to his scarred temple, where one of Angie's bullets had grazed him. She hadn't seen him in four years. Neither the cane nor the elegant blue silk suit, which Nickie recognized as exquisite Italian tailoring, diminished his volcanic animal nature.

Walking a few steps behind him was a heavyset woman whose whole bearing shouted "*paisana!*" Her legs were stubby, and she moved with a slow, oddly shuffling gait, as if determined to keep contact with the earth that had long nourished her.

Z'Maria drew close to Nickie. "Look at him. *Stronzon' bigamo,*" she whispered against Nickie's ear, her breath hot and angry. "The shithead bigamist."

Nickie held her aunt's arm tightly, helping to check her own fury. She watched Tony clasp DiPiano's hand and then give him the ritual kiss on both cheeks—an acolyte bowing to the authority of a bishop. Then Tony turned to the Branzinos, who had moved apart from the others. Nickie never failed to be startled by the cyanic blue of his eyes. They were deep and steady against the mobile coarseness of his grimacing lips and flaring nostrils. He pulled a fat Havana cigar from his breast pocket and lit it as he approached them.

"So this is what's left of the family, eh—one old lady and these two bigshots?" he said contemptuously as he drew on his cigar. "The rest—torn from you." He paused. "They say God pays what you deserve. Every sorrow is a punishment."

Nickie answered with cool equanimity, "You of all people should know that, Tony."

She saw his fingers tighten on the cane. He began to move restlessly, like a dog futilely circling its turned-over bowl. He laughed without mirth. "Look at all a you. Get an education, you think you're smart." He blew out a burst of harsh-smelling smoke. "You don't know nothing."

"Knock it off, Tony," Rocco muttered. "This isn't the time or the place."

Tony ignored him. "The world ain't ruled by fancy ideas; it's ruled by men." Tony's gaze slid over to include both Phil and Rocco in his contempt. "Men with power."

"Enough," Carlo DiPiano said mildly, though there was no mistaking the steel underlying his warning. "We got room enough for everybody." DiPiano glanced at Z'Maria, his sharp eyes revealing nothing. "Tony's leaving Ohio. He's coming to work for me."

Tony's lips drew back. "Gonna be one big happy family, eh?"

Nickie schooled her features into cool indifference, but she couldn't help wondering if they could somehow smell her fear.

Nickie and Z'Maria sat in one of the front rows of the open-air grandstand, oblivious to the musicians warming up and to the dancers in bright ethnic costumes milling about in preparation for the evening show. The two women had their heads bent close together, deep in conversation.

"What can I say?" Z'Maria rasped. "The man no want to forget. Who knows, maybe Tony's not a man but a devil."

Nickie vented her own anger in a soft undertone. "I thought DiPiano was your friend. How could he bring that poison back into our lives?" She rubbed her bare arms irritatedly. "Now when we're just finally getting to be okay."

" 'The crops are good,' we used to say back in the old days," Z'Maria answered. " 'Who knows what disasters are coming?' "

Nickie was not in the mood for her aunt's black humor. "Z', don't give me that fatalistic peasant crap."

"Eh?" Z'Maria shot back, her eyes flashing darkly. "You listen—"

"Signora Branzino?"

Nickie froze when she heard the familiar voice. Oh no, what the hell was she doing here?

"Mrs. Branzino, I thought that was you," Josephine Urbano went on, seating herself in the row behind them as Z'Maria turned to smile. "How are you? How is your family?"

Nickie stared fixedly at the bandstand as she listened to the women's conversation. "I can't tell you how much I still miss Angelina," Mrs. Urbano was saying, her voice at once full of warmth and pain. "Is she . . . is she happy?"

"*Sì sì*," Z'Maria murmured with growing discomfort. "But you remember our Nicoletta, too, eh?"

Nickie had no choice but to turn and acknowledge Louis's mother. The woman's eyes widened for an instant with shock. "Nicoletta," she said coldly, "how charming."

Nickie nodded stiffly as the musicians started up. She never thought she'd be grateful for the offkey playing of the Italian Club orchestra, for their raucous noise served to camouflage the hammering of her own heart. She sat motionless throughout the entire performance, envisioning Josephine Urbano's eyes boring into the back of her head.

Afterward, the woman managed to snag Nickie's arm as they were filing out of the packed rows of chairs. "May I speak to you a moment, Nicoletta?" Her smile was a frozen rictus.

"Go on, Z'," Nickie murmured, avoiding the question in her aunt's eyes. "I'll catch up in a minute."

The crowd drifted back toward the noisy carnival brightness of the amusement park, leaving behind them a sticky detritus of ice cream wrappers and overturned pop bottles. High overhead, the night sky exploded with fireworks. Their boom echoing against the surrounding hills was as ominous as thunder. Intermittent flashes of light illuminated the faces of the two women like flickering figures on a movie screen.

"So the jig's up," Nickie said with an indifferent shrug. "So what's there to discuss, Mrs. Urbano?"

"How dare you be so flippant? I demand to know why you have insinuated yourself into my son's life." Anger and suspicion sharpened the woman's aristocratic features.

"Louis hired me on the basis of my credentials."

"Which you were so confident of that you had to present them under false pretenses." Nickie flushed. "You're the same old Nickie Branzino, aren't you—a brash, pushy sneak determined to grab what she can for herself. How you and Angie could be sisters, I can't fath—"

"How dare you compare me to her?" Nickie cried. "Yes, I'm determined to grab what I can. What other choice did I ever have? I didn't have a fairy godmother to swoop me out of my miserable life. I had to study. I had to battle my father and listen to him call me a whore when I did finally escape. No, you're right, Mrs. Urbano, I'm not like Angie. She had it all handed to her, and she threw it away." Nickie's words came out in short gasps. "Nobody handed me anything. I have worked and suffered for what I've gotten, and I don't intend to let you or anyone else stand in my way."

A fiery roman candle arced through the sky, exploding in a red shower of sparks that bathed the older woman's face in an angry glow. "We'll see about that."

Nickie sank onto one of the folding chairs as Josephine Urbano disappeared into the jostling, laughing crowd. Why did I mouth off that way? Nickie chastised herself. Why do I always have to try to be so tough? Damn it, because that's the way I am. She angrily jabbed the toe of her espadrille against a bottle cap. The silvery metal glinted against the night like a ragged star that had fallen, spent, to earth.

Nickie sat at her desk in the office adjacent to Louis's. The surface was covered with spreadsheets, and she studied them with her usual quick intensity, jotting figures on the scratchpad at her elbow, multiplying percentages and swiftly rechecking her math. From time to time she rubbed the bridge of her nose between her thumb and forefinger, closing her eyes to momentarily clear her head of all the amortization schedules and loan rates whirling in her head. When she reopened her eyes, they focused on the black-and-white line drawing hanging on the far wall. Phil had done the rendering of an Oakland neighborhood: A tree-shaded street of Georgian houses and fanciful stone-turreted mansions curved away into a hazy, idealized vision of the city. She loved the feeling of freedom and privilege that the drawing embodied; for an instant she could lose herself in that beautiful, ordered world of luxury.

Her brother's artwork was the sole personal touch in the small office crowded with file cabinets and shelves loaded with books on banking and real estate. Neat binders held pertinent articles she had cut from the *Wall Street Journal* and the *Pittsburgh Press*. She referred to her books and clippings daily, using them as the basis upon which she suggested deals and loan decisions to Louis—decisions based on what she thought of as "informed intuition." The projects on which she had advised Louis so far promised to be strong validation of that intuition.

The door between their connecting offices opened, and Nickie pulled her glasses down onto her nose. Louis stood in the doorway, regarding her tensely. "Would you come into my office, please? We've got to talk."

"Be right there." Nickie grabbed her yellow legal pad and followed him into his office. "You're early today," she said, her eyes watchful. "What's up?"

Until now their working relationship had been completely harmonious. Nickie had come to greatly appreciate the utter lack of sexual tension between them, that subtle but constant subtext that underlay even the most platonic male-female relationships. Louis's preferences had long since ceased to disturb or even interest her. In two short months a relaxed camaraderie had sprung up between them. This new tenseness put her on edge.

He sat behind his desk, refusing to look at her. He picked up his gold pen from the blotter and began to twirl it agitatedly. "Nicole," he began and stopped, looking up to give her a wounded glance full of suspicion. "Or should I say, Nicoletta . . ."

"So that's what this is all about," she said, pulling off her glasses and dropping them on his desk.

"I'm . . . I'm afraid I'm going to have to let you go."

"Why?" Nickie struggled to stay calm. "Has my work been unsatisfactory?"

"You know damn well it's not because of your work."

"Then why—because of who I am? Because I happen to be Nicoletta Branzino?" she said, angry warmth surging behind the words she uttered with such coolly measured irony. "Nicole or Nicoletta, why should it make one damn bit of difference?"

"Don't be a fool," he snapped, running his fingers nervously through his immaculately coiffed hair. "In the light of . . . of what's passed between our families, I hardly think it would be conducive to a good working relationship."

"You priggish idiot," she fumed, jumping up. "I've never heard such baloney! We work beautifully together and you know it." Resting one hand on the desk and one on the arm of his chair, she leaned toward him. "Why don't we just be honest with each other for a second, okay? Let's face it: This has nothing to do with you or with me. This has nothing to do with my work. This has to do with your mother not wanting me here."

Louis looked up coldly. "You lied to me. To us."

"And I apologize for that," she said, perching on the edge of the desk. "You may not believe it, but what you think of me has come to matter a great deal. I admit I came into your office for that first interview with every intention of deceiving you. You wouldn't have hired Nicoletta Branzino, am I right?"

"Yes, but—"

"Louis, you were kind to me. You gave me a chance. I wanted to repay that kindness by doing a bang-up job for you."

"I want to believe you, but . . ." His fingers moved restlessly to the knot of his tie as if to hide the nervous working of his Adam's apple. It was obvious he was struggling for words, uncertain of how much Nickie truly knew about him. "I . . . I'm afraid I won't ever be able to trust you."

"Louis, look at me." After a moment he lifted his eyes to her face, his expression guarded. "I'm going to say this once, and then it'll never be mentioned between us again." She touched his shoulder reassuringly. "Louis, I know what you are, and I don't care. Your personal life is your own business. I'm not my sister. She's gone. What's past is truly past. What interests me is the future. Do you understand what I'm saying?"

"I'm beginning to," he said, still wary.

"Don't you see, Louis? If I'd been vengeful and wanted to hurt you, I could have done it long before this. That's never been my intention."

"What is your intention?"

"Exactly what you've seen these past few months—to

make myself your indispensable Girl Friday. Look," she broke off, "can we talk honestly for a minute?"

"Do I have any choice?" He laughed ruefully as he turned to the array of pipes on the shelf and picked one up.

"Louis, you and I, we need each other. You've given me a leg up in the business, and I in turn am going to help build your reputation as a banker in this city. I don't want the limelight; I'm perfectly content to work behind the scenes," she said slowly, watching his elegant fingers tamp down the tobacco inside the bowl of the pipe. "Louis, with me at your side, you can continue to make excellent business decisions. You're going to prove yourself not only to your father but to the entire banking community."

He drew deeply on the pipe, then exhaled a stream of fragrant smoke. "In other words," he said wryly, "if I were to fire you, I'd be hurting myself far more than I would be hurting you."

Nickie shrugged. "All I mean to say is that it would be stupid to throw away our partnership—and what I hope is a friendship—because of a petty quarrel between your mother and me."

"Petty." Louis frowned. "Good God, you have an incredible knack for glossing over things."

"I don't gloss over the issues that really matter." She stood up. "Just look at the research cluttering my desk if you don't believe me."

He gave her a considering look. After a long moment he smiled his old lazy smile. "So, tell me, what have you decided on this Winston-Hill merger loan Father's been pressing me to make a decision on?"

Nickie breathed an inward sigh of relief that the battle had been so easily won. But she was no fool. She knew a whole war lay ahead between her and Josephine Urbano. But she wouldn't worry about that now. One step at a time . . .

"The merger looks A-okay to me," she said, making a circle of her thumb and forefinger. "You may give dear old papa the go-ahead."

"Another feather in my cap, Nick?"

She grinned. "I intend to see you president of the

Pittsburgh Bankers' Association within a year." She grinned and bent down impetuously to give him a peck on the cheek. He looked oddly pleased, like a boy basking in maternal approval.

Silly, weak man, Nickie thought, looking down at him. Yet for all her realization of his weaknesses, she felt a sudden rush of affection for him.

24

Nickie looked speculatively up at the house where David O'Rourke lived with his wife, Maura, and their eighteen-month-old daughter. The house was little different from its Delafield Avenue neighbors—one of the modest two-story frame dwellings lining the neat, tree-shaded lanes of Aspinwall. The unpretentious village was sandwiched between the old-money opulence of Highland Park just south across the river and the woodsy, country-club atmosphere of Fox Chapel, where the nouveau riche had begun to build. As she climbed the steps to the front porch, Nickie wondered how Maura Donahue O'Rourke felt about her current status. She was willing to bet Maura had had no inkling that the "for richer, for poorer" part of the marriage vow might one day apply to her.

It was David who opened the door at her knock. "Nickie, come in! Louis and Phil are already here."

"Hello, David," she said as she swiftly assessed his features. It had been years since she had last seen Louis's best friend. She remembered him as warm, charmingly happy-go-lucky, with the smooth ease of manner that Nickie so admired in the rich. From the tight lines around his eyes and a new stubborn set to that handsome cleft chin, she guessed that his decision to leave the family fold had not been an easy one. "I hope I haven't kept you waiting too long."

"No, the extra time just gave Louis an opportunity to rave about your talents." His grin was quick, amused.

Nickie smiled back as he ushered her into the small sitting room, where Louis sat examining a set of blueprints that Phil had unrolled on the mahogany coffee table. From the pleasantly vacant look on Louis's face, Nickie could tell he regarded the detailed architectural prints as only slightly less mysterious than Chinese calligraphy. Nickie had to suppress a laugh as she observed them together. Phil, her brilliantly creative brother, was lost as usual in the beauty he envisioned in his head and totally oblivious to Louis's lack of appreciation.

Louis looked around with relief when David and Nickie came into the room. "Nickie, you look lovely." He greeted her with his usual indolent warmth. "New earrings? They're quite becoming."

Even after four months of working together, Louis's charming attentiveness to even the smallest details of her appearance still surprised her. She had no idea whether it was put on or not; never had she met anyone, other than herself, who was such a clever dissembler.

Nickie reached up to finger her earrings. "Thanks. I picked them up in a little antique shop in Oakland. They're carved whalebone. I thought they had more class than the wood and plastic junk they have been selling at Kaufmann's lately." She laughed. "If this rationing keeps up, we'll all be wearing bearskins before the damned war is over."

"I, for one, wouldn't mind a touch of fur," a high feminine voice spoke from the doorway. "Drinks, anyone?"

They all turned toward Maura, who was balancing a silver tray in her hands. Her long dinner dress with its fuchsia top, plum-colored skirt and jeweled side buttons made her look like a delicate tropical bird. From the looks of the expensive gown, Nickie guessed that Maura still had signing privileges on her mother's department-store accounts. She wondered what kind of battle royale it had taken to win that concession from her husband. Seeing the lines of discontent etched around Maura's pretty mouth, Nickie sensed that those battles were a fairly regular occurrence.

Maura passed around cocktails, smiling with practiced

charm at each man while managing to ignore Nickie completely. "Our dinner reservations are for seven-thirty. I hope you boys get this business discussion over with quickly. It's all been decided anyway, hasn't it?"

"Why don't you check on Katie before the sitter arrives?"

Maura sat down in an armchair next to Phil. "I prefer to stay."

With a shrug, David directed his attention from his wife to Nickie. "Everything *is* settled, isn't it, Nickie?"

When she did not immediately reply, she saw the surface charm slip just a fraction to reveal a cool, steely tenacity that surprised her. In that instant she realized how much psychologically as well as financially must be at stake for him. Both Phil and Louis were regarding her fixedly now.

"Nickie, you know that David and I shook hands on this matter at the club," Louis said uncomfortably. "We have an agreement."

"I have no problem with the basis of the agreement," she said carefully. "But I do have a slight hesitation about the size of the loan you want."

"Damn it!" Phil blazed. "I'm your brother. You think I'm going to welch on a loan?"

"You're an artist, Phil, not a businessman," she replied, peripherally aware of Maura shifting in her chair. "If loans were made strictly on the basis of talent and potential, I'd authorize ten times the amount you've asked for. But we have to look at the situation from the objective standpoint of collateral," she said, her gaze sidling off Phil and resting on David. "To put it baldly, you have zilch."

Maura stirred angrily. "How dare you!"

"Maura, stay out of this," David snapped. He stood up, shoved his hands in his pockets and began to pace. After a while he stopped in front of Nickie, where she sat rigidly on the sofa, as if ready to fend off attack from every quarter. To her surprise, he grinned at her. "Lady, you don't pull punches."

"No."

"But you are forgetting one thing." He sat on the edge of the coffee table, leaning his elbows on his knees so that their faces were inches apart. "My family's name counts for a hell of a lot in this city. The value of that is incalculable."

Nickie nodded. "You're absolutely right, David—theoretically. But let's face it, right now you're not exactly in the good graces of your family. Those connections aren't going to mean anything in the short term, I'm afraid. To be brutally frank, isn't it the case that your father and his cronies regard you as something of a maverick? They see this design-construction venture as a whim, a—"

"A wild hair up my ass?"

Nickie laughed. "I didn't say that."

"But you were thinking it. Admit it."

Nickie realized that she was dealing with a man whose charm was every bit the equal of his intelligence and ambition: a thoroughly attractive but dangerous mixture if your will happened to be at odds with his.

"I won't admit it. David, I'm not your adversary. I'm on your side." Nickie laughed again. "Thank God."

"What do we have to discuss, then?"

She gazed at him steadily. "Enthusiastic as I am about the partnership, I'm not going to yield my earlier point. Establishing a new firm takes time and patience."

"I don't have either, Nickie." David stood up and resumed his restless pacing. "I'm shipping out next month."

"All the more reason to start small and build slowly," she said. "All Phil needs is a pencil, a drawing table, and the freedom to go after projects that will not only pay the rent but will get you a lot of notice from the bigshots downtown—the libraries, the Mellon-supported churches . . ." She turned to her brother. "Am I right?"

Phil's dark eyes gleamed. "Well, yeah."

"Listen, David," she pressed, "by the time the war's over, you two will be in a prime position to be a force in this city's future."

He sat on the edge of the coffee table again. "Why don't we just rent a rear booth down at Woolworth's Grill, so the genius half of O'Rourke and Branzino can get to work?" His grin was teasing. "Would that be a small enough capital outlay to appease your banker's conscience?"

Maura set her glass down on the table with a sharp

click and stood up. She looked at Nickie with ill-disguised malice. "You're relishing this, aren't you? Now that the tables have turned, you think you can lord it over us."

"I'm not lording it over anyone, Maura. I only want what's best for Phil and David, and for Louis's bank." Nickie's glance encompassed all three men. "And I don't think these needs are incompatible."

But Maura was not about to be shunted aside. "What gives you the right to dictate to us? You're a fraud. I've heard all about your ridiculous posing. Josephine confided everything to my mother."

"*Who* confided everything to you?" Nickie cried, trying to will away the slow, hot flush of humiliation suffusing her cheeks. "Interesting, isn't it, how the taste for expensive bonbons and cheap gossip go together?"

"Sticks and stones, Nicoletta." Maura's laugh was as sharp as breaking glass. "The truth is, beneath that veneer you are what you always have been—a greedy little guttersnipe."

"Maura, shut up." David's voice was taut with fury.

"I will not." She rounded on her husband. "I've had it, I tell you. You and your filthy pride! If you'd done what our families thought was best, we wouldn't have had to wind up like this—begging with hat in hand, to her of all people! You'd be staying home where you belong in your father's mills, instead of flitting off to war, and leaving me with the messes you've created."

A child's whimpering cry, soft at first and then rising with urgency, cut through the charged atmosphere.

"Go see to Kathleen," David ordered curtly.

"Go see to her yourself," Maura answered, turning her back on them. "I'm going out."

The front door slammed. David got up and walked down the hall toward the stairs. Nickie looked from Louis to Phil. Louis had pulled a packet of cigarettes from his pocket and now went through an elaborate charade of lighting one, studiously avoiding looking in her direction. Phil frowned at her. She knew he was thinking this was somehow all her fault.

David returned a moment later, carrying a chubby toddler who was the spitting image of her mother. The baby's face was flushed and tear streaked, and her wispy reddish-gold hair stood up around her head like a fiery halo. But she was laughing now, two fingers in her mouth as David whispered something into her ear. All the anger had drained from him, leaving this relaxed, warm, loving man in his place. Playfully he introduced his daughter to Louis, then Phil, and finally to Nickie.

The child's green eyes were vibrantly beautiful but unblinking, expressionless. Nickie suppressed a shiver, unable to imagine being born into a world of perpetual darkness. Louis had described the condition as congenital blindness. It was irreversible.

"Say something, Nickie," David urged. "She loves new voices."

Nickie cooed dutifully, and Katie's whole face lit up.

David set her down on the floor, and she picked her way confidently along, using the sofa and coffee table edge as guideposts. David went to the knickknack shelf and started to pull down a collection of Baccarat animals. Kathleen evidently knew this game because she toddled to her father's side, giggling as he stretched out on the rose-patterned carpet, his head propped up on one arm.

David picked up one of the glass sculptures and handed it to her. "What's this?"

Her fat little fingers moved in a swift, familiar caress over the form. "Wabbit."

"Good girl."

"And this?"

"Duck."

And so it went on. A piece occasionally slipped through her hands to the carpeted floor. She picked it up, and the game would resume. As Nickie watched with fascination, she couldn't help wondering at Maura's reaction to this child's game, played so casually with her priceless collection of elegant French crystal.

25

November 1942

Angie stood in the light of the French doors, waiting with ill-concealed patience as another tuck was taken in her waistband. Madame Francini's elegant drawing room looked like the boudoir of a nineteenth-century courtesan. Sumptuous, lace-bordered dressing gowns, low-cut silk bodices in vibrant hues, flounced velvet skirts were draped over sofas and chairs. A stiff meringue of hoop-skirted crinolines spilled from an overflowing trunk—an irresistible lure for a child. Four-year-old Marshall climbed up onto the sofa arm. Angie reached out to grab him, but the wardrobe mistress gripped her firmly by the waist.

"Hold still, Angelina," Signora Vessi muttered, her mouth full of straight pins. "How do you expect me to finish?"

"Marshall, no!" Angie cried the instant before he dived into the billowy white mound of petticoats.

"Never mind him," Vessi said. "He can't hurt those worn-out rags." Turning Angie to face her, she lifted her wrists to examine the costume's frayed silk cuffs. "Look at this! Violetta is a rich man's mistress. But in this you'll look like a refugee from *La Boheme*. The Germans will scoff."

"Let them." Angie laughed. "After three years of war, you think they're better off than us?"

"Hush," the woman warned, picking the pins from her teeth as if they were tiny fishbones and plunging them into a pincushion she had pulled from her pocket. "Those kinds of jokes are treason nowadays. They consider themselves conquerors and us their poor consorts. Never forget that, Angelina."

"Marshall!" Sarah Langton's sharp voice rang out be-hind them. "Get down at once." He made a beeline for the doors, slipping out onto the balcony before Sarah could grab him. His baby fat had long since given way to a fragile splindliness made worse by poor nutrition. War-time rationing had taken its toll on all of them, but luckily it had not affected their spirits yet.

"Incorrigible little monster," Sarah went on, venting her anger on Angie. "You don't even attempt to control him."

The wardrobe mistress spoke up. "This is not England, Signorina Langton. Our children are children," she said comfortably, "not little *burattinos*." She moved her broad fingers, miming the control of puppets on strings.

"Hmmph."

Angie moved to close the door that her son had left ajar. The northern Italian sky beyond the balcony had the rich blue intensity of a Della Robbia enamel, but its brilliance was deceiving. A chill autumn wind whipped through the piazza, skirling eerily along the electric wires.

Vessi turned toward the doors, her head cocked tensely at the faint, high-pitched sound. "Air raid?"

"No," Angie said, shivering and moving closer to the crackling fire in the grate. "Just the wind."

Vessi followed her, unhooking the row of buttons down the rear of the gown. Angie stepped out of the opulent costume and handed it to Sarah to pack. She rubbed her bare arms to ward off the chill. Standing there wearing nothing but her slip and Renata's gold cross around her neck, she felt vulnerable as a little girl.

Madame Francini stepped into the drawing room, her arms full of music scores. Her eyes swept past Sarah, who had knelt down to refold the jumbled crinolines, and rested on Angie. "It isn't too late to back out," she said. "We can telephone Massarro and tell him you've decided not to go to Berlin with the company."

"I'm going," Angie said, pulling on the white silk crepe blouse that Josephine Urbano had given her years be-fore. She reached up to finger the gold cross. "I know what I'm doing."

"Do you?"

Angie finished dressing swiftly. "You act as though I

have a choice in the matter," she replied lightly. "Vessi was just coaching me on the ways of our German superiors. Rule one: Never say 'no, thank you' to a command performance."

"That's nonsense," Madame said, setting her music sheets down on a table. "What if you'd been taken ill?"

Angie laughed, hurrying over to her. "But I'm not ill, Madame Giulia. I'm hale and hearty," she said teasingly, kissing the woman's thin cheek. "Sound of wind and limb."

"Indeed," Madame retorted, ignoring as usual Angie's impetuous displays of affection. "I see that sparkle in your eyes. I think you actually *want* to go."

"I'd be crazy not to. This is a chance for international recognition."

"What value is recognition from barbarians?"

Angie shrugged off that bitter truth. How could the Germans be any more barbaric than her own father and husband had been? To be able to perform—to affirm her talent and worth—was to acknowledge that in some small, vital way her own will could triumph over whatever evils they represented.

"I want to shake up their Aryan souls," Angie said, her smile full of mischief. "I want to be heard in their magnificent new Staatsoper before the Allies bomb the hell out of it again."

"And if the Americans choose to bomb while you happen to be there—what then?" Madame said dryly. "What about your son?"

"I know that he'll be safe and cared for by his godmother," Angie said, touching the woman's cheek briefly. "Whom he loves very, very much."

Madame impatiently brushed her hand away and turned toward the hall, as if to deny her own strong but buried emotional impulses which Angie seemed determined to draw forth. "You'll need that throat tincture," she said from the doorway. "I know you. You'll sing full out, with absolutely no consideration for the fragility of your vocal cords." Her sharp voice trailed off as she moved down the hall. "You'll return hoarse, and probably with a bad cold to boot."

Vessi shook her head ruefully. "She's right, you know."

Marshall burst into the apartment from the balcony, heedless of Sarah's simmering wrath. "Mama!" he cried. "The taxi!"

Angie and Vessi started throwing the costumes helter skelter into the trunks, while Sarah obstinately continued to arrange the garments with maddening precision, lining each fold with layer upon layer of tissue. Clara bustled in with a cloth-covered shopping basket swinging from her arm.

"Angelina," the rosy-cheeked cook said breathlessly, "I've spent all morning in line at the market. Look what I've brought for your trip!" She folded back the cloth to reveal an enormous salami that looked like the equivalent of the household's meat ration for a month.

Stunned, Angie looked up into Clara's beaming face. "How—"

Clara laughed. "The butcher," she said softly, "you know he has a crush on me."

"I should have guessed. But I can't take that. I don't have enough hands," Angie said, smiling as she picked up her pocketbook and the sheaf of music Madame had set on the table. "Besides, the Germans may be barbarians, but they're not going to starve their own allies. I'm sure they'll manage to throw us a few crumbs in Berlin."

Angie left in a flurry of hugs and admonishments. From the piazza she looked up one last time to the balcony. Madame had lifted Marshall in her arms, and he waved down excitedly. Her heart constricting with love, Angie blew him kiss after kiss. Suddenly, four days seemed like a very long time.

Berlin was cold, grim and gray. The northerly winds blowing down from the Baltic were as penetrating as a knife blade. The linden trees along the banks of the Havel were already barren of leaves. The air held none of the crystalline brilliance that had illuminated the skies above the Austrian Alps. It was as if all life and color had been leeched from the city.

Angie walked briskly down Voss Strasse, her arm linked through her companion's. Sergio Silvestre, a violinist with La Scala, had resigned himself to being Angie's friend since she had made it clear to him long before that she wanted no romantic entanglements. She was glad to be with him now. He had lived in Berlin before the war and had a sardonic irreverence for everything German. His attitude helped ease the strangeness and vague sense of foreboding that had tugged at Angie ever since they had left Italian soil. Sergio's eye followed hers as they moved along the rows of stark monolithic buildings.

"Wonderful Nazi construction, eh? I've heard rumors that Hitler's architects are designing another vast avenue to be lined with captured tanks and artillery, like the Egyptian pharaohs' Avenue of the Rams."

Angie shook her head. "They have no sense of beauty, do they?"

"They have what matters to them—a sense of power."

"So I see," Angie murmured, awed by the gray, blank-faced buildings that seemed to stretch endlessly toward Wilhelmsplatz in the distance. "And that one—what is it?"

"The Reich Chancellery."

"I should have guessed," she said, watching a chauffeur-driven car pull up to the front entrance. Flags with a lightning-bolt insignia fluttered on each front fender. Angie couldn't help but notice the aristocratically handsome blond man who climbed out. "Look at him," she murmured under her breath. "The male model of Aryan perfection." Her eyes moved to the long case he carried at his side. "He must be a musician."

"He's no musician," Sergio said as his hand tightened on her arm.

She turned in surprise. "You know him?"

"Only by reputation." Sergio lowered his voice further, even though there was no one within several feet of them. "He's Heinrich Mahler, the official executioner for the SS, the secret police. That case holds his ax."

"Dear Christ," she whispered under her breath. "What are we doing here?"

"Come on, let's get to the opera house," Sergio said regretfully. "We should have walked the other way along the river. You going to be all right to sing?"

She nodded, trying not to shiver.

Angie stood alone upon the vast stage of the Staatsoper,

holding a mirror up to her face. Tears welled in her eyes. Too late, she thought, staring into the consumption-ravaged features of the dying Violetta. Too late. "Ah!" Angie breathed, heedless of the strain to her larynx as she transformed the high note into a sustained cry of anguish. *"Gran Dio! Morir si giovine."* O God! I am too young to die. Ardor and grief washed through her voice, coloring it with an essence at once dark, sensual and womanly. It was as if the world beyond the footlights no longer existed. The psychological power of Verdi's *La Traviata* created its own reality. Angie wedded herself to that power through her soaring voice. In the final moment before Violetta's death, the bittersweet emotion that engulfed her as she bid adieu to her beloved Alfredo was all that existed for her.

The curtain fell. Angie slowly rose from the stage floor, one part of her psyche still caught up in Violetta's tragedy while the practical part listened intently for signs of the German audience's approval. Could a people so steeped in the quest for martial glory possibly be moved by Violetta's transformation from spoiled courtesan to selfless, loving woman?

The curtain rose, and Angie stood composedly before her judges, hiding her tightly clenched fists within the folds of the white silk dressing gown. After a silence that seemed to spin out forever, the solitary sound of one pair of clapping hands rang out from a box to stage left. As if they had been waiting for that signal, two thousand more hands joined in until applause filled the dark, arching space, a powerful thrum that was a thousand-fold magnification of her own heartbeat. Then the huge central chandelier blazed to life, and its crystalline shards reflected off the bemetalled uniforms in the first rows with an icy effulgence. Angie bowed gracefully. Shading her eyes with her hand, she then turned to acknowledge that first solitary clapping from the private box on her left. But the space was empty, and its red and black swastika-emblazoned banner rippled slightly as if it had been brushed by the occupant's hand as he slipped away.

Enormous bouquets of orchids, gardenias, camellias and white roses filled her dressing room to overflowing.

Angie handed them out to the fellow performers who had crowded into the tiny room with her. But as quickly as she dispensed them, more arrangements arrived, each more lavish than the next. Their cloying aroma reminded Angie of her mother's funeral. She slipped behind the dressing screen and took from her bodice the small photographs that she carried as good-luck charms the way other performers wore scapulars of their favorite saints. An aura of sadness emanated from the painfully thin faces smiling at the camera. She pressed her lips to the blurred photo, then touched the snapshot of Marshall. She kept the two photographs with her always—a family drawn together within the warm imagination of her heart. What more powerful talisman could she possess?

"Angelina!" one of the young chorus singers cried from the other side of the screen. "You have an important visitor."

She hastily tucked away her photographs.

A young Nazi lieutenant stood diffidently just inside the door, his cap beneath his arm. His eyes blinked behind his rimless glasses; his pale face was flushed. He was the least likely Nazi officer she had ever seen. Angie shooed out the young chorus members, who had begun to titter. Then she went to greet him, her hand extended politely.

"You wished to speak with me?" she said in slow but faultless German, her voice rasping. Her throat ached from the performance, but she had schooled herself to ignore the pain. To her it was merely a necessary evil of her art.

"I am Lieutenant Erhard," he told her, his expression full of concern. "But your voice . . . you are not ill?"

"It's nothing."

"*Gut.* But you speak Deutsch." He blinked in belated surprise, finally offering her a shy, tentative smile. "I . . . I was afraid I would have to practice my Italian. It's execrable, I'm afraid."

She smiled back. "Are you the one responsible for this deluge of flowers?"

"*Nein, nein.*" He blushed to the roots of his fair hair. "What I mean to say is, the *Führer*'s ministers and staff . . . after he expressed his approval of your performance . . . they found it fitting . . ."

"Ah, I see."

"My superior officer Herr Feldmarschall von Menzel has sent me to escort you to the official reception at the Chancellery. Will . . . will you do me the honor?"

The shy lieutenant held Angie's arm tightly as they passed through the pair of gates that guarded the Reich Chancellery at the Wilhelmsplatz entrance. They ascended an outside staircase which opened into a large mosaic-filled hall and went up another flight of stairs through a room with a domed ceiling, which in turn gave way to an immensely long gallery punctuated by window niches. To Angie the walk along the polished marble floors seemed endless. She felt at once diminished and overwhelmed by the Nazis' taste for ostentatious grandeur.

They came at last to the reception hall, crowded with local dignitaries, foreign diplomats and German military officers. Very few women were present. Punctuating the masculine atmosphere, four monumental stone figures stood in each corner of the hall. The male nudes had none of the tensile, curvilinear grace of Italian sculpture. These were blocky and oddly lifeless, exhibiting mammoth sexual organs more suitable to horses than men. Angie looked away quickly, noticing now that heads had turned her way. A scattering of spontaneous applause greeted her. She nodded graciously from the doorway, then turned to her escort. "I see my La Scala colleagues are already here, Lieutenant. Would you mind if we joined them?"

"But Fraulein Angelina, perhaps I did not make myself clear," he said, his tone apologetic although his hold on her arm remained firm. "I was sent expressly to escort you into my commanding officer's presence."

Her pulse quickened as he guided her through the crowd to the front of the great hall. A group of high-ranking Nazi officers stood conversing beneath a fierce bronze eagle whose wingspan extended almost the entire length of the wall. Lieutenant Erhard led Angie into their midst and turned to a tall, sparely built man who towered over his companions. Clicking his heels, Erhard announced in a punctilious manner, "Herr Feldmarschall von Menzel, I present to you Fraulein Angelina of the La Scala Opera Company."

The man dismissed his adjutant with a nod and turned toward Angie. She flushed as he bent from the waist to kiss her hand. "An old Austrian custom," he said, smiling, as he led her away from the circle of men. "I hope it does not offend you."

"You are Austrian?"

"On my mother's side."

"You share much in common, then, with your *Führer*."

His eyes flickered over her face, as if suspecting the subtle sting of irony behind her innocuous remark. Angie forced herself to meet his gaze pleasantly. His protruding cheekbones and high, receding hairline made his face a skeletal mask behind which Angie sensed a gloomily romantic nature. His presence touched off an echo in her mind, and a light shiver feathered her spine when she realized who it was he reminded her of. Carlo DiPiano had possessed exactly that air of bloodless charm: the suavity of a man absolutely certain of his sphere of power.

"Would you care for champagne?" Without waiting for her reply, von Menzel signaled to a nearby waiter and selected a glass for her. "It is from the best cellar in Rheims. Who knows, perhaps if we occupy French soil long enough, they will finally succeed in acculturating us barbarians," he said with a sardonic lift to his brow. "Do you not think so, fraulein?"

Nonplussed, Angie looked away toward the corner of the room, where one of the stone giants brooded over the flesh-and-blood assemblage. Von Menzel's cool laughter washed over her. "You seem attracted to Herr Breker's sculpture."

Angie turned back to face her inquisitor, her great dark eyes alert and ironic. "It is like everything else I have seen in your marvelous Reich," she said quietly. "Filled with a sense of its own power."

"We are not all philistines here, fraulein." To her surprise he smiled briefly. "There are those of us who have a deep love of genuine art—an affinity for that fluid, sensual Mediterranean spirit you evoked so wondrously tonight upon the stage. Do you believe that?"

"I . . ."

"Will you permit me to call for you tomorrow at your hotel?"

"I'm so sorry," she said at once. "But we board the train in the morning to return to Milan."

"How convincingly you feign disappointment, fraulein." His eyes gleamed with some hidden amusement. "So convincingly, in fact, that I'm inclined to believe you really would prefer to stay a bit longer."

26

The Berlin station's great arching roof, supported by a heavy filigree of iron struts, seemed to trap every sound and magnify it. Martial music blared from loudspeakers, and arriving trains announced themselves with an ear-shattering shriek of brakes and departed again like snuffling monsters. Angie dug her hands deep into the pockets of her old coat and paced along the southward-bound tracks, her breath misting in the frigid, early morning air. She had left the hotel long before the rest of the company had even arisen. Now she stared down the length of the empty platform, willing the train to pull in. Her head ached, and her throat felt tight and sore. She just wanted to go home, to get away from this strange, frightening country.

She spotted the train as it appeared in the distance, snaking slowly past rows of warehouses toward the station. "Thank God." Moments later, the rest of the opera company started to arrive. Trunks, music cases, valises piled up on the platform. Sergio and several others crowded around Angie, bombarding her with questions about her conversation with the general the evening before. "He didn't say anything," she insisted. "He only wanted to congratulate me on my performance."

"Hey, here comes Cichetti!" someone cried, pointing at La Scala's pompous stage manager. "Look, he's finally got his own cortege—a pair of Nazi guards."

"Probably not real soldiers," a cellist joked. "Just a couple of extras left over from a performance of *Wozzeck*."

Sergio began to hum the German opera's eerily distorted military march in time to Cichetti's ponderous step, making everyone laugh.

"What's all this nonsense?" the manager barked, puffing and out of breath. "I suggest you comedians attend to your belongings. Angelina, wait. I, er, wish to speak to you."

She turned back in surprise. Cichetti, always so arrogant and full of bombast, seemed unsure of himself. "What is it, Signor Cichetti?"

"You . . . um . . . ." He couldn't look her in the eye. "Angelina, you are to accompany these soldiers. There's a car waiting at the station entrance."

"What?" The smile died on her lips. She was aware of a sudden tension around her, as if every member of the company had sucked in his breath at the same time.

"Go on, go!" Cichetti barked into the charged atmosphere. "Apparently other arrangements have been made for your return."

"But—"

He waded into the mass of luggage, examining the tags. *"Ecco!"* He picked up a valise and shoved it into her arms. "This is yours, isn't it?"

"Please," she begged.

He shook his head almost imperceptibly, and for a brief instant his eyes met hers. She read in their depths confusion, anger, an outraged sense of helplessness. Angie realized she had no choice but to do as she was told. Terrified, and aware of the hundred pairs of eyes boring into her back, she walked slowly back through the station between the two German soldiers.

A black Mercedes limousine waited beneath the station portico with its engine running. One of the young soldiers opened the rear door and gestured for Angie to climb inside. Feldmarschall Werner von Menzel sat ensconced against the pale leather seat with a fur wrap over his knees. He leaned forward, holding out his black-

gloved hand to help her in. "*Guten tag*, fraulein." He
greeted her with stiff formality. "So good of you to join
me." Ignoring his hand, she climbed inside and sat with
her back wedged against the door, keeping as far from
him as possible. He laughed. "Come now, surely you
must realize I am not the evil wolf of the fairy tales."
With his gloved hand he rapped lightly on the glass
partition separating the front from the back seat.

Her heart lurched as the driver eased the car out into
the boulevard. "Where are you taking me?"

Von Menzel retrieved an ice bucket holding a champagne bottle from behind the driver's seat. Deftly he
removed the cork and poured out the sparkling, straw-
colored liquid into a pair of flute glasses nestled in a
specially designed holder. When Angie refused the glass,
he merely shrugged.

"Another exceptional cellar," he said, drinking in small,
savoring sips. "This particular vintage was rescued from a
Normandy chateau. Less than twenty cases survived the
bombing."

"What do you want of me, Herr Feldmarschall?" Angie
asked, struggling to keep the quaver of fear from her
voice.

"There are some of us who, for all our loyalty to the
Reich, hunger to escape its austerity from time to time."
Despite the quiet way in which he spoke, his eyes when
they met hers gleamed with an unnerving intensity. "Your
performance last night provided a most magical escape
for me. Now I simply wish to . . . return the favor, if you
will."

Angie looked away, panic-stricken. What did he mean
by that? It had begun to sleet—hard, frozen rain coated
the windshield wipers and made them groan protestingly
with each swish. She stared out through the freezing
mist. They were speeding away from the city center,
skirting an industrial zone heavily interspersed with gaping pockets of bombed-out rubble. The scene possessed
an appalling air of desolation, yet von Menzel did not
seem to see it. He began to chat desultorily about the
Uffizi Gallery in Florence with its fabulous collection of
early medieval Dutch and Flemish masterpieces. His talk
moved on to the genius of Giotto and Cimabue and of

their quest to break away from stylized Byzantine conventions into wholly new terrain. His speech was cultured, even eloquent, yet he spoke with a soulless detachment that chilled her to the marrow. Her stomach twisted into a hard knot. What is it that makes me their target? Angie thought with helpless rage. First it had been Josephine Urbano, then Louis and Tony, each successive victimization more harrowing and degrading as they attempted to capture her essence and twist it into a reflection of themselves. Nothing changed. She had somehow been trapped again, this time in the snares of this cultured Nazi.

The urban boulevard had long since shrunk into a winding country road. They drove endlessly through lonely forest, the tops of the trees lost in gray mist. Finally the car slowed and turned into a graveled drive bordered with thick stands of pine. The road sloped upward, opening onto a vista of a distant hilltop lodge commanding a 360-degree view of forest and field that extended as far as the eye could see. It was a vision out of a Nordic fairy tale, a coldly magical setting that was at once tantalizing and frightening.

Von Menzel stirred from the dreamy reverie into which he had sunk. "Ah, always the same," he breathed. "My beloved Elk's Leap."

The car drew to a stop in front of the three-story manor home that looked as though it had begun as a timbered hunting lodge and been transformed in the intervening decades. Angie climbed out and stood stiffly by the car, unwilling to abandon its relative familiarity. She felt like Gretel in Humperdinck's opera, a lost child frightened by the surrounding darkness of forest. She could almost hear the composer's eerily echoing score, the friendly note of the cuckoo transformed into something mysterious and foreboding.

Von Menzel took her arm and led her up the flagstone steps, where they were greeted impassively by a butler. Angie could not hold back a startled intake of breath as her eyes took in the immense entrance hall. The space was jammed with exquisite objects d'art—antique chairs covered with embossed silk damask; richly gilded commodes and cupboards, their surfaces crowded with Gothic statues; candelabras and goblets that seemed made of solid gold. A half-dozen medieval Flemish tapestries, their fringed borders overlapping, crowded the wood-paneled walls. Angie felt as though she had entered a museum in which the curator's aesthetic discipline had degenerated into concupiscent greed.

Von Menzel stood beside her in the doorway, observing her. "You see now what I meant when I told you last night that we Germans are not all philistines. Here you see none of Arno Breker's monumental mediocrities," he said with arrogant assurance. "I am a connoisseur."

Angie continued to stare, feeling the hall's claustrophobic abundance pressing upon her. "Where—where did it all come from?"

His answer was oblique, evasive. "These works are the finest representation of Teutonic spirit. As such, they belong in the Reich." He gestured curtly to the butler. "Huff, escort the fraulein up to her room. No doubt she would like to refresh herself before dinner."

The third-story eyrie, like every other room and hall in the lodge, was packed with museum-quality items. Here a dozen small paintings hung close together beneath the low-beamed ceiling. As soon as the dour, uncommunicative Huff had put down her valise and left, Angie went to examine the art more closely. She could not believe her eyes as she spied the artists' signatures—Watteau, Fragonard, Murillo, Tiepolo, Lancret. Works of incomparable beauty that had nothing to do with "Teutonic spirit." Driven by curiosity, Angie carefully lifted a painting off its nail and examined the back. Printed in obsessively neat German script was a date, a French city and a name.

Angie moved to the dormer window and stared out over the bleak northern landscape, feeling the hackles rise on her neck. The names on the backs of the paintings had all been Jewish— Rothschild, Rubinstein, Kahnweiler.

She stood outside the drawing room, uncertain whether or not to go in. Despite the large picture window, the room was steeped in gloom. Von Menzel sat in a shadowy corner near a huge, stone-carved fireplace, his head resting against the back of the armchair. His eyes swept down her simple black rayon crepe dinner dress, its neckline set off by pearls. "You look lovely in black." His voice had a soft, almost dreamy quality.

I was married in black, she replied in her mind. It happens to be the color of mourning.

Von Menzel came toward her, a smile upon his lips. As they walked across the hall to the dining room, their steps were muted by thick Persian carpets beneath their feet. He stood back to let Angie enter first and savor her response. She stood stock still in the doorway, her eyes drinking in a feast of Renoirs, Van Goghs, Cezannes, Monets. The Impressionist paintings seemed to radiate their own light, shining limpid and pure from the darkness that had swallowed up their legitimate owners.

"You will not see another collection of this caliber in all of Europe. They are worth millions—however degenerate my esteemed *Führer* may find them," von Menzel boasted, his tone lightly ironical. "The paintings are a fitting backdrop for the supper I have ordered Huff to prepare."

The meal was the most sumptuous Angie had ever been served. Appetizers of Bayonne ham and artichokes served on a pedestal of *foie gras* were followed by lobsters *à la provençale*, rich with garlic, cognac and oil; smoked sausage in crust; young wild boar from von Menzel's estate; fruits, aged cheeses and a different vintage wine with each dish. Angie picked at the food, thinking its lavishness an obscenity, but von Menzel seemed not to notice her indifference. He spoke as if France were his private larder, prefacing each course with an elaborate story of how the foodstuffs came into his hands— the *lanqouste* flown in specially from Brittany, the heady Calvados apple brandy confiscated from the hidden stores of Norman peasants.

"As you can see, I am a man who gets what he wants," he said, his tone oddly euphoric. The pupils of his eyes had constricted to pinpricks. "You would do well, Angelina, to covet my friendship. I can offer protection from the ugly realities of war. You need only look around Elk's Leap to see that."

She offered a conciliatory smile. "I appreciate your

offer, but why would a simple person like myself need protection?"

His dreamy eyes held hers. "War is cruelest to women and children. I can't help but brood over your little family—those two elderly spinsters left in charge of your son. It would be foolish of you to deny them what I can offer."

The fear coiled just beneath the surface threatened to engulf her again. How in such a short time had he managed to learn the intimate details of her life? In the midst of her panic Angie thought of Renata Baldini. What would the beautiful soprano have done if she had been here in Angie's place? Renata's involvements with her powerful protectors had always been a highly relished game in which the goal was to use rather than be used, to reap benefits without giving up anything in return. An ugly, risky game that Angie had no taste for. Yet what choice did she have?

When von Menzel spoke again, his euphoria was tinged by urgency. "What you must understand is that I need—I crave—an ideal of beauty. You must not—you cannot—deny me that." He drained his brandy glass and stood up. "Come, we'll warm ourselves by the fire."

Huff proceeded them into the drawing room. Angie stopped just inside the door when she realized that the only light emanated from the logs burning in the immense fireplace. Von Menzel seated himself in the shadows, while Huff set a silver tray on the table adjacent to his chair. As the butler left, she watched von Menzel roll up the sleeve of his dressing gown, then reach for something on the side table.

"I would like you to sing for me, Violetta," he said as if he were speaking to the air rather than to the living, breathing woman who stood across the room from him. "The 'Addio del passato' from the third act."

Afraid to refuse, Angie began to sing Violetta's haunting lament: "Farewell, smiling dreams of the past . . ." her tremulous soprano acknowledging that it was too late, there would be no more chances for the dying woman whose life had gone astray. As she sang, Angie's eyes followed von Menzel's movements. She watched curiously at first and then with horrified revulsion as he filled a hypodermic syringe from a small vial before plunging it into the soft skin of his inner arm.

Seeing her face, he shook his head. "Come now, why such a look?" he chastised her. "We all have our little ways of escaping. This is nothing to be frightened of." His eyes rolled up into his head. "We live in a mad, evil world, I fear. One must withdraw from time to time in order to preserve one's sanity," he uttered in an eerily drawn-out way. "Go on, my dearest, sing." His head began to move slowly in time to some ghostly music playing in his mind.

As Angie continued the aria, the passionately lamenting notes rising up from her throat faltered badly, but he seemed not to notice. He had begun to sway and move his arms in graceful arcs as if he were conducting an orchestra. Then he started to sing Alfredo's lines: "Come, oh my dearest, far from the city . . ." Still singing, he stood up and tottered toward Angie. Dropping to his knees before her, he wrapped his arms around her waist. Angie was frozen with fear. Before she could do anything, he sank slowly to the carpet. She stared down in horror at his unconscious form. Suddenly the silence of the room was punctuated by a hissing shower of sparks as a log shifted.

Angie tiptoed backward into the hall, her eyes fixed on von Menzel. She prayed his self-administered, enchanted spell would not be broken before morning.

Angie awakened to the thrumming roar of an airplane. She threw back the puffy white eider down and ran to the window. The plane banked left and pointed its nose toward a long, flat stretch of meadow a few hundred yards from the lodge. It touched down bumpily on the grass field and taxied to a stop at the far end. A small truck puttered across the field to meet it. She watched the pilot open the small cargo plane's side doors. Within minutes, several crates had been transferred from the plane to the truck. More loot, she thought in disgust.

A soft knock at her door caused Angie to whirl around. She finger-combed her hair and smoothed as best she could the wrinkled dress in which she had slept. The Louis XV chair she had shoved up under the doorknob the night before seemed a pitiful defense by daylight. Its delicate, painted limbs would have splintered into matchsticks at the first attempt to force the door. Hastily she returned the chair to its rightful place and opened the door.

"Good morning, signorina." Von Menzel greeted her with formal courtesy. "Your plane is waiting."

She gaped at him, thinking she had misunderstood. "I beg your pardon?"

"My pilot is waiting to fly you to Milan," he said as calmly as if announcing a taxi. "I am certain you would not wish to miss your scheduled performance tonight."

Moments later, they stood facing each other downstairs in the hall. "You have honored Elk's Leap by your visit," he said in his curiously stiff, old-fashioned manner. "We will see each other again soon, I promise you." He bent down slightly and brushed his thin bloodless lips across her cheek just as Huff appeared carrying a full-length Russian sable coat, the luxuriant black fur tipped with silver.

She shook her head vehemently when von Menzel draped it capelike around her shoulders. "No, please!" As it settled about her, Angie caught a faint whiff of Chanel perfume. For all the warmth of the fur, Angie shivered.

A scant three hours after they had taken off from Elk's Leap, the swastika-emblazoned Fokker landed at Linate Field outside Milan. Reporters and photographers from the *Prensa* crowded up as Angie stepped from the plane. They peppered her with questions about her triumphant reception at the Berlin State Opera, circling more delicately around the circumstances of her overnight sojourn with the high-ranking Luftwaffe general. Her voice huskier than ever after the cold, drafty flight, Angie fended off their questions with an angry "Just leave me alone. I'm exhausted."

Having seen the deadly effects of envious gossip on operatic careers, she was determined at all costs to keep her personal life inviolate. Angie wanted fame, not notoriety. She was still naive enough to believe that one could be achieved without the other.

* * *

The apartment was quiet when Angie arrived home, although she sensed tension in the air as soon as she stepped into the foyer. Madame came out of the music room, her hands clasped tightly in front of her. "Thank God," she said sharply. "We were worried sick when Cichetti called to tell me you had been detained in Berlin. What happened?"

Marshall, his mouth rimmed with chocolate, burst from the kitchen at the opposite end of the hall and hurtled himself at his mother.

Sarah came out behind him holding an enormous delivery box filled with fresh fruit, Austrian chocolates and bottles of Alsatian wines. "I think it is obvious what has happened, Giulia," Sarah said with cool malice. "Your dear, sweet Angelina has acquired a Nazi lover."

Angie's face went white. "I will thank you not to jump to outrageous conclusions," she said, catching the boy up in her arms. "If you ever speak that way again in front of my son, I will slap your mouth shut."

"Enough!" Madame barked. "Marshallino, go back into the kitchen and help Clara. Angelina, you and Sarah will come into the drawing room. We must talk."

27

In Italy, Christmas officially began eight days before December 25. But in this winter of 1942 there seemed little to celebrate. Thinking back to her first Christmas in Milan, Angie remembered how the grocers' windows had overflowed with colorful abundance: mountains of prosciutto hams formed backdrops for elaborate manger scenes carved out of butter, Sicilian breads decorated with bright marzipan fruits and vegetables, pyramids of tangerines and foil-wrapped chocolates. Wonderful sights that were nothing but memories now.

She tossed a coin to an old Abruzzeze minstrel dressed

in rags. His *zampogne* piped a plaintive melody that
followed her as she hurried past a tired window display of
shriveled carrots, their feathered tops tied with a bit of
red string. Clara's shopping basket bounced heavily against
her hip. Inside it were tins of French *paté* and Russian
caviar, stuffed grape leaves from Greece, Egyptian
dates—a rich assortment of delicacies representing every
nation under Axis subjugation. For the past two months,
the foodstuffs had been arriving in an unending stream
from Werner von Menzel. The little household had shared
the booty with their neighbors, whose gratitude was invariably tinged with curiosity and suspicion. Not that
Angie could blame them. She felt as though she had
opened a Pandora's box. But what was she to do
otherwise—stockpile them? The very idea filled her with
distaste. Her mind still recoiled at the memory of Elk
Leap's groaning cellars, its bathroom cupboards piled
high with enough boxes of milled French soaps to last ten
years. So she carried her overflowing basket to La Scala,
all the while knowing her holiday gifts would be accepted
with ill-concealed disdain.

Angie went in through the opera house's side entrance,
where the alcoholic doorman Federico was on duty. Wishing him a merry Christmas, she handed him one of the
tins, knowing he would trade it for several bottles of
cheap brandy. She walked through the maze of empty
offices and storage rooms toward the stage, where the
company always celebrated its annual "family" Christmas
party. La Scala was indeed a large, close-knit family,
fiercely loyal if one of its members were attacked from
the outside but just as fierce in squabbling among themselves. She followed the sound of laughter and merry-
making, stopping dead at the sight of the real-life *precepio*
that had been arranged on stage. The fat-tailed sheep
and mangy camel, refugees from last night's Aida specta-
cle, were tethered to a makeshift stable someone had
constructed of storage crates. There was a manger, too,
and one of the front-office secretaries with a reputation
for being wild had been costumed, naturally, as the Virgin Mary. The scene filled Angie with sadness. Last year
she would have been in on the hijinks from the very
start. Now she hadn't even heard a word about it.

"But you must have realized the consequences," Madame Giulia had said to her after the newspapers and magazines had played up the photograph of her stepping off the Luftwaffe plane in the luxurious fur coat. Over and over again, Angie had protested to her colleagues that the situation wasn't what they thought. Desperately she tried to convince them that she had accepted his gifts only out of fear, until finally she realized that they *wanted* to believe the worst about her. And why shouldn't they when von Menzel persisted in bombarding her almost daily with packages and long, rambling letters that moved between poetic meditations on *Weltschmerz* and treasonous assessments of the Nazi war effort. His beloved Reich had reached the turning point toward destruction, he wrote to her. The Russians would never let Stalingrad fall; Hitler's glorious eastern offensive had mired down forever on the vast frozen plains. He seemed to be corresponding with himself and Angie was merely a conduit for the outpourings of his tortured soul. He appeared in Milan at unexpected times, whisking her off to dinner and then overwhelming her with protestations of his adoration. She was not a woman to him; he had made her into some idealized dream-goddess.

Angie slowly made her way through the crowd on stage, accustomed by now to the sidelong glances and whispered exchanges that inevitably followed in her wake. Cichetti, the stage manager, stood on an upturned crate, presiding as usual over the party. He had already begun the time-honored Milanese ceremony of cutting the *panettone* and dividing the big porous-textured yellow cake into three slices, which were now being passed hand to hand. Each member of the family had to eat a bite, according to legend, in order to insure good luck for the coming year. Eventually the cake made its way to Angie. She brushed a bit of what she thought was flour from its surface and raised it to her lips. Just then she was overcome by a fit of sneezing.

" 'He sendeth rain on the unjust,' " someone quipped, and a malicious titter ran through the crowd.

Her eyes and nose streaming from the sneezing powder, Angie dropped the bread. As she stumbled toward the wings, she noticed Sergio's eyes on her. Although they were filled with pity, he made no move to come to her assistance.

Marshall bounced restlessly on the train seat, forgetting that Angie had just reminded him to be quiet and not bother Sarah and Madame Giulia, who sat opposite them in the crowded compartment. Lulled by the rhythmic side-to-side clack of the moving train, Madame slept, her head drooping forward on her chest.

"But how will the *Gesu Bambino* know where I am?" Marshall chattered in rapid-fire Italian.

"He'll know," Angie answered him in English as she smoothed back his wild thatch of curls. "Why don't you speak English to me, darling?"

He shook his head. His eyes slid to Sarah, who had her nose buried in a book. "I don't want to sound like her." Sarah looked up disdainfully but said nothing.

"Hush," Angie reprimanded him.

"But . . . how will He find us? We have to . . . to make the *zuppa di cammello*."

"We will, darling."

"Maybe . . . maybe there won't be a place to leave it . . . and He won't find us."

"Hush, stop worrying." Angie pulled him close and turned him around to look out the window. The train climbed slowly, winding past steep fields carpeted with snow that sparkled like diamonds beneath the brilliant Alpine sky. "We'll make plenty of 'camel's soup,' " she reassured him. "We'll use good thick Austrian bread that the camel will love. And he'll be so hungry, he'll gallop up that mountain with the baby Jesus, right to our window, to eat every bite. You'll see."

Marshall squirmed until he got comfortable, nuzzling his head beneath her chin. "And the *Gesu Bambino*— He'll bring me a present?" he asked wistfully.

"Yes, my little love, He will."

Thus reassured, Marshall drifted off to sleep in her arms while she continued to stare out the window, wondering if von Menzel would make an appearance at the *gasthaus* he had reserved for them. He had written that pressing matters would keep him in Berlin; still she wondered and worried. Feeling Marshall's round tummy beneath her arms, Angie felt she had made the right decision in not discouraging von Menzel's attentions. The extra milk and egg rations, the oranges and other foods delivered to their door, had gone primarily to Marshall. He no longer had the drawn, hungry look that had been so familiar to Angie from her own childhood. The ostracism she herself had to suffer—the petty revenge of sneezing powder and countless other mean tricks played on her—seemed a small price to pay in exchange. No matter how grim and destructive this war, her son would survive. She would survive.

Angie stood on the sunny terrace outside her room, drinking in the beauty of the mountain-ringed valley. A brass plaque affixed to the rail indicated west—beyond those jagged peaks—to Switzerland; due north beyond the onion-domed church in the village to Germany; east to Vienna. Here tranquillity reigned, a miraculous niche of sanity and peace isolated within this icy fastness. Angie drew the soft fur of her coat around her neck for warmth. The scent of her own musk and jasmine perfume drifted up, underscored by a fainter essence of Chanel. As soon as she had gotten back to Milan from von Menzel's lair, Angie had taken the exquisite sable to the basement incinerator, intending to burn it. By chance she'd found a hidden inner pocket that had held a note. The elegant French scrawl had been written on ivory vellum notepaper with the Wallenstein family seal embossed at its top. "Jacob insists we flee, but I can't bear the thought of leaving you. Please, darling, let me stay and take my chances with you. Your Nina." The note had still been in its sealed envelope, never delivered. She envisioned the unknown Nina as beautiful, cultured, duplicitous. A woman willing to risk everything for passion. Angie had kept the coat after all, as a sort of touchstone between Nina's hot recklessness and her own icy, steel-willed instinct for self-preservation.

A shout from the long, sloping meadow beyond the *gasthaus* drew Angie's attention. She watched Marshall barrel down on short skis, screaming with terrified joy. His cries broke off abruptly as he took a tumble and landed face first in the snow. Angie held her breath until he got up again, seemingly intact, and pushed off again. The young Austrian ski instructress hurried after him, laughing, with a big black-and-tan Alsatian barking delightedly at her heels. Angie watched until they disappeared from view, then returned inside to study the score of *Don Carlo*, eager to immerse herself in Princess Eboli's character. The deeper Angie burrowed inside herself as a form of self-protection from the world, the more she needed the catharsis of her operatic roles. Sometimes she felt as though they were all that kept her emotionally alive.

A knock at the door interrupted her. Frau Munz, the plump blonde manager of the small hotel, bustled in, bearing a cup of chocolate on a tray. "It's piping hot, fraulein. I thought it might warm you."

Angie nodded distractedly. "Thank you."

The woman stood by the desk, her expression anxious. "Normally we serve fried carp for the Christmas Eve dinner. It's Austrian tradition. But if that displeases you . . ."

"Sounds wonderful," Angie said, her head buried in her music. "Now, if you'll excuse me—"

"Ah, *gut, gut.* Then tomorrow, you know, we have our holiday goose. Herr Feldmarschall has sent a wonderful fat one." A hint of fear breathed through her obsequiousness. "We do everything in our power to please, you understand?"

Angie looked up with a sigh. "Yes. Yes, I do understand."

At midnight Angie and Marshall stepped out onto the dark balcony, carrying a little pot of bread soaked in water that the cook had helped them concoct. She steadied his hands as he plunked the "soup" down excitedly on the balcony rail. It will be a miracle if I can get him to sleep tonight, she thought. Before dinner, Frau Munz had allowed him to help decorate the spruce tree in the corner of the dining room. By the time they had finished, its branches drooped with colored paper, nuts and apples. His excitement had further mounted when she let him light a few of its candles before dinner. His enthrallment had engendered a terribly bittersweet nostalgia in his mother. Looking at him, she saw Gina that Christmas so many years ago in Coalport when the boys had rigged up a tree for her in the parlor.

"Mama!" Marshall cried. "Listen!"

A high trumpet blast, followed by the muted call of a French horn, floated up to them from the village. The harmonic brass chords gradually coalesced into the stately rhythms of an old hymn that enhanced rather than intruded upon the deep silence of the mountain. Across the small valley Angie saw torchlights winking against a steep meadow as a processional wended its way down to the village. She picked Marshall up.

"See them?" Angie said against his ear. "The people are coming to midnight mass. They're going to pray to the Christ Child. They'll ask him to make the war end."

He was quiet for a moment, watching. "But won't they ask for presents, too?"

Laughing softly, Angie hugged him close. His innocence soothed and protected her. Like her music, like the spirit of the vanished Nina, Marshall was a reminder of yet another buried facet of herself.

The wood-paneled room with its large picture window was so quiet Angie could hear the cuckoo clock ticking from the next room. Madame Giulia and Sarah sat like matched figurines on either side of the roaring fire, their reading glasses drooping from the ends of their noses as they dozed. How easily Madame tires now, Angie thought. She had never before pictured the woman as anything but indomitable, ageless. The thought of her one day growing old and helpless upset her. The last four and a half years Madame had been everything to Angie—friend, mentor, a mother to both her and Marshall. What would they have done without her?

Sensing Angie's thoughts were with him, Marshall looked up from his elaborate castle construction and smiled. Angie blew him a kiss and then pressed a finger to her lips, reminding him that he should continue to play quietly. She was delighted that the gift she had chosen was such a big hit. He had worked with the interlocking, handpainted pieces for hours, erecting castle walls and a moat, a keep. It pleased her to think he might possess some of his uncle Phil's flair for design. Marshall was a Branzino. He was hers and hers alone, and he always would be.

The sound of an engine in the valley, distant as it was, splintered the peaceful stillness of the mountain. Angie rose from the sofa and went to the window. She watched the Mercedes limousine laboriously crawling up the winding road. It took every ounce of her willpower not to grab her family and flee to the train station. She had accepted this path with her eyes open; she had weighed the advantages against the disadvantages and chosen not to resist.

As Von Menzel entered the chalet in a flourish, jackboots rang against the flagstoned entrance. Orders were barked to Frau Munz, who scurried to do his bidding. Marshall stared up in wonder at the two young aides-de-camp who proceeded their general into the living room. Von Menzel swept into the room as Sarah and Madame Giulia pulled themselves out of their chairs, looking dazed and apprehensive. He bowed briefly in their direction, then strode over to Angie, who still stood before the window.

"Weillkommen, Herr Feldmarschall." She greeted him with formal correctness as he bent to kiss her hand. She noticed the slight nervous tic at the corner of his mouth, then the extreme constriction of his pupils, and she had a fleeting memory of that hypodermic needle plunging into his vein. "May I present to you my family."

After the most perfunctory of conversations, Madame Giulia swept a protesting Marshall from the room. Sarah followed in their wake, her expression openly hostile and disapproving as her eyes swept over the Germans. With a flicker of his eyelids, von Menzel signaled his officers to leave, and he and Angie were left alone before the fire. Hitler and his generals had gathered at the *Führer's* Obersalzburg retreat a few miles north, and he had only a few hours, von Menzel explained as he withdrew something from the pocket of his greatcoat. Angie murmured her regrets at the shortness of the visit, while inwardly she breathed a sigh of relief.

"I have brought you a special gift," he went on, tossing the coat onto a chair. "I hope it meets with your approval."

Angie opened the package with trembling fingers and lifted out an antique tiara. "It's beautiful," she said truthfully, turning its silver tracery so that its tiny diamonds gleamed in the firelight. "I . . . thank you."

He nodded. "I thought you might wear it upon the stage. It is appropriate to a princess, do you not agree?"

Angie forced herself to meet his eyes and smile. She had been informed three days before that she was to sing the role of Eboli, a decision known only to her, Madame Giulia and Signore Massarro, she had thought. The ruthless efficiency of his spy network frightened her even more than the mad ramblings that filled his letters. "How—how flattering that you concern yourself with the details of my inconsequential life."

"Nothing about you is inconsequential to me." His eyes possessed the glittering sheen of the fanatic—a drug-induced euphoria that bubbled beneath the skeletal harshness of his features. "Put the tiara on. I wish to see you wear it." She slipped the delicate coronet of silver and diamonds onto her head, fastening its sides with a couple of hairpins. "Ah yes," he breathed, his eyes burning into her. "Like a queen."

At his insistence she wore the tiara to dinner, aware of the curious stares of Madame and Sarah. For all the homey warmth of the dining room—the savory smells of the succulent roast goose, the crackling fire in the grate and the cheerful ticking of the cuckoo clock—von Menzel's presence cast a pall over the gathering. He spoke but little, a remark dropped here and there amid the metallic clink of cutlery. Frau Munz, her upper lip gleaming with perspiration, carried platter after platter from the kitchen. All the energy and life in the room seemed concentrated in her frenzied bustling, to which von Menzel paid not the slightest heed. His attention focused on Angie, who attempted to distance herself by acting the imperiously aloof princess role to the hilt. At one point she caught Madame's eye. The woman's head dipped in an almost imperceptible nod as if to say "*Brava*. This is the way to handle him."

A sudden explosion of gunfire outside shattered the silence around the table. An instant later they heard a scream. Von Menzel threw his napkin down and hurried out. Marshall jumped up to follow, but Angie caught him before he could escape through the glass doors that overlooked the high mountain meadows. Holding him tightly with one hand, she shaded her eyes against the glare of the sun as it bounced off the snowy slopes. She could make out the figures of three people scrambling upward frantically, the third lagging well behind the first two. A Nazi border guard raced after them on skis, his rifle fire ricocheting off the rock-studded meadow. Angie's hands tightened on Marshall's shoulders when the lagging fugitive stumbled and fell, rolling back down the slope in a wild tumble. The two farther up the mountain stopped. "Run!" Angie heard a woman's high, anguished cry in German. "Just go!" After a taut, seemingly endless moment of hesitation, the others disappeared into the high reaches of forest at the top of the meadow.

Von Menzel barked an order that the prisoner be brought before him. Sarah, Madame and Frau Munz crowded anxiously behind Angie in the doorway, watching the soldier drag his captive toward the chalet. The woman fought with what seemed the last spark of energy left her. Like a proud cat delivering a mouse to its master, the border guard threw her at the general's feet. Her exhausted eyes slid past von Menzel and rested on the women gathered in the chalet door. Her gaze locked on Angie.

"Please," the woman begged her in harsh, ragged gasps. "Please tell them to let me go." Angie knew that the woman's eyes would haunt her for the rest of her life—so filled were they with wild despair. "I beg of you to intercede for me," she cried beseechingly as the soldier pulled her roughly to her feet. "My family . . ." She turned yearningly to the mountain.

Von Menzel regarded the woman with distaste. "From where have you escaped?"

Before the woman could reply, the huge Alsatian had dashed around the corner of the chalet, barking excitedly. It jumped up onto the border guard's chest. "Down, Fritzi," he commanded irritably. But the dog's high spirits were irrepressible. It whirled toward Marshall, nearly knocking both him and Angie off balance.

"Control the dog," von Menzel ordered. "Now."

In the confusion of the guard's struggle to collar Fritzi, the captured woman bolted from the terrace and started a mad run across the meadow. The dog, thinking it was all a game, started to circle and jump excitedly.

"Enough of this farce," von Menzel said in a calm monotone. "Stop her."

Eager to redeem himself in the general's eyes, the guard slipped the rifle off his shoulder and took aim.

"No," Angie whispered, pushing Marshall's face against her hip to keep him from watching. "Dear God, no!"

The rifle shot cracked, deafening as thunder in the thin mountain air. One instant the woman was scrambling desperately up the slope, the next she slumped forward and lay motionless on the frozen ground. Angie started to shake so badly that Madame Giulia reached out to steady her. Still she could not tear her eyes from the dead woman's blood staining the pristine snow.

Much later, Angie stood alone on the balcony of the *gasthaus*. Although the valleys were steeped in the purplish crepuscular light of wintry dusk, the high peaks to the west still basked in the opalescent fire of the setting sun. Switzerland—and freedom—lay just beyond: an irresistible beacon. She breathed a wordless prayer for the safe passage of the dead woman's family. When von Menzel appeared suddenly behind her, resting his hands on her shoulders, she started and repressed a shudder.

"The Jewess was a fool," he whispered, as if he had read Angie's mind. "There is no escape, Angelina, for any of us."

28

August 1943

A great paved esplanade fronted il Duomo, Milan's fifteenth-century cathedral—a marble colossus bristling with gables and statue-topped spires. Angie took daily refuge there, seeking not only spiritual succor but escape from the oppressive summer heat. She and Marshall would take a shortcut through the elegant, covered walkway of the Galleria past the half-deserted cafes.

Foreboding gripped the city. Von Menzel's mad ramblings had turned out to be frighteningly prophetic. In February the German Sixth Army had surrendered at Stalingrad, an event that signaled the beginning of a strong Russian counteroffensive. An Allied push in the Mediterranean late in the spring had resulted in the conquest of North Africa and Sicily. Now the Americans were inching their way up the Italian peninsula in fierce fighting against the German forces sent in to replace the demoralized Italian army. The once-thriving industrial zone that surrounded Milan lay in rubble from almost daily Allied bombing raids that encroached closer and closer to the heart of the city. Italy's surrender seemed inevitable. Ugly rumors circulated that her capitulation would mean ruthless Nazi reprisals. The terror had been mounting for months.

Angie shepherded Marshall quickly into the cathedral. Here a deep feeling of peace pervaded the cool dark interior. The musky aroma of incense and the low singsong antiphonal response of communicants at mass drifted back to them along the vast length of the colonnaded nave. They made their way to the south transept, where it was their ritual to light two candles before the statue of St. Bartholomew. Then they knelt before the tiers of flickering candlelight.

"God, please bless Mama, Z'Giulia and Signorina Sarah," Marshall whispered in his clear, childish voice. "Bless Z'Maria and *il mio nonno*, bless Z'Filippo, Z'Pietro, Z'Federico, Z'Vittorio, Z'Gina, Z'Nicoletta, and the soul of *la mia nonna* Rosa. . . ." Listening to him rattle off his prayers, Angie felt deeply saddened that her beloved family was little more than a series of names to him, despite all her efforts to bring them alive through her stories.

She herself prayed in silence, fearful for her brothers, who might even now be risking their lives south of here or in the distant Pacific. She prayed, too, for guidance in dealing with von Menzel. His infatuation with her had deepened with every German military setback, until it was now an obsession. He believed in some crazy, twisted way that she could save him from whatever disasters were destined to befall the Reich.

Angie and Marshall emerged from the cathedral into the blinding sun reflecting up off the vari-colored pavement of the esplanade. In the shaded portico adjacent to the Galleria walkway, a few peasants were selling wilted heads of lettuce from their small carts. The line of women waiting to buy extended the length of the Duomo. Angie took Marshall's hand and they went down the steps, moving along the endless queue of women in their worn, drab clothing. Angie was acutely aware of the contrast she presented, her sleeveless Egyptian linen dress and tan crocodile belt expensively elegant. The women's dull eyes followed her enviously as she and Marshall walked to the end of the line.

Angie's hand tightened on Marshall's when one of the women turned. Angie recognized Signora Bertolo's sharp features. The woman, a neighbor in the apartment building, had a daughter who had been rejected by the Scala Chorus. Ever since then, the mother had vented her spleen on Angie, choosing to believe that the only reason Angie retained her position with the opera company was due to political favoritism.

"And what do you do here, eh?" Signora Bertola railed. "Look at her and her son. Does she look like the rest of us, hungry and in rags?" The other women turned to regard Angie with heightened interest. "How dare you compete with us for these few miserable greens! This is all we have, while you . . . you have your German lover to provide every little kickshaw your greedy heart could want."

Angie felt hostility writhing along the line like an uncoiling snake. She backed away slowly, pulling Marshall with her. A crone with arms like sticks blocked her way. She collared Angie and spat in her face. Angie yanked free of her talonlike grasp and whisked Marshall toward the safety of the deserted Galleria.

"*Putana*," the old woman shouted after her in a shrill, cracking voice. "Whore!"

The dank palazzo basement reeked of mildew and the

acrid body odor of the forty pajama-clad tenants jammed inside, seeking protection from the Allied bombers. Angie sat on the stone floor wedged between Sarah and Madame Giulia, while Marshall slept curled up in her lap like a small puppy. She laid her head back against the cold furnace, knowing she probably smelled as rank as everyone else. How long had it been since she'd had a real bath? She couldn't remember. Ever since the municipal service had been cut off, they had had to collect water in jugs from the fountain in the piazza. Now they bathed once a week in the kitchen, standing naked on a towel while sponging down from the copper kettle heating on the stove. She imagined herself lying in a bathtub filled with steaming hot water: She could almost smell the flowery scent of Camay as she rubbed the pink bar slowly into a frothy lather; she could feel her soap-slicked hands sliding down her throat and shoulders, under her breasts and arms.

The keening whistle of a falling bomb intruded into her fantasy. Her arms tightened around her peacefully sleeping son. Thank God for the miraculous resiliency of children, she thought, even as her insides cramped agonizingly. An instant later a horrendous explosion shattered the air, and the ground beneath them shuddered. A low cry swept through the crowded cellar. Somewhere behind them a woman started to mewl like a lost kitten.

Madame turned to Angie. "Close."

"Too close," Angie whispered in a shaky voice. "We might have a gaping new skylight in the music room."

Madame's laugh was a dry husk. " 'E quindi uscimmo a riveder le stelle.' "

"Therefore we came forth to look up at the stars," Angie translated, giving the older woman a curious look. "Shakespeare?"

"Hardly. Those are Dante's words, from his Inferno."

Angie managed a small smile. "Apt."

After what seemed an eternity of teeth-jarring explosions, the all-clear siren rent the air. Marshall stirred sleepily. Angie kissed the top of his head, careful not to jolt him too much as she got to her feet, then extended her free hand to Sarah and Madame in turn to help them up. Sarah ignored her offer of help while Madame accepted gratefully, her bones creaking. These nightly raids were wearing everyone down, physically as well as psychologically.

As they filed up the stone steps and emerged into the dark courtyard, their eyes lifted fearfully to the sky. Although the palazzo itself was intact, the midnight sky beyond the red-tiled roofline glowed luridly in every direction. The lifeless air smelled of dust, smoke and desolation.

The extent of the destruction was driven home much later as the three women stood on the apartment balcony, watching their beloved La Scala burn down to nothing but a ruin of fire-blackened stone.

"It's over, isn't it?" Angie murmured, her voice catching. "I mean, not just for Italy, but for all of us."

"We should have left when we had the chance," Sarah said. "Now what is to become of us?"

"We'll manage," Madame said as she reached up to brush a stray hair from Angie's cheek, the unexpected gesture at once tender and reassuring. "Somehow we shall manage."

Angie took her coffee out onto the balcony the next morning. The sharp smell of burning embers still clung to the air, and wisps of smoke eddied up from the ash-filled opera house. By light of day, the destruction seemed even more devastating. She wasn't superstitious, yet she couldn't help thinking that the fire was an omen of greater disasters to come. In her mind she saw the shooting flames on Dago Hill the night Tony had torched the house next to theirs. She relived the firestorm of destruction that he had unleashed—her mother's death, her own isolation, the mounting sense of self-degradation that had nearly destroyed her. Echoing through her mind, she heard the crone in the cathedral portico shouting *Whore*! Angie's hands started to shake so badly she had to set her cup down on the rail.

She hurried back into the apartment and ran to the bedroom, where she retrieved the diamond-inset tiara from the bottom of her dresser drawer. Then she went to the cupboard and pulled the cotton cover off the Russian sable. The protective aroma of mothballs and crumbled tobacco rose up from its folds. She carried the tiara and coat into the living room and tossed them onto the sofa next to Sarah. "What on earth . . . ?" she cried in astonishment.

Not bothering to reply, Angie fetched a pair of tweezers. Sitting in the sunlight streaming through the French doors, she began the laborious process of bending back the tiny metal prongs that held each gem in place. Sarah hurried out of the room, no doubt to report to Madame this latest madness on the part of "her favorite." Angie worked swiftly, bit by bit amassing a glittering pile of loose diamonds on the coffee table. Madame stopped in the doorway, watching her. Angie dreaded having to explain the intuitive sense of foreboding that had brought this all about, but Madame seemed to comprehend in an instant. The woman called sharply over her shoulder to Sarah, "Bring Clara's sewing box."

"Where did she keep it?"

"I don't have the foggiest idea. Just go, look!"

After scurrying from room to room, Sarah finally located the box in the pantry. They were all a bit lost without Clara since she had left them for the comparative safety of her parents' farm in the mountains.

When Angie began to rip the lining of the fur coat, Madame intervened with her air of crisp authority. "Don't put them in the coat." She left and returned with a nondescript skirt. "Use this instead. It won't attract attention."

Acknowledging Madame's wisdom, Angie took the skirt and picked out two inches of stitching from the waistband with a seam ripper. Madame scooped up the little pile of diamonds and, cupping her hands like a funnel, she dropped the gems into the pocket Angie had opened in the waistband. Angie was just finishing the restitching when a sharp rap on the front door made them all start. The three women stared at one another. The knock came again, louder and more demanding. Angie jumped up and stuffed the skirt and tiara beneath the sofa cushion behind her. She rolled the fur coat into an unwieldy ball, looking wildly for a hiding place.

Madame gestured for Sarah to take the coat. "Throw it in the back of the hall cupboard," she said with the same calm equanimity with which she would have asked her to play a piano selection. "Then please open the door, Sarah."

Werner von Menzel swept into the apartment like a one-man blitzkrieg, leaving his aides posted outside. Angie steeled herself to calmness as he crossed the room toward her. "I will not waste words," he began without preamble, his manner agitated. "I have not much time. The *Führer* has called an emergency meeting at Munich, so I must leave at once. A car awaits you downstairs to take you to Linate Field. You and your family will fly at once to Berlin. From there you will be sent to Elk's Leap."

Where we will be prisoners, Angie thought, standing up.

As Von Menzel went on angrily, flecks of white spittle gathered in the corners of his mouth. "The Italian curs are abandoning us. We will destroy this whole country. You can be certain we will make every last citizen pay for this cowardly abandonment."

Angie crossed her arms over her stomach, her fingers clenched so tightly the knuckles whitened. "Herr Feldmarschall, my son is not here. I cannot leave Italy without him."

He looked at her in surprise. "Where is he?"

"We sent him out of the city to a farm owned by friends. To keep him safe from the bombings," she lied, praying for all she was worth that Marshall would not choose that moment to wake up and come running into the room in his pajamas. Out of the corner of her eye she noticed Madame gesturing sharply to Sarah, who departed to keep a watchful eye on Marshall and muzzle him if she had to. For once, Angie thought grimly, she and Sarah shared the same goal.

"Where is this farm?"

"Southeast of the city," Angie fabricated, situating the mythical farm in the opposite direction from the airfield. As von Menzel mulled over the logistical problem, she offered, "If you could send the car to fetch my son, we women could find our own way to the airfield. It would save time all around. You would be freed to return at once for your meeting."

Von Menzel recognized at once the practical sense of

the suggested arrangement. "Very well, then. It shall be done." He took her hand and bent to kiss it. "When next we meet, my beautiful Princess Eboli, you and your retinue will be safely ensconced within the walls of Elk's Leap."

Then he departed, swiftly barking commands to his waiting aides, one of whom was sent in the second car to fetch the boy from the country. Angie bolted the door behind them and slumped against it.

"Princess Eboli, you are duplicitous," Madame said dryly from the parlor doorway.

" 'All's fair,' " Angie retorted.

"Werner von Menzel might not see it quite that way."

"No."

"Any ideas as to where we might go?"

Angie gave her a weary smile. "As far away as our diamond stash will take us."

Angie and Marshall sat atop a pile of firewood in the back of Martini's rickety three-wheeled truck that looked more like a farmer's barrow. Madame and Sarah were crowded into the front seat beside the dreamy old care-taker, a most unlikely knight in shining armor recruited to carry three women and a child to safety. As the vehicle bounced from side to side across the cobbled piazza, Angie craned her neck for one last look at La Scala. Placards imprinted with the words *Evviva Toscanini* and *Ritorni Toscanini* had sprung up all across the fire-blackened stone facade. The fiery conductor Arturo Tos-canini had been banished from Italy years before because he had refused to play the Fascist anthem "Giovanezza" before opera performances. Now the Milanese were thumb-ing their collective nose at the regime. Angie banged on the tiny round window and gestured for Madame to look at the city's jaunty display of bravado: Long live Tosca-nini! Long live liberty!

The ride through the city seemed endless, despite the fact that the boulevards were eerily empty. Each time a police car or Wehrmacht vehicle passed them, its head-lights blacked out with dark paint, Angie's pulse jumped. She felt a little like Marie Antoinette headed for the guillotine in her tumbrel.

Chaos reigned at the train station in the Piazzale Duca d'Aosta. Hundreds of people shoved and pushed, fighting to get inside. Someone shouted that the express north to Lugarno in Switzerland no longer existed. The tracks had been bombed.

"Where can we go?" Sarah asked fearfully as the three women huddled next to Martini's battered vehicle.

An hour later, the old caretaker dropped them on the highway outside the city. Soon they were picked up by a farmer heading home from his fields. After they lay down in the back, he covered them lightly with hay. Angie clung in terror to her son, knowing that by now von Menzel's men must have discovered her ruse and even now might be combing the area for them.

As the cart bumped slowly along, Angie comforted herself with the thought that the Germans could not hold out long against the Allies. They would soon be free, she tried to convince herself. *Evviva la libertà!*

For five long weeks they made their way south—usually on foot. Enroute they met hundreds of other desperate refugees, fleeing toward Rome in hopes of meeting up eventually with the Allied forces. That's what we are, Angie thought dully—refugees. The charmed life was over. She had a premonition that more suffering lay ahead.

29

Rome, June 1944

The smoky dive on Via delle Quattro Fontane attracted German officers and enlisted men from the Wehrmacht headquarters because it offered them an ersatz taste of home. No matter that the beer was heavily watered and the tasteless sausages had sawdust filler, or that the Italian-

German songstress who serenaded them was in fact an American.

Billing herself as Garrulous Gretta, Angie swayed across the tiny, spotlit dance floor in a low-cut peasant bodice and short aproned skirt that showed off her shapely legs in black mesh stockings. She topped off her incongruous stage costume with a feathered hunting cap tilted jauntily over one eye. The overall effect was outrageously bizarre, and yet it seemed to please the Germans who crowded the club's tables, drinking themselves into oblivion night after night. Angie sang one German tune after another, mixing sentimental melodies with sassy numbers. The audience preferred the melancholy songs, singing along with her while the rumble of Allied artillery south of the city provided an ominous background beat.

For variety, Angie occasionally threw in a torchy Billie Holiday jazz number, "Baby, I know the blues." She sang the English words with an Italian or German accent, according to the inspiration of the moment. She would play the crowded front tables for all they were worth, perching here on a lap and there bending forward to accept the generous tip stuffed down into her cleavage. But always the men would avert their gazes from her face with its garish lipstick smeared around the ugly sores crusting her mouth.

In response to their applause Angie would drop an ungainly curtsy, staggering a little as if she were drunk. "Thank you, thank you very much. My mother was one of you, you know. She sang in a Munich chorus. She sang once for your *Führer*." Between sets Angie doled out these bits of fabricated self-history, her eyes vacant above the disfigured, smiling mouth. Her songs and sexily swaying hips elicited polite applause and an occasional wolf whistle.

The whistles would be from first-timers to the club, Angie knew. She imagined the regulars leaning across to whisper in their compatriots' ears, their breath hot and beery. "Good looker that one, but stay away from her. See those sores? Syphilis. Poor broad's mind is infected, too." Oh yes, the soldiers knew poor Gretta's whole tragic tale.

Occasionally an officer would request an aria from Wagner's *Die Walkure*. Angie willingly sang bits of the opera that she would never have attempted on a real stage, even before these past ten months of nightmare had robbed her voice of its power. She acted out the role of the warrior-maiden Brunnhilde, whose task was to bring fallen heroes to Valhalla, sensing the men listened for the premonitory warning that the somber aria conveyed.

Afterward, Angie would sit alone at the end of the bar and sip the owner's sour homemade wine. Silvio, a short, muscular man with a huge gut and pockmarked, mustachioed face, reigned behind the cash register, while his mousy, sharp-featured wife, Rachele, moved ceaselessly between the bar and the crowded tables. The only time Silvio abandoned his post was to replenish his singer's glass, finding it cheap enough insurance to keep her voice in form. As he approached, Angie pulled a wad of bills from her bodice and laid it on the bartop. "I have a terrible craving for oranges, Silvio," she said. "Can you find me oranges?"

"You want some nice round juicy fruit, eh?" He reached down to grab his crotch. "I will let you suck on these for nothing."

"No thanks," she said, nodding toward her wine glass. "I've had enough piss and vinegar for one night."

Unoffended, he laughed and scooped up the cash, shoving it into his pocket. "I'll see what I can do."

For all his gross randiness, Silvio was harmless. She put up with his nonsense not only because he employed her but because he had superb black-market connections. She knew that by tomorrow evening at the latest she would have her precious oranges. It was Rachele whom Angie distrusted. Sometimes she felt the woman's eyes watching her speculatively, and once Rachele had asked her if she had ever sang at La Scala, which Angie vehemently denied. Angie knew that Silvio's playfully amorous advances to her infuriated his wife. Angie knew, too, that the woman would have fired her long before if she hadn't been such a moneymaking draw.

The club shut down at two in the morning, and Angie would dart home through the dark, empty streets. Even with a pass exempting her from curfew, she did not feel safe. Terror was a constant companion. Rumors that were all too true swirled through the air: tales of torture

houses where the police routinely tore off eyelids in their
bid to "maintain order"; tales of crematories kept busy
outside the city gates of Turin; mass murder of entire
villages in retaliation for German deaths at the hands of
the Italian Resistance. Everywhere people clung to life
and sanity by their fingertips, while below them yawned
an abyss of unspeakable horror.

Angie ducked down a malodorous alley that backed up
to the Tiber River and into the dilapidated building where
she and her household lived in a small, ground-floor
room stuffed with four beds, a rickety table and an ancient sink and coal-burning stove off in one corner. The
hovel made the Branzino house on Dago Hill seem a
palace in comparison. They had long since spent Angie's
stash of diamonds on bribes and false papers that allowed
them to live in comparative safety. Now they scrabbled
for survival along with the other starving citizens of Rome,
waiting in long lines three times a day for bread, for
vegetables and for their inadequate ration of coal. Winter
had been a nightmare that had left Madame Giulia with
an arthritic hip and a persistent, hacking cough that not
even the beneficent warmth of approaching summer could
ease.

That deeply painful cough was the first thing that greeted
Angie as she entered the dark apartment. She crept over
to Madame's bed and lightly touched the back of her
hand to the woman's warm, damp forehead. "Thank
God you're home," Madame whispered. "There were
gunshots earlier—"

"Sshh, stop worrying," Angie whispered back. "Listen, I'll have oranges for you tomorrow. Doesn't that
sound wonderful?"

"And what did you have to promise that buffoon?"
Madame asked with a hint of her old sharpness.

"What he loves most: money." Angie smiled briefly,
smoothing the much-mended sheet that had gotten twisted
around Madame's bony shoulders. "Sleep now. All's well."

Feeling her way through the darkness past the beds
and old table, Angie made her way to the cracked porcelain sink. She lit a short nub of candle. By its dim
flickering light, she scrubbed off her make-up, including
the "sores" around her mouth, which she spent over an

hour applying each evening. Her cheeks and chin were tracked with real scabbed-over scratches, the result of applying make-up that had long since been worn right down to metal foil wrappers. But the realistic results were well worth it. Men avoided her like the plague.

Angie studied her scrubbed face in the shard of broken mirror that hung over the sink. Her cheekbones jutted out like blades and her eyes seemed enormous within the shadowed hollows of their sockets. Not only fear but hunger and exhaustion had left their marks on her. Sometimes she felt as though she no longer knew who she was. Her life had become a multilayered tissue of deceptions geared to that one solid, enduring truth—the need to survive.

Angie slipped out of her tarty milkmaid's costume and flung it over the drooping clothesline that stretched above the cold stove. Next to it hung the prim black dress with its white Peter Pan collar, which she wore for her daytime job—teaching voice at the small convent school where Marshall attended first grade. Sarah had found a job, too, playing organ at Sunday mass even though she herself was a strict Methodist. Between their meager salaries, the household managed to scrape by.

They were a real family now—she, Marshall, Madame and Sarah—christened with the surname *Caruso* by the engraver who had forged their new identity cards at his shop in the ancient Jewish ghetto across the river. A month later, the engraver himself had disappeared, a victim of a merciless roundup conducted by the Germans after they had sealed off the quarter and searched it house by house.

Angie blew out the candle, and on her breath was a silent prayer: Spare us, O Lord, from the slaughter and the hatred.

30

The convent of Santa Cosma rose at the top of a cobbled lane, a medieval gem tucked amid the ruined pagan splendors of the Imperial Forum. Blooming jasmine tumbled over the high stone walls bordering the lane, the vine's glossy leaves starred with thousands of tiny white flowers that gave off an exotic perfume. Angie savored the pastoral illusion of the setting and at times bitterly envied the nuns their cloistered peace. It was as if the world of war and its horrors stopped at the bend in the lane at the foot of the hill. She walked slowly down, savoring the warmth of the afternoon sun, her head still echoing with the pure voices of the nuns uplifted in the ancient, monophonic rhythm of a Gregorian chant. In the distant background she was aware of what she thought was artillery. The promise of liberation seemed as elusive as the nuns' dream of heaven.

When Marshall dashed far ahead of her, she called after him fearfully. A German edict forbade civilians to run or even walk at a fast pace. Angie didn't believe that they would be monstrous enough to shoot at a child, especially not a spindly kid like him; still, one never knew. She called to him again. He turned, waved and kept on running, disappearing around the bend in the lane. He looked so frail nowadays and the circles under his eyes were darker; he was always hungry, as they all were. Yet his sturdy young spirit prevailed, impelling him to run and jump and shout simply for the sheer pleasure of it.

"Mammina!" he cried suddenly, the word rising on a note of urgency. "Come quick!"

Angie's heart leapt with anxiety as she rushed to catch up with him. She came around the corner and nearly dropped to her knees in shock. Advancing slowly up Via de San Gregorio in the shadow of the triple-tiered ruin of the Colosseum came column after column of trucks and tanks three abreast. The words U.S. ARMY were stencilled in white against the drab green background of the vehicles. For endless weeks Rome's frightened, disheartened populace had waited for this moment. Now the miracle had happened, and every man, woman and child in the city was spilling out into the streets to welcome the liberators with one great ecstatic roar. Angie snatched Marshall up into her arms and started to run, eagerly pushing through the mass of laughing, crying, shouting humanity. Oblivious to the bodies shoving against her, Angie stood rooted to the curb. She stared up into the faces of the battle-weary, filthy men who grinned and waved down at the crowds from the backs of the trucks— unmistakably American faces that to Angie were the most beautiful she had ever seen. Tears welled up in her eyes until she saw nothing but a sparkling, blurred nimbus of radiance.

"It's over," she whispered, hugging Marshall fiercely to her. "We've survived! No more war."

Pandemonium reigned in the squalid little apartment. Sarah had upended her mattress and was feverishly searching for her British passport, which lay hidden somewhere in the depths of its stuffing. She intended to storm Allied headquarters first thing in the morning and requisition a supply of honest-to-God English tea. Marshall, delirious with excitement, jumped up and down on his cot, singing a garbled version of "I'm a Yankee Doodle Dandy," which Angie had taught him on the walk home.

" 'Yankee Doodle went to town, riding on a pony,' " Angie prompted him as she changed into her peasant costume. " 'Stuck a feather in his cap and called it macaroni.' " She jammed her ridiculous feathered hunting cap down over her forehead, making Marshall scream with laughter.

"Angelina!"

Angie looked around, still laughing. "What is it, Madame Giulia?"

"Come here, please," the woman said with quiet urgency.

"What's wrong?" Alarmed, Angie took the woman's thin hand as she sat on the edge of her bed.

"You don't intend to return to that disreputable club tonight, do you?"

"Of course I do."

"The cursed Germans are gone. There's no need now to pander."

"But there is still a need to eat," Angie said, lifting her joined fingers and thumb to her lips in the old peasant gesture. "The liberation will not change that. We have four mouths to feed in this house." She had to struggle to keep the irritation and hurt from her voice. Did Madame Giulia think she had enjoyed "pandering" to the Germans all these months? Her nightly cabaret act had kept them from starvation.

Sensing what was going through her mind, Madame grasped Angie's wrist in her bony fingers. "Listen well to me, Angelina. I speak only out of love for you. I fear for you—" She broke off, coughing.

"Shh." Angie grabbed a glass of water from the table and bade her drink. "Don't upset your—"

"Angelina," Madame said sharply, swallowing and fighting to get her breath. "Let me finish. Italy is a small country. It is not like America, where a person could easily lose herself in its vastness if she chose to. What I fear is that if you stay here in Italy, you will suffer unjustly for . . . for naive mistakes you've made. I think," Madame went on, stopping to cough into her handkerchief, "I think it is time you return to America."

"And I think it is out of the question," Angie said, struggling to repress the old feelings of guilt and fear that welled up with unexpected force. "You know my situation."

"The situation is no longer relevant. The monstrosities of this war have dwarfed old sins," Madame said, twisting her handkerchief into a damp knot. When she spoke again, her voice was a barely audible whisper. "Do you honestly believe the American police still care about the death of a gangster hoodlum six years ago? Angelina, your crime—if that is what it was—has long since been forgotten."

"What do the police care about war?" Angie said, her gaze focused on the woman's agitated hands. Their backs were marred by discolored spots, the elegant fingers thin and fragile as bone china. She thought she understood what Madame was leading up to. Unwilling to deal with the issue, Angie jumped up and moved swiftly to the door.

Madame pulled herself painfully out of her bed, brushing off Sarah's nervous cluck of disapproval, and clung for support to the rickety table. "Angelina, what is left for you here? You must take Marshall and return to America!" she cried, demanding that Angie hear her out. "Look at you. You're so thin your voice has diminished to a frail reed. A reed grown coarse and dry from singing in that ugly, smoke-filled atmosphere. Angelina, you must stop feeling responsible for my well-being. You must start your life and your career over again. You must return to America before it's too late. Before you become like me—useless to yourself or anyone else."

"Stop it!" Shaking, Angie turned back from the door. Madame's desperate effort had drained her. She looked gaunt and exhausted, her arms sticking out like spindles from the tattered nightgown. Angie belatedly became aware of the tense, watchful stillness that had settled over her son. How much had he comprehended of their argument? She moved toward Madame Giulia and grasped her shoulders. "Why are you doing this to me?"

"Because it's important. Because you are the future, Angelina."

"There is no future without you," Angie whispered fiercely, terrified as much by Madame's unwonted outburst of despair as by her physical frailty. "We haven't come this far, we haven't suffered this much for me to listen to such nonsense. You've taught me well, Giulia Francini. You've disciplined every ounce of self-pity out of me. Now I think it's time I return the favor. I'm tired of listening to you hacking like an old goose." Angie forced a note of irritation into her voice and was pleased to see a nascent spark of anger in the woman's tired eyes. "I'll be back tonight with oranges from Silvio. You will eat them, Madame. You will sit out in the sun beginning tomorrow and you will get rid of that damned cough. Then and only then will we discuss the future. *Our* future."

A banner hastily painted in red, white and blue hung over the sagging door frame that led down to Silvio's basement dive. "Welcome, GIs!" it proclaimed. "Cold Beer, Hot Dogs and Jazz." Downstairs, the Nazi swastikas and sentimental prints of deer grazing in Alpine meadows had been replaced by yellowing movie posters of Ginger Rogers and Fred Astaire and a battered tin Coca-Cola sign.

She made her way through the maze of small tables still topped with upended chairs. The only customer was an old policeman who sat in his shirtsleeves at the bar, his uniform jacket spread out on the zinc countertop. Angie sat next to him and watched in fascination as he patiently picked out the stitching of the Fascist emblem. Lying ready on the bar was the new *stelleta* insignia of King Vittorio Emanuele's army.

Silvio came in from the storeroom, carrying a large box. "Better take a hint from old Giacomo," he advised Angie. "Wind's blowing in a new direction."

She glanced around. "Nice decor, Silvio. Do you even know what Coca-Cola is?"

"What d'you take me for? Two years I worked in America when I was a boy."

"Also me," the policeman said suddenly, looking up from his clumsy stitches. "I worked in Cincinnati." He pronounced it 'chinchinati.'

"Shaddup!" Silvio roared at him in English. Laughing, he set the box down on the counter and lifted out a sack of oranges with the air of a magician pulling a rabbit out of a hat. "*Ecco,* your oranges," he said to Angie. "Direct from Palermo."

"Sicily?" Angie gave him a sharp look as she reached for the beautiful fruit. "You've hooked up with American suppliers already?"

"And there'll be plenty more from them." Grinning, he caught her arm and tried to pull her close to him across the counter. "If you're nice to old Silvio."

"If you don't behave," Angie whispered between her teeth, "I'll sic your wife on you."

As though Angie's words had conjured her up, Rachele appeared at the top of the back staircase that led to the family's living quarters. Her eyes smoldered in her haggard face.

Sheepishly, Silvio released Angie's arm and called up to his wife. "She paid me for the fruit, you remember!"

"Paid with what, *stronzon'*?" she asked, storming off.

Rachele still hadn't returned by the time the bar opened at seven, leaving her husband to serve tables in addition to his duties as boss. This did not put undue strain on him, since the place was almost empty. Despite his welcoming banner, no American GIs had yet found their way to the cellar. His clientele was limited to a couple of old drunks and three scared-looking kids who Angie guessed were deserters from the retreating Fascist army. She carried a bar stool out onto the dance floor, perched on it and began to sing sentimental Calabrian lullabies that her mother had sung to her when she was little. Soon one of the old men began to sing along with her.

The sound of heavy boots on the stairs cut short her crooning. Silvio jumped up expectantly from his cash register. Shading her eyes against the glare of the stage light, Angie could just make out the figures of two soldiers in white helmets ducking beneath the low arch at the bottom of the stairs. They wore white armbands blazoned with the initials M.P. Military police, Angie thought in surprise, her eyes moving first to Silvio and then to the three young Italian boys who sat rigid with fear at their table. The M.P.s, big husky men with stony faces, ignored the customers. They strode through the rows of empty tables directly toward Angie.

"Angelina Caruso, Italian civilian?" one of them addressed her in English. "Under orders of U.S. Army Intelligence, Fifth Army Division, you are hereby under arrest."

"O my God," she whispered, sliding off the stool. She felt the blood rushing to her head and with it a sharp buzzing in her ears and a panicky sensation of darkness rising up to fill her eyes. She clutched at the stool for support, willing herself not to faint. "But there must be some mistake! What . . . what are the charges?"

"Orders are you're to come with us, ma'am."

"But I can't. Please, my family . . ." she said, the words tumbling out in confusion as they took her firmly by her arms. "Please," she begged, "I have to let them know . . ."

She was marched up the stairs and out into the street like a criminal. Silvio's wife stood outside on the narrow sidewalk, arms crossed over her chest. Her face glowed with vengeful pleasure. "*Putan*'!" Rachele spat, running alongside Angie as the M.P.s bundled her into the back of a jeep. "Nazi-loving traitor! I hope they shave your head!"

The dungeon in which the M.P.s locked Angie was located deep in the bowels of one of the palaces on the Piazza Venezia. All through the night she shivered on a pile of old rags, her back to the mold-slimed wall and her knees drawn up close to her chest. Her thoughts ran in feverish circles. She closed her eyes and felt herself sliding down the steep, snow-covered embankment behind the old house on Dago Hill. Phil had set a trap in the wooded ravine at the bottom and caught a weasel. The wild creature had paced and snarled furiously for hours before finally losing heart and curling up apathetically in a corner of the cage. By morning it was dead. She always believed it had willed itself to die.

She shook off the memory, forcing herself to listen for sounds of life beyond the cold stone walls of her prison. At first she heard only the soft, incessant drip of water trickling into the stinking urinal in the corner. She dozed off for a few seconds. At the distant echo of approaching footsteps, her head jerked up in alarm. A key turned in the rusty lock and the door creaked open. She was about to jump up when a fat woman with stringy gray hair and scuffed slippers stumbled blindly into the cell. The door slammed shut behind her.

Molelike, the woman lifted her head and sniffed the air. Her eyes opened to slits. She peered at Angie's motionless shadow in the corner, then unexpectedly smiled. "At least we're not alone, eh, *tesora*?" The words came out in a breathy wheeze.

Angie stared back at her. "Why . . . why were you arrested?"

"They accuse me of being a spy for the filthy *fascisti* because I denounced a woman." Angie's gaze followed her as she shuffled restlessly about the cell, testing the door, spitting into the urinal. "This woman, she sat next to me on the train, going on and on in a loud voice about how if she were a man she would be a Partisan. The police came through the compartment, so—I denounced her. They stopped the train and . . . ratatatatat." Lifting her arms, she mimicked a chattering machine gun. "Executed her beside the tracks."

The woman's matter-of-fact recital horrified Angie. "But why? Why did you do it?"

The woman shrugged. "I was carrying a whole ham beneath my sweater from my brother's farm outside the Villa Adriana. If the Germans had caught me with it, I would have been the one who was shot. I diverted attention to that loose-lipped *cretina* instead, you know? This filthy war makes criminals of us all." She smiled sadly. "And you? You too collaborated with the enemy?"

"No!"

Footsteps clattered again in the corridor. The cell door swung open again, and this time two M.P.s entered.

"No need to lie to me, *tesora*," the woman wheezed, standing back as the men pulled Angie to her feet. "You and me, we're in the same boat, eh?"

As Angie walked between the stone-faced guards, her rubbery legs barely managed to keep her up. They pushed her toward a narrow, twisting stone staircase. At the top she stumbled, blinded by the light pouring in through the high windows encircling a beautiful Renaissance hall. They prodded her up another set of stairs; these were marble and balustraded with intricately carved wood. The uniformed men they passed seemed oblivious to the elegant surroundings; the beamed and frescoed ceiling glowing high above their heads might as well have been a corrugated tin roof. They seemed more interested in her, whistling appreciatively as she raced past. What a sight I must look in this low-cut milkmaid's outfit and my stockings in shreds, she thought. Suddenly she realized the silly hunter's cap was still pinned to her hair.

Midway down the long corridor, the M.P.s stopped

abruptly before a door and knocked. A muffled voice bid them enter. "Prisoner, sir," the soldier on her right announced crisply, pushing her ahead of him into the room. The officer stood with his back to them, his head bent over hundreds of folders piled on the narrow table behind his desk. Without waiting for his response, the M.P.s backed out of the room and closed the door again, leaving her alone with her interrogator. Her eyes darted nervously around the small room: the serenely innocent smiles of the frescoed cherubs on the ceiling seemed to mock her. She watched the man's back as he searched impatiently through the stacks of documents. What could he possibly know about her, save what the vengeful Rachele had reported? Angie's heart pounded so loudly she was sure he must hear it. At last he found what he seemed to be searching for and turned to face her.

Angie caught her breath sharply.

Numb with shock, she simply stared, unable to believe it was really him. His face seemed fuller, his shoulders broader. His eyes had changed, too, their irrepressible twinkle tamped down to a graver, infinitely darker flame. They frightened her because suddenly they seemed the eyes of a stranger.

"David?" The murmured name was a question fraught with uncertainty. And yet she walked toward him, trusting to the instinct that propelled her.

"Sit down," he said harshly, slapping the folder down on the desk. "Do you prefer Angelina now—or Gretta?" She sank into the straight-backed chair, her hands clutching the edge to keep from trembling.

Still standing, David opened the folder and slowly began to flip through its contents. She watched the news clippings flash by as if they were a nightmarish autobiographical film. In every frame she recognized herself: Angelina smiling among Hitler's generals at the Reich Chancellery reception; Angelina having her hand kissed by Feldmarschall Werner von Menzel; Angelina in black fur descending from a Luftwaffe plane at the Milan airfield; Angelina addressing the Wehrmacht over a radio microphone on La Scala's stage after a command performance of *Carmen*—that last photo left unrecorded her attempt to sneak out of the theater, wrapped in a cleaning woman's shawl, before the broadcast began. The stark black-and-white images reflected only the surface; they did not reveal the shadowed underside of Angie's fear.

"Don't judge me, David," she said, her voice low and urgent. "You don't know what my life has been like these past six years."

"I think it's pretty obvious what your life has been like," he said, not looking at her. He continued to leaf through the dossier, watching the evidence of her complicity pile up before his eyes.

Her fingers tightened on the chair. "I won't offer excuses. I did what I had to do in order to survive. Werner von Menzel was too dangerous to cross."

His eyes flicked up. "Millions of women survived in this country without having to become the mistress of a Nazi general."

"I was not his mistress."

"No?" His voice was that of a stranger, and she recoiled from it.

"You wouldn't understand," she said with icy remoteness.

"Try me, Angie." He propped his fists on the desk and leaned toward her. "Give me one good reason why I shouldn't put you in irons and let you rot for the duration."

"I'll give you three. Surely you know their names," she said, returning his cold look. "You seem to know everything else about me. Surely you know that I have a son whom I haven't raised alone. Giulia and Sarah opened their lives to me when I showed up alone and pregnant on their doorstep. I've spent the last two and a half years attempting to repay their faith in me. I made myself responsible for their survival, as well as for my son's," she said with simple dignity. "What I did I did for them."

"How noble of you."

His mockery smashed through her precarious wall of self-containment. She pushed herself up out of the chair, shaking with suppressed rage. "Nobility had nothing to do with it!" she shouted. "I did what I needed to in order to survive. I said I wasn't von Menzel's mistress, but if he had taken me to his bed, I wouldn't have resisted. Being a man's chattel isn't new to me, David. My father and my husband trained me well." Tears welled up in her eyes and she brushed at them angrily. "Their ugly lessons weren't wasted on me."

"I don't want to hear—"

"Damn it, let me finish!" She swallowed back a sob. "I decided that if I had to be a victim again, then by God I'd be a victim with some measure of control over what happened to me. I used von Menzel as much as he used me, do you understand? I kept four people alive and healthy while there was starvation all around us. I bought new identities with his diamonds. Von Menzel was a sick, evil man. I despised and feared him, but I played the role of his muse willingly—gladly, even." Starting to cry, she pulled the feathered hunting cap from her head and flung it to the floor. "The world looks at me and sees nothing but a dancing, clowning whore. What it doesn't see is that von Menzel never touched me here, inside." She laid her fist against her chest. "None of them ever did—not my father, not Tony, not the Germans. What I possess here is invio—" Her voice broke. "Inviolate."

The word echoed around the room, diminishing at last into silence. Angie stood, her head unbowed, and waited for judgment.

Slowly David shut the file and held it out to her. She stared at him uncomprehendingly. "Here, take it," he said, and she heard the weary undercurrent of disgust in his voice. "I've never seen the dossier. I've never seen you. You're free to go."

Unwillingly, she took it from him. "David?"

He shook his head, refusing to meet her eyes. "Just go."

31

Leaning over the cracked sink, Angie scrubbed stretched-out bras, torn panties and ragged slips, using the same sliver of soap that they had been husbanding for months. All the while she kept one eye on the pot of beans boiling atop the coal stove and stopped to stir it from time to time. At last she hung the dripping lingerie over the line that she had stretched above the stove. Drying her hands on her skirt, she turned to look at Madame. The woman was sitting up in bed reading to Marshall, who had cuddled next to her, listening raptly.

While Angie had been in jail, Sarah had stormed Allied HQ, returning not only with the tea she so sorely craved but with some sort of new horse pill, which she had been forcing on Madame Giulia. The Englishwoman had condescendingly explained to Angie that the pills contained "sulfa," talking as though she herself had singlehandedly researched and discovered the wonder drug. Much as Angie hated to admit it, Sarah's medicine was working. Madame's cough already seemed better, and her skin no longer had that frightening gray tinge.

Angie knew she should have been grateful; instead she was wracked with jealousy. Sarah had become the household heroine, returning from her daily forays with a pint of milk, a few eggs, a chunk of salt pork—luxuries they hadn't tasted in months—while Angie had not ventured outside the apartment since her release three days before. She felt as though she bore a scarlet letter branding her a collaborator. Her cheeks burned with humiliation each time she relived the scene in David's office. She heard again his disbelief, his disgust. It was as if his lack of faith in her had sapped her will.

A clatter at the door announced the Englishwoman's

return. Now what has queenie brought home? Angie thought as Madame called for Sarah to leave the door open to the cooling breeze off the river. Marshall jumped off the bed and rushed to examine the basket that Sarah set on the table.

"Did you bring oranges?" he asked excitedly.

"No, I did not."

"Why?"

"Because they are impossible to get." Exasperated, Sarah pushed him away.

"But Mama can . . . she can get oranges." He ran over to Angie. "Mammina! Me and Z'Giulia want some oranges. Can't you go sing at the Germans'? They're your friends, they'll give you some—"

Angie's hand shot out, connecting with his face. The ugly slap reverberated through the room. Sarah froze, her hand inside the shopping basket, while Madame winced as if the blow had been aimed at her. But what tore at Angie's heart was Marshall's look of shock and pain. Never had she raised her hand to him. She had vowed that her son's childhood would not be like hers—a life of dodging fists and living in perpetual fear of Pap's rages. Even Sarah, the self-appointed mistress of corporal punishment, had learned never to touch Marshall in Angie's presence. Now Angie herself had lashed out with venomous rage and hurt him. In that instant of self-loathing, she felt as though she finally understood her father. While his fury had landed on his children's heads, she realized that the true object of his hatred and bitterness had been himself. *He had wanted to give his children so much.* Angie remembered her mother's dying words. "*Wound up giving nothing.*" How clearly now she understood Pap's pain, his sense of failure. Full of remorse and sadness, Angie pulled Marshall close and hugged him with fierce tenderness. "Forgive me," she murmured over and over again, stroking his hair. "Forgive me, Marshallino. *Ti amo.* I love you."

The awkward, terrible moment was saved by Sarah. "I suppose you've burned the beans," she said witheringly. "And my salt pork with them."

The sharp criticism was so unexpected and yet so like her that Angie laughed through her tears. "Don't worry," she answered shakily. "I may be an ungrateful witch, but I'm not foolish enough to bite the hand that feeds me. The beans and your precious pork are just fine." Sarah sniffed indignantly and started to move toward the stove, but Angie blocked her path. "Go on, go sit down. You've been on your feet all day. I'll serve."

Madame called, "Sarah, I think I feel well enough to come join all of you at table. Will you help me up? Marshallino, come sit next to me," she said, lightly kissing the cheek that was still red from Angie's slap. "I'll tell you about the time the great Gandolfo came to sing in my parents' poor village and the townspeople showered him with presents."

Marshall nodded eagerly. "They gave him . . . gave him Easter bread and . . . and a whole tray of ravioli 'cause they were poor and didn't have anything else."

"Yes, little one." Madame laughed. "You know the story as well as I do by now."

Angie ladled out the beans, doling out a mere spoonful for herself while filling Marshall's bowl to the brim.

"Angelina," Madame said over the boy's head, her eyes sharp and knowing, "I do not approve of pointless, guilt-ridden gestures."

"For your information, Dr. Freud, I'm not hungry."

"No?" Madame answered dryly, picking up her own spoon. "Now that you have given up eating, how do you propose to build up the strength to sing? There is no room in opera for half-starved canaries."

"Where were you thinking I ought to audition?" Angie asked as she carried the empty pot back to the sink. "In the ruins of La Scala?"

"What has gotten into you, Angelina? The world hasn't ended simply because you spent a night in a cell."

Angie didn't reply, for her attention was arrested by a moving shadow outside. She stared toward the open apartment door while Sarah answered Madame with cutting wit: "Indeed, our Angelina should be grateful. Think what the experience will do for her prison tower scene in act four. *Il Trovatore* will never be the same."

"*Buon giorno*," David O'Rourke called, ducking his head inside the door. "Anyone home?"

"What are you doing here?" Angie said in a small,

defeated voice, wondering how much he had overheard. Her gaze moved to the laden box in his arms. She started to back away, until her head bumped against a damp brassiere on the clothesline behind her. She felt the hot rush of color suffusing her face. "What do you want?"

"May I come in?"

Madame, Sarah and Marshall turned, wide eyed, to stare at the uniformed stranger on their doorstep. David's presence seemed to fill the cramped room. His vitality—his sheer maleness—was an affront. Watching him, Angie burned with resentment. He had no business barging into their private lives.

Madame Giulia rose from the table and extended her hand. "Good day, sir. I am Giulia Francini. May I present Sarah Langton and this is Angelina's son, Marshall." She made the introductions with an air of composed dignity. "And you are . . ."

"O'Rourke. Major David O'Rourke, U.S. Army." He smiled as he shook her hand. "But please just call me David. I'm an old friend of Angi—Angelina's family."

Angie blanched as Madame's eyes darted questioningly to her, but she said nothing.

"As you can see, Major O'Rourke, our table is meager," she said with cool formality. "But you are welcome to take a glass of wine with us."

"You're very kind." He set the box down on the table and took the chipped tumbler that Madame had filled with the last of Silvio's lousy wine.

Marshall reluctantly tore his eyes from the American and stared at the box, from which emanated wonderful scents: real coffee, sugar, oranges. The lure was too great. As he reached across the table to peek inside, he accidentally knocked the water pitcher over. Sarah rapped his knuckles sharply with her spoon, and he started to whimper. "That is quite enough, young man." Turning on Angie, she said, "Your son's manners are intolerable."

Though flushed with anger, Angie had no intention of engaging Sarah in a cat fight in front of David. Taking her cue from Madame, Angie spoke with a dignified air. "You must excuse us, please. These last few days have been a strain on all of us." She watched David pull an orange from the box and hand it to a delighted Marshall.

"Come on, darling," she said stiffly, her hands on her son's shoulders as she guided him to the door. "I think we should go out and get a breath of fresh air."

Angie walked swiftly down the short alley that opened onto the river quay, turning with impatience to Marshall, who dawdled along behind, engrossed in trying to peel his orange. She could just imagine David's thoughts as he had made his way through the dilapidated clutter of the neighborhood. Patched sheets hung from lines strung from one crumbling mansion to the next formed a billowing canopy for the shouting boys who had improvised a game of soccer with a rotting cantaloupe. Marshall stared up in awe at the scavenged cigarette butts dangling from the corners of their mouths.

"Hurry up, Marshallino," Angie called, anxiety sharpening her tone. She had to get her son away from this squalor. Maybe Madame Giulia was right. Maybe it was time to go home. Marshall finally caught up to her, and she threw a protective arm around his shoulders. "Come on, darling, let's practice our English while we walk."

"Ma non voglio."

"Why not? You'll live in America some day."

He shook his head mutinously. *"Io sono italiano."*

Exasperated, Angie lightly tweaked his ear. *"Testa tosta!* What am I going to do with you?"

They had just turned onto the boulevard fronting the river when David's deep voice called at their backs: "Angie, wait!" She stiffened as he jogged up to them. "Can I walk with you?"

"Suit yourself."

As they strolled side by side, she refused to look at him. Her eyes roamed past the island in the river to the ruins of Caesar Augustus's theater on the opposite bank, made luminous by the soft golden light of late afternoon.

"This city's beautiful," David said, following her gaze. "Even in war it's beautiful."

She stopped and turned to face him. "David, what do you want—information about von Menzel? Things I might have overheard in the club where I sang? I'll cooperate. I owe you that much in return for my freedom. Just please stop with the phony friendship business. I can't bear it."

"Christ, you think I came to butter you up with bribes? Angie, I'm here because I care about what happens to you. Damn it, we were friends!"

She looked at him mistrustfully. "That was a long time ago."

"Not so long as all that." Noticing that Marshall was already halfway across the bridge, he asked, "Does he know where he's going?"

"He's headed for the piazza on the other side. He loves the big carved mask on the church that they call *la bocca della veritá*."

"The mouth of truth?"

"Yes." She gave him a sidelong look. "The legend is that it'll bite the hand of anyone who has a lie on his conscience."

David's mouth twisted wryly. "Would you settle for an old-fashioned American 'cross my heart and hope to die'?" He sketched an X on his chest. "I'm not lying to you, Angie. I would never lie to you. I'll admit I was upset when I read your dossier, but after you left, I thought about what you said. I thought about it for a long, long time."

She waited.

He smiled ruefully. "Will you forgive me?"

Her answering smile was tentative.

They sat at a cafe table beneath the branches of an umbrella pine. Pink and white oleanders bloomed in profusion around the perimeter of the peaceful plaza. Beyond the baroque fountain in its center, the graceful belltower of the church rose into a clear sunset sky that burnished the red-tiled roofs of the surrounding buildings to a dark coppery richness. Marshall had long since gulped down his ice cream and abandoned the adult company. He had raced around, exploring every inch of the old square, and was now trying to launch a stick in the fountain.

"Funny," David said, idly turning his empty cup in its saucer. "This was how I thought my honeymoon here was going to be—Maura and I drinking espresso in the evening, absorbing every nuance of this gorgeous country." His laugh was harsh, self-mocking. "How goddamned naive could a guy be."

Angie watched the impatient movement of his hands, the way they dwarfed the miniscule cup between them. The tanned hands were beautiful, the long fingers dusted with black hair below each knuckle. She could easily imagine those strong, supple fingers wielding a pencil or a brush—or caressing the curves of a woman's body. Feeling herself begin to blush, Angie said quickly, "Maybe it's not too late for you two to start over again."

"It's way too late. The only good thing to come out of our marriage is Katie," he said, his eyes roving around the piazza before coming to rest on Angie again. "Then, I guess you'd understand that."

"Yes."

Marshall came back to the table, looking happy but exhausted from his adventures. "Come rest," Angie said tenderly. Her heart constricted as she imagined Gina at his age. She hadn't been able to believe David's news: Her little sister had died four years before in a polio epidemic. Angie would never see her again.

Marshall climbed onto her lap and soon drifted off to sleep. The waiter brought more cups of the watery ersatz coffee. Pushing away her sadness, Angie pressed her companion: "Now, tell me more about Nickie, how she looks. Everything."

The deepening night and the soft glow of light from the splashing fountain invited confidences. Angie wished they could sit like this forever, wrapped in the warm cocoon of their conversation.

David stretched and grinned. "Look, I didn't mean to talk your ear off tonight. It just . . . it feels so good being able to sit and talk like normal, civilized human beings. Christ, but I've been lonely—and down."

"Me, too. I could go on listening for hours, even though I'm beginning to understand how Marshall must feel when I tell him about my childhood. It all has such an air of unreality, like I'm listening to stories about wonderful, exciting strangers. I'd give anything to be able to see my family again! It's been a purgatory for me, not knowing how they all were, what their lives had become." Sadness breathed through her voice. "Sometimes I wonder if I'll ever see them again . . . if they'll ever get to know Marshall."

David leaned across the table. "Angie, if you want to go back, I can arrange it."

She bit her lip. "It's so tempting."

"Look, if it's Malfatti you're worried about—"

"Madame Giulia doesn't believe I'd be tried for his murder."

"No, you won't be."

Something in his tone alarmed her. "What do you mean? How can you be so certain?"

"Angie, you're not a murderer." His expression was troubled. "Tony Malfatti is alive."

"But I watched him die."

"Angie, you wounded him badly. But he's very much alive."

Trembling, her hands tightened around her sleeping son. "O God, no."

As the tears slid down her cheeks, David was reminded of the way she had cried on the ship so many years before, a silent outpouring of grief that had touched him deeply. Looking at her, he couldn't believe that she and Nickie were sisters. Nickie reminded him of so many of the kids orphaned by this war. Their eyes were cool and hard. The world couldn't offer up any more ugly surprises than it already had. They were tough, smart, twisted beyond redemption. Like his wife.

Then there was Angie, who seemed to have escaped her sordid background unscathed. An aching fragility breathed through her, and yet—as she had told him—no one and no thing truly touched her. It was her recondite core that drew him. He was in love with her. He had been since their chance shipboard meeting, maybe even before that. He loved the mysterious challenge of her; he sensed a depth of passion that excited him beyond all reason. Yet he knew he had to resist any attempt to possess her. He knew that would only drive her further into herself.

David stood up. He shrugged out of his jacket and placed it gently around her, then lifted Marshall and laid him against his shoulder. "Come on," he said. "Let's get you home."

She stood up slowly. "David, I'm afraid."

"Angie, listen. Malfatti's not going to find out he has a son. And he's not going to find you."

"How do you know that?" She asked, her voice clogged with tears. "You found me."

"Because I knew where to look." His eyes glimmered darkly. "You don't think this was all chance, do you? I don't keep dossiers on every beautiful woman in Italy."

32

A warm breeze streamed into the jeep as it raced alongside the Tiber. The scent of pine wafted down from the woods surrounding the Renaissance villas that ringed Rome's seven hills. Her hair whipping in her face, Angie turned to smile at Marshall in the back seat. He sat sideways, using the picnic basket as a headrest, and his face was turned up toward the bright sky like a sunflower. She laughed with sheer exuberance and David looked over, laughing too, as if he understood. Around the bend in the river rose the great bulk of the Castel Sant'Angelo, its Roman walls augmented with fifteenth-century watchtowers and octagonal bastions. To the west she glimpsed the twin semicircular colonnades of St. Peter's Square before the boulevard jogged right and they crossed the river over the Ponte Margherita. Ahead of them loomed the monumental Piazza del Popolo with its terraces, statues and fountains. The tapering Egyptian obelisk at its center was an arrow pointed at the vast gardens of the Villa Borghese in the hills.

The jeep circled up to the left of the piazza, and David braked to a stop on the Pincio terrace. All of Rome lay before them—palaces, Baroque churches, the huddled rooftops of Trastevere and the ancient Jewish ghetto. Sunlight glinted off the dome of St. Peter's, set like a jewel within the thick walls of Vatican City.

David scrambled up to sit on the backrest of the driver's seat and leaned his elbows on the windscreen. As

Angie watched the breeze ruffle his short dark hair, she couldn't quite believe he was the same tense, grim-faced man who had confronted her across a desk ten days earlier. He seemed almost boyish again, full of the light-hearted joy that she remembered so vividly from her life with the Urbanos. He looked down at her, his green eyes brimming with a passionate intensity that she found irresistible.

"I can't believe this city, Angie! It's like a living museum. All the beauty that man can create—it's right out there in front of your eyes." His laughter was full of joy and wonder. "What an inspiration. I can't wait to get home and create something for a change rather than destroy everything in my path."

Marshall jumped up and down in the back seat. "*Ma dove siamo oggi?*" he cried excitedly.

"*Veni*—come on," David said, speaking to him in an improvised patois, which he called Engl-italian. "I'll show you the vista. It's *molto bella*. Very beautiful."

Angie watched them run to the end of the terrace, David leaning down to point out various sights to her wide-eyed son. He had indeed opened new vistas for her and Marshall, swinging by to pick them up whenever he could spare an hour or two from his duties. The long months under German occupation had been an exercise in survival. Their world had been limited by harsh rules and curfews. Even a short outing to get water had been fraught with peril. Angie's dreams still rang with terrified cries of "The Germans!"—the shouted warning echoing down the street moments before a Nazi patrol appeared in search of "volunteers" to be sent to labor camps in Germany. Now, under David's enthusiastic tutelage, she and her son were learning what it meant to live again rather than merely survive.

They drove through the rolling meadows of the Villa Borghese, past the cardinal's palace and the pine-shaded amphitheater. They stopped to watch the king's cavalry exercising their horses on the long oval course of the Galoppatoio, then drove on, coming to a stop finally above a small, exquisite lake surrounded by botanical gardens.

"Welcome to paradise," David said, lifting Marshall out of the jeep.

"Mammina! *Guarda le nave!*"

David laughed. "Translation, kid?"

"Boats! Boats!" Marshall cried, dashing down to the lake edge. "Look at the boats!"

Angie shook her head, her eyes bright with amusement. "How do you get him to do that?"

"Do what?"

"Answer you in English. He stonewalls me every time."

David winked. "Guess he just wants to be one of the guys."

"You're right about that, I think," Angie murmured, turning to watch her son. "You're really the first man he's spent a lot of time with—roughhousing, looking under car hoods, turning over rocks to look at bugs. Poor kid, I never thought about how claustrophobic it must be for him, stuck in a household with three women." She turned to David again. "The change in him this past week is amazing. I . . . well, I just want to thank you."

He shook his head. "No . . . I'm the one who ought to be thanking you."

"For what?"

He leaned back against the jeep and crossed his arms over his chest. Squinting, he looked past her toward the horizon. "I don't know," he said. "It's like all the destruction and the horror I've seen the past two years rubbed off on me. Now . . . now I suddenly feel good about life again." His eyes shifted to meet hers, and she could almost feel their caressive warmth. "You've made me feel good about living."

His words touched her deeply, yet she was uncertain how to respond. "David, please," she whispered, putting two fingers on his lips. "Stop."

He caught her hand and held it to his mouth, kissing her fingertips. A tumult of confused emotions washed over her. Gently she withdrew her hand and busied herself getting the picnic things out of the back of the jeep. They walked in silence down the hill and spread a blanket beneath the shade of a coral tree. Marshall was halfway around the small lake, talking animatedly to the old man who rented the boats.

Angie opened the basket and pulled out a bottle of wine while David stretched out on the blanket beside her.

"Just like old times, isn't it?" he said, watching her pour the wine into two tumblers.

She smiled ruefully. "Not quite."

He took one of the glasses and clinked it lightly against hers. "To the end of the war."

"And to your safe return home."

"What about you?"

"What do you mean?" She lifted the glass, barely noticing how the rough wine burned her throat. "What about me?"

"You know what I mean. You're coming with me, aren't you?"

She bit her lip, refusing to meet his gaze. "David, please, don't pressure me."

"I've got to. My unit's going to be advancing in a few days," he said. His voice became low and urgent as he reached out to take her hand: "We might not have time to talk again. Angie, listen to me. It's going to take years for Europe to rebuild, for life to get back to the way it was before. Christ, half the opera houses on the continent are in ruins! What are you going to do in the meantime—demean yourself and your talent by singing in lousy clubs?"

"Please." She shook her head. "I've been through this a hundred times with Madame Giulia."

"Angie, Angie . . ." His thumb rubbed a caressing whorl on the back of her hand, gentle but insistent. "Look, I didn't mean to upset you. I'll shut up."

She stared out over the shimmering lake, willing her spirit to be soothed by the tranquil beauty of their surroundings. Finches whistled to each other from the treetops, their call quick and urgent, as if they, too, were demanding a response from her, a decision. She sighed. "It's so hard for me, David. Now that I know Tony is alive, I can't go back, knowing I'd be in virtually the same situation as when I left—a victim. I'd feel threatened all the time."

"But I'll be there, Angie." His hand tightened on hers. "I can help you."

She shook her head. "You don't understand, David. You couldn't protect me from him. No one can." She sighed again. "No, for now I'm staying in Europe. When the war's over, I'll start again. I'll work and sacrifice until I get to the top. I did it once, I can do it again."

"Damn it, aren't you listening?" He shifted restlessly. "Most of Europe's in ruins."

"There's still Stockholm, Geneva, Paris. . . ."

She reeled off the names of the cities in a dreamy way that irritated and scared him, for he sensed her withdrawing to a place he could not reach. Turning away, he sat up and hooked his elbows around his knees. "Sounds damned lonely."

Angie inclined her head slightly, observing him. How attractive he was. She longed to reach out and trace the laugh wrinkles around his eyes, to smooth the taut line of his mouth. God, she was so tempted. She knew that this was a man she could so easily love and lose herself in.

As Angie faced David across the small restaurant table, her eyes twinkled with amusement. He had finally convinced her to go out—just the two of them, without the comfortable, distracting buffer of Marshall—and they had wound up at a tiny *trattoria* where the Allied liberation was still being celebrated two weeks after the fact. The white-aproned waiters jostled amid the crowded tables, their arms laden wtih heaping plates of fried *calamari* rings; they sang lustily, drowning out the battered mandolin being strummed by a tipsy patron in the corner.

Laughing, Angie lifted her brimming wine tumbler. "To life!"

"To us," David responded. Lifting his glass to hers, he turned his hand slightly so that his knuckles caressingly brushed the back of her hand. "To love."

As he smiled into her eyes, the din and bustle of the crowded room receded: She saw and heard only him.

"Come on," he said, "let's get out of here."

Outside, the bright summer sun beat down on the throngs surging past the fountain at the base of the Spanish Steps. Linking hands to keep from being separated by the jostling crowd, David and Angie raced like children up the majestic sweep of steps.

At the top, he caught her in his arms and kissed her. The hungry warmth of his mouth excited her. As his tongue lightly flecked against hers, his mouth tasted of tobacco and wild honey—a harsh strength tempered by sweetness that was inexpressibly wonderful. Suddenly the thought of his leaving Rome—the possibility that he might die in battle and never kiss her again—filled her with terror.

"David," she murmured, "I—"

"Listen," he interrupted, his eyes lambent with desire, "I know a little place not far from here. . . ."

She nodded quickly.

The drab boardinghouse possessed a certain down-at-heels charm. The old-fashioned bed in their high-ceilinged room looked as comfortable and welcoming as an old pair of slippers, yet Angie felt a rush of fear as David closed the door. Turning away from him, she opened the narrow shutters and stared sightlessly out at the city.

No man had touched her since her marriage. She squeezed her eyes shut against the remembered pain that flooded through her. She felt Tony plunging into her over and over again, until she felt like bloodied sandpaper. Sex meant ugliness, violence, domination.

David touched her shoulder, and she recoiled. "Angie, what is it?"

Almost inaudibly she whispered, "I'm afraid."

"You know I would never hurt you," he murmured, bending to kiss the nape of her neck. "Don't you?"

She nodded, shivering as he gently unzipped her dress. He pushed it off her shoulders, then eased the straps of her slip over her arms, tugging it down over her hips until it slid off her body. Slowly, savoringly, he undressed her until she stood completely naked in the golden afternoon light. He carried her to the bed and knelt beside her. She could not look at him, her fear mingling with embarrassment and shame.

"You're so beautiful," he whispered, likening the grace of her limbs to a ballerina in a Degas drawing, the ripeness of her breasts and hips to a Renoir, her strongly delineated features to an exotic Gauguin. As he talked, his fingers traced the outline of his words against her skin. Like a painter's brush, they embellished, feathered, whorled. The combination of his voice and the gentle touch of his hands was hypnotic. Her shame and fear gave way gradually to a languorous, engulfing warmth. She felt herself sinking deeply into the bed; she felt heavy and full like ripe fruit. A hot, melting sensation spread between her hips.

"You're so beautiful," he whispered as the tips of his fingers softly stroked circles on her inner thighs. "Someday I'll paint you."

She felt sensually feline; she wanted to purr and rub herself up against him. Driven by an instinct older than time, she opened her legs to him, arching her hips. When he lay atop her, she felt her flesh merging into his. He bent his head to her breast. His teeth grazed her nipples, and he began to suck and tease. The hot moistness of his mouth made her writhe with pleasure, and she pulled his head impatiently to her other breast.

She reveled in this unexpected interconnectedness of tenderness and passion, hungry to know him and for him to know her. Until this moment, she realized, she had never known what it was to enjoy a man's touch. David had awakened something in her that she had no idea she possessed. She was awed by the flowing undercurrent of femininity that surged up through her. She felt complete, alive in a dark, pulsating way that drew from some hitherto untouched core.

Later, as he lay propped beside her on an elbow, stroking her hair, David whispered, "I'm so damn crazy about you I can't think straight. But we have to. We need to talk about—"

"Sshh," she said against his chest, feeling the beating of his heart, so strong and vital. This moment was complete; it had neither beginning nor end. They dared not spoil it by talk of a future that might never exist for them.

Angie hurried out of the empty Renaissance palace that had temporarily housed U.S. Intelligence, shielding her eyes against the glare of the hot morning sun. Army trucks were parked in endless convoy formation, filling the great curving space of the Piazza Venezia. Watching the hundreds of soldiers milling about beneath the immense, blinding-white marble memorial that dominated the square, Angie felt a stab of fear. How in God's name would she ever find David in this crush of men and equipment?

She hurried from soldier to soldier, asking over and over again: "Major O'Rourke?" They shook their heads, shrugged. No one seemed to have seen him. Fighting back her rising panic, she kept racing from group to group until the soldiers blended together into a faceless sea of army green. She spied an M.P. who towered over the assemblage and tugged on his sleeve like a child. "Excuse me," she said breathlessly. "I have an important message for Major O'Rourke. Can you please help me locate him?"

"Saw him just a second ago, ma'am," he drawled in a strong Southern accent as he scanned the scene. He pointed finally toward a group of jeeps parked in front of a church, their snub noses pointed toward the Via del Corso. "Over there. Might want to shake a leg, ma'am. Looks like they're about ready to pull out."

Angie dodged through the crowd, oblivious to the curious stares that followed her. She nearly fainted with relief when she saw him finally, leaning against a jeep with another officer as they smoked and studied a sheaf of orders. She stopped to catch her breath and smooth back her hair. What was she going to say now that she had found him? When he had come by the apartment one last time to say good-bye, she had told herself she was glad he was leaving. She wanted no emotional entanglements to cloud her future; she hungered for success, and the money and security that went with it, the way a barren woman hungers for a baby. That obsession had to exclude everything else. She simply could not take the risk that a man's needs and wants might conflict with her own. And yet as she stood there looking at David, imagining him gone, she felt an ache of loss.

He looked up and saw her. Shoving the papers into his companion's hands, he rushed over. "Angie, what are you doing here? Is something wrong?"

"No, no, nothing like that," she said quickly as he pulled her into the cool shade of the church portico. "It's just—I wrote a letter." She reached into the pocket of her beautiful white linen dress, her last remaining touch of luxury. "I thought maybe you could give it to Nickie."

"Angie, who knows when I'll be Stateside? You sure you—"

"I'm sure," she said, holding up the envelope. "I . . . I want you to give it to her yourself. It doesn't matter how long it takes. I didn't mention Marshall, though. You understand?"

His hand closed over hers. "Don't you know by now you can trust me?" His eyes moved slowly, lingeringly, over her features. His gaze elicited a rush of melting warmth, like a sweet ache, that set her hips and thighs on fire.

"David. David, I can't lie to you," she murmured, her face flushed with heat. "I had to see you one last time."

He reached up to gently trace her thick eyebrows and graceful line of her nose, to circle the soft rose blush of her mouth with its faint shadow on the upper lip, as if to imprint on his fingertips a tactile memory of her. She inclined her head, curving her face into his warm, callused palm. "Oh God, David, what's going to happen to us?"

His mouth closed over hers. For all the hungry urgency of his kiss, it was sweet as nectar to her. She wanted only to melt into him, to let this final moment of mutual possession spin out forever. But it was not to be. The clatter of approaching boots cut through the encircling cocoon of their desire.

"Major O'Rourke! Excuse me, sir," the young soldier called into the shadows where they stood. "We're ready to move out."

"All right," he answered curtly, his eyes holding Angie's. "I've got to go. I'll write," he whispered.

She nodded, not trusting herself to speak. He kissed her once more, then was gone.

Angie went to the end of the covered portico, where the edge of the cool shadows bled out into the merciless sunlight. Shading her eyes, she watched the convoy pull out. She stood there until long after the last truck had disappeared, and the piazza echoed with a ghostly silence.

33

August 1945

August 1945

Nickie waited outside Horne's Department Store at the intersection of Ferry and Stanwix. Phil was late as usual. She walked to the corner and idly stared out over the wasteland of crumbling warehouses and seedy taverns encroaching uptown from the Point—Pittsburgh's historic heart, where the Monongahela and Allegheny rivers joined to form the Ohio. The grand old department store reminded her of a dowager fighting off the attentions of grimy panhandlers. But not for much longer, she thought. The city's newly passed urban-redevelopment law would put muscle behind the dream of razing the entire blighted area and replacing it with a park and eventually, if the rumors were true, a complex of high-rises.

Nickie walked back to Horne's main entrance, impatiently fiddling with her flexible gold watch band, which she wore twisted twice around her wrist like a bracelet. The costly piece was at once feminine and elegant— deliberately chosen to offset the severe lines of her gray silk suit. She put as much time and thought into her appearance as she did into her banking appraisals. Her male colleagues found her at once businesslike and attractive, an advantage she had learned to use shamelessly. Because she spent so much on clothes, she was always broke. But not for long, she reminded herself. As soon as the war ended, Pittsburgh would be on its way up, and she intended to scale the heights right along with it.

Phil loped around the corner with his long, even stride. A bunch of rolled-up blueprints were tucked under his arm. "Hi, Nick." He greeted her breezily, oblivious to the fact that he was late. "Come on, I'm taking you to lunch at the Penn. You've got to see these plans for the Point area. Collins said he'd try to get me a liaison role with the New York guys who're going to design this stuff. It's like a dream come true!"

Nickie let him chatter on enthusiastically as they walked back uptown. Typical Phil, she thought, envisioning magnificent skyscrapers while he still lived with Pap in the ramshackle Dago Hill house. Sometimes she envied him the world of beauty he inhabited in his mind. But damn it, she thought, one of us has to be practical.

Every time James Collins's name cropped up in conversation, Nickie felt a niggle of guilt, which she immediately suppressed. Collins was a powerful member of the Allegheny Conference on Community Development—an odd alliance of Republican money and Democratic political muscle spearheading Pittsburgh's renaissance. The man had put Phil on his planning team, choosing him over the dozens of other local architects clamoring for the plum position. Only Nickie knew the reason why her brother had been favored. It had begun the previous December when an unexpected snowstorm had dumped fifteen inches of snow on the city, stranding thousands of Christmas shoppers downtown. Nickie, who had stayed late at the bank, trudged across the street to the William Penn, where she bumped into Collins at the jam-packed bar. One thing led to another, and they had wound up in bed together in the hotel's spacious presidential suite, oblivious to the hundreds of people taking refuge in the lobby downstairs. Nickie, who found sex with Collins boringly unpleasant, tried to glamorize their sporadic couplings by comparing herself to the famous consorts in history who had used sex as a springboard to become the powers behind the throne.

"Are you even listening to me?" Phil complained.

"I'm listening," she said sharply. "That's all great, but you have to keep things in perspective. The Point project should be a strictly back-burner thing for you."

"You out of your mind?"

Nickie sighed. "Think of it from the point of view of those big New York designers. You think they give a shit about you?" she asked with coarse bluntness. "No. You have to build your own power base, Phil. And where does power come from?"

"Yeah, I know," he said glumly. "Money."

"I knew I'd get through to you one of these days," Nickie said, laughing. "Yes, money. And I have an idea for a project that'll provide all the capital you and David are ever going to need." She patted the burgundy envelope clutched under her arm. "I worked up some stats for a big housing subdivision."

"Tract houses?" he groaned. "I might as well still be designing army Quonsets."

"Don't think of them as thousand-square-foot boxes. Think of it as your contribution to the American Dream," Nickie said. "Listen to me, Phil. Congress has approved millions of dollars worth of home loans to returning GIs. You and David will handle the design and construction, while Louis and I take care of the financing. This idea's going to make us all rich!"

"Tract houses. Hell."

"If you won't think of yourself, then think of David," she argued. "He's been risking his ass overseas for three years. Don't you think he deserves something real to come home to in this partnership, instead of some pie-in-the-sky dream that's five years down the road?"

Nickie knew that was a cheap shot. Phil had never gotten over his guilt of having a medical deferment and a cushy stateside job designing for the government, while his peers were being killed on the battlefront. War had ended in Europe in June, but the Japanese were still fighting every bloody inch of the way. David had been sent directly from London to the Pacific, though Nickie had the feeling it wasn't heroics alone that drove him: If it wasn't for his daughter, David probably wouldn't care if the war lasted forever. Fighting the Japs had to be more pleasant than facing that bitch Maura. Nickie cast a sidelong look at Phil as they started across the street to the William Penn. She wondered if Maura had gotten him into bed yet. God knows she'd slept with every other available male in the city. But then Phil was more brainy than brawny, and she had heard Maura preferred them low-class and tough.

Suddenly a roar that seemed to shout from every building

on the block cut into Nickie's uncharitable thoughts, and she clutched Phil's arm. "What's going on?"

"I don't know!"

His reply was swallowed up in another tumult as hundreds of people poured out onto the sidewalks and into the street, jostling them from every direction. As they stared open mouthed, guests on the upper floors of the Penn flung open their windows. Masses of sheets, pillows and towels came cascading out the windows of the elegant hotel like gigantic pieces of confetti. The staff scurried out and collected the bedding in great armfuls, only to have more stuff dumped on their heads.

Nickie started to laugh. "The whole world's gone nuts!" Before she knew what was happening, a scrawny kid in a Western Union uniform had slung his arm around her waist and began waltzing her around in the middle of the packed street. "What's going on?" she shouted over the euphoric roar of the crowd.

"Japs have surrendered! Just came on the radio!" Then he started to sing to the tune of a polka: "Japs have surrendered, we'll have a barrel of fun!"

Phil eventually found Nickie again in the milling crowd and caught her in a big bear hug. "Can you believe it, Nick?" he shouted, tears in his eyes. "It's finally over! All the boys'll be coming home!"

She grinned at him. "And we'll be ready for them."

It had been one hell of a year—a snowy, bitterly cold winter followed by destructive spring flooding in March, and then rain, rain, rain all summer. Now Mother Nature had decided to grant a reprieve. As if in celebration of war's end, she had blessed western Pennsylvania with a glorious, golden autumn.

Nickie stood at the top of the woods ablaze with flaming maple trees and the deeper burnished russet of oaks. She envisioned hundreds of small frame houses marching down rows of terraces to Morgan's Run Road at the bottom. If the dry weather lasted, they could have the site graded and ready for construction in the spring. She had persuaded Louis to invest his own resources in the project, while she and Phil had kicked in everything they had. David O'Rourke was the last hurdle.

She was waiting for him now, leaning against the hood of the battered old Ford coupe Phil had bought as soon as gas rationing had ended. When she learned Phil had invited his partner to the big block party that the Mitchell Avenue neighborhood was throwing for their returning soldier boys, Nickie casually asked David to stop off on the way. It wouldn't look as though she were pestering him so soon after his own return home. Nickie was eager to go with this project now before others saw the need. It was critical that they be ahead of the pack.

Hearing a car engine chug up the hill, Nickie straightened and fluffed out the skirt of her coral jersey dress. A flash of expectation raced up her spine. She wondered what three years of war had done to him. She had always found David attractive, not in the bluff *maschile* manner of Italian men but in a low-key, soft-spoken way that hinted at the steel underneath.

He climbed out of the Buick, and she hurried over to meet him. "David, welcome home!" she said, giving him a quick hug and peck on the cheek. "It's so good to see you."

"Thanks, Nickie." He smiled. "It's good to be home."

She realized that the smile did not quite reach his eyes; they seemed darker and more shadowed than she remembered them. The lines around his eyes were deeper, the set of his cleft chin harder. She sensed that whatever he had seen and done in war, the experience had tempered him. He seemed tougher, more self-possessed and less eager to charm—a man accustomed to taking his own counsel. She got the feeling she wouldn't be able to manipulate him the way she could Louis and Phil, nor, she realized with surprise, would she enjoy it if she could.

"So," he said as they walked together along the high ridge of the hill, "what are these big plans you've got cooking for O'Rourke and Branzino?"

She abandoned the Katie angle she had thought would appeal to him—the line about how he could bring his daughter out and she'd hear kids playing in the streets, smell the aroma of baking coming from kitchens, feel the nice green grass growing and realize that this was something her father had created. Instead she said simply, "I see this as a jumping-off point for you guys. A quick-off-the-ground project that'll attract community good will and recognition. More important, it's going to provide a ton of seed money for O'Rourke and Branzino to go after the projects that will make you guys the biggest in the state."

"Sounds fine," he said distractedly as he strolled along beside her, his eyes focused on the steep furrowed fields across the valley.

She stepped her pitch up a notch, talking about return on investments and yields, holding the Katie angle in abeyance in case she had to throw that at him, too.

Finally he shook his head. "Nickie, relax, okay? I was convinced this was a good idea as soon as I heard about it."

Nonplussed, she stopped and turned to look at him. "Then why were you so anxious to meet me out here? I don't understand."

"I had an ulterior motive."

She gave him an arch smile, reaching up to smooth the lapels of his suit. "You're stealing my tricks, David."

"Listen," he said, gently disengaging her hands and reaching into the inner pocket of his jacket. "I've got a letter for you."

"A letter?" She laughed. "What are you talking about?"

"It's from Angie."

"Angie?" The laughter died on her lips. She stared at him in shock. "My sister?"

"Yes."

She looked at the crumpled envelope, refusing to touch it. "Is this some sort of a joke?"

"For God's sake, help me out a little on this," he snapped. "I saw her last year in Rome. We hooked up . . . by chance. She asked me to give this to you personally."

"Angie's dead," she said, rubbing her hand nervously along the side of her face. "I mean, I convinced myself she was dead, that Malfatti had killed her and buried the body or something." Her questions tumbled out: "Why now—after seven years? Why didn't she write before this? Where was she? Why has she stayed away?"

"Nickie, why don't you just read the letter?"

Her hands shaking, she took the envelope and stared down at the familiar handwriting. Emotions churned through her, murky and dark as river water: love undercut by anger, relief swirling into bitterness. She shoved it unopened into her purse. "We better get going," she said tightly. "We'll be late for the party."

The neighborhood *festa* was in full swing by the time they pulled up at the end of the street blocked off by a rope festooned with American and Italian flags. A pack of screaming kids chased each other back and forth beneath the flags, knocking them askew. Old men with handkerchiefs draped over their bald heads stood in the sun, playing the ancient hand game of *mora* with fists and fingers, shouting out *due, sette, otto*. Behind them the women argued over which foods were to be set on which tables. The wheezy tenor of a concertina breathed beneath the whole cacophonous uproar, like a nostalgic theme song only dimly heard.

"Welcome to the Hill," Nickie called wryly to David as he pulled up next to her and got out of his car. "Better brace yourself. You may not survive the shock of dancing the tarantella with a hundred Calabrians."

David grinned. "After six months in Italy, I think I can handle it."

Six months, she thought as they threaded their way through the gauntlet of women neighbors eyeing her rich 'merican companion with avid curiosity. She wondered how much of that time had been spent with Angie in Rome. Nickie had a million questions, but she sensed David was reluctant to answer them. In fact, she had the distinct feeling he was hiding something. She pressed her pocketbook close under her arm, desperately curious about the letter she carried, yet afraid of it, too.

Superb actress that she was, Nickie showed none of this inner tumult as she laughingly greeted people she hadn't seen in months. Pap sat on the sidewalk in an old chair that someone had lugged outside for him. Her father reminded Nickie of burning paper: a remnant of flame glowing through the fragile gray husk, vulnerable to the least wisp of breeze that would disintegrate it at last into formless ash. Still he clung to life, too stubborn and mean to die.

She turned away, drawn by her brothers lively jamming on an improvised platform: Freddie, home after sixteen harrowing months slogging through France and Germany, pumping Pap's old concertina as if he had never left the Hill; Pete strumming on a guitar, skeletal after two years in a Jap prison camp, his deep-set eyes gentle and faintly merry, reflecting none of the horrors he must have witnessed. Her heart twisted imagining handsome, dark Vic between them with his clarinet—he had stepped on a land mine in Belgium and been blown to smithereens.

Nickie shook off the sadness and turned to David with a smile. "Bet you never figured Tommy and Jimmy Dorsey would be playing here."

He laughed. "You think they'll play 'Same Old Shillelagh' for me?"

"Would you settle for 'Santa Lucia'?" Still smiling, she took David's arm and led him over to her aunt, who was marching down the sidewalk toward them carrying an enormous Dutch oven.

"Late as usual," Z'Maria carped as Nickie kissed her cheek. "*Sempre la donna d'affari*. Business, always business."

"Z', I want you to meet Phil's partner, David O'Rourke."

Z'Maria looked him up and down, refusing to relinquish the huge casserole, which he offered to carry for her. "Nobody touch my ravioli but me."

Phil came up the stairs from the house and hailed his partner. As David walked over to greet him, Z'Maria beckoned Nickie to lean closer and whispered, "I thought he had a wife, that one. So where is she?"

"You wouldn't want to meet her, Z'," Nickie whispered back. "His wife's a witch—a redheaded witch."

Z'Maria clucked her tongue. "*E pazzo*?"

"Z', you've got to forget those old superstitions," Nickie scolded her. "Just because someone's got red hair it doesn't mean they're nuts."

"Well, is she?"

Nickie laughed. "She's got her problems."

"*Ecco*," Z'Maria said, satisfied. "See? I'm not such a stupid after all." She plunked her Dutch oven down on one of the long tables that had been set up crosswise on the street. "Sit down, Nicoletta. *Mangia*."

"I'm not hungry, Z'."

"*Ma che*?" the woman answered, lifting her joined fingertips in a gesture of annoyance. "Look at you. *Troppo* skinny. Work too hard. When you gonna settle down, find a nice man?"

"Where would I keep him?" Nickie joked. "My place is too small."

"*Che cazz'*!"

"You're the one who should get a man, Z'. All by yourself in that house for twenty years." Nickie whispered maliciously, "I hear poor Carlo's wife died. Maybe you should make your move—what do you think?"

"And the poor woman just a month in her grave. *Gesu cristu mari'*, what talk!" Z'Maria blessed herself hastily, then snorted, "Besides, I no need a man."

"There, see? You and me, we think alike, Z'."

The woman shoved a plate into her niece's hands as the men came over to join them. "Nicoletta, here, make yourself of use. Fix a plate for David." She pronounced it "daVEED." "Filippo!" she said. "Go pour him a glass of my wine, eh?"

Nickie sat opposite David and Phil at the long table, wishing she could be absorbed into the music and the laughter, the excited buzz of conversation swirling joyfully around her. Even as a kid, one part of herself had always stood apart, watchful and calculating. Her gaze strayed to the end of the street, where a shiny, brand-new car pulled up amid the battered old heaps. Drawn like flies to honey, the kids rushed to inspect it. Tony Malfatti climbed out from behind the wheel, his thick shoulders thrown back at a cocky angle. Nickie wondered whom he'd had to bribe in Detroit to get the car. He came through the crowd, his gait rolling and slightly off kilter, swinging his polished hardwood cane as if it were a replacement for his lost potency. Some of Nickie's feelings crept into her face because she noticed David eyeing her curiously. He turned around to see what she was staring at.

"Who's that?"

Phil turned. "Son of a bitch," he swore softly. "Someone should hang him by his heels the way they did Mussolini."

"Who is he?" David persisted.

Nickie smiled crookedly. "Who do you think? That's our beloved ex-brother-in-law, Tony Malfatti," she said, watching David's mouth tighten.

Tony stopped at their table, biting off the end of a cigar he had retrieved from the pocket of his suit. "Too bad about Vic," he said in his guttural drawl, spitting out bits of tobacco from his tongue. "Like I always say, some families, they're meant to suffer, eh?"

"Then there's some people who never seem to suffer enough," Nickie answered quietly, her eyes cold with malice. "No matter how much you want them to."

The music trailed off. Every ear inclined without seeming to in the direction of the Branzinos' table.

"You know what, Nicoletta?" Tony lit his cigar and inhaled deeply. "You shoulda never gone to the city. A woman don't belong down there. It ruins her. She starts talkin' tough and ugly like a man—a man has to start treatin' her the same way."

"I'd like to see a man try."

Tony winked. "Better watch out what you wish for, *bambola.*"

Nickie pushed her plate away and stood up. Ignoring everyone's stares, she walked away. From her vantage point at the fence above her father's yard, she listened to the slow, deliberate tap of Tony's cane as he moved off to join Carlo DiPiano and his cronies. The music started again, and she felt the tension seeping out of the air as the crowd's attention refocused elsewhere.

A moment later David joined her. "Are you all right?"

She ignored his question. "So how much did Angie tell you?" she asked. "It would have been like Pollyanna to gloss everything over, to pretend her marriage was all sweetness and light."

"She didn't gloss over anything."

"No? But did she tell you Tony's a mad dog, held on a short leash by that one?" she said with sudden ferocity, gesturing behind her toward DiPiano. "His tongue's rabid. Don't get too close—the poison may drip on you."

"I don't get it," he said slowly. "I don't understand how your family still talks to Malfatti."

"Because Italians are like this," she said, twisting the fingers of her hands together. "Love, hate, loyalty, betrayal, it all goes on right inside the heart of the family, the community." She laughed bitterly. "When you're Italian, you're never really alone. You're caught up in an emotional milieu that's as binding as chains." She sighed. "Do you have a cigarette?" He shook one out of the pack in his pocket, and she took it with trembling fingers. "You know, I still hate my sister sometimes," she said, her eyes drifting toward the curtain of gray smoke veiling the clanking mills down in the valley. "The way she just abandoned us. Then other times, I wonder how the hell she got the courage to cut herself off like that. To make it alone." Her mouth twisted as David lit the cigarette for her. "I mean, look at me—I always thought I was a thousand times tougher than her. And here I still am. Stuck in the same old bullshit."

"Nickie—"

She brushed him off. "If you're smart, you'll go finish your ravioli, David," she said curtly, angry with herself for having revealed so much. "My aunt never forgets an empty plate."

Before he could say anything further, she hurried down the steps into Pap's yard. The house had the fusty smell of an invalid's room. How did Phil stand it? she wondered. She noticed the fresh coat of paint on the walls and the new linoleum underfoot, but it was like putting make-up on a corpse. The place should have gone up in flames ten years ago, along with the hovel next door, she thought.

She sat at the scarred kitchen table where she and Angie had once kneaded dough every Saturday morning and took the letter from her purse.

Dearest Nickie, she read, *where do I begin? Being apart from all of you has been an agony for me. . . . God, the ridiculous irony of it. I had to run out of desperation and fear because I thought I had murdered Tony. And now to think I have to stay away because I find that he's alive. I know him. His thirst for revenge won't ever be slaked. I have no doubt he would kill me if he were ever to find me. . . .*

Nickie read on, scanning the pages feverishly, unable to believe that this woman writing with such eloquent passion was her sister. Her head whirled with the idea of Angie, an opera diva, performing on a wartorn continent. Nickie saw her in her mind as a portrait in *Vogue*—one of those society women who always seemed possessed of such a soignée aloofness.

I try to envision you and Phil as you are now, but my imagination can't fill in the spaces between child and adult. For now, I have to be content with my memories—nurturing the hope that this separation won't be forever. As always, your loving sister, Ange.

Nickie's eyes blurred with tears. She felt like she was fifteen again, a gawky misfit avidly pouring over Angie's letters home, her mind filling the spaces between the lines with wonderful fairy-tale images that made her own life seem so drab and narrow by comparison. Secretly she believed that somehow Angie was the better part of herself—beautiful, larger than life, a woman who had reached the maturation of her powers—an utterly feminine strength augmented rather than diminished by the compassionate warmth underlying it. As much as she despised her sister, Nickie realized more than ever how much she longed to be like her.

Nickie lifted her head with a start. How long had the phone been ringing? She hurried to answer it. "Louis!" she said, shocked. "Why are you calling here? What's wrong?"

"Thank God I got you, Nickie." His voice was tear-choked. "My father's had a heart attack. Mother and I are at Shadyside Hospital. They—" He bit back a sob. "They don't think he's going to make it."

"Louis, I'm so sorry. Do you want me to come?"

"Would you?" he answered with almost childlike relief. "Mother's so damned remote, locked in her own grief. I just—"

"Louis," she interrupted with unwonted gentleness. "I'm leaving right now."

The private hospital had the hushed air of an expensive hotel, down to the thick carpet runner muting Nickie's footsteps as she made her way quickly to the east wing.

At the end of the corridor she saw Louis pacing and wringing his hands with an urgent restlessness, as if to wash away the accumulation of guilt. He turned and hurried to greet her, his eyes glassy with anxiety and shock. "Thanks for coming." He took her hands in his icy grasp. "It's been awful."

"Take it easy, Louis. You'll be fine," she reassured him, leading him to a chintz-covered sofa in a lamplit alcove. They sat down and she began chafing his hands, trying to bring some life and warmth back into them. "You know you can always depend on me, don't you?"

He nodded, his relief almost palpable.

The door to Mr. Urbano's private room opened. A nurse hurried out, followed by Josephine Urbano. "Louis," she called to her son, "your father is asking for you." Her voice was a ragged, grief-filled whisper.

He got up and Nickie rose with him, her arm unobtrusively supportive under his. As he hurried into the room, Nickie stopped before Mrs. Urbano. The woman's face was drawn and white with fatigue. Nickie had never seen either of them look so vulnerable. "Please, Mrs. Urbano, may I help in any way?" Nickie asked quietly. "May I at least get you some coffee?"

The woman looked into Nickie's eyes as if she just realized who she was. "How dare you intrude at a time like this?"

The woman's animosity stung Nickie to the quick. "Mrs. Urbano, Louis asked me to be here. Whether you choose to accept it or not, we are friends. I would do anything for Louis."

"You mean you would do anything for yourself," she snapped. She brushed past Nickie with a dismissive gesture and went back into her husband's room. Nickie caught a brief glimpse of a white-coated physician shaking his head and Louis sobbing over his father's motionless form. Then the door closed, shutting her out with a sharp click.

34

In deference to her employer's death, Nickie wore black to work all week. Today it was an Omar Khayyam design in rayon crepe. The loose, Russian-blouse jacket over a slim skirt was elegantly dramatic—chosen to remind one and all of the depth of her grief. She stopped at the desk of Madge Sinclair, the gray-haired secretary whom she and Louis shared. "Any word yet from him?"

"I'm afraid not, Miss Branzino."

Frowning slightly, Nickie went through to her office and shut the door. He had disappeared the day of the funeral and hadn't shown up since, though she had a pretty good idea where he had fled. She picked up the telephone and put a long-distance call through to the Waldorf-Astoria in New York, asking to speak directly to the hotel's manager. Identifying herself as Louis's secretary, Nickie explained that she needed to speak to him urgently.

Ten minutes later, the manager returned her call. "I'm afraid there's a slight problem, Miss Branzino," he said. The discomfort in his voice was apparent even over the loud crackling of the long-distance wires. "It seems Mr. Urbano has not spent the night in his room since he checked in late Monday evening." As Nickie digested this information, the man went on: "Shall I . . . do you wish me to contact the police here?"

"No!" Nickie said quickly. "That won't be necessary."

After reassuring him that it was probably a misunderstanding, Nickie sat back in her chair, chin in hand, and debated what to do. Although Louis's occasional trips to New York were ostensibly bank related, she knew his real destination was a certain Harlem bar. The trips provided an escape valve within the safe anonymity of a distant city. But part of the agreed-upon routine had been that he would check in with her daily so she could keep him posted on office matters. This disappearing act was something new and potentially dangerous.

Don't do something stupid now, she berated him silently. Everyone's counting on you to take up the reins. Don't let the pressure get to you. Damn it, Louis, I'm here for you. Don't you understand that?

Nickie was about to pick up the phone again when the intercom buzzed. "Yes, Madge?"

"Mr. Smithton would like to see you in his office, Miss Branzino. At once, he said."

"Thank you. Tell him I'm on my way."

What could he want? Nickie wondered. As chairman of the bank's board, the old man had stepped in provisionally to keep things on an even keel until Louis Junior had assumed the presidency in his father's place. Had the board somehow gotten wind of Louis's New York escapades?

Smithton was hunched behind his desk, his back to the tall window that overlooked the noisy congestion of Fifth Avenue three stories below. Josephine Urbano stood at his side, plucking at the tips of her black gloves. Seeing her, Nickie felt a prickle of unease. The woman had always remained in the background, seemingly indifferent to the day-to-day running of the family bank. What had caused this sudden turnabout?

Smithton rose slowly and came around his desk. "So good of you to come, Miss Branzino," he greeted her in his old-fashioned courtly manner. "Do sit down, please."

She perched on the edge of the chair, seeking some clue from his watery blue gaze. "As you might realize, we on the board have not been totally blind to your, er, contributions to this institution. But with the untimely demise of the elder Mr. Urbano, we have been compelled to examine your position in a, er, new light. Our operation here is, we think, rather confining for one of your, shall we say, far-reaching ambitions." He started to glance over his shoulder toward Mrs. Urbano, then apparently thought better of it. "Therefore," he went on, choosing his words with care, "we have decided to give you the opportunity to seek more fitting outlet for your skills . . . elsewhere."

"In other words, you're canning me."

"Good heavens, no! Oh my, no." Flustered, he fumbled for the long envelope on his desk. "In fact, as a measure of our appreciation, we have decided to give you this."

Nickie took the envelope and glanced inside. The amount written on the check was substantial. "Quite a bribe," she said, tossing it back down onto the desk and glancing at Josephine Urbano's inscrutable face. "Shame on you, Mr. Smithton. You should know me better than that by now."

He looked helplessly toward Mrs. Urbano. "Thank you, Arnold," she said, her voice soft but firm. "Would you mind leaving Miss Branzino and me alone for a moment?"

With palpable relief, the man shuffled quickly out of his office. "I'm disappointed," Nickie said quietly, standing up. "I wouldn't have expected such a cheap shot from you."

"And I wouldn't have expected you to understand, Nicoletta. I've lost much in my life. First my beloved Julia, then . . . Angie, and now my husband." The black mesh veil of her hat did not quite disguise the puffiness under her eyes. Yet for all her grief, the older woman exuded a certain singleminded tenacity that surprised Nickie. "I am not about to lose Louis to you."

"Louis and I are colleagues, Mrs. Urbano. We have a cordial business friendship," Nickie said coolly. "I work for him, I answer only to him. Our relationship has nothing to do with you. Therefore, I really don't see the point of this conversation."

"Don't you?" Mrs. Urbano's smile was bitter. "I've watched you these past several years, Nicoletta, the way you've wormed your way into my son's life like some female Svengali, trying to control his every decision."

"That's ridiculous."

"I allowed it to go on only because . . . because I didn't want to jeopardize Louis's new closeness with his father. Louis was deluded enough to believe that you were the one who made their reconciliation possible— that you were responsible for his successes here at the office." She toyed with her emerald-encrusted bracelet, twisting it around her gloved wrist. "Now that my husband is gone, I see no reason for continuing this pretense. Louis has taken a few days to think things over. In the end he'll realize that what I want is what's best for him. There's no point in your hanging on."

Nickie listened, sensing with quickened interest that the woman was actually afraid of her. Mrs. Urbano was no fool, after all. Although she obviously knew nothing about Louis's secret life, she did know perfectly well how weak her son was. She was not about to relinquish her guiding role in his life to a dangerous upstart. The gauntlet had been thrown.

Nickie moved toward the door. "I'll say it one more time, Mrs. Urbano: This conversation is distasteful and pointless. The decision about my future is not yours to make. It's Louis's."

"My son adores me, Nicoletta. In the end, he will always do what I want him to do."

Her parting shot reverberated in Nickie's head as she hurried back to her office. That's what you think, lady, Nickie thought as she stopped at her secretary's desk.

"Get Allegheny Airlines on the phone for me, Madge. I'm taking a trip."

Nickie stood in the elegant portico of the Waldorf-Astoria, waiting for the doorman to hail her a cab. A sultry heaviness lay on the night air, at odds with the electric energy pulsing along the streets. Nickie liked the feel of New York. It made her think of the high-gloss movies of the thirties—a crackling, tap-dancing atmosphere of bright perpetual motion. By comparison, Pittsburgh seemed a clanking dragon sinking in the smoking earth from which it had arisen. She could understand New York's appeal for Louis. Its quicksilver nature was more tolerant of human frailty than the masculine intransigence of his hometown.

The doorman opened the cab door for her and she slid into the back street. "Lenox Avenue and One-Twenty-Fifth Street," she told the cabby.

He turned to look her up and down, assessing the sheen of her thickly braided gold necklace against her classy black suit, the snappy forward tilt of her high-crowned hat. "You sure, lady? That's Harlem."

"If I wanted a tour guide, I'd have hired one. Just drive."

"It's your money." Shrugging, he threw the cab into gear and eased out into the snarled Friday-night traffic. They inched along the bottom of a canyon bordered by towering office buildings, emerging finally into the darker reaches of upper Manhattan. The cabby slowed as the glowing marquee of the Apollo Theater loomed ahead. "Here, lady?"

"Keep driving." She rummaged in her purse and found an old matchbook cover that she had taken from Louis's desk drawer. "You know the Esmeralda Club?"

"Heard of it, yeah." He shot her a sharp glance in the rearview mirror.

Despite the tension coiling in her stomach, Nickie almost smiled.

The street got narrower, dirtier; a rank smell of garbage wafted in through the cab's open windows. At last they drew to a stop. Nickie peered up at a torn padded door dimpled with studs. Nothing advertised the place as a bar except for that door. The entrance reminded her of Cheech Ignacio's Dago Hill joint—low profile and definitely low class. "You sure this is it?"

"What were you expectin'—the Ritz?"

"I want you to wait for me," Nickie said as she climbed out.

"Look, lady—" She silenced his protests with a ten-dollar bill. He shoved it into the pocket of his loud shirt. "Ten minutes, you got it? I don't want nobody mistakin' me for no fruit."

Bebop music washed over her as she pushed open the door and stepped inside the dim, smoky club. Men jammed the short bar and wedged into the maroon booths. A *tootzun'* band played on the tiny stage, seemingly oblivious to the white guys shuffling across the tiny dance floor with their arms entwined around each other. Everyone turned to stare at Nickie. She swiftly scanned the crowd, ignoring the suspicious stares and her acute discomfort. She had thought of herself as worldly, but nothing in her experience had prepared her for this bizarre, bluesy Sodom and Gomorrah.

A beefy kid with rolled-up shirtsleeves and slicked-back hair sidled up to her. A cigarette dangled from his lips. "How ya doin', babe—looking for a good time?" The voice sounded tough but curiously reedy.

Nickie noticed the outline of breasts beneath the baggy men's shirt and realized the voice wasn't that of a young kid but of a woman. "No thanks," she said neutrally. "Not my type."

The transvestite shrugged and turned away. Nickie made her way through the crowd, searching frantically for Louis. She found him in the last booth: His head lolled on the neck of a swarthy, mustachioed giant who in turn had his arm draped over Louis's shoulder and was nuzzling his hair. His hand was inside Louis's unbuttoned shirt, caressing his chest.

"Louis!" she called sharply.

"Take a hike, broad," his friend growled, revealing a wide gap in his front teeth. "Can't you see he don't want what you got?"

Louis stirred. He looked up, his eyes unfocused.

"Please, Louis, come with me," she urged. "It's important."

The giant pushed out of the booth, towering menacingly over Nickie. "I told you, take a hike."

Though petrified Nickie stood her ground. She looked the big guy up and down, noting the ornately tattooed MOTHER on his forearm. "Look, mister," she said in a conciliatory tone, "I don't want any trouble. I just came to take my brother home. Our mother's sick. She just wants to see him. . . ."

Louis staggered out of the booth. "What happened to Mother?" he wailed, slurring his words as if he were speaking underwater.

By this time a curious crowd had gathered, pressing in on them. Nickie slipped her arm around Louis's waist and tried to push through the men. No one budged.

"Let 'em go," Louis's mustachioed Romeo suddenly growled.

The men backed away, their hostile stares following Nickie as she led Louis outside.

They stumbled into the cab. The driver watched them in the rearview mirror. Louis slumped down, his head resting on the back of the seat. He reeked of cheap booze. "What's happened to Mother, Nickie?" he moaned.

"Nothing. She's fine."

"But that's the reason you've come, isn't it? I knew what she was up to. She's so sure I can fill the old man's shoes that I don't need you. But she's wrong. O Christ," he moaned, "what am I going to do?"

Nickie had to fight the urge to slap him. "Everything's going to be okay," she murmured soothingly as he drifted off to sleep. "I think I've got it all worked out."

Nickie stared down at the wakening city from the hotel-room window. Rain had fallen, imparting a licorice sheen to the empty avenue. She had sat there all night, watching the rain and then the soft, watery sunrise. Behind her, Louis snored on the bed where the bellhops had dropped him the night before.

She rose as soon as she heard the soft knock on the door and admitted the room-service waiter with his cart. The pot of extra-strong coffee she had ordered smelled wonderful. She was just pouring herself a cup when Louis stirred and looked over at her, bleary eyed. "Nickie?"

"How are you feeling?" She brought the coffee over to him and sat on the edge of the bed.

"Stop shouting."

"I'm not. Your head must be ready to explode. What was that stuff you were drinking last night? It smelled like moonshine."

"O God, I *didn't* dream it." He gulped the scalding coffee. "You were there, weren't you? Lord, I'm sorry."

"Louis, listen to me. I don't expect apologies or explanations. We're friends, and I accept what you are," she said, taking the empty cup from him and setting it on the bedside table. "I've never judged you and I don't intend to start now."

"Thank you, Nickie." He rubbed his fingers in a circular motion on his temples. "What a monstrous hangover."

She shrugged. "What do you expect after a three-day binge?"

"Three days?" he looked shocked.

"You know, you're lucky it was me who found you. Someone else might not have been so understanding." She got up to pour coffee for herself and to get a couple of aspirin for him. "Frankly, I don't think you can afford to take any more risks like this, Louis. You're the president of a bank now. People will be relying on your integrity and character. Discretion is more vital than ever." She looked over at him. "Otherwise you run the risk of being destroyed both professionally and socially."

"Don't you think I know that?" He closed his eyes. "You should have heard the old man blathering on before he died, about what a model son I'd become, a credit to the family. Good God, what a scene! I had to run. This is the only place where I can be myself and not have to pretend."

"You don't have to pretend with me." She poured a glass of water and handed him the aspirin. "Here, take these." She smiled as he swallowed the tablets. "I can take care of you, Louis. I understand you. You know that, don't you?"

He groaned. "All I know is that I feel trapped between you and my mother."

"Louis, listen to me: You don't have to choose between us. I've been sitting up thinking about the situation all night. And I've reached a decision."

He cocked one eye open wearily.

She came back to the bed, sat down and took his hands. "I think you and I should get married."

He sat up so quickly he had to grip his head against the rush of pain. "But we can't do that," he said, stunned.

"Why not marry a woman who understands you, a woman who would never make any demands of you?" She smiled. "Obviously, I wouldn't be expecting a conventional marriage."

"You are certainly not Angelina, are you?" he murmured.

Nickie bristled. "My sister was a romantic fool. I'm a realist, Louis, and so should you be." Annoyed by the reference to Angie, she got up and started pacing restlessly before the window. "If you want me to outline the benefits of such a marriage, I will. First, as president of Urbano Bank, you will be more in the limelight. As long as you're single, these kind of 'lost weekend' escapades are going to make you extremely vulnerable. Second, a man in your position must have a wife as a cover, if for nothing more than an adornment on his arm at social and political functions. Think of not having to run the gauntlet of all those tiresome matrons throwing their ugly daughters at you."

"They aren't all dogs," he said, a flicker of his old teasing self filtering through.

"I'm surprised you'd notice," she retorted, not missing a step in her rapid pacing. "Third, in my own way I do care about you. I'd make you a good wife. No demands; only strong and loving support. Finally, and most important, once we're married, your mother will have no choice but to accept me."

He groaned. "You make it sound so simple and straightforward. But how in God's name can I face Mother and tell her I'm going to marry you? She'll never accept it."

"I've thought that through, too. We'll present it to her as a fait accompli." Nickie crossed her arms and grinned. "We'll get married here in New York."

Act Four

35

Angie rode her rusty old bicycle through the maze of streets that made up the Marais. She never tired of peeking into the tiny workshops where craftsmen painstakingly repaired bent silver and broken ivory, as their forebears had done since the Middle Ages. Grimy hovels crowded the courtyards of the noble mansions lining the boulevards of the impoverished arrondissement, but enough of the district's former grandeur still remained for Angie to be enchanted by it.

As she bicycled along, a soft spring breeze ruffled the full skirt of the summery print dress she had carefully tucked up under her. She couldn't afford to get any axle grease on her clothing because cleaning fluid was severely rationed—along with everything else in Paris, from coal and cooking utensils to meat and coffee. The *salles Boches*, as the French referred to the Germans, had bled the country dry in their long wartime occupation. Not only had they skimmed the best of France's foods, but they had stripped the nation bare of featherbeds, copper pots and iron garden spades. Nor had they spared Paris's wonderful bronze lampposts and statues. These had been torn away as well to feed the maw of the German war machine. The war had been over for two years, but the French continued to suffer severe shortages. The citizenry sardonically referred to their plight as the great hardship of peace in Paris.

Angie smiled ruefully to herself as she parked her rickety bike outside the butcher shop, marked by a painted horse head. In Rome she had fantasized that the French capital had remained miraculously untouched by war.

The reality was this: spending hours cycling from shop to shop with her fistful of ration tickets from the local prefecture, overjoyed to be able to purchase a few hundred grams of horse meat or tripe.

She came out of the shop, wedged her small package amid the others in the basket wired to the front handlebars and wheeled out into the street. An old Citroen zoomed wildly past, grazing her and sending the bike careening into the curb. Angie flew forward, banging her crotch painfully on the bar. She jumped off the bike, more concerned about damage to her conveyance than to herself, knowing if it had been wrecked, there was no way she could scrape together the money to buy another. "Damn idiot," she fumed at the long-gone driver.

The French seemed gripped by madness. They drove with wild erratic glee through the streets, drunk from the sheer excitement of holding a wheel again. All their pent-up anxieties and fears bloomed in an insatiable hunger for stimulation. Art galleries, cinemas, restaurants were packed at all hours. Angie was grateful for this mass mania for entertainment, since it provided her chorus jobs at the Folies Bergere, where she couldn't kick her heels as high as a real showgirl but high enough to satisfy the somnolent after-lunch crowds. The Paris opera, a tightly closed community obsessed with the idea of its own superiority, had been a harder nut to crack. Angie had wangled her way in first as an unpaid extra. Then several months before she had graduated at last to the chorus, where she had risked the ire of the temperamental director by outsinging everyone around her. Her ploy had worked, however, and she had captured his attention, along with the coveted understudy position to the ill-tempered diva Francoise Duvall.

Angie circled around the church of St. Nicolas-des-Champs to the tiny cobblestoned street that was now home. They lived on the top floor of a nineteenth-century building with a mansard roof. Madame Fouchet, the concierge, had a face like Roquefort cheese and a personality to match. She watched Angie's comings and goings with rheumy-eyed suspicion. Whenever Angie received a package from David—Maxwell House coffee, powdered milk, Hershey's chocolate, occasionally a whole canned ham—la Fouchet would sniff it out. She tolerated the lowly foreigners in the top flat, keeping her mouth shut about their false residence papers in exchange for bribes of food. Her son, Jules, was the only reason Angie didn't begrudge the mean-minded concierge her demands. The poor man's hands twitched uselessly, the result of nerve damage inflicted from a near-fatal Gestapo beating. No one had escaped this war, no one.

Angie climbed the narrow, twisting staircase two steps at a time, full of stamina after bicycling miles every day to shop and work. Their low-ceilinged flat was little more than one big room with peeling wallpaper and warped floorboards, but it was sunny and even had a tiny balcony lined with geraniums. At night, cheery accordion music would drift up from the *bals-musettes* around the corner, piercing Angie with longing for her childhood, for the fierce, loving closeness of the family that had been so long lost to her.

Marshall sat at the table, bent over his schoolbooks. Life here had been hard for him; the French kids' ostracism had left its mark. Angie bent to kiss the top of his head. "How's it going, *mon petit*?"

"Better," he said more cheerfully than she had heard him in a long time. "Today when that *porco* Pierre Lambert called me a greasy wop, I punched him in the stomach."

"Oh my," she said, sliding into the chair beside him. He would be nine soon, halfway to manhood. Sometimes she found herself searching out traces of Malfatti in him, fearful that Tony's ugly aggressiveness would explode suddenly from her quiet, sensitive son. "The only problem with hitting," she said finally, "is that once you've done it, you have to be willing to do it over and over again. It's like starting a war—people don't know what they're in for until it's far too late."

"I'm glad I hit him," he said stubbornly.

Angie didn't argue. Let him be a boy, she told herself. Let him fight his little battles and be the stronger for it.

She went over to Madame Giulia, who lay dozing in the afternoon sun on an old wicker chaise that they had rescued from a corner of the garden. Her stiff hands gently stroked Cherie, the stray tabby who had popped in through their balcony door last summer and adopted them. Madame had aged greatly these past three years. The sunlight ruthlessly exposed the wrinkles in her fine skin, though it was more kind to her hair, brightening the dull brown-gray to silvery highlights. Her once-beautiful fingers had become gnarled from arthritis. The last two winters of frigid cold and severely rationed coal had taken their toll. Her hips pained her, too, and she rarely left the apartment because the steep stairs were too much for her.

"*Bon jour, madame!*" Angie called to her in perfect mimicry of a Frenchwoman's gay, singsong greeting. "Look what I've brought—the first apples from Provence."

Madame Giulia stirred and smiled, taking one of the hard fruits. "How lovely!" she exclaimed. "Just like the ones we'd pick in my father's orchard when I was a girl."

She spoke often of her childhood now, drawing Marshall with her into that comforting world of long ago. The two of them had developed a deep bond that delighted Angie and annoyed Sarah.

Speak of the devil, Angie thought wryly as Sarah swept into the apartment, little wisps of hair escaping from her usually tidy bun. She had always been thin, but the war had sharpened her angles even more, giving her the brittle, quick air of a grasshopper. "Telegram for you, Angelina," she announced breathlessly, waving it as if it were a flag. "From the United States. Madame Fouchet just handed it to me."

Angie snatched the thin yellow envelope from her hands and tore it open. As she skimmed the words, her fear gave way to tremulous agitation. "David's coming," she told them, her eyes fixed to the flimsy typed sheet as if afraid the wonderful words would evaporate like a mirage. "He's bringing his daughter. There's an eye surgeon here in Paris who's done amazing work on soldiers with damaged vision. She must be what?" Angie murmured to herself. "Six?"

Marshall jumped up, full of excitement. "The American man!" he shouted. "John Wayne!"

Angie laughed, hugging him. Ever since American films had flooded the French movie houses, Marshall had equated every Hollywood star with the big American soldier who had visited them in Rome. Even in her own mind, David had acquired that same larger-than-life image. He's coming for his daughter's sake, she told herself over and over again. Not mine. Yet when her heart filled with longing, she could not stop it from flooding her entire being.

Angie sat in the first row facing L'Opéra's vast stage, hand-stitching a dress whose design she had filched from one of the couturier shows. She had worked on it every spare moment since David's telegram had arrived, vowing he would not find her the same pinched ragamuffin he had left in Rome. As she sewed, she kept one sharp eye on the stage, where they were running a dress rehearsal of Puccini's *La Fanciulla del West*—The Girl of the Golden West. Angie glanced over at the stagehand commandeered to babysit Duvall's poodle Maxi, a ridiculous froufrou creature clipped *en papillon* with pompoms, fur cuffs and a fuchsia bow. The man held up the tiny dog and gestured with it toward the stage, as if to say it could do a better job than its mistress. Angie grinned, knowing he was right. Francoise Duvall sang the role of the saloonkeeper Minnie like a haughty queen dressed up in calico and boots for a costume ball. But even the French diva's mannequin performance couldn't completely spoil the opera for Angie. Her favorite part was approaching, in which Minnie at the end of Act II cheats the evil sheriff at cards in order to save her bandit lover's life. The saloonkeeper was an earthy, complex heroine that Angie longed to explore.

No, no, no! Angie thought, watching Francoise stiffly pluck the aces hidden in her stocking, so concerned about the fluid purity of her G sharp that she had forgotten her character. Suddenly in her head Angie saw Z'Maria mimicking the way rich 'merican women walked—"like they have a broomstick up their *culo*." She almost laughed out loud. The description fit the iron butterfly on stage to a tee.

Monsieur Perrin, the director, shouted, "*Mais non, non, non,* madame! This action calls for finesse coupled with desperation—Minnie is risking her *honneur* to save the life of Johnson." He pronounced it "zhonsawn."

Angie got a kick out of the production. Although Puccini's orchestration and Debussy-inspired harmonies were wonderful, the idea of L'Opéra—so grand and sublimely French—staging an Italian composer's exotic vision of the American Wild West smacked unintentionally of farce. Angie knew the only thing that could make the whole silly thing work was a strong, believable soprano, which Duvall emphatically was not.

The diva went around and around with M. Perrin. "And I say it cannot be done!" she shouted back, her lovely bosom heaving with indignation. "Imbecile! All you're fit to direct is traffic in the Rue Auber."

Angie dropped her sewing in her lap as the argument grew heated. When Duvall forgot her nightingale image and got her dander up, Angie grudgingly had to admit she had a strong enough stage presence. But M. Perrin wasn't regarding the situation from quite the same objective standpoint. He had run his fingers through his thin brown hair until it stood up on his head like a rooster's comb. As he turned toward the auditorium, Angie could see his face was about the same mottled shade of red.

"Mademoiselle Angelina!" he barked, seething from Duvall's scathing insult. "Come here at once!"

"*Oui*, monsieur!"

The tense silence in the cavernous theater was broken only by the clatter of Angie's heels as she hurried across the stage.

"Angelina, go sit at the table with Charles. Now we shall see if this can or cannot be done. We shall see who should be out in the Rue Auber . . ." M. Perrin said with exquisite contempt, his eyes raking Duvall, "plying another trade."

The woman drew in her breath sharply. "How dare—"

"Play!" he roared into the orchestra pit.

Duvall stalked off in a snit. She grabbed Maxi out of the stagehand's arms and murmured her complaints against the poodle's ears in a loud stage whisper.

The musicians, distracted by the lively display of tempers, launched raggedly into the score. Angie took advantage of the momentary confusion to warm up with a few nervous trills under her breath. Charles, the baritone singing Sheriff Rance's role, gave her an encouraging wink. She took a deep breath and closed her eyes for an instant. Her wounded lover's life was riding on this poker game. She envisioned David slumped in the chair nearby, rather than the fussy, egotistical tenor Claude Marrast who sang the role of Johnson.

The music swelled in unison. Rance shuffled the cards, and Angie turned her upper body so that she leaned forward on one elbow, at once distracting him with her cleavage and taunting him as if she expected him to cheat in the deal. With her free hand beneath the table she subtly pulled up her skirt and slipped two cards into the top of her stocking.

They each won a hand. Finally, when it looked as if Rance was going to win the third, Angie shifted in her chair, shooting an anxious look at the bleeding, unconscious Johnson. Then she dropped her cards on the table, announcing that she must have something to drink if they were to continue. As soon as Rance turned, she pulled the aces from her stocking, her furtive movements fueled by a reckless panache that she hoped illuminated Minnie's desperation. With a flourish she tossed down her winning hand and Rance stalked out.

The music trailed off, and a spontaneous smatter of applause broke out among the stagehands. Angie made a comical little bow.

"Enough!" M. Perrin shouted, his eyes fixed on Duvall. "There, madame, as you see, it can be done."

Duvall stormed forth from the wings, enraged by the impromptu ovation given her understudy. "All I see is a slick italienne wallowing in her own cheap passion."

Angie was suddenly glad she had not scolded Marshall for punching fat Pierre in the stomach, because she had the almost overpowering urge to inflict the same punishment on the insufferably arrogant Duvall.

36

On opening night, Francoise Duvall had her backstage
retinue in a tizzy. A singer was entitled to her superstitious rituals, but this woman's preperformance shenani-
gans took the cake. Angie watched the goings-on from
the open doorway of Duvall's dressing room. Tucked
behind a painted screen was a cookstove, from which
emanated the wonderful aroma of grilling filet mignon.
What killed Angie was that the exquisite meal was not for
Duvall, who like all singers ate sparingly before a performance, but for her spoiled pet.

Angie's own ritual was simple: Before going on stage
she kissed first the photos of her family and then the tiny
gold cross. She smiled as she remembered how Renata
Baldini had slipped it around her neck the night Marshall
was born. What a far cry this insufferable Frenchwoman
was from warm, generous Renata. Angie thought longingly of her beautiful friend who had retired from the
stage and married a dashing, wealthy Argentine rancher.
Duvall couldn't hold a candle to the Italian diva, Angie
thought, watching her hurry toward the stove. Now what?

"*Mais non*, you call that chopped finely?" she railed at
the chef in a frantic whisper, ever fearful of straining her
tender voice.

The chef, whose real job was in the prop department,
pretended not to have understood her. "Pardon, madame?"

"Idiot!" she cried, straining her whisper to the utmost.
"You heard me. Those slabs would choke an elephant.
Here, give me that knife."

Angie wasn't the only one observing the proceedings.
The clipped and beribboned Maxi sat atop a tasselled
pillow, his round black eyes jealously watchful. He growled
when his mistress let out another strangled hue and cry,
this time berating a wardrobe girl because she had al-

lowed the little pot of heating milk to boil. Maxi jumped up and nipped sharply at her heels as the girl rushed past to set the scalded milk on the windowsill in the corridor.

Drawn by the commotion, a small crowd gathered around Angie. One of the carpenters surreptitiously kicked Maxi in the behind, sending him squealing back into the diva's dressing room "Insufferable little bugger," he growled, pulling a flask from his pocket. "I'll fix his curly ass." He poured a healthy shot into the cooling milk.

Angie smiled at the prank, only the latest in a time-honored tradition of stagehands taking revenge on haughty stars. She watched with concealed glee as Maxi finished his elegant lunch and lapped up his fortified milk.

Duvall called for her sleep mask and earplugs, and everyone was summarily shooed away while she lay down to rest before the evening performance. When Angie was sure the coast was clear, she crept back and peeked inside. Maxi tumbled off his pillow and staggered toward her, his eyes glazed. Taking pity on the poor dog, Angie picked him by his scruff and set him out of harm's way in the clean chamberpot by the door.

"Sweet dreams, pooch," she laughed softly.

Not long afterward, Angie sat on the stained sofa in her own meager dressing room, her legs curled up under her as she put the finishing touches on her new dress. She had no idea when David would be arriving in Paris; his telegram had been maddeningly vague on that point. Warnings niggled at the back of her mind. He was married, he had a family, a home, a business—a whole life that excluded her. She had no right to expect anything of him but friendship, and she knew it would be foolish to allow herself to feel anything more than that in return. Then too, she was frightened of the power men wielded over women: not so much the brutish dominance she had experienced at the hands of Pap and Tony, because she knew she would never allow herself to be so controlled again, but the willingness with which women subsumed their identities in the men they loved—bending, deferring, always yielding, until the world existed only as seen through the man's eyes. These past nine years she had schooled herself to be aloof, to maintain at all costs the

clarity of vision that kept her true to her own inner self. She
feared that loving a man would mean having that essence
stolen from her; she didn't believe the two could coexist.
And yet, paradoxically, she longed for David's presence.

A sudden high-pitched wail from the corridor startled
her, making her prick her finger with the sewing needle.
Licking the blood, she jumped up to see what was going on.

Down the hall, Duvall stood at the center of the vor-
tex, shouting furiously as the drunken Maxi lolled uncon-
sciously in her arms. "I will have the culprit fired! I swear
it!"

Angie hurried to her side. "Madame Duvall, you better
calm down," she counseled. "Your voice—"

"Shut up! Someone call the veterinarian at once."

Another timid voice ventured, "But Madame Duvall,
it's Saturday evening."

"Then get a doctor. My baby's sensitive little stomach
may need pumping. Hurry!"

An hour before the performance, the opera manager
and director arrived in haste at the diva's dressing room,
not because of concern over the fate of the universally
despised Maxi but because of Duvall's throat. M. Gumery
recommended a hot poultice while M. Perrin advised
various herbal teas and tisanes. The doctor who had been
called in was more conservative in his medical advice; he
ordered complete rest for twenty-four hours.

Angie hovered in the background. She felt vaguely
guilty, even though she had done nothing herself and
couldn't know that the stagehand's mean-spirited fun would
give the diva a full-blown case of hysterical laryngitis.
Angie had little time to think about the incident further,
however, because M. Perrin was pulling her out of the
star's dressing room and down the hall, giving her hurried last-minute directions about the role she was to take
over.

"I feel badly, monsieur," she managed to say when he
took a breath.

"*Non, non, non!*" he answered in his rat-a-tat style.
"You are a fine *artiste*, Angeline. Your voice is strong,
your acting superb. Believe this when I tell you: You will
make a far finer Minnie than that pompous bag of nerves."

Angie bit her lip nonetheless. As much as she had

coveted the role, she was not happy to have won it as the result of a backfired practical joke. Her triumph had a slightly bitter taste.

The black taxicab sped down the Rue de Rivoli. To the left rose the Louvre and the long shadowed perspective of the Tuileries Garden, glimpsed briefly before the cab turned right onto the resplendent Avenue de L'Opéra. David turned away from the window and looked at Katie, who sat staring straight ahead, locked in her self-contained world of darkness. He reached across the seat to squeeze her hand. "You okay, sweetheart?"

" 'Course, Daddy."

Her cheerful matter-of-factness reassured him. However he viewed her blindness, it was obvious she didn't regard herself as a tragic victim. With a blind person's sixth sense, she turned her head expectantly toward him. "Are we almost there?"

David looked out the window again. The grand, brilliantly lit Place de L'Opéra loomed just ahead. "Almost."

"What's it look like?"

"The opera house?" He relaxed, glad to have their favorite game to fall back upon. "Well, I guess it looks like a fancy cake with a . . . I don't know, a big green onion stuck on top."

"Green onion?" She giggled. "What kind of green— soft green like grass?"

"Not exactly."

"Cool like mint gum?"

"Nope."

"Slimy green like my fish pond?" She wrinkled her nose. "Or rough green like the old kettle in Poppy's kitchen?" Poppy was Poppandreu, a Greek immigrant in Oakland who cooked in Katie's favorite eatery.

"Boy, it took you awhile," David teased, making her giggle again. "I was getting worried there for a second."

Sometimes he closed his own eyes and tried to envision a world of colors experienced only as texture against a finger, a taste on the tip of his tongue, but his attempts at empathy were fleeting. They depressed him too much.

As they left the cab and made their way inside, David described everything to her: the Grand Staircase of white marble, the elaborately carved and frescoed ceilings, the lavish rococo adornment of every surface that bewildered the eye. He found that in having to describe things aloud, it sharpened his own visual sense, forcing him to see things in more focused detail.

As soon as they had settled in their seats, Katie assumed that intense aura of concentration that so intrigued her father. Sometimes she reminded him of a mouse in the way she gently sniffed the air. The vast gold and crimson auditorium before him faded; in its place he smelled the bouquets of flowers adorning the balconies, the dizzying melange of perfumes, the aroma of varnished wood on the stage sets and of dust clinging to the velvet drop curtain; his newly attuned hearing caught the rustlings of women's silk gowns and the scrape of a bow across a violin down in the orchestra pit. Katie sat back finally, wriggling excitely in her seat, the toes of her black patent Mary Janes pointed straight up at the chandelier. It was moments like this that his love for her was so intense it felt almost like pain.

A man clad in a rusty-black tuxedo marched out onto the stage before the closed curtain. He carried a heavy wooden pole, which he knocked three times against the boards. "Attention . . ." he intoned as a hush fell over the noisy, glittering crowd.

"What's he saying, Daddy?"

"Something about a change in the program, I think."

Angry hissing whispers spread through the house like fire. Katie turned anxiously to her father. "How come they're all mad now?"

"Shhh," David hushed her as the curtain slowly rose on a goldrush-camp saloon.

The audience settled down a bit as Puccini's wonderful music filled the theater, evoking the hard-drinking, hardgambling atmosphere of miners far from home: Sheriff Rance threatened a cardshark. The Wells Fargo agent arrived seeking news of a bandit plaguing him. Rance threatened one of the patrons with his pistol when he mocked the sheriff's intentions to marry the saloonkeeper Minnie, but someone knocked his arm away as he fired.

The wild shot was Minnie's entrance cue. As soon as the soprano appeared, the Parisian audience jumped to its feet in a fury, hissing and booing loudly. Someone began to shout "Duvall, Duvall!" until the whole crowd picked up the chant.

David stood up, too, staring in shock at Angie, who looked like a beautiful Annie Oakley in a long suede skirt and scoop-necked embroidered blouse. She lifted her warm voice above the audience's rhythmic chanting, smiling and laughing as she moved among the men on stage—accepting a bunch of wildflowers from one, a ribbon from another—seemingly oblivious to the audience's rebellion. David felt like turning around and smashing his fellow theater-goers left and right. God damn it, will you just give her a chance? he wanted to yell. He saw the conductor wave his baton at the orchestra, signaling them to play louder.

For a while it was touch and go; then gradually the audience started to quiet down. David sat tensely through the whole first act, tapping his rolled-up program on his leg. What the hell was she doing up there in a starring role anyway? The last time she'd written, she had just managed to slip into the chorus, complaining that the Paris Opera was a closed union. By the end of the first act, the audience was mollified enough to give a round of lukewarm applause. By the end of the second act, they were rather more enthusiastic. By the time the curtain had dropped on the third act, the brave and tender Minnie had the crowd eating out of her hand. The applause was thunderous.

David slumped back against his seat and breathed a huge sigh. Katie stroked his arm consolingly. "Daddy, tell yourself what you tell me—it's only a story, it's not for real."

He laughed. "Did you like it?"

"Yeah! The lady sounds pretty."

"She is." He stood and swung Katie up into his arms, suddenly feeling buoyant and full of optimism. "Someday maybe you'll get to see for yourself, angel."

Angie made her way through the backstage maze of the opera house, surrounded by a laughing, bubbly crowd. What an incredible feeling to have won over an audience like that. Heads popped out of dressing rooms, shouting congratulations. She smiled and nodded her thanks, savoring the sweetness of the moment as she made her way down the corridor. When she passed Francoise Duvall's room, the door opened and the diva appeared, regarding her with complete disdain. "They cheered you tonight, but you're nothing, Italienne," she whispered, every word a strain. "Nothing but fool's gold—a glittery flash in the pan."

Angie smiled tightly. "The public will be the judge of that, madame."

Even as she spoke, the delivery boys paraded down the corridor toward her dressing room, their arms laden with congratulatory bouquets.

Floral arrangements soon filled the tiny room, scenting the overheated air with jasmine, gardenias and roses. The massed flowers reminded Angie, as always, of a funeral. She might save one of the small arrangements to bring home to the apartment; the rest she would have sent to hospitals and orphanages.

Angie wasn't about to have her head turned by an audience's shouts of "Brava!" The future was no less precarious than it had been before. She knew from bitter experience that success made one a target for hatred, jealousy and revenge. She would have to be on her guard.

37

David sat alone at a café around the corner from his hotel, nursing a beer. A warm breeze ruffled the leaves of the plane trees lining the *quai*, carrying with it the aroma of newly baked bread. The bursting fullness of the spring day, the cool green surge of the river, the sunlight glinting off the rose window in the south facade of Notre Dame Cathedral—all were lost on him. He was still back in the hospital, breathing in its medicinal odors as he stared down at Katie, looking tiny and vulnerable in the narrow iron bed. Dr. Maurier had articulately explained the limits of the new ophthalmalogical procedure he had developed. He would examine Katie thoroughly. Before that, he would offer no prognosis. "You must have patience, Mr. O'Rourke," he had said. *Patience!* David thought. He wanted answers, he wanted Katie to be whole.

As soon as he left the hospital, he had called Angie. He couldn't wait to see her—to hear her voice rich and warm as honey when she laughed, to breathe in the subtle scent of her perfume, to lose himself in her beauty for a few hours. Restlessly his eyes scanned the bridge that linked the two islands in the Seine. He had just convinced himself she had changed her mind and wasn't coming when he picked out her familiar stride amid the crowd. Angie didn't mince or sway. She moved with lithe, sexy ease, as if she meant to embrace the world with her limbs. His throat tightened as he watched her approach.

Angie had blown twenty francs on cab fare because she wasn't about to ride up on her bicycle like a peasant. Nervously she scanned the crowded café tables as she crossed the bridge. What if something had happened to Katie? What if he had been called back to the hospital? What if he had left Paris without seeing her? David had sounded so tense and lonely, but Angie had been forced to keep her own voice neutral. The apartment building's only phone was in Madame Fouchet's little cage, and the nosy concierge was notorious for eavesdropping.

Then she saw him. He must have spotted her, too, because he had stood up and was waving. She hesitated a moment, smoothing the skirt of her soft, scoop-necked dress. Her throat was bare of jewels, for what she had loved about the design was its look of unadorned sensuality. Now, suddenly, she worried: Was it overdone? Would he find her too changed?

Setting aside her fears, she hurried forward to greet him. He caught both her hands and held her at arm's length to look at her. The expression in his eyes made her glad she had gone to all the effort over the dress.

"You look wonderful," he said, pulling out a chair for her.

"Thank you," she murmured quickly, still feeling nervous. "When did you get in town?"

"Two days ago. I wanted to take Katie to the opera." He smiled briefly, easing the tightness around his mouth and eyes. "You make a terrific Minnie."

"I sort of fell into the role." She felt herself blushing and was relieved when the waiter appeared. She inquired about various aperitifs, finally ordering a Dubonnet—aware of David's eyes on her the whole time.

"You speak French like a native," he said after the waiter left.

"I just happen to have a talent for mimicry. Makes it easier to fit in."

"He obviously didn't mistake you for a tourist."

"Stick around," she said lightly. "I'll show you the real Paris no tourist ever sees—the butcher shops and coal cellars; backstage at the Folies with a dozen sweating showgirls cursing their bunions . . ."

"Sounds great," he teased as he leaned his elbows on the table, still staring as if he couldn't get enough of her. "Nothing I'd like more."

Flustered, she looked away, her gaze following the snakelike flick of a fishing line as an angler cast out from the far riverbank. "How long are you staying?"

He sighed and sat back. "Depends on what the surgeon says." He sounded downcast. "It all depends on what Katie needs."

Angie looked at him. "You must love her very much."

"When I went into the service, she was two. When I saw her again, she was four and a half. It was like I was a stranger." He shook his head. "I guess I'm trying to make up for lost time. I want to give her everything."

"I'm sure just having you back is enough."

"You don't understand. I want to give Katie her sight." The intensity with which he spoke startled her. It struck her then how superficially she knew him.

A silence ensued between them, heightened by the cheerful conversations buzzing at the other tables. She had been longing for this moment for so long, and now that she found herself with him she hesitated to talk about the things that really mattered. It was safer to skim the surface, to laugh and joke. Perhaps this meeting had been a mistake.

The waiter brought her drink, and she toyed with the stem of her glass, debating a moment before she asked with feigned casualness, "How is Maura?"

He shifted restlessly, turning to watch the Seine where it broke and surged to either side of the tiny island's point. His eyes had that same glinting green shimmer as the river, bright and dark at the same time, she noticed. "Maura is Maura. She doesn't change," he said finally, his intensity fed by a current of anger. "You don't see her here, do you?"

"Maybe she was too afraid of being disappointed. It's got to be hard for her, too."

David's laughter was sharp, full of suppressed hurt. "What's hard for her is not having Katie there to remind the world what a noble mother she is. Maura eats up that role. Hell," he swore, "she's the one who should be on stage."

"We're all actors, David. We're all chameleons."

His eyes raked her. "Why are you so eager to defend Maura?"

Because, she thought, if I knew you truly belonged to her and Maura belonged to you, then I wouldn't be tempted. As she sipped her bittersweet aperitif, she gave him a sidelong look. "I suppose," she said aloud, "because we're both women."

He gave her a wry look. "That's no damn answer at all."

"Let's walk for a bit, okay?"

He threw several bills down on the table, then pulled her up beside him and kissed her lightly. "I've missed you," he said huskily.

Her face flooded with warmth. "Come on, let's walk through the open market."

They crossed over the bridge onto the Ile de la Cité, past Notre Dame with its rows of buttresses like massive arms bent under the weight of history. The Gothic spire of Sainte Chapelle rose above the slate turrets of the Conciergie, where Marie-Antoinette had languished for two months before dying at the guillotine. Angie stared up at the golden chapel spire, imagining it snagging one of the cotton-puff clouds that drifted along the sky, un-ravelling it into long, smoky tendrils.

"We rarely come down to this part of the city," she said, her eyes still on the lazy clouds.

"Why not? The Marais isn't too far."

Angie smiled. "I can see why the Europeans resent Americans, even if you did just win the war for them," she said, turning to look at him. "You always act like everything is so simple and straightforward."

"No, you're wrong," he said, reaching up to toy with a curl that had fallen free of her small Basque beret. "The trick is to focus on a single thing that you want, to go after that with every ounce of will you've got—one small step at a time until the objective's won." He tucked the curl behind her ear, allowing his fingers to linger a moment against the warmth of her neck.

"I see what you mean," she murmured, resisting the temptation to yield to the promise of his fingertips. "I'd be a little worried if that strategy were directed at me."

He laughed. "Come on. I'll buy you a red rose. When I think of you, it's always in strong colors—red and black and white, like a gypsy."

"Gypsy!" She laughed as well, and the easy sound broke the subtle tension between them. "I always sort of pictured myself as a mysterious Mona Lisa."

David closed one eye and lifted his thumb, pretending to examine her as an artist might. "Uh-uh," he said with a shake of his head. "You're too vibrant, too alive for that quiet dame."

An open-air flower market filled the narrow street that wound around the hospital of Hotel Dieu. Jonquils, vio-lets, daisies, roses, sprigs of blooming dogwood all over-flowed from the water-filled jars. David bought her a red rose, and she tucked it beneath her watchband like a wrist corsage. The bird-sellers had their rows of cages set up, too, and the air was alive with the melodic twittering of canaries. Near the Chatelet Bridge a ruddy-cheeked farmwoman sat between two huge baskets, one overflow-ing with ginger-colored kittens and the other with tiny black and white puppies. Angie bent to pick up one of the puppies, holding it close to her cheek. He wriggled and licked her face. "How adorable," she laughed. "Marsh has been agitating for a dog of his own, but it's impossible where we are now." She knelt down to put the puppy back, although she continued to stroke his soft fur. "I keep promising him that someday we'll have a real home with a garden." She stood up, her gaze still focused on the squirming bundles in the basket. "I want so badly to give him that kind of normal life. Sometimes I feel he's missed out on the warmth and comfort of a real family."

"Angie—" David began, but she cut him off with a shake of her head and an overbright smile, fearful of having revealed too much.

She glanced down at her watch. "David, I really have to run!" she said hurriedly. "I've got a rehearsal. Will you promise to let me know how Katie is?" She backed away toward the bridge. "Call me, no matter how late it is."

He stared after her retreating figure in frustration. She was like trying to capture a butterfly—always fluttering just beyond his reach. Without warning he was pierced by loneliness. He turned and retraced his steps toward the hospital, even though he knew it would be hours before the surgeon delivered his prognosis.

Angie parked her bike inside the dark vestibule of the old apartment building, humming her lilting second-act aria from *La Fanciulla*. The performance had ended at eleven, and she'd just bicycled the mile home. She should have been exhausted, but the strong adrenalin rush from performing left its bubbly residue inside her. She felt totally alive, every sense honed.

Happily, Angie's success on stage had recharged Madame Giulia, too, eliciting reserves of stamina and will that had ebbed dangerously low in the past several years of hardship. They'd also had heartening news from Italy: It was rumored that the great Toscanini would return to the newly rebuilt La Scala after his long years of exile. Giulia Francini had begun talking with longing of her homeland. Change was in the wind, Angie sensed, for all of them.

She crossed the dimly lit foyer, glancing into the concierge's room, where the night watchman, Denon, snored blissfully, his broken-veined nose pressed to the desktop.

She was halfway up the first flight of steps when she heard the shrill ring of the telephone. She stopped. After the fifth ring, Denon stirred and picked it up. "*Qu'est-ceque c'est?*" he bellowed into the receiver. Lightly Angie ran back down the steps, hovering in the doorway. "*On-di-don!*" Denon exclaimed with curt impatience. "*Je ne comprends pas, monsieur!*" She wrested the phone from the bleary-eyed watchman and spoke quickly into the receiver. "*Bon soir.* With whom did you wish to speak?"

"Angie, thank God."

Her stomach tightened. "David, what's wrong?"

"I need to see you. Can you come?"

"I'll be right there."

Angie gave the cab driver the address of the small hotel on the Ile St. Louis. She stared out at the blur of shuttered store fronts as they sped down the empty avenue, her thoughts in a whirl. David's grief-filled voice had terrified her. The cab crossed the bridge onto the tiny island, its laboring engine loud and intrusive in the elegant silence of the sevententh-century stone facades. They drew to a stop finally in the rue St.-Louis-en-l'Ile.

Angie rang the buzzer beneath a copper carriage lamp and was immediately ushered inside the exquisite, Persian-carpeted foyer by a concierge attired in tailcoat, striped tie and white gloves. He seemed less a doorman than a custodian of luxurious comfort, entrusted with the task of holding the harried modern world at bay beyond the beveled-glass entrance. He accompanied her up in the wire-caged elevator to the fifth floor. "Room twenty-one," he said crisply, pointing toward a door at the end of the hall.

Her nervousness made her knock way too loudly. As David flung open the door, she stared at him in shock. His eyes were red rimmed; the collar of his wrinkled shirt open wide. He looked incredibly weary, his expression shuttered, wary of revealing whatever was eating him inside. Instinctively Angie wrapped her arms around his waist and leaned her head against his chest. He stood stiff and unresponsive. Then it was as if a clenched fist somewhere deep inside him relaxed. His arms went around her, and he laid his cheek against the top of her head.

For several minutes they stood in wordless communion, simply holding each other.

A tentative knock pulled them reluctantly apart. The chambermaid entered, wishing to turn down the bed. Angie spoke to her swiftly in French, asking that she bring a bottle of brandy, along with a bit of bread and cheese, even though David looked as if food were the last thing on his mind. "Monsieur has been ill and needs to regain his strength," she whispered to the wide-eyed maid, who bobbed her head sympathetically.

David had gone to the fireplace, where a bright blaze warded off the cool, damp breeze blowing in through the open balcony doors. He stood with his back to Angie, staring into the fire.

She came toward him but stopped a few feet short, feeling suddenly awkward and uncertain, chary of intruding on his intensely private pain. "David," she said finally, "what is it?"

"Maurier can't do anything for Katie. He says she'll be blind for the rest of her life. I spent the whole evening just wandering the streets; I couldn't face her." He slammed his fist on the carved mantel. "I've never felt so damned helpless in my life . . . so much to blame."

His harsh self-censure took Angie aback. "How can you possibly blame yourself?" she murmured. "Why do you want to punish yourself this way?"

"Why?" He turned, his pain-filled eyes reflecting pinpoints of light from the fire. "Because I wanted a child for all the wrong reasons. Katie's suffering for my selfishness."

"But David, that's nonsense!"

The maid knocked again and Angie went to the door, taking the lace-lined silver tray that had been set with a midnight repast for two—cheeses, bread, butter, lettuce with a cruet of oil. Thankfully, she had not forgotten brandy.

"Good food will cure anything," the maid whispered conspiratorially. "Bon appetit."

Angie set the tray on the mahogany butler's table before the small sofa. She poured the brandy into a crystal tumbler and brought it to him. He swirled the liquid, staring broodingly into the glass. "David, please don't turn your back on me, after I've come all this way. Please."

He downed the brandy in one gulp and set the empty glass on the mantel. "I'm sorry. I shouldn't have dragged you into this."

"Into what? David, look at me." She took his face between her hands and turned him gently to face her. "You are the most unselfish man I've ever known. Warm, sensitive and kind. You're being too hard on yourself."

He shook his head. "You're one of the few good things in my life, Angie. I hate having you so far away from me. Every night I dream of you. I've tried to get you out of my mind, but I can't. I need you so badly."

"David," she breathed. His confession rekindled the passion that had lain dormant since that afternoon in Rome long ago. He had given her so much. Now she only wanted to give in return—to assuage his pain with her lovingness.

She drew his mouth to hers and kissed him deeply. Then she lightly kissed his eyelids and the line of his jaw. Her hands dropped to the front of his shirt. Slowly she unfastened the buttons and nestled her mouth between the opened plackets, caressing his chest and teasing his flat hard nipples. Then she knelt down, quickly undoing his belt and zipper. Her unwonted boldness—this pliant desire to please and arouse him—fueled her own rising excitement. Gently she guided him down onto the bed. When she crossed the room and turned off all the lights, the only illumination came from the dying fire in the grate and the shafts of cool moonlight flooding the open window.

She went toward the bed and very slowly began to undress, aware of his eyes following her movements. She drew her hands caressingly up her thighs before unhooking her stockings. As she reached behind her back to unfasten her bra, she heard him groan. She caught the lace cups in her hands and slowly let her breasts fall free.

"Angie, you're like a dream. So goddamned beautiful," he whispered huskily, holding his arms out. "Come here."

"Sshh," she murmured as she climbed astride his legs and began to caress his stomach and thighs.

Her hands teasingly skirted his groin, and his member reared up gently as if to beckon her touch. She grasped it between her hands, her caresses long and languorous, yet insistent.

He gasped. "Christ, Angie . . ."

She felt a trembling flutter in her belly, a rising warmth that quickened her own breathing. "Yes, I know . . ." Lifting her hips, she drew him slowly into her. "Oh, David."

He reached up to fondle her breasts, his thumbs gently tracing her engorged nipples. Then his hands dropped to grip her thighs as she began to sway and circle above him in a rhythmic, sinuous dance of mounting pleasure. She caught her breath. The tiny bursts of excitement deep in her loins gathered and focused until she felt as if her whole being was one exquisitely tuned nerve quivering on the edge of incandescence. Her climax erupted in a flash of brilliant, silent explosions, pulsing inside her like summer lightning.

Exhausted, her breath escaping in ragged gasps, she eased down beside him. "David." Her sweat-dampened curls feathered his face as she bent to kiss him. "You give me so much more than I could ever give you."

He laughed against her hair, his voice low and warm, surfeited with pleasure. "I wouldn't bet on that, angel face."

Later, they lay in each other's arms, eating food from the tray, talking desultorily. Angie reached over to stroke his bare chest. "What did you mean when you said you had a child for the wrong reasons?"

"Maura didn't want to get pregnant."

"But you insisted?"

"Yeah." His breath escaped in a noisy sigh as he poured himself another glass of brandy. "I figured a baby would keep her occupied while I went back to school. That she'd have some other focus in her life besides hounding me about the decisions I was making." He looked at Angie uneasily. "What's the matter—what are you thinking?"

"Nothing!" She rolled over and bent her arm up over her head, staring at the ceiling. What he'd said upset her, for she realized how little she understood what drove him.

He caressed her arm. "I would never manipulate you, you must know that, Angie. What I've found with you I never had with Maura." He bent over her and brushed his lips against her breast. "Angie, I love you. I have for a long time."

They made love again, and the joyous, exhausting physical pleasure banished the doubts that nagged at her. Much later, as she hovered between wakefulness and sleep, she heard her heart whisper: "Hold this moment."

Marshall led Kathleen by the hand along the curving path, plucking flowers for her and naming them in French. Usually so quiet and reserved, he had taken instantly to the girl in a tenderly protective way that was touching to watch. Giggling, Katie bent to sniff the flowers, her bright red-gold hair glinting like a new penny as it brushed against a leaf. They had been strolling leisurely for two hours through the grounds of Versailles. Angie and David trailed behind the children, drinking in the peaceful sunlit ambience of the formal flowerbeds, the ornamental lakes and elaborately sculpted fountains. They walked close but not touching, their newfound intimacy too private and fragile to risk exposure to the world. Still, the pleasure of last night's lovemaking resonated between them like the echo of an exquisite melody.

"Katie's got your joie de vivre, David," Angie said softly. "She's such a happy child."

"I try to convince myself of that."

"You don't have to convince yourself of anything. Just look at her," Angie said with a laugh as Katie knelt down to bury her face in a patch of aromatic thyme and then jumped up, sneezing. "Whatever else may be wrong with your life, David, you're very fortunate to have her."

He turned to Angie. "You like her?"

"I adore her!"

They smiled into each other's eyes. How changed he seemed today, lighthearted and boyish with the breeze blowing his hair, the lines around his eyes crinkling with pleasure. The thought of how easily she had fallen in love with him frightened her.

"Come on," she said quickly, "we haven't seen the Petit Trianon yet. The kids'll love it."

They walked past the gray stone mansion to the tiny village nearby. The picturesque mill along the manmade babbling brook and the little dairy farm seemed strangely out of place against the regal grandeur of the rest of Versailles. Katie and Marshall invaded a small pen filled with lambs, chasing them until the caretaker shooed them off. Then Marshall pulled some peanuts from his pocket and they tried to lure the swans from the pond.

Angie and David strolled beneath the trees in the orchard. "Can you imagine how disillusioned poor Marie-Antoinette must have been with court life to have gone to all the trouble to build this fantasy place?" Angie murmured. "I read that she used to dress up as a shepherdess and tend to the animals, like a little girl playing with dolls. And all the time the real world was closing in on her. Sad, isn't it?"

David turned her to face him. "I get the funny feeling you're not talking about some queen who's been dead almost two hundred years. You didn't choose this outing by chance, did you? You're trying to make some kind of point."

She bit her lip. "I guess I am. It's just . . . about last night. It was wonderful, magical, but . . ." She sighed. "It seems we're destined to have nothing more than stolen moments together. What we have has nothing to do with the real world."

"You're denying what happened between us last night?"

"No!" She reached up to stroke his cheek with the back of her hand. "I'll always cherish it. David, you taught me things about myself I'd never known before."

He caught her hand and kissed it. "Come back with me to the States, tonight. I'll ask Maura for a divorce. I want to marry you. Angie, I love you."

"Stop saying that." She pulled away. "David, haven't you been listening? What we had was magical, but realistically it can't ever be. I wish more than anything that Katie and Marsh were ours together, that our lives were meshed. But we can't torture ourselves like this by yearning after an illusion." Her eyes swept Marie-Antoinette's make-believe world. "Your life's in Pittsburgh with Katie and Maura. And my life's here with my career and my son. David, we live in two different worlds."

"Damn it," he said fiercely. "Don't my feelings for you count for anything?"

She shook her head, tears blurring her eyes. How she longed to tell him that she loved him, too, but to make even that commitment of words would be like jumping off a precipice. At all costs she had to remain in control of herself. She could not allow emotion to entangle her, to deflect her from what she had to do.

"David," she whispered brokenly, "I'm sorry."

"Christ, *you're* sorry!" All his bitterness and pain washed over her.

Marshall came running through the rows of trees toward them. "Mammina!" he called, laughing as he rushed up. Angie put her arm around his shoulders.

She watched David go to Katie, where she sat at the pond's edge, playing with the cat-tail reeds. He picked her up in his arms and they headed back across the gardens through the long shadows cast by the late-afternoon sunlight. At the end of the path he stopped and looked back, as if waiting. Angie had to steel herself not to run to him. Finally he turned and walked away.

Watching him go, Angie felt her heart breaking. "I love you, too," she whispered so softly the words barely rippled through the silence.

38

Drawn by the charming theme of Disney's *Snow White*, David stopped in the doorway of his daughter's bedroom. Beyond the pristine loveliness of the canopied bed and French provincial furniture was a small archway that led to the space Katie called her "kingdom." He himself had designed and cut the passageway into the spare room closet to give her a cozy nook all her own.

He tossed his dinner jacket on the satin bedspread and ducked inside. He smiled when he saw her stretched out on the floor like a lazy ginger cat despite the flouncy party dress she was wearing. Her feet in their patent shoes wiggled in time to the music on the record player.

He squatted down beside her. "Hi, pumpkin."

"Daddy!" She grinned in delight. "Come listen. You can really feel the music when you lie down."

Obligingly, he stretched out on the thick carpet beside her. She was right—you could actually feel it. As he listened, his eyes swept around her lair: toys scattered helter skelter, the much-loved Baccarat rabbit with one ear broken off. An intriguing collage of what looked like corrugated cardboard and wadded-up tissue paper sat half finished on her work table. It astonished him sometimes that this irrepressible little life had somehow sprung from his seed.

The music trailed off into an ear-wincing screech. Maura shut off the record player. "For God's sake, David," she snapped, "must you encourage this kind of behavior?"

The long-festering tension between them had deepened ever since he had returned from Europe and suggested a trial separation. Maura had coldly threatened him, "If you even think of divorcing me, I'll take your daughter away. By the time I'm done with her, she'll hate you."

David watched her pull Katie to her feet. "Look at you!" Maura scolded, fluffing out the child's layers of petticoats before retying the big bow at the back of her dress. Maura herself looked stunning, her evening gown of bronze chiffon over crinoline subtly defining her flawless figure. Her obsession with perfection extended to her daughter, as if a perfect appearance could somehow make up for Katie's incurable imperfection—her blindness. "And your hair," she went on, irritated, pushing at unruly wisps of red curls escaping out from the intricate braid. "I don't know why I bother."

"Damn it, Maura," David said sharply. "It doesn't matter."

"Doesn't matter?" She rounded on him. "But we'll be at the club!"

"Let's cancel the dinner reservations. I don't feel a hell of a lot like celebrating."

"Don't be so selfish. Katie's been looking forward to this all week, haven't you, darling?" She knelt beside the child. "You want to go out with Mummy and Daddy to celebrate his birthday, don't you?" she cooed, looking back over her shoulder at him. "Surely you wouldn't want to disappoint her."

Maura's sarcasm made him itch to slap her. "She's used to it by now," he whispered tightly as Katie moved through the archway ahead of them. "You do it all the time."

The Fox Chapel Country Club, situated well back from the road amid rolling lawns, exuded a comfortable elegance. The black-and-white tiled entryway opened onto twin sets of stairs that led down to a vaulted, glass-domed garden room. Maura swept ahead of them into the dining area. Its ornate ceiling was patterned with white rococo medallions, and a wall of French doors overlooked the wide terrace and the emerald sweep of the links beyond.

David, matching Katie's step, was so intent on the eager way in which she moved into an unfamiliar environment that he was caught totally offguard by the shouts of "Surprise!" and "Happy birthday!" Friends and family crowded around, laughing. David tried to smile as he moved through the sea of faces.

Some time later, he overheard his mother say to Maura, "I must compliment you on the party. It's nice to see your attention focused on your family for a change." Then Maura's cool retort: "I'm always concerned about their well-being. My gift to David will show just how important my family is to me."

Wondering what she was up to, David turned. He watched Phil introduce Maura to his date. Ignoring the girl, Maura put her mouth to Phil's ear and said in a stage whisper, "Everything ready?" At his nod, Maura drifted away to greet other friends.

David grabbed his partner's arm. "Come on, buddy, give! What have you and Maura cooked up?"

Phil grinned. He was bubbling over with creative energy—just the way he got when he had some fantastic design brewing. Before David could grill him, Louis and Nickie came up. Marriage seemed to agree with them both. Nickie, in an elegant dinner dress and close-fitting hat with rhinestones sprinkled in its netting, looked as if she had been born to the high life. She was reveling in the wealth her veterans' housing project had created for them all. In fact, O'Rourke and Branzino's lucrative home-construction subdivision had become the firm's backbone.

Nickie reached up to kiss his cheek. "You're sure ageing well," she teased him, turning to include Louis. "Both of you."

Louis smiled lazily. " 'Thirteen was a very good year."

Maura drifted back and linked her arm possessively through David's. "Hullo, Louis," she said, adding almost as if it were an afterthought, ". . . Nickie."

Nickie's smile sharpened. "Life's just a long, luscious fairy tale for some of us, isn't it, Maura? Castles in the air . . ."

David saw Maura's expression darken warningly. What the hell was going on—was the whole world in on whatever dubious surprise she had engineered?

After dinner everyone gathered around the alcove, which had been curtained off. Maura, her arms resting lightly on Katie's shoulders, beckoned to David to come closer so that the three of them stood as if posing for a portrait. Maura smiled at the crowd. "Those of you who have been in on my little secret know what a tremendous amount of love and effort have gone into the preparation of this very special gift." She turned to Phil. "Ready?"

A gasp went up when he drew the curtain and revealed a three-dimensional home model, complete with an indoor-outdoor swimming pool, a solarium, a music room, and a gracefully curving staircase that seemed to float in mid-air. Phil's wonderful design was detailed down to the carved patterns incorporated into the walls and around the doorways. He explained that he had created the textured motif as a guide rail for Katie, at which point Maura interrupted to emphasize that the entire home had been designed around the child's special needs.

Nickie watched this show with narrowed eyes. What a sly, manipulative bitch, she laughed to herself, moving to join Louis and his mother as they examined the model. "Beautiful, isn't it?" Nickie murmured. "You know, I think we should commission Phil to design a winter home. Palm Beach is delightful, I hear. You two could golf, play bridge with the other snowbirds—"

"You'd just love that, wouldn't you, Nicoletta?" Josephine Urbano snapped. "Having Louis and me off the scene while you're here in *my* home, in *my* husband's bank, running the show."

Nickie smiled sweetly. "Now, Mother," she said, knowing how much she hated when Nickie called her that, "I was simply thinking of you and your arthritis, especially now that you're getting on."

The elder Mrs. Urbano moved away in a huff, and Louis shook his head. "Good God, Nickie, must you always bait her?"

"You know what cats women can be. It doesn't mean a thing. We just have to let off steam once in a while," she said. All the while her observant eyes followed David as he went through the motions of looking pleased. Louis was one thing, weak and malleable, torn between the conflicting needs of the women who dominated his life. But David was something else again. Just how long was he going to put up with Maura's crap? Nickie had a hard time figuring what he wanted for himself. The business was rolling in bucks now, compounded by the fact that

Daddy O'Rourke and his cronies had started to come around. Nothing bred success like success. Yet David seemed restless, almost indifferent to everything except Katie.

Across the room David continued to nod and smile, while inside he felt cornered. Using his devotion to Katie as the snare, Maura had trapped him so that he would have no choice but to build this magnificent showpiece. Resentful anger ate away at him. It's about time I start going after what I want, he thought. His love for Katie and the creative challenge of his work could not fill the void left by Angie's absence in his life. He needed her, now more than ever.

"Don't you love the house?" Maura enthused, kissing her husband in a show of affection. Her lips tasted metallic to him, as if they exuded some poison.

The drab, uninspired stone facade of the New York Metropolitan Opera was thick with decades of grime. David stared up at the block-square monstrosity, while traffic inched along on Broadway behind him. So this was the famed Met, the heart of American high culture—the mecca for every aspiring singer in the world. He felt a pang of disappointment.

Inside, the doorman gave him directions to the executive offices on the 39th Street side. Nodding, David detoured slightly to take a look at the massive stage. Offseason, the place was almost deserted, its echoing silences unnerving. He craned his neck to watch a scenic artist on the unrailed paint bridge forty feet above his head. The man worked swiftly, retouching a forest scene on an immense canvas drop that reached to the stage floor. David turned back to gaze out into the auditorium. Above the private boxes of the rich, the galleries extended dizzyingly upward. His disappointment gave way to excitement: He envisioned Angie enthralling a packed house with her sensual, powerful voice. His misgivings at what he was about to do vanished as he stood there. I'm doing this for her, he told himself.

"Mr. O'Rourke?" a female voice called from overhead. He turned and stared in surprise at a woman in a business suit perched on the paint bridge as casually as if she had been a trapeze artist. "I'm Mr. Boursault's secretary. He sent me to see if you'd gotten lost. You can use the elevator around the corner. It'll bring you right up to his office." She grinned. "That way you won't have to cross the bridge."

Paul Boursault, manager of the Met, was a portly, balding man with a hearty handshake that radiated energy. "O'Rourke? Pleased to meet you. May I introduce Harrison Fredricks—scion of one of our most prominent New York families. Been on the board here for thirty years. He's privy to every decision, major and minor, made in this company."

David turned to face a distinguished elderly man. Fredricks nodded curtly toward a chair. "Have a seat. We're all ears."

David caught the sardonic edge to his tone, but he chose to ignore it as he sat down. "I've done my homework, gentlemen. I know the Met runs perpetually in the red and that you rely on the city's wealthier citizens to subsidize your operations." He nodded in Fredricks's direction. "But I figured there's always room for one more philanthropist."

The opera manager smiled. "Your point, Mr. O'Rourke?"

"I'd like to finance the Met's talent-hunting trip to France this summer—all expenses paid."

Fredricks grunted. "Very generous of you. And the catch?"

"I want the scout to discover a young Italian soprano who's with the Paris opera. Her name is Angelina. She uses no last name—just Angelina."

Fredricks's eyes glinted with youthful sharpness, a contrast to the drooping pouches of skin beneath them. "Your interest in this Angelina is strictly professional, I assume?"

Cynical old bastard, David thought in amusement. "Whatever my interest in her, I guarantee my proposition will be much to the Met's advantage."

Boursault looked up from the figures he was scribbling on a yellow legal pad. "We're prepared to accept your offer, Mr. O'Rourke. However, if this soprano proves disappointing, our scout will be under no obligation to recruit her. If he passes her over, you can't come back here bellyaching about how we reneged on our deal. Understood?"

Smiling, David stood up. "She won't disappoint him."

Outside again on the hot pavement, David glanced at his watch. He had an appointment with the real-estate agent in twenty minutes. With luck they could conclude their business in time for him to catch the afternoon flight back to Pittsburgh, and no one would be the wiser.

He moved briskly down the busy sidewalk. By autumn Angie would be here in New York, rehearsing for her Met debut. She would never be out of his reach again.

39

Lugano lay at the base of the Alps on the Swiss-Italian border. Angie and Marshall had already spent two days here, riding the steamer which plied the region's lakes, exploring gemlike Borromeo Island with its seventeenth-century palace and exotic gardens, and splurging on meals in picturesque outdoor restaurants. Now she was about to leave him at one of the Swiss villas that had been converted into a boarding school.

Mother and son walked hand in hand through the school grounds, breathing in the nippy air that shimmered off the silvery-leafed olive trees at the base of the mountains. She looked out over the soccer field and horse stables, the rolling meadows that served as ski and sledding slopes for the students every winter. "You'll be happy here, I know it," she told him.

"I'd rather go with you to America."

She smoothed back the thick hair that fell over his forehead in dark, lustrous waves. At ten he was a handsome, solemn boy, his brilliant blue eyes arresting against the dark olive of his skin. "Marshallino," she said softly, cupping his face in her hands, "we've been over this a hundred times. I won't have a second for myself, let alone for you, once I start work."

His eyes pleaded. "I wouldn't complain, Mama."

"Here you'll be with kids your age. You'll make friends."

"I don't want friends. I want to be with you."

"I . . . I know, darling." Angie's voice caught in her throat. "But Z'Giulia is close. Milan's only a few hours on the train. Now that she's settled back there, you'll see each other all the time. You know how much she loves you—how much we both love you!" Angie bent to kiss his forehead. "This is only for six months, darling. It's what we've worked toward for so long!"

Even to her the words rang false. As if the Met could mean anything to him, she thought, anguished at the prospect of their separation. Six months was a lifetime to a child. Yet she had no choice but to leave him here, safely out of Tony's reach. The boy knew nothing of his father, nothing of the vengeful nature that could destroy both mother and son. As far as Marshall knew, his father was an anti-Fascist Resistance fighter killed by the Germans.

Dr. Ablier, the school director, crossed the gravel driveway toward them. He was a charming, courtly man whose wife taught languages. He smiled kindly. "Your son will be in good hands, Signora Branzino, I assure you."

"Yes, I know that," she said, her eyes fixed on Marshall. He looked as if he was about to cry. "Good-bye, darling," she said quickly, kissing him again. "The time will go fast!"

She climbed into the waiting taxi, waving to him as they drew away. Suddenly Marshall tore away from Dr. Ablier and dashed headlong down the driveway after the taxi.

"Stop!" Angie yelled to the driver. "Wait, please!"

She jumped out, and Marshall ran into her arms. Tears streamed down his face. "Mammina." He was out of breath, sobbing. "Don't go. Don't leave me!"

She clung to him until at last his sobs subsided, then she knelt at his side. With shaking fingers she reached around her neck and unfastened the gold cross. Gently she slipped the crucifix over his head and folded his hand over it. "This is our connection, Marshallino. It will bind me to you, mother to son, my life to your life: They are one and the same. Wear it and know my thoughts are with you every minute, no matter how far apart we may be." She kissed him again, breathing in the wonderful sweetness of him, the little-boy smell of open fields and sticky candy. Gently she pushed him away before she broke down in tears. "Go on," she said, her voice thick with emotion. "Be strong, like Mama has to be."

He stood rigid as she climbed into the taxi. As it picked up speed on the winding road, she turned to stare out through the rear window. Marshall stood alone in the driveway. Then the taxi rounded a curve, and he disappeared from sight.

Sometimes she felt as if her life would be nothing but one long series of good-byes, Angie thought as she stood facing Giulia Francini outside the Milan train station.

"I'm not sure if I'm doing the right thing," Angie said.

"You are," the older woman murmured, her hands clutching the head of her cane whose necessity she despised. "Angelina, I know you're apprehensive, but you must concentrate on what you're going back to America for. You will sing, you will be a success."

Angie took Madame's hand and raised it to her lips. "Thank you so much for your faith in me. I would never have made it this far without you. You know that."

"Angelina, you are like a daughter. I care very deeply for you and our Marshallino. I . . . I shall miss you." Sunlight caught the glint of tears in her eyes. She brushed them away in irritation. "You must go now, and do what you have prepared yourself to do all these years. We will be here waiting. And when you return, it will be a joyous occasion."

Angie hugged her. The tears that she had fought to hold back in her son's presence poured forth. "I'll miss you so much."

Brusquely Madame Giulia smoothed Angie's hair back. "Go on now, child," she whispered, lifting her hand in farewell.

How strange it felt, Angie thought much later as the train rolled northward through France's verdant Rhone Valley and onward along the sun-drenched vineyards and undulating countryside of Burgundy. It was as though she were heading backwards in time, when her son had been nothing but a seed in her womb and she herself had been a battered, fearful girl, ravenous for life. A decade later and she was a woman now—stronger, more confident of her powers, determined to succeed; and yet, lingering beneath the surface, lay that same fearfulness, ready to explode.

Desperately she tried not to think about Tony. What connection would a low-life Ohio hoodlum have to the New York opera world? None, she consoled herself. I'll be safe. Besides, she felt she had no choice but to grab this chance to sing at the Met. It might never come again.

As she drifted off to sleep, she thought of David. Even though she knew she should forget him, she couldn't help hoping that somehow he would find her and they would be together again.

The next morning, the orchards and lush pasturelands beyond Rouen gave way to the busy outskirts of Le Havre. New construction had sprung up everywhere. Here Angie found no signposts to the past. The old port as she remembered it was utterly gone. The *Ile de France* stood majestically in its berth, a trio of red and black funnels thrusting skyward above the white superstructure of the grand old ship—an anachronism in the modern shipyard complex rising from the ashes of war.

Angie was met at the dock by the Met representative, Lyle Carson, a cadaverous man with hunched shoulders. "Right on time," he said, glancing at his watch. After directing the porter to take her small trunk aboard, Carson explained, "I did a bit of advance P.R. with the captain. He's a big opera fan. He—"

"Monsieur Carson!" a female voice fluted. "Here I am!"

Angie turned to see Francoise Duvall climbing out of an overloaded taxi, her huge traveling cases tied to its roof. She carried Maxi on her shoulder as if the poodle were a baby. Just who I need to lift my spirits, Angie sighed. The French diva returned the sentiment, her mouth forming a moué of disdain at the sight of her junior rival. Neither could fathom why the other had been recruited.

"Listen," Carson said, addressing them in his fluent

but badly accented French, "the captain's asked that you both sing at a gala the night before the ship docks. You'll sit at his table. I've already accepted on your behalf. You can choose your own music."

Excited and nervous, Angie almost ran up the gangplank. Lalique crystal lamps blazoned the way along wide corridors graced with statuary, bas reliefs and artistic ironwork. The smiling steward led the two women to cabins opposite each other. Angie gazed around in amused delight. "I can't believe they're already treating us like stars."

"I *am* a star," Francoise said arrogantly. "I deserve this and more."

As the steward unlocked Francoise's door, Angie made a mock bow. "Age before beauty."

The diva's eyes glittered angrily. "What is your youth? Nothing! You are like cheap champagne that effervesces too fast and dies quickly." The woman swept into her cabin and slammed the door.

Being thrown together for the duration of the voyage only sharpened their mutual derision. At intimate stateroom parties to which they were both invited, their rivalry became a source of amusement to the bored first-class crowd. Once she saw their smiles, Angie changed her tactics immediately. She began to defer to the older diva's opinions with an almost exaggerated respect. Duvall was no fool either. When she realized what Angie was up to, she neatly turned the situation on her by emphasizing Angie's youthful gaucheness. Eventually Angie played right into the sly Duvall's hands, when at the last party the woman accused her of not being able to hold her liquor. The challenge was too much for Angie, who felt compelled to prove her sophistication by drinking almost a whole bottle of Mumm's champagne by herself. She got so tipsy that two stewards had to help her back to her cabin, with Duvall tut-tutting maternally behind them all the way.

And so Duvall had gotten the last laugh.

With a flurry of whistles and foghorn blasts, the *Ile de France* was warped to the French Line pier on the Hudson. Angie, bleary eyed and queasy, shaded her eyes against the late-afternoon sunlight. She was thankful her ghastly hangover was almost gone.

The carnival-like mood that reigned on deck—streamers flying and voyagers calling down to friends and family waiting on the dock far below—helped lift her spirits. She walked gingerly toward the disembarkation area, telling herself that she would not be sick all over the classically tailored Lanvin suit that she had scrimped for all year and bought on sale at the fashion house.

The captain, a tall, corpulent man with a silky white mustache, hailed her over the heads of the first-class passengers who had begun to disembark. "Mademoiselle," he cried, "we were so sad that you were indisposed last night. What a farewell feast you missed. Our chefs truly outdid themselves—a whole roast oxen, mind you, and souffles the size of their hats." Angie covered her mouth. "But the pièce de résistance was the entertainment. La Duvall gloriously filled the breach of your absence. A truly—"

"Did I hear someone mention my name?" a voice trilled behind them.

"Ah, madame," the captain said, bowing to the diva, "I was just commiserating with your unfortunate colleague."

Duvall smiled sympathetically. "Yes, poor thing."

They were interrupted by a well-dressed American couple. "Miss Duvall?" the woman began. "I just wanted to say how much we enjoyed your singing last night. We intend to get tickets for the Met. May I have your autograph for my daughter?"

Other passengers milled around the diva, crowding Angie back toward the rail. Idiot, Angie berated herself. At least her self-directed anger had the effect of clearing her woozy head. She was searching for a steward to bring her trunk down when a deep, excited voice called, "Angie!"

Unable to believe it, she whirled to see David striding up the gangway. Laughing and crying, she ran to fling herself into his arms. "What on earth are you doing here?"

"I wanted to welcome you home," he said huskily. "And to apologize for walking away from you in Paris. I've been planning this moment ever since I got your letter."

"But you must be so busy, your work . . ."

"Shut up," he growled, both teasing and loving. He drew her close and fixed her with a hungry kiss that melted her bones. "Haven't you figured it out yet? You're the one thing that matters to me, Angie. All the rest is just marking time."

"David." She buried her face in his neck. His appearance had banished the loneliness and depression she had been struggling against since she had left Europe.

As their taxi sped along, the flashy neon signs downtown formed giant pinwheels against the fading sky. The honking cars, the streaming throngs of pedestrians, the towering buildings themselves emitted a high-voltage, razzle-dazzle energy. Angie had forgotten that the American pulse beat so strongly. She felt exhilarated, as if she were on a wild carnival ride. She had the sensation that she was being spun towards events whose outcome she could neither predict nor control.

They drew to a stop before an elegant apartment building opposite Central Park. Angie turned to David, smiling. "This doesn't look like the Barbizon Hotel."

"A surprise." He held out his hand. "Come on."

Once upstairs, he handed her a key. She laughed. "What is this?"

"Open the door and find out."

She turned the key and stepped into a spacious apartment overlooking the park and city skyline beyond. Soft lamplight illuminated a curving sofa angled toward the view. "It's wonderful," she breathed. "Yours?"

"No. Yours."

"David, it's too much," she protested. "I can't accept this."

Brushing aside her protests, he pulled her inside and showed her all around. As he switched on the bedroom light, Angie gasped in startled delight. Brilliantly hued designer gowns draped the bed and matching slipper chairs; they hung from the curtain rod above the wide balcony doors, dazzling the eye with their sumptuous colors and textures. In a daze she wandered through the collection of exquisite fabrics. There were gowns of sea-green silk taffeta and absinthe-yellow chiffon, smoky gray velvet and starkly dramatic black faille. A mirrored armoire stood open, one door festooned with a silver-blue mink cape and the other with a long evening coat of padded, cherry-red silk. She recognized the lavish designs of Jacques Fath, the rich detailing of Balenciaga and Molyneux. The one-of-a-kind gowns must have cost more than the furnishings in the entire apartment. Such reckless generosity left her speechless. Finally she turned to him. "This is crazy, David. You're crazy!"

"Crazy about you," he said, leaning against the doorway, his hands thrust in his pockets. "Once I started buying, I couldn't stop. You should be drenched in drama and color. I've always said that, haven't I?" He grinned.

She smiled back at him uncertainly. "It's all lovely and wonderful, but . . ."

"But what?"

"David, what do you expect of me?" she asked, her voice low and intense. "I won't be your mistress. It would demean us both."

"Is that what you think?" he said tightly. "That I'm trying to buy your affections with all this? That I want to manipulate you to satisfy my needs? Christ, Angie, I offered you my life in Paris—to share all of it, and you turned me down! I was hurt and bitter. Then I realized I was only making myself more miserable. Listen to me: I'll accept whatever you choose to share of yourself. Just don't shut me out completely. I couldn't endure that."

Though still doubtful, she came to him and slipped her arms around his waist. She leaned her head against his chest. "Oh, David, why does it have to be so difficult?"

He stroked her hair. "Angie, let's make this our refuge. When we're here the rest of the world won't exist. Nothing will—except us."

He makes it seem so easy, she thought, lifting her mouth to be kissed. How she had longed for this in her dreams, relived a thousand times her sensual awakening in his arms. Feverishly she helped him as he struggled with her buttons. She felt no shame or fear this time, only a joyful eagerness to join her body to his. Yet she was still too shy, too new to the idea of emotional intimacy with a man to tell him how much he excited her, how she had longed so many lonely nights for his caresses, for his murmured endearments that made her feel so beautiful, so desirable, so quintessentially woman.

As they lay back against the coolly fragrant sheets, she whispered his name over and over again.

Their foreplay was slow and languorous, a sweet rhapsodic exploration that meandered and teased, arousing in her a breathless fire that radiated from her center in delicious shock waves. "Make love to me, damn it," she whispered finally, laughing, her tongue teasing his chest, "before I explode."

Their quick, fierce coupling left the barely perceptible imprint of his teeth against her throat and red scratches from her nails across his lower back. Like primitive clan markings, they were physical proofs of the bond that had been sealed by this act of love, this act of affirmation and trust.

Afterward, they lay nestled together like spoons. He put his arm around her, and she held it close between her breasts. "This is almost perfect," she breathed in soft contentment.

"Almost?" he teased her, nuzzling her hair back so that he could kiss her warm neck.

"The lovemaking was perfect, you know that." She sighed. "It's just—I miss Marshall so much."

"We'll send for him."

Angie turned, her eyes huge in her face. "No! Nothing's changed. You must understand that, David. Tony is so close it frightens me. I'm taking a risk. But under no circumstances will I risk my son's life."

"Angie, sweetness, the man's not going to touch either one of you. He's ancient history."

"You're so wrong about that," she whispered, staring past him toward the moonlight that lay in a silvery pool below the balcony door. "You've never had to deal with the Latin thirst for vengeance, David. No, it's never going to end." For all the warmth of their snuggled bodies, she shivered.

David stroked her bare arm. "Angie, don't think about it. We can't let him taint this night. Everything's going to be fine, I promise you."

But long after she had drifted off in his arms, sleep eluded him. He looked down at her relaxed features, so soft and vulnerable as she slept. Their innocence was so at odds with the strong-willed presence she radiated by day. Bit by bit, apprehension and the first faint stirrings of guilt crept into his mind. Maybe he had been wrong to manipulate the Met into bringing her home. No, he tried to convince himself, it'll all work out. No matter what, he would protect her.

40

Nickie stood at the back of the Met auditorium, waiting for her eyes to adjust after the blinding brilliance of the snowy streets outside. The stage was a beehive of activity. Swelling music competed with the cacophony of carpenters hammering and shoving scenery around. She heard the conductor in the pit shouting at his musicians: "First violins, slow down . . . Gulden, you're a quarter-beat off!"

What a madhouse, she thought. Beneath all the brouhaha she detected the clickety-clack of radiators and steam pipes hissing away. Not that the heating system was doing much of a job, she thought, drawing the thick collar of her honey-colored fur close around her throat. The place was cold and drafty; it smelled stale. So this was Angie's glamorous world.

Angie sat in the third row with the *Tosca* score spread open on her lap. She hadn't sung the role in seven years and longed to do so again. But it wasn't to be. Millar, the director and an avid francophile, had given the part to Francoise. This season Floria Tosca was destined to be an overfed tigress. Angie tried not to dwell on her bitter disappointment as she sought comfort in Puccini's wonderful symphonic melodies.

A movement in the aisle caught her eye and she looked up in puzzlement at the elegant blonde wrapped in fur. Then the woman smiled tentatively, a crooked half smile that twisted Angie's heart. She jumped up, heedless of the pages of music slithering to the floor. "Oh, my God!" She raced toward the aisle and flung her arms around her sister.

Nickie stiffened, then finally hugged her back. Without warning she felt tears pricking her nose. She hadn't meant to cry; she had meant to be aloof, polite, on guard. What she hadn't expected was this maelstrom of emotion washing over her.

Angie drew back, laughing and crying as she wiped the tears from Nickie's face. "You're so beautiful, so damn grown up. I . . ." She paused as her voice broke. "Dear God, I can't believe we're actually standing face to face!"

"I've missed you, Ange," Nickie said with husky fierceness.

"I've missed you too, Nickolodeon." Angie's smile was tender, full of love. "You gave me a shock. You weren't due in until eight."

"We caught an earlier train. I conned your apartment super into letting us in. Z's already cooking up a storm."

Angie laughed through her tears. "How is she?"

"You know Z'Maria—she never changes," Nickie said, sniffing. "Look, you want to grab a cup of coffee somewhere?"

"Nickie, I can't leave."

"Of course," Nickie said, rummaging nervously through her purse until she found her handkerchief.

"It's just that dress rehearsal's about to start, and I'm understudying the role."

"Understudying?" Nickie's brows lifted. "From what David's been telling Phil and me, I thought you were a star."

Angie shook her head. "Long story. But I fought and got a good mezzo role at least. Carmen's such an alluring character. . . ."

Nickie nodded, not really listening. She couldn't help marveling at how wonderful Angie looked. Yet her polished air of savoir faire had not tainted the charming sweetness that so endeared her to people. When Nickie told the Met doorman she was Angie's sister, the old guy's face had lit up. "She's a doll, that Miss Angelina," he'd said. "So friendly and considerate. Never high-hat. We'd do anything for her." So what else was new? Hadn't

Josephine Urbano once succumbed as completely to Angie's charm?

"To think this all started in Father Lucatta's kitchen," Nickie said, looking up at the stage. "Fate's strange."

"I know. Sometimes I find it hard to believe my own life—the twists it's taken . . ." As she trailed off, Nickie turned away, disconcerted by her sister's wistful, almost pleading expression, as if suddenly she needed Nickie's absolution.

"Are you here to stay?" Pent-up resentment bled through Nickie's husky voice. "Or are you eventually going to run again?"

Angie gave a helpless shrug. "That's not fair."

The opening notes of the opera—three menacing chords reverberating through the vast auditorium—signaled that rehearsal had begun. Further conversation was impossible. "Listen, Nickie," she said hurriedly, talking over the music, "we'll discuss it tonight, okay?"

Before Angie had even turned away, Nickie could see that she was already lost in her dramatic, imaginary world.

At the end of rehearsal, Angie was standing at the back of the stage, watching Duvall sing her final aria as she climbed to the top of the parapet. The last note died away, and the diva leapt unconvincingly to her death. She landed on a mattress a couple of feet below the fake castle wall, complaining loudly when someone didn't rush over fast enough to help her up.

"Geez," a heavily accented Bronx voice whispered to Angie, "that broad never lets up, does she?"

"Hi, Jimmy." Angie turned to smile at the small, wiry stagehand whose showbiz career had begun as a janitor and some-times performer with Barnum and Bailey. They watched Francoise flounce past, rewarding them each with a glare.

"What's her *problem*?"

Angie laughed. "She thinks the whole world owes her homage."

"You hear she had my cousin's buddy fired last week over nothin'?" Jimmy added feelingly, "Friggin' witch."

"She's a witch all right," Angie agreed. "She's been giving me grief for the past two years."

"Two years? You deserve a medal." His eyes sparkled with mischief. "Ya know, I got an idea how we could all get even with that Frenchie cream puff."

"Jimmy . . ."

"Hey, I didn't say nothin'," he demurred, turning to stare speculatively at the mattress where Duvall had landed.

Angie stepped inside her airy Central Park apartment, and the aroma of simmering tomato sauce instantly transported her back to Coalport. Suddenly she felt like a little girl, excited and scared at the same time. She peeked into the kitchen. Z'Maria, a dishtowel tied around her waist, was banging pots around and muttering, totally at home. Angie could almost convince herself that her long absence had never happened. Z'Maria was ageless, changeless. Watching her, Angie felt a sense of peace steal over her.

"Z'," she called softly, as not to startle her.

The woman turned. "Madonn'," she gasped, tears starting in her eyes. "Angelina!"

Angie held out her arms. The women clung to each other, too overcome by emotion to speak. Finally Z'Maria drew back, holding her eldest niece at arm's length. "Look at you," she keened, her small eyes bright with tears. "Europe has changed you. It's put the sadness in your blood."

Angie swallowed. "Can you ever forgive me, Z'?"

"Madonn', my beautiful girl, what is there to forgive, eh?" the woman said, hugging her again as Nickie came out of the guestroom. "The important thing is that we are all together again."

"I'm afraid, Z'. I'm afraid of Tony."

"You no worry about him," her aunt answered fiercely. "Carlo gave me his word he would keep Tony from your throat. But don't get me started on that *stronzon'*, you'll make me burn my ravioli." She turned to the bubbling pot and stirred it vigorously.

Angie leaned over to kiss her aunt's cheek. "Thank you so much, Z'," she said simply. Knowing that she had been promised a measure of protection, Angie felt as if a huge weight had been lifted from her shoulders.

The woman waved her off. "For what?"

"The ravioli," Angie teased her, hovering by the stove. "What did you do—carry them up in your suitcase?"

The woman puffed out her chest. "How else?"

Nickie came through the door and leaned against the counter. "You should have seen us, Ange," she said wryly, lighting a cigarette. "Just like a couple of dagos fresh off the boat—lugging Z's wine, Pete's homemade sausage, hot peppers from Freddie's garden. They thought you've been starving all these years."

"I have been in a way," Angie said, the quiet words eclipsed by the radiant smile she gave them. "I'm so happy you're both here."

Long after the food had been eaten and the wine drunk, the three Branzino women sat at the table reminiscing about the past. Angie refused to dwell on anything unpleasant, nor would she discuss her life in exile. Her homecoming was too precious to be marred by discord.

After Z'Maria had gone to bed, Angie stood at the sink, her silk blouse rolled up above her elbows as she scrubbed a pot with a scouring pad. Nickie stood beside her, drying forks. Neither had spoken a word in five minutes, aware of the constraint that had begun to seep between the cracks of their surface camaraderie.

Finally Nickie tossed her towel onto the dish drainer and reached for the cigarettes she had left on the counter. "So, what aren't you telling us, Ange?"

"What are you talking about?" Angie said defensively, scrubbing the already gleaming pot harder.

"Come on, we're not blind. You got jumpy every time we started to ask you anything."

"You're imagining things."

"Really?" Nickie murmured sardonically, dragging on her cigarette. "By the way, did I mention I'm on the board of the Pittsburgh Opera Guild? Me, who wouldn't know a B flat from a C minus." She laughed on an exhalation of smoke. "I haven't stayed awake through a performance yet." She gave Angie an openly challenging look. "You've chosen a strange life for yourself, big sister: standing up in front of sham scenery, singing ridiculous love duets with overweight Casanovas in girdles. After ten years of that crap, do you think you even remember what reality is?"

"My little sister, the philistine," Angie snapped, stung by Nickie's sarcasm. "I've probably learned more about life—real life—from opera than you'll ever learn from behind a desk. It may be all those silly things on the surface, but at its core the music is a metaphor for passion, for everything crazy and illogical that makes us human. You of all people should know that, Mrs. Urbano. I mean, you're living an opera libretto yourself, aren't you, in that improbable sham of a marriage."

"Louis is a friend," Nickie said tightly, jamming her cigarette into the sink with shaking fingers. "I happen to care for him deeply."

"Spare me the gory details, if you don't mind." Angie edged past her, intent on gaining the refuge of her bedroom. But something made her hesitate and she turned around. Intuitively she realized that beyond Nickie's brittle facade lurked the cockily defiant girl who had always been hurting inside. "Nickie, what's wrong with us?" A contrite smile hovered on her lips. "Why are we punishing each other?"

"I don't know." Nickie laughed wearily. "Too much of Z's dago red?"

They both laughed then, a little shakily.

Angie made a pot of coffee and they drank it, sitting side by side on the sofa in the dark living room.

"I resented you for so long," Nickie said, her gaze fixed on the etherealized city skyline beyond the window. "It's like you were an escape artist—always managing to slip away while the rest of us had to slog through the shit."

Angie sat on the edge of the sofa, staring into her empty cup. "You may think my life hasn't been tough compared to yours, Nickie, but it was tough because I lived it," she said ruefully. "You can't possibly know the pain of always having to leave a part of yourself behind. Don't you think it tore me apart to have to go with the Urbanos? Then I married Tony and it was infinitely worse. I had to run. Pieces of my life are scattered here and there." Tears suddenly came to her eyes and she wiped them with the back of her hand. "Now I'm here and part of me is still in Europe."

"What are you talking about?"

"Nothing." Angie rubbed her temples. "God, how I wish I'd killed Tony," she said with a sudden ferocity that startled them both.

Nickie stared at her. "I used to think I could read you, Ange," she said, her voice husky with emotion. "Now I don't know who or what you are."

Angie stood up and started to pace. "I'm just a woman like you, Nick. Fighting to make something of my life, to preserve what's mine."

"To preserve what—your precious career?"

Stung, Angie retorted, "If that's what you think, then you really don't know me at all!"

"Tell me then!"

Angie debated for a long moment before answering. "Nickie, I have a son," she said almost inaudibly. "A ten-year-old son."

"Tony's?" Nickie said in disbelief.

"His name is Marshall. He's a Branzino. He's ours, understand? Not Tony's! Do you see now why I had to stay away?" Angie crossed her arms over her stomach, the pain of missing her son a physical ache deep inside.

"O God, Ange, if Tony finds out—"

"He won't."

"How the hell naive can you be? Tony's always got his feelers out."

"He won't find out," Angie repeated fiercely.

Chandeliers blazed in Sherry's restaurant on the second floor of the Met. Huge wall mirrors caught the light and refracted it with a scintillating brilliance to match the diamonds sparkling on throats and wrists around the room. Opening night of the new opera season brought out the *creme de la creme* of New York society.

Angie glanced across the table, where Z'Maria was cozily huddled with Harrison Fredricks. Neither seemed to notice the vast social chasm that should have kept them at arm's length. Fredricks, with his white leonine head and patrician features, towered over Z'Maria, who had begun to look like all the other crones on Dago Hill, her rounded shoulders belying the vigor of her spirit. Nickie, on Fredricks's left, smiled at something he said. Her sister, elegantly radiant in an evening dress of taupe silk faille with a scarf of baum martens and long kid gloves, looked entirely at home in this chic environment. How did she pull it off? Angie wondered, then realized with an inward laugh that Nickie was every bit as good an actress as she was.

From her evening bag Angie retrieved her densely jeweled compact—one of David's myriad other "surprises." The tiny mirror caught the gleam of her diamond earrings, the pale curve of her bare shoulders above the cuffed decolletage of her strapless Balenciaga gown. Angie noticed Nickie's eyes resting speculatively on the compact. Let her wonder. Angie's apartment, her clothes, her jewels were her own business. She wasn't ready yet to share the knowledge of her ties to David with anyone.

"Well, ladies," Fredricks said, his smile lingering longest on Angie, "are we ready?"

Angie nodded regally and stood up, giving a little swish to the graceful sweep of the gown's draped pannier as she turned. She had chosen the most muted of David's lavish gowns to wear, and its two tones of gray in velvet and taffeta were as silvery and cool as she meant her demeanor to be that night. She was well aware that all eyes were on her as she swept out of the restaurant ahead of her party, aware that they knew she was the mysterious young Italian soprano who had been passed over in favor of Francoise Duvall. Let them read in her face that she knew her own value, even if the director didn't.

Fredricks, a doting host, settled everyone in his box and passed around glasses of champagne. Angie barely touched hers, for she was hardly in the mood to celebrate her rival's debut. She had to struggle against the disapointment that threatened to engulf her. She was thirty, approaching the prime of her career. How ironic that the role she most coveted eluded her now when she had the capability to truly do it justice.

Fredricks leaned toward her. "By all rights you should be the one debuting on that stage tonight, Angelina," he whispered with an adoring gaze. "The role cries for a woman of your passionate vitality."

She looked at him, wondering if he had somehow read her mind. He was such an intriguing man. She never knew what to expect from him. When they had first met,

he had been abrupt and almost rude, but over the past
two months he had done a complete turnabout. No doubt
the whole world assumed she was his mistress.

The theater lights dimmed and the curtain rose. Duvall's
soaring bell-like voice lifted with seeming effortlessness,
but in achieving that purity of tone and line she sacrificed
expressivity. For Angie the evening dragged on. She
breathed a sigh of relief as Duvall moved toward the
parapet for her fatal leap. Crying out to the evil baron to
meet her before God, she jumped. Then to the utter
astonishment of the audience, the diva reappeared, bouncing into the air beyond the low castle wall, her screams
reverberating through the auditorium. She went down
and up again, staggering as she tried to get her balance.

"What in the . . ." Angie felt a giggle beginning deep
in her stomach. Jimmy, you devil, she thought. A
trampoline!

Inexplicably the curtain remained open throughout this
deliciously mad, hypnotic debacle, so that the audience's stunned silence gave way to furtive giggles and
finally a wild hilarity. Z'Maria and Nickie were holding
onto each other, laughing like banshees.

Even the dignified Fredricks had to pull out his handkerchief. Through his laughter he reached over to take
Angie's hand. "Somehow, my dear," he managed to say,
wiping away his tears of mirth, "I think you may be
taking over this role sooner than I had hoped."

41

Spring 1949

Nickie sat at her desk, reviewing the paperwork gener-
ated by the joint venture between Urbano Bank, O'Rourke
and Branzino and G. & O. Steel. The project had been
Nickie's baby from day one. She had nursed it through

all the channels, smoothed ruffled egos and personally lobbied city-council members to speed up the demolition of the old utilities building downtown. Now the results of her efforts were about to bear fruit. She had circled the last day of the month in red on her calendar: 9:00 A.M. groundbreaking ceremonies for the thirty-five-story G. & O. Steel Building, which Phil had designed but which she herself had masterminded.

As she leaned back and stretched her cramped back muscles, Nickie noticed the Pittsburgh Opera Guild envelope next to the phone. She opened it up and idly scanned the contents. She did a doubletake when she read the name "Angelina" printed in big bold letters. Feverishly she read the release about the ravishing new soprano who would perform at the local charity gala. Nickie dropped the sheet. Is she out of her mind! she thought, seething. Before she could pick up the telephone, the intercom buzzed and Madge Sinclair's crisp voice rang out. "One-second warning, Mrs. Urbano. The *other* Mrs. U. is on her way in."

Josephine Urbano swept into her daughter-in-law's office. Her eyes swung briefly toward the framed eight-by-ten photo of Louis and Nickie on a nearby credenza. "I won't keep you. Please draft a check for ten thousand dollars," she said briskly. "I've committed the bank to finance the benefit gala next month."

In a bid for time, Nickie made a show of straightening the scattered papers on her desk. "I'm a member of the board. Why wasn't I informed about this ahead of time?" she demanded.

The elder woman stared at her incredulously. "Since when have you been interested in our decisions? You know as well as I that your so-called 'involvement' is just another of your pretenses."

"That's neither here nor there," Nickie snapped, irritated beyond measure because the woman was right. "The point is, I'm tired of seeing bank funds committed to your pet society projects. What makes you think you can regard this institution as a private piggy bank you can dip into whenever you feel like it?"

Her mother-in-law went white. "You seem to forget, Nicoletta," she said, enunciating each syllable as if she were biting off bits of ice, "my husband founded this institution. And as his heirs, Louis and I control all final decisions." She met Nickie's angry stare measure for measure. "Now, draft that check at once."

Josephine Urbano marched out, check in hand, and Nickie punched the intercom. "Get me New York, Madge."

Five minutes later, Nickie was embroiled in another argument, this time with Angie. "So you're under contract, so what? The Met doesn't own you. You could have weaseled out of this."

"I'm coming." A hint of steel rang behind Angie's warm musical voice. She sank down onto her apartment sofa, not wanting to hear Nickie's objections. She had made her mind up weeks ago.

"You're crazy," Nickie persisted. "You know that."

"I may be crazy, but I'm not stupid," Angie replied, exasperated. "I phoned Carlo DiPiano myself. He reassured me—"

"Bullshit," Nickie swore. "If Tony wants to get you, nobody's going to stop him."

"For God's sake, what do you expect me to do? Cower here in New York like a little mouse, estranged from the people and the place I love because of that monster? No!" Her fingers toyed nervously with the telephone cord. "Nickie, I've finally made something of myself. I want everyone in Pittsburgh to know that—to share my triumph with me."

"You dreamy-eyed, egotistical—"

"Call me all the names you want, Nickie, I don't care. I said I'm coming and that's final. Believe me, I've thought it through. This confrontation with Tony is inevitable," she said tightly. "Better on my terms, than his."

"Angie—"

"Good-bye, Nickie."

Nickie hung up, feeling oddly deflated. She envisioned how Louis's mother would be delighted when she realized that the famous diva Angelina was her beloved companion Angie from the old days. A stab of jealous insecurity twisted Nickie's insides.

She turned in her swivel chair to stare out over the changing city. Inevitably her thoughts circled back to the issue at hand. I'm the one who made this bank grow beyond anyone's wildest dreams, she thought angrily. Yet, when it got down to the nitty-gritty, she had no real power at all.

What can I do? she asked herself, absentmindedly twirling the jeweled watch that Louis had given her on their second anniversary. How can I secure the power—make sure it's mine once and for all?

Geographically, the steep ridge of Mount Washington and its houses running along the rim of Grandview Avenue reminded Tony Malfatti of the inaccessible villages of his youth. But there the similarity ended. The southern Italian landscape had been a bony hand squeezing the life and blood out of a man. This place was another story, he thought as he crested the hill in his new Chrysler. Up here a man could feel like a king. All of Pittsburgh lay at his feet, like a fat chicken waiting to be plucked.

He parked outside the luncheonette that Pete and Freddie Branzino owned, irritated that Carlo DiPiano always had to rub the family in his face. Not that he had a personal gripe with Pete. How could he hate a guy with the eyes of a saint?

"Hiya, Tony." Pete greeted him amiably from behind the bar as Tony headed toward the tables in back. "Pour you a beer?"

"Sure, kid." Every time Tony saw him, Pete had racked up another fifteen pounds or so; they said he ate so much now because the Japs had starved him in the war. *Pazzo*!

Tony's annoyance flared up again when he saw that DiPiano had invited his son, Rocco, to the meeting. But he covered it with a gladhand smile for the guys playing pinball in the corner and a respectful kiss on the cheek for the old man. He barely grunted a hello to Rocco, however. Carlo sat with his back to the wall of glass overlooking the city. Rocco sat next to his father, so that Tony had to sit opposite them and squint into the sun.

Carlo got down to business right away, complaining about the construction unions downtown that were balking at playing ball. "There's a Frank Yaminsky, head of the bricklayers," he said to Tony. "I want you to have a little talk with him."

"Right." Tony lit a cigar. "I'll have my boys take care of it."

"Forget your boys," Carlo said, his eyes sharp as glass. "I'm telling you to take care of it personally. *Capito*?"

Without waiting for Tony's reply, Carlo turned to his son and started talking the big-money end of things, the legit wheeling and dealing that formed their real base of power. All the rest—the loan-sharking, the whores, the pinball and bootleg cigarettes—was penny ante compared to what was coming down the pike. Tony hungered so badly for a piece of that power he could taste it. But the old man saw him as nothing but muscle, a whip hand without a brain in his head. Carlo turned back, and Tony began, "I got some ideas, you know, about funneling union—"

"Not now, Tony. There's something else we gotta discuss. Something important," Carlo said slowly, as if measuring the effect of what he was about to say. "I got word Angelina's coming back. And I'm telling you right now, I don't want no trouble. You understand me, Tony?" Carlo's razorlike gaze sliced through him.

The very mention of her name sent a searing pain through Tony's gut. "How long you known that? Where is she?" he said hotly. "I gotta right to know, goddamn it!"

"Shuddup and listen," the old man said, never raising his voice. "You stay away from her. Me and the Branzinos, we been friends a long time." He gestured toward Pete, polishing glasses behind the bar. "I give the boys here a sixty-forty break on the pinball. We all get along, you understand me, Tony? I watch out for my family—*all* my family. After all these years, I don't want no trouble."

It's my manhood, my fucking honor he's talking about, Tony raged inside, but he don't give a shit! Fury choked his throat, filling his mouth with bitter bile. He yearned to smash Carlo's face. Then he realized that Rocco was watching him, and he forced himself to smile affably. "Yeah, I understand, Carlo."

"I want your word, Tony. You're gonna let this go."

"Yeah, yeah, yeah."

Nodding, Carlo rose and left with his boys. Rocco didn't budge; his shrewd eyes impaled Tony for so long he had to resist the urge to squirm. Finally Rocco spoke, his voice a low-key echo of his old man's. "I can read your mind, Tony. You're thinking you can appease my father for a while because he's old, and sooner or later he's going to be out of the picture. But that's an illusion. Because once he's gone, it isn't going to make any difference. You'll still have to answer to me."

"You talk real fancy, lawyer boy, but you don't know shit."

Rocco stood up. "What happened between you and Angelina is water over the dam, Tony. We need your energy focused on what's important for the organization. We don't want it dirtied with a cheap vendetta that's going to call attention to us."

A muscle worked in Tony's cheek. "Keep your stinkin' nose outta my business, Rocco."

"Just a little lawyerly advice." Rocco smiled fleetingly. "No charge."

Mealy-mouthed asshole, Tony thought. What had Rocco ever done to prove himself a member of the organization, the way Tony had proved his loyalty—with blood. Rocco was weak, and eventually Tony would exploit that weakness. Once the old man was gone, things would be different, all right. It was only a matter of time before all the pawns fell into place right where he wanted them— including that bitch who had left him for dead.

Tony smiled suddenly. "Hey, Pete!" he roared. "You got any champagne in this joint? I'm in a mood to celebrate."

After the war, Bathsheba Green had relocated her small dressmaking business to a modest storefront downtown, assisted by a loan from Urbano Bank. Success hadn't changed her much. Bathsheba looked up from her sewing machine as the bell on the door tinkled and Nickie, still her best customer, swept in.

"Hi, Sheba," Nickie greeted her, untying the silk babushka that covered her head.

The black woman blinked when Nickie pulled the scarf off. "I thought scalpin' went out with the red folk," she said dryly, unable to take her eyes from her severely shorn hair.

Nickie struck a pose. "Think I'll turn some heads at the opera gala?"

"Honey, them heads, they'll be swivellin' clean off once they get a gander at you!" Her laughter was belly-deep.

Nickie grinned. "Is the outfit ready?"

"Oh, it's ready, all right," she said, gesturing with her head to the curtained fitting room. "I jus' don't know if this town's ready for *it*."

Nickie quickly changed, then stood on a stool while Bathsheba did the final fitting. "Now, you listen to me," the woman teased her. "If they like it, you tell 'em I'm the one responsible. But if they don't, which I 'spect to be the case, you tell 'em you rented it down at the costume shop." The woman stepped back to survey her handiwork. "Lordy, lord, I have made up lots of things for you, girl, but this . . ." She shook her head. "You sure you haven't done gone too far this time?"

Nickie laughed. "I hope I have."

42

Angie had taken great pains with her dressing room backstage in Pittsburgh's Carnegie Hall. A brilliant paisley scarf covered the dressing table and set off her silver brushes and crystal scent bottles, while the white mohair throw on the couch gave the room a cozily elegant touch. Framed photos chronicling her career stood before the vases poised in readiness for postperformance bouquets. As Renata had shown her long before, the dressing room was simply another stage where the star could shine.

The room began to fill with Opera Guild patrons and other wellwishers before the evening performance. Angie moved smilingly from group to group, telling amusing anecdotes from the glamorous part of her life in Milan and Paris. Her wealthy guests had paid for this evening, donating bundles to the city's new school for blind children. The least Angie could do was give them a good show, off stage as well as on. Looking across the crowded room, she caught Harrison Fredricks's eye, and he flashed her a brilliant smile. Gallant old dear, she thought affectionately: He had insisted on accompanying her on this trip. The man's devotion touched her. He had proposed marriage several times, but she always turned him down gently.

Angie was telling a woman the story of Maxi, the pampered poodle, when a messenger arrived with an envelope on a silver tray. Swiftly she opened it.

I've waited a long time for this, Angelina, she read. *I've seen you in the darkest hours every night. Now you're here in the flesh, and I can't tell you how good that makes me feel. I'll be waiting for you, Angelina, in the upper lefthand balcony.*

She recognized the handwriting even before her eyes slid to the arrogantly scrawled T at the bottom of the page. Her hands began to shake uncontrollably.

As she walked out onto the stage, Angie steeled her features into a semblance of calm confidence. But her eyes gave her away, darting anxiously as they did to the balcony. She stared up in shock at the lone figure sitting in the midst of an empty block of seats. Dear God, she thought in terror, would he dare kill her in front of a theater full of witnesses?

Tony's thousand dollars had bought him a block of twenty seats in the balcony that partially overhung the stage. He felt like God, sitting up there alone. He remembered something he had heard once, something about the whole world being a stage. Well, Tony felt like master of the world tonight. Absentmindedly he rubbed the nubby scar on his temple.

Music swelled from the orchestra pit. Angelina tossed the hair wildly framing her face as she began to move in time to the slow Spanish rhythm. Tony's eyes followed the sinuous movement of her body in the deeply cut, red ruffled dress, and he felt the traitorous answering movement of his loins. Fucking cunt, he breathed, filled at once with loathing and desire. Then she began to sing from *Carmen.* "Gypsy love is a roving rapture, a wanton bird that none can tame, not a bird for a fool to capture. . . ." The texture of her voice—warm, powerful, incredibly sensual—was something he had not even imagined. Yet, instinctively, he knew that this part of her had always existed, hidden away. It had been rightfully his, but she had kept it from him.

In that instant Tony knew that it wasn't her death that he wanted. Once long ago he had tried to possess and control this elusive bird, to keep her caged for his own private amusement. But she had flown free, taunted him with her freedom. Go ahead and sing, canary bitch, sing while you can, because I'm going to drag you down bit by bit, he vowed. Down to your worst nightmare.

The vast foyer of Carnegie Hall resembled the baronial reception chamber of an Old World castle. Flames crackled in the immense stone fireplace at the far end, glinting off the richly patterned floor of imported marble. Colonnades of massive *vert tinto* pillars soared to the ceiling—an intricately wrought baroque fantasy of antique gold from which three chandeliers hung suspended like a dowager's jewels. A bar had been set up at the other end of the foyer, ready to serve the eighteen hundred people who had poured out after the concert.

Angie stood in the shadows of the theater anteroom, her eyes feverishly scanning the crowded foyer. She was still shaken by the image of Tony sitting up there all alone. Fear had leant an element of poignancy to her performance; ironically, she acknowledged to herself that she had sung better that night than she had ever sung in her life. Where was he now? Even though she had extracted a promise from Carlo, Angie didn't trust Tony. But you can't stand here skulking in the shadows all night, she told herself angrily. She fluffed out the skirt of her ivory silk evening gown with its embroidered golden velvet flowers. Above the low-cut bodice she wore the diamond necklace David had sent her—a lacy pattern of stones that ringed her throat with delicate sparkles. She touched it briefly before moving out into the light with a regal smile.

Admirers thronged around her, drawing closer until she felt like a fish caught in a net. It was Phil who came to the rescue, pulling her away by her gloved hand. "Come on, Ange," he urged her, "the family wants to see you. They still can't believe it was really you up there on stage!"

Her heart filled with gladness as she saw them at the entryway. Z'Maria acted as if she owned the place, while Pete and Freddie huddled shyly next to Pap on his folding chair. She hugged and kissed her brothers, then knelt down before her father and took his almost weightless hands in hers. Nickie had tried to warn her, but nothing could have prepared her for this pathetic shadow of the brutal man who had dominated the Branzino household. All her revilement, her bitter resentment momentarily faded. In his frail, drawn face she saw an echo of her mother; she saw a part of herself that would soon be no more. "Papa," she said, tears sparkling in her eyes. "Papa, are you proud of me?"

"Angelina," he whispered, his thin chest struggling with each breath he took, "my first born. I thought I no see you again before I died."

"Papa, I'm here." She swallowed. "*Ti amo*, Papa."

Phil intervened. "Come on, Angie, let him rest. There's someone else who wants to see you."

Reluctantly she allowed herself to be pulled along, until she realized he was taking her to the Urbanos. She hung back. What on earth could she possibly say to Louis?

Then Josephine Urbano turned and saw her. "Angelina!" she cried, her whole face lighting up. "I can't believe it's really you. After all this madness dies down, we have to sit and talk. I'm so thrilled, so proud of what you've become," she gushed, enveloping Angie in a warm hug.

Angie closed her eyes, breathing in the floral cologne that transported her back into the Urbanos' car the day Louis's mother had come to the Hill to take her away— the day that had changed her life forever. "Mrs. Urbano," she said, her smile strained, "how lovely to see you!" Then she turned to Louis—handsome, duplicitous, charming Louis who had long ago swept her off her feet. Looking at him now, she saw the same lazily affable charm that had so completely taken her in as a girl. "Hello, brother-in-law." She greeted him with quiet irony.

"Angelina," he said, looking uncomfortable and rather embarrassed.

A stir of excitement from the entrance saved them the necessity for making awkward small talk. As all eyes turned, Angie heard Josephine Urbano breathe a horrified, "O my God!" Then Nickie swept into view, moving with lithe, boyish grace through the crowd that parted in shock for her. "Disgraceful!" Angie heard someone else mutter. "Outrageous!"

Outrageous, audacious, unpredictable Nickie. Angie laughed inwardly as she took in the pencil-slim black satin slacks that her sister had paired with a man's evening tails. Never one to do anything by halves, Nickie had also donned a man's starched white shirt fitted with a silver lamé cummerbund and black bow tie. But the coup de grace was her hair—scandalously short, parted on the side and slicked back. She looked like a masher from the twenties.

Nickie's eyes glinted with mischief as she joined them. "Angie," she said, laughing sharply, "you really didn't think you could upstage me, did you?"

So that's what the game's all about, Angie thought, her own smile bright and lively. "I'd ask you to dance, little sister," she shot back, "but I think you've already caused enough heart attacks for one night."

"Coward." Nickie turned to her husband and bowed. "My dear, may I have this dance?"

Looking as nonplussed as the others, Louis reluctantly allowed himself to be pulled into the middle of the room as the orchestra struck up "All or Nothing at All."

Standing at the bar with a bourbon in hand, Tony had no interest in Nickie's antics. His eyes continued to track Angelina, a vision in ivory, as Phil led her out to dance. His attention was so intent on her that he didn't notice the woman next to him until she asked for a light. He gave her the once-over. Christ, what a looker, he thought, a pouty little bitch with strawberry-blond hair that he could tell didn't come out of a bottle.

She smiled into his eyes as he lit her cigarette. "I'm Maura O'Rourke."

"Malfatti." He smiled back. "Tony."

"Not one of the Branzinos, then?"

"No," he said tightly, turning back to check out where Angelina was. "But you might say I got ties to the family."

The woman laughed. "Well, I'd stick around, Tony, but I see you've obviously got other things on your mind." She stubbed out her cigarette and picked up her drink. "See you around sometime?"

"Yeah, right," he said, watching her luscious behind as she sashayed off. He slugged down his drink and headed toward the dance floor.

As Phil swept Angie around, he said, "Remember the last time we danced together? It was at my high-school graduation party."

"We had a lot of good times." She smiled. "I've missed you all so much."

David came up and touched Phil on the shoulder. "Would you mind, buddy?" David took Angie into his arms and twirled her expertly around the room. "You look radiant tonight."

"We really shouldn't be dancing together." Her expression was rueful, tender. "People might guess."

"Might guess what—that I'm in love with you?" He grinned. "As if every other man in the place hasn't fallen for you tonight."

Despite her tension, David's lovingly teasing banter warmed her to the marrow. She was about to tease him back when she glimpsed Tony elbowing his way through the crowd in their direction. Before she could warn her partner, Tony was next to them.

"My turn," Tony said, rudely cutting in. When David hesitated to relinquish her hand, Tony persisted. "What's your problem? Me and the lady here, we go back a long way."

Feeling David's anger and terrified that Tony might sense there was something between them, Angie said formally, "Thank you for the dance, Mr. O'Rourke." She allowed Tony to slip an arm around her waist, but she refused to meet his eyes. As they danced, she stared past his shoulder with a patently false smile etched on her lips. When he tried to pull her closer, she held her elbows rigid, refusing to allow it.

"Ten years I waited for this. I figured you had to

surface sooner or later." Her skin crawled as she felt his warm breath on the side of her face. "I been a patient man, Angelina."

"You can't touch me," she said through her smile. "Carlo won't stand for it."

"Right now you're thinkin' you won, huh, Angelina? On top of the world." He laughed harshly. "But let me tell you something. Life's like a rollercoaster. Up 'til now it's been takin' you higher and higher. But you made a mistake when you came back, because from now on, bitch, it's gonna be a downhill ride all the way."

Angry with himself at having given in, David strode back onto the dance floor. "I think it's my turn again," he said, coolly wresting Angie from his grasp before Tony could make an issue.

As he whirled her away, Angie murmured: "Stay out of this, David, please. It has nothing to do with you."

"It has everything to do with me," he said grimly. "I promised to protect you, and I will." The music stopped, but he continued to hold her.

"He did his best once to destroy me. I absolutely refuse to stand by and let him destroy you," she said. "You *must* stay out of this." Pushing David from her, she turned and walked away.

Frustrated, David stared after her.

Someone touched his arm and he looked around, startled, into Nickie's worried face. "Remember what I told you when you came up to the Hill after the war?" she said softly. "I tried to explain the old dago mentality to you then, but unless you've lived with these people all your life, you can't fathom what we're about. People like Tony live by the old code—an eye for an eye. He's not going to stop. Nothing's going to stop him."

Listening to her, David felt helpless for the first time in his life. Nickie was right—nothing in his experience had prepared him for this. He lived in a milieu where wealth, power and influence could control any situation. But brutal men like Malfatti were out of his ken; he couldn't touch him without becoming like him. Too late, David realized that he had unleashed a dark force that he was incapable of controlling.

Dimly, through his haze of guilt and self-directed anger, he heard Nickie murmur, "I'm afraid for my sister, David. I truly am."

Still dressed in her *outré* evening clothes, Nickie knocked on Louis's bedroom door. "It's me. May I come in?"

He had draped his dress pants over the suit tree and stood unfastening his cufflinks. It was the first time, she realized, that she had ever seen her husband's bare legs. Nickie held up a bottle of Dom Perignon that had been chilling in the refrigerator.

"What's gotten into you?" he said with a weary smile. "You've been behaving bizarrely all evening. Why did you do that to your hair?"

She poured out two glasses of champagne and held one out to him with a teasing smile. "Let's drink a toast!"

"To what?" He eyed her wearily over their clinking glasses.

"To us."

Nickie sipped the expensive champagne, her eyes never leaving his face. "Tell me, Louis, do you find me attractive?"

"You're a lovely woman."

"I don't mean that," she said impatiently. "I mean, do you find me attractive in this get-up?"

"I . . . you look intriguing, like a boy dressed up in his father's evening clothes."

"Coming from you, that sounds like 'attractive,' " she teased him. "Go on, drink. The night's still young, and I feel wonderful." She did a little waltz around the room and came back to him, her eyes dancing. "May I have a cigarette?"

He withdrew his case and handed her one. She held it up to her lips, waiting for him to light it. As he brought the match up, her hand closed lightly over his to steady it. She saw that he noticed her fingernails. They had been cut off squarely like a man's. She laughed huskily. "What do you think?"

"Ab . . . about what?" he stuttered.

Without replying, she drifted toward the balcony doors and opened them. The May air felt soft against her skin as she stepped outside into the moonlight, which softened her boyish profile into silvery shadow. She reached up and unzipped her slacks, gracefully sliding them down over her hips. Her panties followed, until all that remained were the tuxedo tails partially obscuring her pale round buttocks. "Louis," she beckoned to him gently.

As in a dream he moved toward her.

She stood patiently, waiting, knowing that he was staring at the tempting illusion of male youth she had created in the semidarkness. "You don't even have to look into my face," she murmured, her voice enticingly low. "Fantasize, darling . . ."

Mesmerized, he slipped an arm around her and buried his face against the shaved nape of her neck. "O God," he murmured, "why are you doing this?"

Nickie reached behind her and unzipped his trousers. She fondled his swollen member, pleased to find him already excited. Unerringly she guided him into her feminine depths. They made love like that, standing up. For Nickie their coupling was exotic and strangely erotic. Hearing his helpless groan of pleasure, she smiled with satisfaction.

43

The summer had flown past more quickly than Angie thought possible. Only David knew where she had gone, darling David who was privy to everything in her heart, her joys as well as her sorrows. She had spent a marvelous six weeks with Marshall traveling through Italy and Greece, a wonderful idyll that had exploded when Marshall realized he was not going with her to America. Their parting was terrible.

He had written, pleading with her: *Mammina, please send for me. I would stay out of your way while you're working. I'm big now, eleven. Madame Ablier taught us how to make* croque monsieur *sandwiches with ham and gruyere cheese. So, you see, I could even cook for myself. Please, Mammina, I don't understand why we have to be apart. . . .*

His desperation, the thought of his anguished loneliness, made her want to weep. Why hadn't she simply told Marshall the truth about Tony from the start? The truth would have bound them closer. As it was, the lie she was forced to perpetuate had driven a wedge between them. She realized it was her destiny to have her life torn like this: forever having to choose between her love for her son and the passion and ambition without which she would not be whole.

She hurried along 40th Street in the brisk fall afternoon, her eyes scanning the unending river of traffic and pedestrians. Ever since her return to the States, she seemed to be constantly looking over her shoulder for Tony. She almost wanted to laugh. How in God's name could he hurt her more than she had already hurt herself?

As she passed a newsstand, her eye caught the two-inch high headlines blazing off a scandal sheet: MET DIVA WAS NAZI MISTRESS! Angie snatched up a copy of the paper and stared at the smiling photo of herself with Feldmarschall von Menzel. Her hands shaking, she started off down the street.

"Lady, hey, lady!" an outraged voice called at her back. "You gonna pay for that or what?"

She dropped the paper and melted into the crowd, feeling that everyone's eyes were on her. She crossed Broadway toward the front entrance of the Met but stopped abruptly when she saw the crowd of reporters and photographers milling excitedly out front. Turning on her heel, she ran back around to Seventh Avenue and lost herself in the jumble of trailer trucks offloading scenery and props from one of the Met warehouses. She sneaked inside and crept up a set of back stairs, frantic to reach the privacy and security of her dressing room.

Thank God, at last! She slipped inside, locked the door and leaned back against it with her eyes closed, panting. She felt like a fox being hunted by a pack of hounds. Breathing deeply, she smelled the cloying perfume of massed flowers. Flicking on the light, she blinked at the enormous bouquet of spiky black and purple gladiolus on her dressing table. As if hypnotized, she moved toward the funeral arrangement and plucked out the card with trembling fingers.

"Better hang on, bitch," she read. "The rollercoaster ride's just started."

She dashed the flowers to the floor, then tore up the note and threw the pieces onto the broken blossoms. A hand pounded on the door outside, and she whirled. "Who is it?"

"Mr. Boursault wants to see you up in his office."

"Coming," she called, struggling to keep her voice from cracking. She turned on the amber-colored lights that ringed her dressing-table mirror. The face staring back at her was shiny with perspiration. She hastily blotted her cheeks and nose with a handkerchief, then fluffed on loose powder, brushing it to a smooth matte finish. She squared her shoulders, schooling her features into a look of calm self-possession. It did not mask her desperation.

She stood rigidly before the opera manager's desk as he gestured toward the newspaper poking out of his wastebasket. "I expect you've seen the headlines."

"Yes. I—"

"Look, Angelina," he interrupted her. "I'm willing to ride this scandal out if you are."

"What?" She stared at him, speechless. "Oh, Mr. Boursault, how can I thank—"

"Enough already." He raised his hands. "This has nothing to do with any soft-heartedness on my part. What you may or may not have done during the war, I'm not going to judge. I'm no moralist. What I am is a businessman and, if I may say so, a damn shrewd one at that." His phone began ringing, but he ignored it. "My job is to make this opera house a paying proposition, you understand? And in my book, notoriety for one of my stars is as good a way as any to draw in the paying public." The phone continued to ring. He lifted the receiver and set it down on the desktop. "Like I said, if you're willing to put up with the heckling and the insults, then I'm willing to let you go on."

"I'll do it," she said without hesitation. "The opera's my life. I don't know any other."

* * *

In the week that followed, Angie never saw Tony Malfatti, yet he made certain that she felt his presence. The doorman informed her that a guy was lurking around asking questions about her, and someone else said they had seen the same guy dining with Françoise Duvall. The very idea terrified Angie: What if the Frenchwoman mentioned Marshall?

As if the week hadn't already been harrowing enough, the abuse heaped upon her by the outraged opera fans who filled the house each time she performed was petrifying. Yet she went on.

Elsie, the wardrobe mistress, had just fastened the last of the gold-braid couplings up the front of Angie's red Chinese silk gown for *Turandot* when one of the chorus members burst in. "We've got to evacuate—bomb threat! Everyone out!"

Hiking up the billowing costume around her knees, Angie dashed out behind Elsie into the corridor and joined the throng of frightened staff rushing pell-mell for the stairs. In the confusion Angie lost her black wig with its carved ivory pins, but she didn't dare stop to retrieve it.

As they rushed out onto Seventh Avenue, the whine of approaching fire engines filled the cold night air. Shivering in the thin silk, Angie started to pace. She heard her name and turned to see Boursault hurrying toward her. His normally dapper appearance was shot to hell. He looked as if he had just come through a war zone. "Angelina, I'm very sorry," he said, pulling her aside behind one of the big moving trucks. "But there is someone who most definitely does not want you on the stage. I just had a phone call. He said that if you're scheduled to go on again, there'll be another . . . incident like tonight's."

"You can't give in to him!"

"Angelina, listen to me: My first obligation is to the Met. We can't risk another disaster. Fleeing patrons nearly started a stampede at the Broadway exit. It's a miracle no one was killed!"

She swallowed. "O God."

"Angelina, who is this mad man?"

"An old enemy," she whispered. She felt tears smearing the thick, elongated rim of black liner around her eyes. "An old enemy who wants to destroy everything that's ever mattered to me."

44

Pap's body lay in a bronze casket against the parlor wall. Tall candles burned at each end of the makeshift bier. Angie sat on the worn sofa, still wrapped in her mink cape against the drafts that crept into the ramshackle house. In her lap she held the old recordings of Caruso that had been Pap's pride and joy. Angie would take them as his legacy to her. Pitifully little else remained. Except for the small olivewood crucifix that her mother had brought to America and a pair of topaz earrings edged in gold filigree that must have been her wedding gift from her bridegroom, all the rest would go to the junkyard. Her heart constricted at the thought. Their lives seemed so pathetic, so insignificant.

"Angie!" Full of vitality, Nickie swept into the sloping-floored parlor.

Angie stirred, suddenly aware of the life going on around her. Rich cooking odors wafted in from the kitchen. Sauces thick from simmering and redolent of beef and garlic overrode the subtler scents of roast chicken and hot peppers, the yeasty sweetness of *panettone*. She heard a pot lid clattering to the floor and Z'Maria's strident voice raised in argument over how much basil should go into the sauce. The neighborhood women had slaved over the funeral feast for two days.

Nickie perched on the sofa beside Angie, her pregnant stomach concealed by the pleat of her brown worsted wool skirt and unbelted suit jacket. "What are you doing in here all by yourself? It's so damned grim," she said, looking around with distaste. "Appropriate, though—an ending that fits the man and the way he lived."

"Nickie, not now. I'm in mourning, if you don't mind."

Nickie's narrow, tilted eyes dissected her. "You haven't forgiven the old bastard, have you?"

"I could never forgive the things he did, but I've come to understand why he did them." Angie sighed. "It's so strange. Somehow I never thought he would be gone." She got up and went to the back parlor door. "He was like those old oaks," she said, staring down at the sturdy, bare-limbed trees in the ravine. "No matter what—droughts, floods, disease—they've always survived. Indestructible."

"Stop idealizing him," Nickie flung back angrily. "He was a mean, bitter man who hated everything and everyone around him."

"He only hated one person," Angie said quietly. "He saw his whole life as a failure, a waste. So he did the only thing he felt there was left to do—he lashed out." She turned to look at her sister. "You know, in a twisted way, I think Pap was in part responsible for our successes. His temper and cruelty taught us to survive. If it hadn't been for my childhood, I don't know if I'd have made it through the tough times I've gone through since." She smiled sadly. "I have him to thank for my inner reserves of strength—my will to go on. Mama encouraged us to have dreams, but it was Pap who forced us to fulfill them. I don't know—maybe, in a way, that was more important."

Nickie stood up, unwilling to listen to any more.

Angie took the topaz earrings from her cape pocket and held them out on her gloved hand. "Here, I found these in his cufflink box."

"Mama's?" Nickie asked softly.

"They must be. I thought you should have them, in case your baby's a little girl."

"Do you think it will be? Louis is so typically male sometimes. He's hoping for a boy."

Angie, consumed with curiosity about her pregnancy, saw her opening. "What does Josephine have to say?"

"The old battleaxe is thrilled. She's actually condescended to call me Nickie after all these years."

"You've pulled off quite a coup."

"Haven't I, though?" A wicked grin lit her face. "Louis is more of a man than you thought."

"It is his, then?" Angie laughed softly. "I should have known."

"When I want something, I go after it."

"I'm surprised you want a child."

Nickie shrugged. "I got tired of being an outsider. I figured that if I couldn't be an Urbano, then I'd produce one." Evading Angie's eyes, she began to move about the tiny parlor that Pap's coffin seemed to fill.

"God, sometimes I wish I had more of your ruthlessness," Angie murmured, her tone as much amused as shocked.

Nickie whirled. "What?"

"You heard what I said."

"Angie, you'll never be like me. You're another Phil—brilliant and creative, but with no grounding in reality. You live in a dream world," she said witheringly. "Didn't I try to warn you about Tony? Didn't I tell you he'd find a way to get at you?"

Stung by the implication that she was somehow less savvy than her sister, Angie rounded on her. "I'm sick of you denigrating my 'dream world.' I studied, I fought, I connived and wheedled. I made sacrifices every step of the way." Angie clutched her precious opera recordings. "I won't allow you to belittle what I've achieved in my life, and I'll be damned if I allow Tony to take it from me!"

St. Mary's was located on Central Avenue, amid Slovak taverns, Italian spaghetti joints and 'mercian stores in downtown Coalport. The warm brick bulwark of the church had comforted and uplifted the Branzino family from birth to death. They had been baptized at its font; they had cried as Rosa's coffin had been trundled out; they had celebrated with Freddy when he married his childhood sweetheart, Leonora, at its altar. Now the tower bell pealed its relentless death knell for Pap.

Angie and Nickie climbed out of the Urbano car, which Louis parked behind the hearse. They paused a moment, glancing at the old parish house where they had worked in exchange for food. Angie adjusted the mesh veil that fell from her black Basque beret with its jeweled insignia, while Nickie drew her fur tighter around herself. Their argument back at the house forgotten, the sisters walked arm in arm into the church.

Angie loved the Catholic ritual, the medieval drama enacted against a backdrop of candles flickering before the massive crucifix above the tabernacle. The priest—resplendent in his black chasuble and intricately embroidered crimson and gold yoke—lifted the chalice of consecrated wine high above his head. The altar-boy rang a silvery bell, and the kneeling congregation beat their breasts while the saints gazed down from their pedestals.

By the end of the long Requiem Mass, the black candles flanking the pall-draped coffin at the foot of the altar had almost burned out. From the organ loft, the first swelling notes of "In Paradisium" sounded, and the priest swept down the steps to make the final blessing. An altar boy gently swung the censor, which clanked against its triple chains. Smoke drifted back through the church, filling it with the odor of incense.

What incredible pomp and pageantry, Angie thought, to mark the end of an existence lived in such mean poverty. Yet Frank Branzino's life force persisted, bright and indomitable, in all of his children. Papa, she cried inwardly, how can I let let you know that I'm grateful for what you did give us?

The young cross-bearer began leading the exit procession down the center aisle, followed by two acolytes carrying candles. Impulsively Angie rose and left her pew, ignoring the curious swivel of heads as she marched toward the back of the church. She spotted Tony at the end of the second pew. "How dare you?" she wanted to scream as she passed him. Feeling his eyes on her back, she hurried up the stairs that led to the organ loft.

She gestured to the surprised organist to stop playing, and the soaring music echoed away in silence. She advanced to the rail and watched the coffin being wheeled slowly down the aisle. Taking a deep breath, she began to sing, "Va, pensiero, sull'ali dorate," the operatic tribute Verdi's adoring countrymen had sung as the composer's coffin passed through the streets of Milan. Angie offered it up to the memory of her father, whose life had echoed the furious vitality of Verdi's music. As her powerful soprano filled the church, she realized that she was singing for herself as well, a heartfelt cry that her own spirit would prevail.

Leaving their tears behind at the grave, everyone on Dago Hill crowded into the Branzinos' old house to eat and laugh and reminisce. A proud coterie surrounded Angie in the kitchen.

Like she's some kind of queen or something, Tony thought, watching the *gumbaris* ply her with cookies and wine. He walked into the hot kitchen, rolling his shoulders like a boxer warming up. Instinctively the other women drew back until he stood face to face with Angie. "Quite a comedown from the Met, ain't it?" he sneered. "Singin' for your supper in a milltown church."

As she eyed him coldly, her gaze fixed on the angry white scar at his temple. "What do you want here?"

His sneer turned into a menacing growl. "I got a right to be here. Frank Branzino was my friend. We understood each other. He understood that Antonio Malfatti is a man's man." Tony punched at the air with the burnt-down nub of his cigar. "He respected that."

Nickie came up to stand next to Angie. "Too bad Frank isn't here to speak for himself, or we might have heard differently," she needled him. "You said what you had to say—now why don't you take off?"

"Shuddup! Look at the two a you with your high-class gloss. Underneath, you Branzinos ain't any different from how you started out." The bruised blue of his eyes ogled them up and down insolently. "But you don't want me around remindin' you of that because you're goddamn phonies—all a you with your college educations and your fuckin' Johnny Bull friends."

Hearing the ruckus, some of the men came out of the parlor. Phil and David started forward, but Carlo DiPiano raised his hands placatingly. "Tony, enough," he said in his silken voice. "We gotta show some respect here in this house, eh? Respect for the dead at least." His hand clamped on Tony's shoulder and he led him back into the parlor, where the men were talking and drinking *chiquets* of whiskey.

As Phil and David hurried toward her, Angie stared at Tony's retreating back, feeling a bone-deep weariness. Where was this psychological torment going to end? She felt as though she had reopened a wound that had never healed properly; now it had begun to suppurate, the poison threatening her whole body. She turned to her sister.

"I've got to leave, Nick, I've got a train to catch," she said, her vibrant voice quenched. "Sorry to leave you with the mess."

Nickie smiled crookedly. "I'm used to it."

David spoke up. "I'll drive you downtown."

As they drove slowly through Coalport, the cold mist fogging the car windows made Angie feel closed in, trapped. Edgily she touched the back of her hand to her lips.

"You okay?" David asked. When she didn't reply, he steered the car to the curb and reached for her. "Angie, I've never seen you so down." Gently he caressed her face. "Let me help, let me do something."

She sighed. "David, I'm just so tired. I need to get away and think—to plan what I want to do with the rest of my life."

"Don't shut me out," he said, refusing to let her pull away. "Listen, Angie, we can go away. We can take Katie and Marshall with us. We'll start over fresh, the four of us—a family, the way you wished it could be."

"David, darling David, your romantic side is so appealing." Her laughter was sad and faintly chiding. "But you know that's impossible. I couldn't marry you even if Maura would give you a divorce. I wouldn't dare expose you to Tony's wrath. I love you too much to risk that." Reluctantly she pulled out of his arms and turned to stare out through the freezing mist rising up from the valley. "I've got to insulate myself."

"Angie, you need me," David said urgently. "I could talk to Boursault—he's got connections in South America. He could arrange for you to go on tour for a while until things calm down."

Angie stared at him. "What do you mean, you can talk to Boursault? You act like you know him."

"You introduced us."

"Stop being evasive." She watched his face clench shut. "I sensed when I introduced you to Harrison Fredricks at the gala that somehow it wasn't the first time you'd met, but I didn't think much of it at the time. How do you know these people? David, what have you done? Tell me!"

"You're imagining things."

She sat in silence for a long while, her thoughts whirling. "It wasn't a coincidence, was it, that the Met scout found me in Paris? You . . . you arranged that, didn't you?" She felt numb as she realized her talent had not been a factor, after all. "You paid them to 'discover' me."

"I set a few things in motion," he admitted grudgingly. "But that's as far as it went. You did the rest."

"You bought my way into the Met," she said coldly.

"Damn it, no! Aren't you listening?"

"I've heard all that I need to hear." She jumped out of the car and started to march back toward the center of town.

David rolled down the passenger window and backed up alongside her. "Goddamn it! Get back in the car."

"You used me, David," she cried, her hurt pride breathing through her angry words. "You're no different from the others who wanted to control me."

"I did it for you! Because I love you and believe in you."

"You did it because it was convenient to have me closer!" she shouted, not caring that passersby were listening. "You didn't do it for me, David. You did it for yourself."

As a bus lumbered around the corner, she hurried up to the bus stop. David jumped out of the car, determined to stop her, but she pushed him away. "I'll be damned if I give you another chance to interfere in my life. Goodbye, David." Oblivious to the curious stares of the other passengers, she climbed aboard without looking back.

45

Nickie waddled around the office, feeling like a hippopotamus. Her legs ached and she knew she looked like hell. Outside the sleet-obscured window, a tall Christmas tree shone in a blur of lights. She wished the holidays were over; she wished it were February. Two more months to go. How will I be able to stand it? She came to work early, took lunch in her office and left late in order to avoid the judgmental looks from her staff. Louis had taken over all her business appointments; clients were so scandalized by her condition that she was worthless in a meeting anyway. She might as well have been living in the Victorian age. Louis's mother harped daily about her taking a leave of absence, but Nickie knew she'd go stir-crazy lying around. Whoever had extolled the joys of pregnancy had to have been out of their minds.

She opened a file drawer and retrieved documents relating to a new venture the bank was partially underwriting for David's father, who was board chairman of G. & O. Steel. The man always had an eye to the future. The company's projected forty-million-dollar Southside expansion was getting publicity nationwide as the first public-private project of its kind. Nickie couldn't have invented more wonderful P.R. if she tried.

"Junior," she said, patting her stomach proprietorially, "we're going to build quite an empire."

The intercom buzzed. "Mrs. Urbano, you have a visitor."

"Who is it, Madge?"

"A Mr. Malfatti."

"Tell him I'm out."

"He's standing right here," Madge whispered in a strained voice. "He says he'll wait all day if he has to."

Nickie racked her brain for an out, finally deciding it would be best to see him and get rid of him as quickly as possible before anyone recognized him. "Send him in," she said sharply.

Tony was all spit and polish from the top of his balding head to the toes of his expensive loafers. "Nickie, glad you could make time for an old friend."

"What do you want?"

"That any way to greet a *paisan*'?" He wandered around the office, examining the books on the shelves and the view from the window. Finally he stopped before the photo of her and Louis. "What's the matter with that husband a yours—no balls?"

Nickie stiffened. "What are you talking about?"

"Hey relax, Nicoletta. Just a joke. I only meant I wouldn't let no wife a mine out in your condition."

"I don't care for your jokes. I never have," she snapped. "Get to the point."

He dropped his hat on the edge of her desk. "I got a business proposition for you."

"This is a bank, not a bookie joint, Tony."

"I don't care for your jokes, either," he said, gritting his teeth. "Now, you better listen, because I'm not gonna say it twice. I'm planning to build some warehouses. I want you to put up the loans, at a couple a points under prime."

"Sounds like legitimate real estate, Tony," she said, stalling, wondering how she was going to get rid of him.

"No kidding." He looked irritated.

"And it also sounds to me like you're infringing on Rocco DiPiano's terrain."

He started really fuming now. "This is my baby. I planned it, you understand? And I'm gonna prove to that asshole I can make a deal 'pencil out.' That's where you come in, Nickie. You make the loan at a nice rate, I kickback a little for your trouble—we're in business. Carlo's gonna see his spawn ain't the only one with smarts."

Nickie made a show of getting up and resting her hand on the small of her back, although her grimace of discomfort wasn't entirely put on. "You got me at a bad time, Tony," she lied as she came around the desk. "The last thing on my mind right now is business."

"I'll come back, then."

"Tony," she said, choosing her words with care, "doesn't Rocco have banks he already works through?"

"This don't got nothing to do with him, I told you," he said furiously. "This is mine, and you're gonna help me." He picked up his hat and set it lightly on his head, running his fingers around the brim. His eyes moved briefly to the photo on the credenza before coming back to rest on her face. "Like I said, I'll be back. Tomorrow, the next day . . . I'll be a real regular customer."

"Why us, why Urbano Bank?"

"Because your family owes me."

"And if I don't cooperate?"

Tony smiled. "You know me better than to ask that." He stalked out, slamming the door after him.

Nickie crossed her arms over her burgeoning stomach. Seven years of her life she had poured into this bank, long years of working and scheming to solidify her position. And that scum waltzes in to threaten it all.

The Villa Vittoriale Palace Hotel was a fabulous gem within the walled medieval village of Sirmione on Lake Garda near the Italian-Swiss border. In summer the wide terrace and surrounding park with its pathways winding through the trees brimmed with life. But now in the dead of winter—the trees bare and paths sodden underfoot, a steady chill rain falling beyond the window—there was a sadness in the air, a sense of life held in abeyance.

Maybe the sadness is just in me, Angie thought, twirling her wedding rings around her finger. The exquisitely cut marquis diamond glittered in its palladium setting, but its radiance gave her little joy.

"Angelina, you're worrying me."

As she turned from the window, her negligee of tawny pink silk chiffon swirled around her. Handsewn beige Chantilly lace edged the matching chemise underneath. Harrison had spent a fortune on his bride's trousseau. They had married in a whirlwind. He had proposed and been turned down by her so many times that her acceptance at last had left him momentarily stunned. Diffidently he had confessed that he could not offer her physical love, and she had assured him that it didn't matter. What she needed from him was the protection his money could provide for her and her son.

He was sitting up in the large walnut-carved bed, a cup of tea in hand and American newspapers spread open on his lap. He looked at her over the tops of his reading glasses. "Come sit and talk to me, dearest."

She went to the bed and perched beside him, not resisting as he took her hand and gently chafed it between his big gnarled fingers. "Harrison, I'm so afraid I've lost him."

"Nonsense," he said, faintly irritated. "The boy's just disappointed. Children have a wonderful way of bouncing back from little disappointments," he said, cheerfully brushing off her concern. "Now look at this, my dear: What would you think of my building you a winter home in Los Angeles?"

"Harrison, don't you understand? I've made so many promises to Marshall and I've broken them all. Children never forget those things."

"You're making altogether too much of this," he chided her. "You did what you had to do. When he gets a little older he'll understand. I think the best thing we can do now is get on with our honeymoon and let him get back into his regular routine. In a few days he'll forget about all of this and everything will be back to normal."

He set the teacup on the bedside table and reached for her. As she curled up next to him, he placed his arm around her waist. Gently his hands caressed her hair the way a father might console a daughter, the way her own father had never consoled her. She closed her eyes, thinking again with anguish of their awkward, terrible meeting with Marshall.

He had come running to her through the entrance of the drawing room at school, tall and spindly as a colt for all the grown-up look of his blue blazer and gray flannels. As Angie introduced him to Harrison, Marshall had shot him a look that was at once shy and full of curiosity. "He's to be my papa now?" She could still hear his high, sweet voice tinged with hope.

"In a way, darling, yes."

"And we'll be a family now? Live together?"

"Not quite yet, my love."

"Why? Why not?" The quiver of tears behind the words had wrenched Angie's heart.

"I can't explain to you yet. You have to be patient, my Marshallino. You know I love you."

"You don't love me! You love that old man. I hate him. I hate you!"

The bitter resentment that had flowed out of him terrified her.

Perhaps this is my punishment, Angie thought. She'd had to return to Pittsburgh and show off, flaunt her success to Tony and the world. Now everything was ruined.

She had lost David and married Harrison, ashamed because she knew deep-down she regarded her adoring, elderly husband as expendable. Did Harrison sense that? Was that the basis of his seeming indifference to Marshall —a childish desire to get even?

I've made a mess of everything, she thought in despair. She could not risk another trip to Switzerland. The danger was simply too great that Tony might track her movements and discover Marshall's existence.

Her hasty, ill-conceived marriage had protected her from nothing, least of all from herself. She felt trapped and alone. Too late she realized that ego had clouded her judgment, perhaps with irrevocable consequences.

46

December 1950

The glittery New Year's Eve costume ball thrown by jeweler Harry Winston was a high point of New York's winter social scene, a razzle-dazzle send-off for the idle rich before they headed south to their yachts in the Bahamas and villas on St. Croix. Angie swept through the ballroom of the Waldorf-Astoria on Harrison's arm, her head held high. She caught the excited twitters, the self-righteous disgust on faces before backs were pointedly turned. The taint of Angelina's past and the wide age gap between Harrison and her were lively sources of gossip.

This was the couple's first social outing since their return from four months on tour in South America, where Angie had sung throughout the continent. Around her neck she wore a *navette* diamond pendant, the unusual cut of the stone resembling a ship's hull. Harrison had given it to her after her much-praised performance in Berlioz's *The Trojans*. Tonight she had come to the ball as Helen of Troy, her hair swept up and a thin ribbon banding her forehead. She wore an off-the-shoulder empire-waisted gown of white linen, which fell in narrow soft folds to her feet. Her severely classical look was reminiscent of an ancient Hellenic vase. But for all the elegance of her carefully chosen costume, Angie felt naked and cheap before the stares and snubs of Harrison's compatriots.

In their year of marriage his interest in Marshall extended solely to monthly checks, for which Angie was not ungrateful. He had also done a masterful job of insulating her from the world and from the threat of Tony. Except for their months away, Angie's life had centered around the hushed elegance of their luxurious Park Avenue apartment, with occasional forays via limousine to exclusive shops and restaurants. A pair of low-profile yet highly visible bodyguards accompanied them wherever they went.

It was Angie who had asked that the South American tour be arranged. Let me work, she had thought; maybe work will cure me. Belatedly she realized nothing could cure the malaise of spirit that weighted her down. The worst of it was that her need for insulation from the world was the very thing that was causing her suffocation. Harrison made every major decision concerning their lives, purposely cutting himself off from the social and cultural life of the city he loved. His life revolved totally around her. The whole focus of his energy went to fulfilling her every whim, as if by doing so he could somehow command her love. Their marriage had caused them both suffering, and she could not forgive herself for that. His obsession with her had taken its toll. He had aged tremendously in the past year.

"Angelina," a familiar female voice called behind her.

Both she and Harrison turned. Francoise Duvall stood before them. She had come to the ball as Marie-Antoinette, and the elaborate jewel-sprigged wig on her head balanced the deep plunge of her decolletage, which she had accentuated with a heart-shaped velvet beauty mark. "Where next?" she said to Angie. "Too bad vaudeville is a thing of the past." She flashed a triumphant smile. "Did I not warn you, Angelina? You would not last?"

Harrison said sharply, "I'll thank you not to harass my wife, Miss Duvall."

Duvall's eyes widened in mock surprise. "Ah, you do have a voice, monsieur," she said loudly. "So it is true what they say: Money does talk."

A suppressed titter rippled through the room.

Harrison turned to confront the elegant crowd. "What do all of you know?" he shouted as Angie tried to quiet him. "You have no inkling of what my precious wife has been through!"

"Harrison, please," Angie whispered, frightened by the unnatural pallor of his complexion. "Let's go."

As they hurried out, she saw that he had begun to perspire.

Downstairs she needed the help of their chauffeur, Charles, to get Harrison settled into the back seat of the Rolls. Gently she wiped his cold, damp forehead. She was worried, but she did not want to alarm him. "Harrison, darling, we should take you to a hospital." She exchanged a quick glance with Charles. Without a word, he put the car into gear and swung out into the traffic.

As Harrison slumped exhaustedly against the seat, Angie slipped out of her fur and bundled it up behind his head for support. "Angelina," he whispered, groping for her hand, "I . . . I just want you to know one thing—"

"Shhh, don't try to talk," Angie said, frightened.

"You must know." His voice was low and strained, every word an effort. "This past year I have been a very happy man. No . . . no regrets."

His head slumped forward. "Harrison?" she whispered, the velvety timbre of her voice thick with fear. "Harrison! Don't leave me!"

47

"I'm glad you decided to come home, Ange."

She reached across to touch Phil's hand on the steering wheel. "There wasn't anything left for me in New York."

Angie looked out the side window again. The woods with their feathering of verdant spring growth seemed to rush past them as they sped along the newly completed airport parkway into town. Her eyes fastened on a billboard with foot-high letters: O'ROURKE, BRANZINO AND URBANO—WORKING TOGETHER TO BUILD A NEW PITTSBURGH.

"Phil, I'm impressed! Whose idea was that?"

He grinned. "One guess."

"Motherhood hasn't slowed her down a bit, I see." Angie shook her head. "I can't wait to hug my new little niece."

"She's a dollbaby. It's a damn shame Pap didn't live long enough to see his first grandkid."

Angie bit her lip. She thought of her son still locked away in Europe. The enforced estrangement was tearing her apart. She feared that Marshall had begun to hate her, but even if it meant losing Marshall, she had to keep him away from Tony. His last letter had been so cold, so adult for a twelve-year-old boy. *Thank you for the check, Mother,* he had written in a neat, controlled script almost unrecognizable from his usual enthusiastic scrawl—as if he could no longer allow himself the luxury of revealing his feelings in any shape or form. *The Abliers took me to Milan, and I bought a bike. We visited Madame Giulia. She pretends to be fine, but her arthritis is bothering her. I can tell. Sarah was the same as always. I know she doesn't like me. She never has. I'm used to that. . . .*

The matter-of-fact way he spoke of Sarah's dislike smote Angie to the core. He had long since grown used to being hurt—by everyone in his young life.

She shifted uncomfortably in the passenger seat. She could not change that, not yet. She flared with anger at her son's coolness, though she knew she was to blame. As long as she knew he was safe, she would simply have to get on with her life. She had lived as a fugitive recluse with Harrison. Pampered though that existence had been, it was the life of a fugitive all the same. She was through running from Tony, from her own fears.

Phil swung his sporty red Studebaker up Grandview Avenue and drew to a stop before a cantilevered restaurant of wood and stone that stood on the former site of Pete's modest luncheonette. A small sign announced "PIETRO'S, Fine Italian Cuisine."

"Phil, your design is out of this world!"

He beamed. "You really like it?"

"Yes! But what about Pete—how's he handling being a full-fledged restaurateur now?"

"You know him. He never changes," Phil said with wry affection. "Shuffles out of the kitchen in his apron and brings samples around. The diners love it. Freddy makes sure the place stays in the black."

Pete, more rotund than ever, greeted them merrily and led them to the best seat in the house, a corner table overlooking the two rivers where they merged beyond The Point. Angie rested her arms on the table and gazed down at the city. The steel framework of three high-rises rose behind the open grassy park that had replaced the industrial wasteland of decrepit warehouses and rusting train tracks. They were calling Pittsburgh's transformation a new renaissance.

She turned back to her brother, hoping her eyes didn't reveal the sadness, the sensation of being lost and adrift that had beset her during her time with Harrison. "It's exciting to see a new city spring up out of the ashes of the old," she said quietly. "I hope I can do as much with my own life."

"Look, Ange, I hope you don't mind, but I, um, I took the liberty of discussing your idea with David."

"Phil, it was so tentative!" She looked away again, not wanting him to see her distress. She had cautiously broached her idea of building an opera house downtown, the cost of which she would partially underwrite with the fortune Harrison had bequeathed to her. He had loved the opera as much as she did. She thought the gift to Pittsburgh would not only be a fitting tribute to him but an outlet for her own creative impulses. She intended to make the contribution contingent on her being appointed director. But she wasn't ready to deal with David yet; her feelings about him were too confused. She pretended to be absorbed in smoothing the collar of her smoky gray wool suit as she said, "What was David's reaction to the idea?"

"Feasible, he thinks. Highly feasible."

She felt a stab of disappointment. "That's all?"

"He'll come around. Look, Ange," Phil went on excitedly, taking a pen from his pocket and grabbing a napkin. He started sketching, and the building that took shape beneath his long artist's fingers was strangely beautiful, like a pair of unfolding wings. "This is my idea. I think it has the potential to be the jewel in the renaissance crown."

"Understating things as usual," Angie teased her brother. "With your usual humility, I might add."

He grinned.

Pete shuffled over to the table, bearing a huge plate covered with what looked like stuffed mushrooms. "Whaddaya think, you guys?" he asked, watching their reaction as they bit into his new appetizer. "Crab, white wine, a touch of garlic, lemon . . ."

"Scrumptious," Angie pronounced. "Pete, you're a genius in the kitchen."

"I just like to eat, that's all." He smiled. "Never trust a skinny cook."

Over lunch, Phil kept to the subject of the opera house, explaining how he had already begun to research acoustics and materials.

"You've got to rein in a little," she said in dismay. "This is still just the germ of an idea."

"Hey, didn't I tell you?" he said with feigned innocence. "You're presenting the plan to the Opera Guild on Wednesday. And I'm going to unveil my design."

Angie looked at him, stunned. Things were moving much too fast for her. Yet maybe that was what she needed after this past year of emotional and physical hibernation.

The taxi drew to a stop before the Highland Park home. Lights filtered out into the early spring dusk through the mullioned windows, casting shadows across the ivy that softened the great expanse of gray stone. Angie climbed out of the cab, feeling a tremor of agitation as she headed up the sidewalk with her small bag in hand. The house was unchanged, though its inhabitants had undergone so many transmutations. Here she was, fifteen years later, coming full circle on a journey that had begun right here.

Josephine Urbano opened the door at once in response to her tentative knock. "Angelina, welcome!" The woman hugged her. "Come in! May I get you tea?"

"No, I'm fine. Z'Maria and I went visiting on the Hill. You know how that goes—we ate everywhere," Angie said, her eyes sweeping around the wide lovely foyer before coming to rest on Josephine again. "I . . . I hope I'm not intruding. It'll only be for a week or so, until I can find a place."

"Nonsense, Angelina, I want you to think of this as your home," Mrs. Urbano said firmly. "You must know how much I've wished—"

"How's the baby?" Angie interrupted quickly. "I'm dying to see her."

A soft smile wreathed the woman's patrician features. "Come up, then. She's beautiful. She looks just like my Julia when she was a baby."

Angie hesitated outside the door that led to the nursery. This had once been her room, and before her it had been Julia's. She thought, How strangely interwoven all our lives have become! The nursery was washed in the same soft pink tones that Angie remembered so well, but the bed was gone, replaced by a brass crib draped with netting. A white-uniformed nurse stood over it, deftly straightening the baby's blankets.

Angie looked down into the tiny face, which stared wide eyed up at her through busily waving fists. Angie lifted the infant and cuddled her against her neck. At the fresh innocent smell of her, the strong sense of life emanating from the warm body, Angie felt tears starting in her eyes. She carried her to the rocking chair and sat down, softly crooning the Calabrian lullabies that she had sung to Marshall and that her mother had sung to her. Except for the slightly tilted eyes that were an echo of Nickie's, little Rosa Josephine looked only like herself. Whatever Angie might have thought about Nickie's motivation for bringing this child into the world, she had to applaud the lovely gesture of naming her after her two grandmothers. Angie looked at Mrs. Urbano. "You're right—she's beautiful." She laughed softly. "Such a feminine, delicate little thing. I adore her."

"Nickie's already calling her RJ," the new grandmother said with a disapproving shake of her head. "Rush, rush, rush, that one. I suppose we should be lucky she takes time for her daughter at all."

"Did I hear someone mention my name?" Nickie said from the doorway, looking stylishly slim once again in a tweed dress, over which she wore a blue fox fichu. She glanced from Angie, rocking the baby, to her mother-in-law. "Well, Mother," she said coolly, "it looks like you've seen to it that Angie made herself thoroughly at home."

Angie stood up and handed little Rosa Josephine to the nurse. "I think I'd better go freshen up. Which room . . ."

"Come on," Nickie said, "I'll show you."

Nickie lounged on the green satin slipper chair in the guestroom while Angie unpacked her small suitcase. "Where's Louis?" Angie asked conversationally, anxious to steer the conversation away from the scene in the nursery.

"New York." Nickie hesitated fractionally before adding, "On business."

Angie continued to tuck her things into drawers, aware of her sister's eyes following her every movement. Nickie said finally, "You're certainly traveling light these days."

"I have a couple of trunks coming tomorrow by train. All my worldly possessions." Angie sighed. "I sold Harrison's furniture along with the apartment."

"I see." Nickie stood up. "So you are intending to stay in Pittsburgh."

Angie gave her an exasperated look. "You knew that. Why are you acting like I've just dropped a bombshell?"

"Will you continue to sing?"

Angie turned, closing the drawer with her hips. She leaned back against the dresser, her arms crossed in front of her. "Nickie, I feel like this is some sort of inquisition. If you didn't want me here, you should have spoken up. I could have gone to Phil's or Z'Maria's."

Nickie pushed her hair back and went to the window that overlooked the sprawling rear gardens. After a moment she turned back. "Sorry," she said, although she didn't sound as though she meant it.

Angie kicked off her shoes and sat on the bed. "I was hoping we could talk about my plans—Phil must have told you."

Nickie shrugged. "What's there to say?"

"Damn it, why are you hedging? I value your opinion, you know that."

Nickie moved away from the window. "All right, you want to know what I think? I think you're crazy for coming back. I think you could've gone anywhere. Why here? Why put yourself right in the eye of the storm?"

"I came back because I thought I had something of value to give to this city. I want to make a cultural contribution, to share some of the bounty I've received in my life."

"How noble of you."

Her coldness wounded Angie to the quick. "What did you expect me to do—sit in my Park Avenue castle and count gold coins? I want to give something of myself. But that's only part of the reason." Angie slumped back against the pillows. "I came home because I'm tired of running and because I'm lonely. I want my family around me. I feel that I need you—all of you."

"Poor little rich girl," Nickie said ironically. "You have family—in Europe. I can't help wondering how Marshall feels about your decision."

Angie flinched as if she had been slapped.

"Don't like the truth much, do you?" Nickie pushed. "You're so damned selfish—all you've ever thought of is yourself. It won't change. While you've been living the high life with Harrison Fredricks, I've been paying for your sins, as usual."

"What are you talking about?"

"Just that with you so inconveniently out of reach, Tony had to find another target: me."

"How? What's he done?"

"You wouldn't want to know." Nickie smiled crookedly. "Good night, Angie. Sweet dreams."

Angie slid off the bed and ran after her. But Nickie had crossed the hall and slammed her bedroom door shut. "Nickie!" Angie knocked sharply.

Nickie locked the door and leaned back against it, willing her to go away. Finally Angie gave up, and Nickie put her hands over her face. How at home Angie had looked in the nursery with RJ. She made Nickie feel like the outsider. Go back where you came from, she felt like screaming. Stay out of my life.

48

With its arched windows, columns and glowing stone and terra-cotta facade, the Pittsburgh Athletic Association building epitomized the city's old money. Angie paced the sidewalk out front, waiting for Phil. She wondered what he thought of the opulent structure that so much resembled a sixteenth-century Venetian palace. Renegade that he was, he probably liked it. She knew Phil had little use for the bland, Bauhaus-inspired boxes going up at The Point. The current vogue for severity of form went against the lyrical grace inherent in his own very personal style. She thought again about his sketch for the opera house, but her pleasure was undercut by nervousness. The Opera Guild board was waiting for them now in one of the P.A.A. conference rooms. She glanced down at her watch. Phil was even later than she was. She couldn't wait any longer; she was going to have to beard the lion's den alone.

The Italianate elegance of the building's facade spilled over into the lobby. Angie drank in the Old World beauty of the sunken-paneled ceiling and stone fireplace with its carved escutcheons and arabesques. A movement caught her eye and she turned. "David!" Seeing him against the backdrop of this European ambience, Angie had the sensation of being transported in time back to Rome, to the joyfulness of their brief interlude together . . . the poignancy of their bittersweet parting. Nostalgia engulfed her. She had to fight to keep her voice even. "I . . . I thought Phil was going to be here."

"He got called to Baltimore," David said quickly, and yet Angie sensed his reluctance, as if he were chary of carrying on even that minimal bit of conversation with her. "A problem came up on one of our projects."

Angie couldn't keep her eyes from him. She noted the faint silvering at his temples, the finely etched facial grooves mirroring an inner life deeply felt. She wanted so much to touch him, but his implacable gaze stopped her. His remoteness was like a knife blade in her heart.

"We'd better go in. The board's getting restless."

"Yes," she murmured quickly, "of course."

Fiona Donahue was chairing the meeting as they entered. The svelte matron looked little different than she had in Father Lucatta's parlor so long ago. ". . . But I really do think whatever director we choose should be someone from within the community. Someone who knows our cultural needs." Listening to her, Angie thought ruefully, some things never change.

"I agree with my mother," said Maura Donahue O'Rourke, her metallic voice an echo of the older woman's. "I hardly think this city is so desperate we have to succumb to an outsider intent on buying her way in."

A murmur went around the table, and angry color suffused Angie's pale features. "May I remind you, Mrs. O'Rourke," she said quietly, "I was born and raised here. This city is my home, as much as it is yours."

Maura sniffed. "Only when it suits your purposes to call it—"

"Ladies," Nickie intervened, standing up and looking around until she was sure she had everyone's attention. "I've done some research into the running of an opera house. Invariably, the director is a shrewd, hardheaded businessman who knows the ins and outs of negotiating deals."

"A man like yourself, in other words," Angie quipped.

Nickie frowned angrily, refusing to meet Angie's eyes. Instead, she focused on her fellow board members. "My sister is a gifted soprano; her talent on stage is breathtaking. But in all truth I can't see her enmeshed in the grinding day-to-day struggle of running an opera house. In the end I think it would hurt her, and it would hurt us."

Angie stared across the table at her, stunned by her betrayal. The room grew so quiet, Angie became aware of the distant muffle of traffic on Fifth Avenue, the rapid beat of her own heart. It was obvious the others were as shocked as she by her sister's defection.

"Thank you, Nickie," Mrs. Donahue said, gratified. "I would think you are more qualified than any of us to judge Mrs. Fredricks's strengths and weaknesses." She turned toward David, who had sat on the windowsill throughout the meeting, waiting to present Phil's drawings. "Now, David, if you will please accompany her out into the hall. There are obviously serious reservations about her generous offer that we must discuss."

David pushed off the sill. "I'm not going anywhere until I've had my say." He put his hands in his pockets and slowly circled the conference table, eyeing each woman in turn. "You know what I think? I think you're all acting like petty fishwives." He ignored their outraged gasps. "You pay lip service to this town's cultural development"—Angie saw him look toward Maura, who gave him a murderous look in turn—"but now you have this windfall dumped in your laps, you're worried that Ang . . . that Mrs. Fredricks is an outsider, that she's too soft . . . too this, too that." He shook his head in disgust. "Who gives a damn? That point is that what she's offering—not just the building itself but the scholarship fund she wants to set up—is going to benefit the community for decades to come." He paused. "Isn't that what you all want? Isn't that what you've been working toward since you started the Guild?"

"Well spoken, David," Josephine Urbano murmured.

"Thanks, Mrs. U., but I'm not done." He smiled briefly. "My partner, Phillip Branzino, was to come here today to present his architectural concept of the performing arts center that he and"—again he stumbled over Angie's married name—"and Mrs. Fredricks have planned together." He nodded toward the tissue-covered renderings on an easel. "Phil couldn't be here today, so I'm here to speak for him. As you all know, Angie Branzino Fredricks is Phil's sister. And I know that if he were here, he would have spoken up in her defense." David's eyes rested briefly on Nickie's cool poker face. "He would have insisted that you acknowledge his sister's intelligence, her determination, her ability to set goals and achieve them, her sensitivity to the musical arts, the nurturing warmth of her personality that . . ." His deep, confident voice trailed off abruptly. "The point is, Pittsburgh needs what she's offering, and you'd be foolish to turn your backs on it, for whatever personal motives."

Touched beyond measure by what he had said, Angie closed her eyes and pressed the backs of her fingers to her lips, afraid she might cry.

Mrs. Donahue coldly thanked her son-in-law for his input, then once again asked them to wait outside in the corridor.

As soon as they were alone, Angie turned to him with glistening eyes. "Thanks so much for what you said in there, David. It meant a lot to me. . . . I can't tell you how—"

"I did it for Phil, Mrs. Fredricks," he interrupted, refusing to meet her gaze. "He's put a hell of a lot of effort into this. I spoke up because I know this would be a showpiece for this city, and it would get Phil the national acclaim he deserves."

"I see." Angie blinked back her tears. "Nevertheless," she went on in a hushed voice, "thank you anyway."

Nickie rode the elevator to the twentieth floor of the new G. & O. Steel high-rise downtown and emerged into the carpeted foyer of Rocco DiPiano and Associates. While the receptionist announced her arrival, Nickie looked around. The moss-green carpeting extended to paneled walls hung with English hunting prints and glowing oils. Everything about the place breathed permanence, old money, a sense of Johnny Bull rectitude. For all the desperateness of her mission, Nickie couldn't help but smile at the irony.

Rocco came out of his office to greet her. A double-breasted gray silk suit, impeccably tailored, accentuated his well-built shoulders and torso. Nickie felt the old sexual spark, the inevitable shiver up her spine, as he gave her a welcoming hug. She found herself half wishing they could have connected somehow, but as quickly as the thought surfaced, she pushed it away. It wouldn't have worked, couldn't have . . .

"Hello, Rocco." She greeted him huskily. "I appreciate your seeing me. I know how busy you are."

He led her into his beautifully appointed office. "Never too busy for an old friend. Sit down," he said as he perched on the edge of his desk. "You look great, Nick, but then you always do."

She had worn a dress to the meeting, the surplice-wrapped olive silk softer and more feminine than the suits she usually wore. The corner of her mouth lifted in a crooked half smile. "I was just thinking the same about you."

A hidden current of electricity raced between them, poised as if waiting for some indefinable signal to allow it to break the surface. It was Nickie who looked away first, glancing at the photograph behind the desk of his 'merican wife, Kelly, and their two children.

"So what can I do you for, Nickie?"

When she looked at him again, she saw that although he still smiled, he was now all business. "Rocco, I'd like you to intercede for me with Tony," she began, terse and matter-of-fact as always. "He did a little arm-twisting and forced me to give him a deal on several loans." She shook her head. "I hoped that might appease him, but it just seems to have whetted his appetite."

"So, what's a loan?" Rocco said, unconcerned, picking up a box of gleaming marquetry inlay from the desk. "Cigarette?"

She took one and tapped it nervously on her crossed leg. "He came back last week. Now he's asking me to set up dummy accounts and manage them for him." Her voice tightened. "You understand what I'm saying? The son of a bitch wants me to launder money. It's blatantly illegal—a federal offense. Rocco, Urbano Bank's respected, we're a partner in the city's rebirth. I've got a child myself now. This is her legacy. I don't want everything I've worked like a dog for tainted by Mafia filth."

Rocco leaned forward to light her cigarette. "There's no such thing as 'Mafia,' Nickie."

"Yeah, and the moon's made of green cheese," she said sardonically. "Rocco, you don't have to play semantic games with me. I came to you, friend to friend, asking for your help. Your . . . whatever you want to call your nonexistent organization must have banks of its own in Philly, New York, New Jersey, that can handle what Tony wants. Why target mine?"

Rocco went around the desk and sat down. He picked up a paperweight of rough stone and hefted it in his hand before reaching across the desk to set it in front of her. "Know what that is? A piece of Calabria, Nickie, a piece of the pitiless land where our parents started out. Carlo brought this with him to America as a reminder, a warning to himself. Your father and mine, Nickie, they sprang from the same hard soil. All those Calabrian *paisan'* broke their backs together in the coal fields. My father still talks about it."

"Rocco—"

"The point is, Nickie, my father knows what Tony's up to, and, frankly, he likes the idea. This is something he's always wanted—the younger generation working together, consolidating their talents and their brains and their resources, like a family, sticking together against the outside."

"This is the twentieth century, Rocco," she fumed, "not the Middle Ages."

"You're missing the point," he said softly. "What I'm talking about is something that goes bone-deep—in all of us. How come you never left Pittsburgh? Why did I come back? I had some good offers, Nickie—law firms in New York and L.A. But I'm here, basically, because I don't want to cut myself off from my family."

Nickie laughed in disbelief.

"I am not bullshitting you now, Nick." His dark eyes bored into hers. "I did a lot of soul searching, but in the end what it boiled down to was that my father needed me. I figure my task is to bridge the old ways to the new, so that by the time my boy grows up, the majority of our operations will be legitimate, within the mainstream of good old American capitalism." He paused, smiling. "What are you looking at me that way for? I'm no idealist, Nickie. If I had been, I'd have become a Jesuit instead of a lawyer. The way I see it, the world is evil. My goal is to try to make it less evil. There's good and bad in everything—it's no different in families."

Nickie stood up. "Rocco, you can yak all you want about lesser and greater evils. To me it's all philosophical baloney. What I'm talking about is reality: an ugly, dog-eat-dog reality called Tony Malfatti. The guy's an evil that can't be controlled—by any of us—and the sooner you wake up to that fact the better off we're all going to be."

She stubbed her cigarette on the chunk of Calabrian rock and stormed out of his office, her anger mixed with fear. Rocco had been her last hope, and he had let her down. She could almost feel Tony's teeth against her throat. She had a bad feeling that, slowly but surely, he was going to bleed her dry until there was nothing left.

49

Nickie slouched down Pittsburgh's Liberty Avenue past the dingy bars and pool halls, the peep shows and tattoo parlors, that attracted the detritus swept out of the downtown bus terminal. Her raincoat and dark head scarf were as much disguise as they were protection against the drizzle spotting the uneven sidewalk.

She stopped finally, hesitating a moment before stepping inside a noisy, dark pinball arcade. Guys with greasy hair and even greasier smiles turned from their games to eye her up and down. She hurried toward a rear door that led down to Tony's basement office. A heavily made-up girl with sagging breasts lounged on a sofa against the wall, exchanging wisecracks with a couple of thugs wearing shoulder holsters. The men were obviously his chief lieutenants in the business of shakedown, protection, debt collection, street prostitution. Tony himself sat behind a battered metal desk in his shirtsleeves, talking a mile a minute into the phone.

"What is this?" he said, eyeing Nickie's garb as he hung up. "You look like some peasant straight off the boat."

"I dressed appropriately. I knew I was coming to see you," she said, watching his nostrils and neck muscles flare like a cobra preparing to strike.

"Nickie, don't you ever learn? Every smart-ass crack outta your mouth is costing you. All these years I been keepin' tab."

"So have I."

"Yeah? Well, I got news for you: I got the upper hand here, and I'm not gonna tolerate any more a your shit." He signaled abruptly with his head for the thugs and the girl to get out. "You made a big mistake when you went behind my back to Rocco. A big mistake. You went back on your word, Nickie. You see, now I know I can't trust you. From here on in, I gotta be sure you're gonna do what I want. That's why I sent for you."

Struggling to control her fear, she watched him open a bottom desk drawer. He pulled out a large envelope, a whiskey bottle and two shotglasses. "You ever been to New York, Nickie?" he asked conversationally as he opened the envelope and spread its contents on the desktop. "A tourist can take a lot of interesting pictures." She stared at him, refusing to look at the photos. "They got some weird bars, especially down in Harlem. Joints that cater to real perverts . . . the kinda perverts that'd turn the stomachs of the upstandin' people in this town." He poured out a couple of *chiquets*, then smiled up at her. "You know what I mean, Nick?"

"Yes." Her voice came out like a frog's croak.

His smile broadening, he handed her one of the brimming shotglasses. "Here's to us, to our long and profitable partnership."

She choked down the whiskey, feeling its burning path through her entire body.

Syria Mosque was a concert hall decorated in Mideastern motifs. A frieze of Arabic script ran around the building's exterior, and exotic desert scenes flanked the stage inside. It was a few blocks up from resplendent Carnegie Hall, where Angie had made her glamorous Pittsburgh debut.

She had long since exchanged the glamour of an ivory silk ballgown for a serviceable pair of beige linen slacks and a short-sleeved white cashmere sweater embedded with sawdust and soiled with chocolate—from a Hershey bar she had appropriated from one of the pint-sized chorus extras. She looked up from the ladder she was experimentally sanding. "Ray!" she called to her prop man. "I think the glitter will adhere fine if we just sand it down a little more."

An officious voice interposed itself at her back: "I don't see why you can't use the ladder as is."

Her patience strained to the limit, Angie turned to face the short, fat music professor whom the Opera Guild board had hired to dog Angie's every step. "Mr. Spode, this is a mystical dream sequence in which fourteen angels descend from heaven. The ladder has to look like it belongs to them, not to Carpenters' Local 431."

His protruding eyes glared. "You are not at the Met now, Mrs. Fredricks. This is a small city opera with modest aims. What matters is the performance, not emphasis on picayune details." With his bug eyes and wattled neck, he looked more like a Mr. Toad than a Mr. Spode. "I will see that Mrs. Donahue gets a full report of your intransigence."

"You do that. In the meantime, if you don't stay off my back, I'll have you rehearse the children's chorus."

The prospect of facing that bunch of wild Indians is enough to shut Spode up for a few minutes at least, she thought.

She turned her attention to the young soprano rehearsing Gretel's opening song with the pianist. Laura McCormick, home from Juilliard for the summer, was the daughter of one of the Guild's board members. Although she had a light, clear voice, it was lacking in emotional tone.

"Laura, you've mastered the music beautifully. Now, wouldn't you like to begin focusing on characterization as we discussed last night?" Angie began, careful to couch her suggestion as a question. "Gretel's a lively girl; I'd like to see you bring some of your own exuberance to the role. Don't you think she'd have a mischievous, teasing note when she dares Hansel to drink out of the milk pitcher?"

"I know what I'm doing," Laura said rebelliously.

Her mouth tightening, Angie turned away. She thought she'd won three months before when the Guild members had swallowed their misgivings and narrowly voted approval not only of Phil's design but of her appointment to direct the fledgling opera company. But it had turned out to be a Pyrrhic victory. She had worked doggedly, eighteen hours a day, pencilling budgets, hiring people, carefully weighing options as to which operas would generate the most enthusiastic community interest and support. She had settled on Humperdinck's *Hansel and Gretel* because it combined a familiar, much-loved folktale with rich Wagnerian orchestration. Yet at the same time the composer had written clearly separated melodies that had the engaging simplicity of nursery rhymes, tunes an audience would come out humming. She had spent days at Southside schools, auditioning children for the chorus—determined to include the city's blue-collar element and demonstrate that opera wasn't just for highbrow snobs. For all this, her reward was rebellion and snide gossip on all sides.

Something inside of her snapped. She had tried being kind, conciliatory, charming, but no more. She realized that the situation called for a show of force.

Nickie slipped in the front entrance of the concert hall, working her way around the curving wood-veneered walls that separated the foyer from the theater proper. She had

been avoiding Angie for three months, torn by conflicting feelings of guilt and anger. Then the telegram had
come, a terse ultimatum bringing things to a head: IM-
PERATIVE WE TALK Stop COME TO MOSQUE
AFTERNOON Stop IF NOT, I'LL BE AT BANK A.M.

When Nickie entered the auditorium, Angie stood in
the middle of the stage with her arms crossed. She looked
madder than hell, oblivious to the noise and chaos on
stage. Christ, there were even kids hanging from the
rafters. The *Press* had made much of what they nick-
named Angie's "knothole gang," praising her effort to
involve children from lower economic strata in the company's first production. Nickie had figured that all the
favorable publicity would lure Tony out from his hole.
But he continued to lie low.

Nickie was shaken out of her reverie when Angie suddenly shouted, "Everyone! Sit down, I have something to
say!" The place went dead quiet. Even Nickie held her
breath, waiting. "I have had it up to here with you
people grumbling and gainsaying me, trying to impede
me every step of the way. I've been through a lot in my
life, and what you people are dishing out is pablum
compared to the struggles I've faced. I rose above them;
I will rise above you and your petty nonsense. From here
on when I give an order, I will expect immediate compli-
ance. Offenders will be thrown out. I don't care who you
are, or who your mother or your employer happens to
be. Do I make myself clear? I am the boss here. Not the
board, not Mr. Spode." She stopped. "All right, take a
half-hour dinner break. When we come back we're going
to work, and we're going to do it my way."

Nickie stared, watching the elegant, smooth-tongued
Angelina Fredricks revert to scrappy Angie Branzino
from Dago Hill—ready to duke it out if someone tried to
bully her or give one of the younger Branzino kids a hard
time. For all her sense of estrangement, Nickie felt a
surge of warmth.

Angie's backstage office had an air of comfortable
chaos. Costume sketches and scenic designs lay scattered
atop the baby grand and spilled over onto the record
player and sagging couch beneath the frosted window. A
tabby cat jumped from the top of a bookshelf to the

piano keyboard, striking a discordant note and sending pages of musical score flying.

Angie plugged in the hot plate to warm up some coffee. "This is called 'winging it,' " she said to Nickie, who stood in the doorway surveying the mess. "Nine-tenths of the time I feel like I don't know what I'm doing, or why I'm even here."

"That was quite a speech you gave to your mutinous crew."

"You heard that?" Wearily Angie sat down at the piano and ran her fingers over the keys. "I'm determined to make this company work. I don't care who opposes me." She glanced around at Nickie. "Are you coming in or not?"

"Just for a minute," Nickie said curtly. "But if you're expecting me to apologize for what I said to the Guild, I'm not going to."

"I don't expect an apology," Angie said, standing up. "An explanation, maybe, but not an apology."

"Is that why you sent for me—so I can 'explain'?"

"No, I asked you here so that we can make peace, Nick. I want us to be friends—I need a friend." She smiled ruefully. "I also need someone who knows the ins and outs of this city. You've made wonderful connections, political as well as financial. I'd like your help in getting the city's backing to get the opera house built. I'll go it alone if I have to, but it would be easier if I had you to count on."

"Looks like you're doing okay on your own. You should have heard yourself out there—you sounded like a drill sergeant." Nickie shook her head. "I forgot how tough you could be."

"You and I are more alike than we are different," Angie said, pouring out two cups of muddy coffee. "I'm as much a product of the Hill as you are, Nickie. Believe me, I know what dirty fighting's all about."

Nickie took the cup Angie handed her. "You used to be my hero, Ange. You were what I always wanted to be. I guess somewhere deep down I still need that to hang onto." The words escaped in a husky surge of anger. "My own life feels so tainted sometimes."

"Some hero you picked," Angie said gently. "As you've

reminded me more than once, my son is in Europe and I'm here. I made a monumental mistake in lying to him, and now I'm suffering for it. What's worse is that Marsh has to suffer, too, and he doesn't understand why." Angie lifted her cup, scalding her lips with the bitter coffee. "Not exactly the perfect ideal, am I?"

"Yeah, tell me about it." Nickie sat on the sagging sofa, her smile tentative and rueful. "Josephine is back to 'Nicoletta.' The temporary ceasefire is over—she harps constantly about the way I ignore RJ. But I've got all that crap with Tony to deal with. . . ."

Angie flinched at the tight, worried look on Nickie's face. "I'm sorry. I suppose you still blame me."

"Only about fifty times a day."

Angie put her cup down and rubbed her temples. "I get the feeling he's thrown a net over us and slowly, very slowly, he's going to reel us in." She shook off the feeling of foreboding that came over her. "Sometimes I see him sitting in his car parked down in the street. But he never does anything. He just sits and waits like a spider."

"You were right about one thing, big sister," Nickie said with grim humor. "You should have killed the son of a bitch when you had the chance."

50

The summer passed swiftly, swallowed up in long days of rehearsals and nights of planning. The three-night run of *Hansel and Gretel* had been a Labor Day weekend sell-out, despite competition from a crucial Pirate-Dodgers series at Forbes Field. David had surprised Angie by showing up backstage before the first performance. When he asked her how she was, she had replied, "Lonely." He'd said nothing in response, but she had glimpsed in his eyes an echo of her loneliness and beyond that festering pain. She had not understood until that moment that he must have viewed her marriage to Harrison as a betrayal of his maleness in the deepest sense: She had chosen the support and protection of another man over his own.

Now September was rapidly drawing to a close, and she had not seen him again since that awkward backstage exchange. She tried to console herself with the thought that he must be missing her as badly as she missed and needed him.

With the success of her first production proving that opera could draw crowds, Angie immersed herself in preparation for the real opera season, for which the end-of-summer performance had been just a teaser. No matter how busy she was, she scheduled a few hours each day for public relations, for she was determined to build community support at all levels.

Today, ten students from the Pittsburgh School for the Blind were backstage with Angie and her crew in the prop room. Maura O'Rourke, who had accompanied the children along with three other mothers, had barely acknowledged her. As Angie began to explain how stage boulders were made out of mesh and plaster of paris, Katie O'Rourke piped up excitedly, "I know you. I know you from Europe!"

Angie blanched in sudden fear. Afraid the child would blurt something else, she hurried through her spiel, explaining that youngsters were often used as supernumeraries, or extras, and that she loved working with children and animals onstage because they added the essential ingredient of reality and warmth. Then she passed out feather boas, plastic swords and other props, hoping to distract the children's attention.

But Katie, an adorable redhead with her mother's creamy complexion, wasn't about to be distracted. She turned from draping a boa around her friend's neck. "Mrs. Fredricks, is your little boy a supe-superary?"

Startled Angie said quietly, "No, no, he's not." She briskly started toward the door. "We'd better get a move on. The rehearsal's going to start any minute!"

Katie dawdled, enjoying the moment of attention. "My daddy took me to the opera in Paris, and we heard Mrs.

Fredricks sing," she told her friends animatedly. "Then we all went to a big park with fountains. Me 'n Marshall, we chased lambs!"

As the other mothers shepherded the children out into the corridor, Angie started to follow, but Maura placed a detaining hand on her arm. "How interesting. I didn't know you had a son." Her smile was brittle, her eyes searching. "How old is he?"

Angie summoned up all her acting skills to disguise the terror she felt inside. "I make a point to keep my family out of the limelight, so they can live as normal a life as possible," she said evasively, her smile as brittle as Maura's. "Now if you'll excuse me, I've got a rehearsal to direct."

Angie moved out into the hall, aware of Maura's eyes boring into her back like a searchlight. She slipped into her office, and after locking the door with fumbling fingers, she ran to the phone and dialed David's office. "Yes, David O'Rourke, please. . . . When will he be in? . . . Yes, have him call Angie Branzino. And, please, tell him it's urgent."

David lazily swam the length of the pool underwater, savoring the coolness and serenity. He closed his eyes and imagined himself in Katie's world, a daily penance he endured as payment for his need to control and manipulate people. He swam up toward the shimmering afternoon light and broke the surface, then he kicked off the wall. He swam hard and fast, working off his tensions and the repressed frustrations he felt about Angie. Having her so close and yet so distant was the most difficult penance of all. *I know that she wants me and, God knows, I want her too.* But she had hurt him badly.

When he swam his vigorous, punishing crawl, David splashed all over the place, and Maura would bitch about water marks on the interior terrazzo. Typical Maura, he thought grimly—everything for show.

He hauled himself up out of the pool and was toweling down when the front door opened and Maura and Katie came in. Before he could even greet them, Maura said sharply, "Katie, please go to your room. I have to talk to your father."

"But Mommy, I want—"

"Go!"

David watched Katie climb the stairs, then turned to Maura in irritation. "What's this all about?"

"I want to speak to you in the study, please," she said with frigid formality, turning her back on him.

The soaring room with two-story windows faced west. A golden and salmon autumn sky shone on rolling lawns that sloped toward the woods in the distance. David regarded the room as his private sanctuary, where he could dabble at painting or just stretch out on the deep flokati rug before the fireplace and listen to music. The fact that Maura chose his own ground to attack him fueled his irritation even more.

"I'm waiting," he said coldly, watching her pour a glass of scotch from the liquor tray.

"Why didn't you tell me you saw Angie in Paris six years ago?"

He shrugged, wary but determined to play it cool. "Come off it, Maura. Since when are you interested in anything I do?"

"I certainly would have been interested to know that the soprano Angelina was Angie Branzino from the old days," she said, fiddling with her glass. "What did you do on that trip?"

Her inquisitional style infuriated him, but he tried not to show it. "The hospital experience was traumatic for Katie. I cast around for something memorable to do afterward and decided on the opera."

"Oh, really? And naturally you had to let Angelina know you were in town." David let that one slide. "What about this child of hers?"

Shit, where was she coming up with all this? "I don't know," he said with studied casualness, pouring a finger of scotch for himself. "I didn't ask about her personal life. Figured it was none of my business."

Ignoring his ironic tone, she persisted. "How old is he—this Marshall?"

"I really don't know."

Maura gulped her drink and started pacing. "Wasn't there a story that after Louis dumped her, she married some gangster?" She stopped, her eyes glinting speculatively. "In fact, I think he was at the gala when she sang. . . . You were dancing with her when he cut in. As I recall, you seemed awfully tense that night."

"Maura, I think you're the one who's worked up. What the hell's gotten into you?"

"How long have you and she been friends? Did you see her during the war?" she badgered him, her voice rising stridently. "For all I know, this child could be yours! Your feelings were so obvious when you spoke in her defense before the Guild. No one was fooled when you pretended to speak on Phil's behalf. You humiliated me," she said in a self-pitying tone.

That was the bottom line, David thought with mingled aggravation and disgust. Her attack was motivated neither out of love nor a desire to keep her threatened marriage intact. She was upset that her pride was wounded. Some of what he was feeling showed on his face, because she was looking at him with hatred now.

"Maura, you're fantasizing," he said evenly, moving toward the door. "This conversation is pointless."

"You're a liar, David," she cried shrilly after him. "I will find out the truth. So help me, God, I will."

The last light of sunset filtered into Angie's office as she sat at the piano, learning the score of *Aida*. The mental discipline kept her from driving herself mad with speculation over what Maura would do now. Her fingers flew over the keys, playing the sweeping lines of the tenor's aria "Beauteous Aida" that ended with an ascent from F to high B flat dying away in a haunting pianissimo. Not that she had ever heard any tenor—egocentric and applause-hungry creatures that they were—sing it with the kind of subtlety Verdi had intended.

She jumped when someone knocked on the door. "Who is it?"

"It's me, David." She rushed to the door and stiffened with fright when she saw his taut, strained features. "Angie, we have to talk."

She nodded. "Can we get out of here? I need to walk. David, I'm so afraid."

When he put his arms around her, the gesture felt as easy and natural as breathing to both of them. She nestled against him for a long moment, taking sustenance from his strength.

Outside, the air was crisp and cold. A presage of winter hung in the air, like a faint wisp of smoke. They walked down Bigelow Boulevard, their feet crunching the leaves skittering about them in the freshening wind.

"David," she said, shivering. "What am I going to do?"

"Angie, this is our problem, not just yours," he said, tucking her hand into his arm. "Let's not worry too much yet. Maybe this'll blow over."

Angie shook her head. "No, I don't believe that. Maura's vindictive. She despises me. She won't be able to resist crowing to the world that I've got a child tucked away. . . ." She was unable to finish.

"She won't if I confess that we had an affair during the war and Marshall's mine. Believe me, I know her," he said sardonically. "She's hardly going to crow that her husband cheated on her and fathered an illegitimate son."

Angie stopped and turned to face him. The streetlight on the corner threw his strong cheekbones and lean jaw in sharp relief. The very fierceness of his expression buoyed her. "You would do that for me?" she whispered.

"Angie, whatever you want or need, I'm here to give it to you. Christ knows, I've tried to hate you, but I only wound up loving you all the more."

"I know." She nodded, her eyes bright with unshed tears. "I feel the same . . ."

He bent to kiss her, the warm connection of their lips a refuge against the cold fragility of the night.

The society matron had called and asked him to meet her at a hotel outside of town. Tony parked the car and hunched his shoulders against the cold night wind blowing across the parking lot. All the way over, he'd been racking his brain over what she'd want to see him about.

Maura O'Rourke opened the door and invited him into her suite. In her gray silk and pearls she looked like Miss Prim-and-Proper.

"May I offer you a drink?" she said, indicating a cocktail tray.

"Whiskey straight up," he said, following the luscious

curve of her backside that didn't match the mold at all.
He remembered her, all right.

"Mr. Malfatti," she drawled in her upper-class voice as
she handed him his drink, "I'm sure you must be wondering why I wanted to see you."

Right, he thought to himself, what the hell am I doing
here? He did not smile, did not say a word. Let her carry
the ball for now.

She sat down on the sofa and crossed her silk-clad legs,
smiling slightly when she saw his eyes linger on the curve
of her thigh beneath the thin silk. "I'll get directly to the
point. I think you may have some information that I
need."

"Information?" He grimaced. "What kind of information would I have that you need?"

"A bit of background regarding Angelina Branzino
Malfatti." The woman smiled her sly cat's smile again.
"You two were married at one time, weren't you?"

Prying cunt, he thought. He drained his glass and set it
down. "What d'ya want to know for?"

His belligerence got her dander up. She wasted no
more coy smiles. The real self came out—the hoity-toity
looking down on the riff-raff. "I have reasons that don't
really concern you," she said arrogantly. "I could have
hired someone to obtain the information, but it would
have taken a lot longer. I'm in a hurry, so I'm offering to
pay you instead. Quite a substantial sum."

The mention of money angered Tony—treating him like
hired help. But for the moment he held his anger in check.

"Mr. Malfatti, above and beyond money, I think you
and I may have a common interest. I have a feeling you
nurse some sort of grudge against your ex-wife."

His eyes narrowed to slits. "So?"

"I have reason to believe Angelina had an affair with
my husband, and I would like more than anything else to
see her punished." The cat's smile was back. "I suspect
that the child she's got tucked away somewhere is illegitimate. Otherwise, why keep him under wraps?"

"What are you talking about?" Tony said, galvanized.
"What kid?"

"My, my, and I thought you people were so ruthlessly

efficient," she said ironically as she stood up. "My mistake. I apologize for your wasted trip."

Tony advanced on her. "What kid?" he said, gritting his teeth.

She laughed. "You aren't threatening me, are you, Mr. Malfatti?"

Her cool, provoking laugh infuriated him. "I'm through with fucking cat-and-mouse games." His hand shot out and he grabbed the back of her neck, twisting his fingers in her hair until her head bent at an awkward angle. "I'm asking you one last time." He brought his other hand up, ready to slap her. "What kid?"

Their faces inches apart, he stared down into her wide eyes, expecting to see fear. Fear was there all right, but along with it he read desire. He grabbed her chin and kissed her, an invasive, brutalizing kiss that ravished the inside of her mouth. "Tell me, bitch."

She laughed breathlessly, her lipstick smeared like blood around the edges of her mouth. "Make me."

He slapped her, and she took a step back. He slapped her again, as they moved in a sadomasochistic tango back to the bed. He pushed her down. Maura moaned and writhed, lifting her throat and breasts toward him. He jerked the pearls from her neck, sending them flying, then dug his fingers into the V-neck of her dress and ripped downward. The soft, protesting shriek of torn silk rose in tandem with her excited panting. Tony felt the stirring of desire in his useless member. He started to really hit her now. But she seemed to like it, even begging for more. He felt an aphrodisiacal rush of power. To think I, Antonio Malfatti, have the power to bring this rich bitch to her knees. His sexual drive had always been fueled by a need to dominate and punish. He toyed with the idea of having one of his boys come in and drill her while he watched, but he didn't have time for that now.

He shoved her off the bed with his foot. "Get up," he snarled. "You're not worth fucking." He grabbed the telephone on the nightstand and dialed. "Russo? Malfatti here . . . yeah. Look, I gotta job for you. There's somebody I want you to find. Hang on . . ." He turned to Maura, who was pulling on her coat. "Bitch, you know anything else about the kid?"

"His name," she said softly, finding it difficult to talk through her swollen lips bruised by Tony's brutal kisses. "Marshall."

Tony repeated the name into the phone, watching Maura as she slowly pulled on her coat over her torn dress and left the room. "Yeah, I know it ain't much, but use our connections. And Russo? If you find him, I'll take care of you real good."

Alone, Tony paced, feeling vengeful rage licking at his insides like fire. The woman who had robbed him of his manhood and of an heir had a son.

51

The headquarters of O'Rourke and Branzino occupied a complex that the partners had built on a hill overlooking Schenley Park and nearby Carnegie Tech. Angie stood at the conference-room window, her eyes following the rough-and-tumble antics of a group of boys in the park. Behind her she heard the festive pop of a champagne cork and good-natured laughs from the staff, which had planned the surprise birthday party for Phil. His draftsmen had presented him with a detailed model of his performance center. Seen in solid 3-D form, the design was indeed spectacular. Frozen music, Phil had called it—a building whose sense of harmony would echo the city's rivers and hills.

Outwardly Angie smiled while inside she was tied in anxious knots over what the unpredictable Maura might do. David had been tight lipped all week, saying everything was okay. God only knew what had occurred between husband and wife.

"Penny for your thoughts?" David's warm, caressing voice spoke at her side. She looked around, trying to smile. "Come on," he said, handing her a glass of champagne. "Let's toast . . . to the future."

"I'm afraid I don't have much faith in the future anymore," she said, her eyes focusing disinterestedly on the model. "None of this matters. I feel like the world's pressing in on me."

"We'll work through this. I promise you."

"You know I never wanted to cause trouble between you and Maura."

David's laughter was low and bitter. "Maura makes her own trouble." He gazed out over the rolling hills of the park. "Angie," he said suddenly, "let's get away for a few days. Put all the ugliness behind us for a while. We can drive up to Bedford Springs. The countryside's beautiful this time of year."

She gave him a faintly teasing look. "You think a mineral bath will cure what ails me?"

"Sure." His changeable green eyes glimmered for an instant with answering amusement. "That and other things—cuddling up by a fire, breakfast in bed, long lazy afternoon walks . . ."

Suddenly Angie realized that what she loved most about him was his wonderful capacity to buoy her, to make even her worst fears recede. Invariably he brought her joy and comfort and laughter when he sensed she was most in need of them.

"I'd love it," Angie said simply, her smile full of tender gratitude.

The great forests of the Allegheny Mountains blazed gold and russet and scarlet as David's convertible wound along the rural highway past stone dairy barns, fields dotted with cows and sheep, farmhouses with chimney smoke curling up lazily into the clear blue sky.

They stopped at a roadside stand to buy a crock of honey and fresh-baked bread. The Amish woman, modest and shy in her bonnet and gray dress protected by a snowy white apron, smiled at Angie. Her inner tranquillity reached out, woman to woman, a tacit communion that filled Angie with warmth. Although Pittsburgh was only three hours behind them, she felt as though she had crossed some sort of emotional boundary—an alien yet familiar world that had always existed deep inside of her.

They took the Bedford turn-off, and David, his hair blowing across his forehead, regaled her with a tale about President James Buchanan, who had made the Springs his summer White House. Coerced into a wild coach ride with a visiting horsewoman from Maryland, she had taken him dashing through town—much to the horror of the locals, who thought the lady was eloping with the hapless bachelor.

Angie laughed. "Poor Mr. Buchanan."

"Not at all." David grinned. "They said he looked resigned to his fate—whether it was marriage or a broken neck. So nobody interfered."

The Revolutionary War era stone taverns and storefronts soon gave way to immense Victorian mansions flanking an elegant avenue. Beyond the town the avenue shrank to a winding country lane that brought them eventually to the Bedford Springs Hotel. Its white clapboard facade seemed to stretch forever along a narrow, curving valley graced with meadows and a pretty creek.

Their suite was a third-floor eyrie furnished with a canopy bed and cherrywood antiques. Fresh flowers stood in a vase on the dresser, and the fireplace had been laid with birch logs.

"David, it's perfect," she cried. She went out onto the balcony, drawn by the rhythmic clip-clop of hooves in the driveway. As David joined her, he slipped his arm around her waist. Together they watched a horse-drawn surrey stop at the Barclay House entrance. A liveried driver leaped down from the coachman's seat. Glancing up, he saw them on the balcony and waved jauntily.

Angie looked at David, laughing. "Do we dare?"

"I think I'd better find out your intentions first," he murmured, nuzzling her neck. "What do you have in mind for me—marriage or a broken neck?"

She turned and slipped her arms around him. "Neither at the moment," she teased him, standing on tiptoe and feathering her lips softly around his. "David, I just want you. However much or little of your life you can spare for me."

By afternoon the brilliant day had taken on the warmth

of Indian summer. They hiked across the foot bridge that led to the springs and walking paths beyond the wooded hillside. David carried his sketchpad and charcoals, Angie a small blanket from the car. The other hotel guests preferred the more civilized delights of the golf course and indoor bathing pool, and they didn't meet another soul as they walked.

Angie had bent down to entice an inquisitive chipmunk with a crumb of bread when she glimpsed a shaft of light beyond the shadowy gloaming of the woods. She called ahead to David. Picking their way through the trees, they emerged into a sun-filled meadow, green and golden and warm as a Monet landscape. Neither of them spoke, both afraid to dispel the quiet magic of the place. Angie spread out the blanket while David unfolded his camp stool. She lay back, propped on her elbows, her face upturned to the caressing warmth of the sun. A breeze rustled through the leaves and teased the loose curls around her face. She heard the distant cry of starlings and, softer yet, the scratch of David's charcoal pencil across his sketchpad. Then she felt his fingertips against her jaw, gently tilting her toward him, and Angie realized that he was drawing her.

The idyllic afternoon ebbed slowly, like a dream. She half dozed, her only connection to the world David's light, warm touch as he brushed her hair back off her shoulder or gently eased her peasant blouse off one shoulder. Each time he touched her, his hand lingered as if she herself were the painting and his fingertips were brushes stroking her skin, drawing out the colors of her soul.

They dined that night in their room, sitting cross-legged before a crackling fire as they picnicked on bread and honey. Later they made love in the big canopy bed, the sweet merging of their bodies a celebration of the day's harmony, an exquisite mutual knowledge that went beyond words or thought. Long after David had drifted off to sleep, Angie lay awake within the protective circle of his arms, savoring the lassitude that enfolded her. How long had it been since she had felt so complete—so connected?

The green banker's lamp on Tony's desk cast a pool of light on the notepad in front of him. The loud jukebox in the bar next door blasted through the walls. He had to jam the telephone against his ear. "Yeah, Russo, I can't hardly hear ya! Speak up, for chrissake. Yeah . . . F . . . R . . ." Quickly he scribbled the name. "Francini, Giulia Francini . . . yeah, I got it . . . Huh? Nah, uh-uh, I'm gonna handle this one myself." He hung up and leaned back in the chair, lacing his fingers behind his head.

He let his mind replay all the hatreds he had nursed for so long. You robbed me of a son, he said to the beautiful phantom of a woman who moved across the stage inside his head. Now you're gonna have to pay the same price.

52

Tony's fingertips impatiently drummed the wheel of his rented black Alfa Romeo as he waited in the queue of traffic inching through the border station into Switzerland. He whistled tunelessly, feeling good. So far everything had gone like clockwork. The old bitch in Milan had given him trouble, but he had gotten what he needed in the end.

Tony eased the Alfa up to the checkpoint. "Good afternoon, sir," the Swiss guard greeted him, glancing cursorily at Tony's passport. "Is this trip business or pleasure?"

"A little a both, you might say," Tony said, smiling at his own wit. He was still smiling as he braked to a stop in the circular gravel drive outside the private boarding school in Lugano.

The school director smiled cordially across the desk at his unexpected visitor. "And how is your sister?"

Tony shifted in his chair. "Fine, great." He glanced at his watch. "Look, we don't got much time here. And I'm sorta anxious to see my, uh, nephew before I fly back out tonight."

Before the man could respond, his office door opened and Marshall stepped inside, glancing between the two men before coming to rest inquisitively on Tony. "Come in, Marshall," Dr. Ablier said heartily, "and say hello to your uncle."

Tony stared at the thin, dark boy. So this was Angelina's pride and joy, he thought sourly, watching the boy come toward him. Christ, the kid has to be twelve years old! When I was his age, I was already bustin' my balls chopping wood for ten cents a day. This one looked like he never did anything but open a book.

Marshall greeted him in impeccable but accented English. "I am very happy to meet you."

At that moment Tony noticed the kid's wary eyes, a brilliant blue against his dusky olive skin. The vengeful hatred that had consumed and driven him ebbed in a mist of shocked confusion. It couldn't be. It was a trick of his imagination. . . .

On Sunday night, quiet reigned in downtown Pittsburgh. Angie cuddled next to David in the car, which he had parked beneath the portico of the William Penn. He kissed her once more. "Promise me," he murmured against her lips. "No worrying. Everything's going to be fine."

"As long as I'm with you, I can almost believe that," she breathed, disengaging herself reluctantly. She opened the car door. "Good night, David."

Still warm from his kissess and the kindling glow of their weekend, Angie walked through the hotel foyer, humming the impressionistic score of Debussy's *Pelleas* under her breath.

"Angie!" She turned in surprise to see Nickie hurrying toward her from the bar. "Where have you been?"

"What's wrong?"

"You got an urgent message from Milan—a Sarah Langton got hold of Josephine. We had no idea how to reach you."

"Madame Giulia must be ill," Angie said half to herself, rubbing her arms anxiously as they rode the elevator to her suite. "God, please don't let it be anything serious." Yet she knew that if Sarah had called, it must be. For the next hour, as she waited for the hotel switchboard operator to put through the call to the hospital in Milan, Angie paced ceaselessly. Nickie offered to send down for a drink, but she waved off the suggestion. She felt terribly cold suddenly, as if the magical interlude with David had been nothing but a mirage. Here was reality—this agony of waiting, of fearing, of not knowing. An agony that had to be suffered alone.

The telephone rang at last and she nearly broke her ankle rushing to pick it up. "Hello . . . Sarah? . . . Sarah!"

The woman's familiar voice, distorted by crackling and distance, finally reached her. "Angelina? She's in a coma! My darling Madame is dying. . . ." Even through all the distortion, Angie could hear the terrible pain in her voice.

"Sarah, what happened?"

"Beaten . . . the apartment ransacked." Sarah, who had never visibly expressed an emotion, began to sob. "It's all your fault! You and that son of yours!"

Angie's heart began to pound like a jackhammer. "What about Marshall?"

Sarah murmured brokenly, "What will I do when she's gone? She's been my whole life."

"Sarah!" The line clicked dead.

Fighting back hysteria, Angie scrabbled through a desk drawer for her address book.

"Angie," Nickie cried, watching her rush around like a mad woman, "what the hell's going on?"

Angie picked up the phone again and frantically flicked the button with her fingertip. "Yes, another overseas call . . . DeVilliers School, in Lugano, Switzerland. This is an emergency."

While she waited for the operator to ring back, Angie pulled out a suitcase and started throwing things inside. "Nickie, please do me a favor. Go down and call David from one of the lobby phones. I don't want to tie up the line here. Tell him I'm going to New York and from there to Switzerland."

"Angie, calm down," Nickie said, although she was starting to look scared, too. "Come on, sit down," she said, forcing Angie into a chair. "Tell me what's happened."

Angie resisted, her whole body shaking as if she had chills. "I've got to go, Nickie. Marshall needs me."

The phone rang, and she jumped. Nickie motioned her

to sit and went to pick up the telephone. "Yes . . . yes . . . thanks for trying." Nickie hung up and shook her head. "No answer. The operator just reminded me it's five in the morning in Europe."

"It doesn't matter now." Angie dragged the suitcase off the bed. "I've got to get over there."

Angie accepted the cup of coffee that Dr. Ablier handed to her without even looking at him. Her eyes were fixed on the Swiss police detective who sat on the windowseat in the school director's office. He was observing her calmly.

"You must help me," Angie said, trying to keep her voice low and measured. She felt haggard and groggy after the endless air flight, on the verge of hysteria. Still, she sensed the importance of appearing rational before this phlegmatic policeman.

"Very well, Mrs. Fredricks, let's go over it step by step. This man who appeared at the school was not in fact your son's uncle."

"That's correct."

"They did not know each other, then?"

"No!"

"But this man, he knew you, Mrs. Fredricks?"

"Yes. He's a killer, he's vindictive, he could do anything—"

"And your relationship to this Antonio . . ." the man interrupted, glancing down at his notebook, ". . . Malfatti."

Angie took a deep breath. "We were married at one time." Seeing the look exchanged between the two men, she added hurriedly, "The marriage was annulled."

The policeman nodded. "Hm. Tell me this, then, Mrs. Fredricks: Who is the father of your son?" She shook her head. The policeman's voice, uninflected and somewhat pedantic, persisted. "Mrs. Fredricks, I must insist that you answer me and answer truthfully, otherwise I cannot help you."

She closed her eyes. "He was."

"Pardon? I don't understand."

"Antonio Malfatti was . . . is my son's father."

"I see." The man methodically closed his notebook and stood up. "Mrs. Fredricks, you must realize that this puts the matter in an entirely different light. It is no longer a matter for the police."

"It is!" Angie jumped up. "Monsieur, please, how can I make you understand what a vicious man my former husband is? He's capable of murder."

"I am sorry," the detective said, his words perfunctory and without feeling. "As far as this prefecture is concerned, there has been no crime. No kidnaping. The boy was removed from the school by a parent. The disagreement is a family matter. If you wish to see your son, I can only suggest that you speak to his father."

Angie had forgotten how the northern Italian light could illuminate the sky with such brilliant intensity. The sun sparkled off the granite stones in the hillside cemetery; it caught the silvery sheen of the olive trees in a neighboring field and glinted off the spires of the cathedral in the distance. Madame Giulia's grave lay facing the city she had loved. Angie couldn't help but think she would have been pleased by that.

The priest made the final benediction, the chill autumn breeze catching his maniple as he sprinkled holy water over the lowered coffin. Angie made the sign of the cross and bowed her head. One by one the other mourners drifted away until only Angie and Sarah were left. Angie touched her shoulder tentatively but Sarah jerked away. Her grief-ravaged eyes were fixed on the open grave, as if all her hopes and dreams had died with Giulia.

"Sarah, please don't rebuff me," Angie murmured. "I loved her, too."

"Love?" Sarah spat back, her voice swollen with misery. "You loved what you could get from her. She took you in, she made you a star. She . . ." Her voice broke. "That man, that vicious husband of yours beat her mercilessly, but she refused to talk." The words seared Angie. "I came home and found her lying in her own blood. He broke her skull. . . ." She swallowed. "If I had been there, she would still be alive. I would gladly have exchanged your son's life for hers. Gladly!" Sarah stared at her with hatred. "Go to the apartment—go and see what she endured for your sake."

*   *   *

Old Martini, the caretaker, was gone. Fiats filled the graveled courtyard that he had once raked with such methodical pleasure. Otherwise, the dark stone palazzo with its olive-drab shutters seemed unchanged, solid, enduring.

Angie climbed the steps that she had climbed so long before, afraid and alone, as a young pregnant girl. The door stood ajar and she went inside, half expecting to see Madame sweep out of the music room, her acerbic smile concealing a spirit that was so wonderfully compassionate. But the apartment was eerily silent.

She moved down the hall to the glassed-in parlor and stopped, staring in shock past the police cordon at the wreckage inside the room—furniture upturned, the contents of the desk scattered. Her eyes traveled slowly around the chaos, coming to rest finally on the balcony doors. Reddish-brown splotches radiated outward from a single shattered pane. She stared in puzzlement until she realized that the dark stains were splattered blood. Angie turned away in horror.

"*Mea culpa*," she whispered in Latin. She had let that monster into their lives. "Forgive me, Giulia," she prayed. "Please forgive me."

Despite her fog of exhaustion, Angie drove straight from the airport to Tony's home in the South Hills. The long driveway led up to a rambling two-story brick house, well isolated from the neighbors to either side. Angie's mouth twisted, remembering the ramshackle Ohio farmhouse from which he had run his bootleg business. The facade might have gotten fancier, but it harbored the same hoodlum mentality. In his world a man's worth was measured by the power and control he wielded over others—a power maintained by extortion and murder.

As she rang the doorbell, conflicting feelings of hope and despair filled her heart. Only let my son be alive, she prayed. One of Tony's armed thugs opened the door. "I have to see your boss," she said. "Now."

"I dunno." He grinned, looking her up and down. "My boss, he don't entertain women at the house."

"Get him now," she said with barely controlled fury. "I have to see him."

Just then Tony himself sauntered down the hall stairway, a dark silk dressing gown tied at his thickening waist. "Angelina, I been expecting you." He gestured with his head for the thug to get lost as she stepped into the foyer. "So, how you like my place? Nice, huh?"

His false bonhomie enraged her. "Where is he, Tony? Where's my son?"

"I don't like your tone of voice. It ain't ladylike," he said, toying with her. "What happened to the songbird, huh?"

He turned and went through a pair of double doors off the hall, leaving her no choice but to follow. He pulled the stopper from a crystal brandy decanter and poured himself a glass, then went to the old-fashioned mahogany desk and picked up a cigar. He moved with the swaggering, prancing grace of a boxer. She saw that he was enjoying this moment immensely.

"Angelina," he addressed her with mock solicitude, "for you to come out this late, it must be important. You need some kind a favor?"

"I know you have him," she whispered, her strained nerves edging the words with desperation. "I want him. I want my son back."

Tony circled her slowly. "Your son. You want your son. Well, ain't that interesting." He breathed deeply and slowly, as if to disguise his rising excitement, the thrill of a dangerous game that he seemed certain of winning. "You mean the kid you left in Europe while you were busy playing Madame Butterfly and fucking your rich lovers? Is that the kid we're talking about here, huh?" Angie shut her eyes. He was so close she could smell his dark animal maleness. "I almost killed him," he said in an easy conversational tone that chilled her to the marrow. "Your son. Then I looked into his eyes, Angelina, and I knew he wasn't just yours. He's *my* boy. A boy I never knew existed. Twelve years of his life passed already, and I never knew it." Tony stopped in front of her, his liquored breath hot against her face. "I'm a stranger to my own kid, and it's your fault. You kept him from me all these years, but that's over. Because he's where he belongs now. He's mine. You understand? Mine!"

"You can't do that," she said softly. "Tony, I'll fight you, I swear it. I'll go to court . . . get legal custody."

"Legal custody." He laughed. "Angelina, I thought you knew me by now. I'm so far beyond the law—"

"Tony, listen. Let me see him, then. I'm his mother, for God's sake."

"You don't know the meaning of the word 'mother,' Angelina. Now get outta here," he said, dismissing her. "Be thankful I didn't kill him."

Angie grabbed his arm beseechingly. "Please, Tony, I beg you, just let me see him for a moment."

He shook her off and walked to the door, calling to one of his bodyguards. "Bring Tony Junior down."

The words made Angie cringe. She began to pace, frantically searching for the right words to say. Then she turned and saw Marshall in the doorway. She rushed over and enveloped him in her arms, clinging to him. But he was as unresponsive as a statue. She dropped her hands to her side, watching in despair as he went to stand next to Tony.

"Leave me alone," Marshall said, his young voice full of contempt. "I never want to see you again."

His words struck her more powerfully than any blow Tony had ever inflicted. She bowed her head as Tony murmured, "It's okay, kid. Go on up to bed now. I promise she ain't gonna bother you anymore."

As soon as the boy had left, Tony swung around to face her. His expression was hard, merciless. "Now you listen, bitch. I'm only gonna say it once: If you ever come near my son again, I'll kill you."

Act Five

53

Fall 1952

Dago Hill in autumn smelled like nowhere else in the world. The rich, heavy odor of fermenting grapes over-laid the ever-present sulphuric pungency that spewed up from the coke works, drenching Angie in the past. Her memories were sharp and clear as the October sky.

From her vantage point on the bench beneath the oak tree, she watched her aunt lift three-year-old RJ out of a crate of grapes and admonish her. It might have been Angie herself thirty years earlier who was being scolded and hugged at the same time. Purple juice stained RJ's pudgy cheeks and her cotton overalls; she had bits of stem stuck in her light brown hair. "Gwapes!" she shouted, her radiant grin full of mischief. "I like 'em!"

"Ecco, sì. Tì piagge la uva," Z'Maria repeated in Italian, turning her head away as RJ tried to shove a grape into her mouth.

Nickie, clad in dungarees and one of Louis's shirts, came up the cellar steps with an armload of empty crates. Except for the lines of tension grooving her face, she might have been a twelve-year-old tomboy again, agitat-ing to sneak off with her pals around the corner. She dropped the crates by the sloping cellar door. "Hey, Z'," she called, gesturing a thumb toward Angie, "look at her just sitting on her *cul'* while I do all the work."

The old woman put RJ down and hefted a full crate onto her shoulder. "What?" she said to Angie. "The queen, she forgets how to use her muscles?"

"Okay, okay," Angie said, "I'm coming."

"Hey, Z'," Nickie groused, only half teasing, "I don't know how you conned us into this. We're rich women now. We can afford the best French wines."

"*I francese*," Z'Maria spat with exquisite contempt. "What da hell they know about wine?"

Angie and Nickie exchanged rueful glances. A new closeness had blossomed between the two sisters in the past year: a lovely flower in the midst of the thorns Tony Malfatti had sown around them. Like an evil wizard in a fairy tale, he had spirited away what mattered most to each of them. Feeling like an empty shell, most of the time, Angie had turned and found her sister.

She lifted one of the full crates and followed behind RJ, who was laboriously negotiating the steep stone steps by inching down on her behind. The old cellar smelled like a freshly pulled wine cork, musky and dark. Z'Maria's press with its slatted wooden sides and huge rusted iron crank on top was a creaking antique. They poured the grapes into the press, while Z'Maria climbed up on her stepstool and started cranking away until the juice trickled from the spigot at the bottom. RJ rushed over and stuck her mouth up to it. Shaking her head, Nickie whisked her up into her arms. "Little dago through and through, I can't believe it."

Z' called, "Let her drink, Nickie. *La fatto bene!*"

"Mama, down!" RJ said imperiously.

"Sure, Z', it'll do her good," Nickie said, setting RJ down again. "Just like the wine shampoo I caught you giving her when she was a newborn."

"Eh," Z'Maria agreed, ignoring Nickie's sarcasm. "Make the hair healthy."

"Some things never change, Nickie," Angie said from her perch on the bottom step. "Don't you remember her doing the same thing after Gina was born?"

"No," Nickie said, looking away sharply at the mention of Gina's name.

Funny, Angie thought, how the pain of loss lingered— Gina, Vic, Mama, Pap. Even though Nickie might pretend to be tougher than other women, Angie knew she felt it as keenly as Angie herself did. Each loss was like a soft gap in the mouth where a tooth had once been. Again and again the tongue returned to the spot, uncomfortable with the emptiness it found. Her exiles from Marshall had always felt that way, but this past year had been the worst. Despite Tony's boast that he was above the law, Angie had exhausted every legal route in attempting to get custody of her son. But Tony's posturing had not been empty. Even superior court judges could be paid off, she had found out to her bitter dismay. Now, in her darkest moments, she sometimes felt that Marshall had truly died to her.

She had toyed with the idea of killing Tony, completing the job she had started fourteen years ago. But each time she reached for the pistol she kept hidden in a drawer, something held her back. If she killed him, she knew she ran the risk that her son would hate her forever.

Nickie came to sit on the step beside her. "I saw Marshall yesterday," she murmured.

Angie touched her sister's arm. "How is he?"

"He's okay."

"You're sure?"

Nickie shrugged. "He's as okay as a kid can be who has a man like Tony for a father. It didn't take Marshall long to get disenchanted."

Angie persisted. "But Tony doesn't mistreat him?"

"You kidding? He treats him like a prince. I've told you that a hundred times." Nickie smiled crookedly. "Tony doesn't know how to act around him—Marsh is so cultured and refined. Every time I look at him I'm reminded of our own Phil or Vic."

"I'm glad," Angie said quietly. "He'll be fourteen next month. Sometimes . . ." She stopped, biting her lip. "Sometimes I almost can't remember what he looks like at all. My own son."

Marshall had become like one of those ancient Roman mosaics—an incomplete portrait made up of myriad tiny pieces that she could no longer quite put together into a whole. She knew that on the surface the boy did not want for anything. Tony sent him to Catholic school, lavished him with clothes and records and cash. But what did that mean? Nothing.

Nickie regarded her sister's stricken features. What a damn tragedy, she thought. Although she always tried to put the best light on the situation for Angie's sake, Nickie feared for her nephew. She sensed when she saw him now that he was being held against his wishes, as much a captive as Angie had been when she had been Tony's wife.

Realizing that Angie was looking at her, Nickie winked. "How bad off can a kid be who owns his own thorough-bred?" she said lightly. "They keep it out at DiPiano's country place near Latrobe."

"You've been there?"

"I see Tony out there when . . . when we have to talk business."

Angie heard the tell-tale stress in Nickie's voice, and her fear was for her sister now, too. "What kind of business?"

Z'Maria stepped down off her stool. "Pshhh, pshhh," she said, imitating their low whispery voices. "What you think this is—a 'merican funeral?"

RJ tugged at Z'Maria's dress hem. "Can I have a cookie?"

"*Menagg'*! KooKEE." The woman mimicked. "You no can say *biscott'*?"

"Cookie!" RJ insisted.

"Nicoletta, take this *testa tosta* upstairs and get her something before I . . ." She raised her hand and mimed a spanking, but in such a teasing way that RJ giggled.

Watching Nickie and her daughter climb the stairs to the house, Angie suddenly felt tears starting in her eyes.

"Tell me, Angelina," Z' said simply. Angie shook her head, unable to speak. "You miss your Marshallino, eh?"

"It . . . it's not just that," Angie managed finally. "I'm so afraid for him . . . what will become of him."

"Angelina, open your ears and listen to me," Z'Maria began in her crusty peasant Italian. "Your son, he is not dead to you, you understand me?" Her small dark eyes held Angie's. "In Calabria there is a woody bush, strong and sweet smelling. The mother bush, she sends off many small shoots, like this . . ." Z' held up a gnarled finger, her hand like a worn tool. "The farmers, they break off the shoots and plant them. The little stems grow into strong new plants with many shoots. *Tu capish*, eh, Angelina? This is nature's way. The branches that are our children must break away from us. This makes them strong—makes us stronger, eh? You were torn away, now it is your Marshallino's turn. He's a good boy, that one. Tony can't destroy what is good in him, because you are his strong mother plant, you see?"

"I want to understand, Z'," Angie murmured. "I want to believe that."

"It's true." Z'Maria shrugged impatiently. "And it goes for that other one . . . David." DaVEED she still called him.

Angie looked up, startled. "What's he got to do with this?"

"The good father, too, is like the strong plant."

"So?"

"So." Z' lifted her shoulders eloquently. "So tell him to leave that crazy wife of his and marry you. Before you're both too old to produce more tender little shoots."

Angie uttered a warm, deep, delicious laugh that broke the coldness lodged around her heart. "You're a gem, Z'," she said, getting up and kissing the woman's cheek. "What would we have ever done without you?"

Louis Urbano sat at his father's old teak desk. Its surface was littered with unopened files waiting for his signature, but he had swiveled around in his chair to stare out at the marvelous fall day. Maybe instead of a game of squash at the P.A.A., he'd go for a long, leisurely walk before lunch. He stretched contentedly, his gaze coming to rest on the photo of Nickie and RJ on the low credenza. What in the name of heaven had he ever done to deserve his life? Whatever his faults might be, lack of self-knowledge wasn't one of them. He realized that he was weak willed and lazy, his sybaritic tastes more suited to life in ancient Greece than to puritanical America. And he knew perfectly well that Nickie had manipulated him into marriage for her own ambitious ends. But in return, she accepted him the way he was and shielded him. He was terribly fond of her and he adored RJ, their miracle child. Sly, sly Nickie! Louis thought. He had anticipated marriage as a dull duty but was pleasantly surprised to find himself content. Whoever said one can't have it all was a damned liar, he thought with wry amusement.

There was a brisk knock on his office door. Turning

swiftly to the desk, he opened the topmost file before calling out in his curt I'm-a-busy-man tone, "Come in."

As soon as he saw his mother he relaxed again. "Hullo, Mother," he greeted her, taking in her imported tweed suit. "You look lovely today."

She shook off the compliment impatiently as she approached his desk. "Louis, we have to talk. We have a problem regarding Nickie."

"What now?" He grinned lazily. "You heard her swearing again in front of RJ? I'll have to talk to her."

"Louis, don't be flippant. This is very serious." She dropped a folder with a label bearing the name of an independent auditing firm onto his desk. "You must see this."

He opened the folder and scanned the contents. As he read, he felt his mouth going dry. "This simply can't be," he said faintly, looking up at his mother in disbelief. "Nickie would never do anything illegal. The bank's reputation is as important to her as her own integrity."

Mrs. Urbano's lips tightened. "I anticipated that you would try to defend her." She turned toward the door and called out sharply, "Madge!" Nickie's secretary entered the office, nervously smoothing her gray hair. "Go on, please," Louis's mother urged the woman, "tell Mr. Urbano what you've seen."

Madge looked at him with stricken eyes. "I admire your wife a lot—you know that, sir. I . . . I didn't want to have to do this."

"Just say what you have to say." Fear put an angry edge on his tone.

In her precise, practical manner, she described the couple of times Tony Malfatti had come to Nickie's office. Unabashedly she admitted eavesdropping on their discussions and to snooping through her boss's files. "I had to do it," Madge defended herself spiritedly. "Much as I admire and like your wife, I've only worked for her for a few years. I worked for your father for twenty years. I felt I owed him and your mother the greater loyalty. You can be assured I won't tell anyone else."

"Yes," Louis answered coldly, "I can see that the ethics of someone who eavesdrops and snoops would, of course, exclude gossiping."

Reddening, Madge looked toward Louis's mother for support. Mrs. Urbano gestured that it was all right, that she would speak to him.

Madge was barely out the door before she started in on him. "Louis, how could you?" He shook his head, trying to fend off his mother's angry hectoring, but she persisted. ". . . only trying to avert scandal, you know that, Louis. We must stop this quietly. I will not allow your father's institution to be sullied because of Nicoletta and her gangster connections. You and I will have to deal with this alone. I personally hired the auditor to verify what Madge Sinclair confided in me, and I'm the only one who received a copy of his report. There's no need to involve the board. You and I will speak to her tonight at dinner. We have to convince her she must resign."

Louis lifted his hands placatingly. "Mother, please, stay out of this. I'll . . . I'll talk to Nickie alone first." He swallowed. "There must be some logical explanation."

"Louis, if you have one fault, it's your determination to see only the good in people." She reached across the table to stroke his head. "You must wake up, darling," she said more softly, although it didn't quite disguise the steel beneath the mothering tones. "It's imperative that you see her for what she really is—for all our sakes."

The lovenest was a one-room cottage on the edge of a farm that Tony rented. Maura had laughed at the decor the first time she had seen the place, as if red plush and gilt hadn't been good enough for her, "Early bordello," she had called it in her snooty tone. When he told her none of his other dames had ever complained, she had raked her elegantly manicured nails down his bare chest. "But I'm not one of your low-class 'dames,' am I?"

He had caught her jaw and squeezed it. "No, you're lower."

She had simply laughed at that and whispered huskily, "Show me how low."

It was a match made in heaven. Each time the attacks had become more vicious, yet she had always come crawling back for more. Until now. Bitch had the nerve to say she was bored, he thought. That she was through. Like she was the one calling the shots. He had made a mistake long ago in letting one like her get away. Angelina had slipped out of his grasp, but no woman would ever do that to him again, especially not one of these high-class broads who thought the world owed them something.

"I don't owe you shit," Tony said contemptuously as he stared down at her unconscious form. Flecks of blood speckled the white satin sheets. He walked to the door and called to his boys playing cards in the Chrysler parked behind Maura's sportier roadster.

"Gino," he barked. "Take her and the Jaguar outta here. Make it look like an accident."

54

For a year Angie had drifted through the empty rooms of the house as if she were a ghost. She had bought the place on impulse, a Tudor mansion with a park view that reminded her of Europe, of her bond to Marshall. The house was everything she had promised to him from the time he was a baby. Now that he was lost to her, she lived here alone, punishing herself with reminders of what should have been. It had taken Z'Maria with her crusty wisdom to shake Angie out of the emotional limbo into which she had fallen and make her realize how unfair she was being, both to herself and David.

The only room she had even made a pretense of furnishing was her study, with its huge windows overlooking the gardens and distant city. It contained her piano, a black leather sofa, a jewel-toned Persian carpet, and an antique drop-leaf desk opened to reveal silver-framed photographs of Marshall, Giulia and Renata Baldini, of the Branzino kids lined up on the sidewalk above the old house on Mitchell Avenue. Propped on the mantel, side by side, were two portraits—the drawing Phil had made of Mama the year before her death and the charcoal sketch David had done of herself in Bedford. Even now, even after all the grief and anguish that had engulfed her, she could look at herself in the finely pencilled drawing and recapture the magical peace of that afternoon.

She bent down to put a match to the kindling in the grate. Soon the blaze crackled to life, reflecting off the eighteenth-century marble facing and the gleaming parquet floor. Hearing the doorbell, she hurried to answer it, her feet echoing along the empty hall.

When she flung open the door, David looked up in surprise. Her silk lounging pajamas with a teal-and-amethyst abstract pattern was a pleasant change from the somber tones he'd become accustomed to seeing her in. "You look beautiful."

Angie took his hand and pulled him inside, her smile at once playfully seductive and loving. She led him to the study, where again he stopped short in surprise: the brightly blazing fire in the grate, a bottle of champagne chilling in a silver bucket, long-stemmed roses gracing a crystal vase atop the Steinway—the whole room was vibrant with life as Angie herself.

An inquisitive smile tugged at the corner of his mouth. "What are we celebrating?"

She turned from putting a record on the hi-fi. "Us," she said simply. She returned to his side and slipped her arms around his waist. "It's about time, don't you think?" Her low musical voice melded with the intimate, strumming chords of Rodrigo's *Concierto de Aranjuez*.

"What's happened to you?" he breathed, his lips brushing her temple as the warm Mediterranean ambience of the music flowed over them.

"I've woken up, David," she said, leaning her head back to stare into his eyes. "I finally realized how unfair I've been. After Tony stole Marshall away, I stopped caring about everything, until I was in danger of not even caring about us anymore." She shook her head. "I was wrong. I refuse to let myself die inside. I need you, David. I want you to bring me back to life. I . . ." She took a deep breath. "I want us to get married. I want to be your wife."

He kissed her tentatively, as if she were a fragile piece of glass. She responded with warm, hungry eagerness. How good it felt to be in his arms, she thought.

Hours later they nestled in a corner of the sofa with a wool blanket over them, watching the fire burn down to glowing ashes. David kissed the side of her cheek and she bent her head slightly, shivering with pleasure as his lips moved down her sensitive neck. "This was all Z'Maria's idea, you know," she murmured lazily, her eyes half shut.

He laughed. "What are you talking about?"

"She said our kids are strong and don't need us anymore—we should get on with our lives."

"She's right," he said against her hair. "But I don't think it's that they don't need us anymore. They never really belonged to us in the first place. They belong to themselves."

"I guess," she said, her soft voice edged with pain. "Still I'm afraid for them both. What . . . what'll you do if Maura takes Katie?" Angie felt David's whole body tensing.

"I'm not worried about that anymore," he said with unwonted sharpness. "Maura's made her own sordid bed—and she's going to have to lie in it."

"David, you said that once before." She twisted around. "What do you mean—what is she doing?"

"Angie, shhh, it doesn't concern you." The words were uttered so convincingly, yet she sensed that he was lying.

She pulled away and sat up, her eyes watchful. "Please, David, we promised not to keep things from each other, even if they might hurt."

But he shook his head. "Not this—"

She was about to press him when the telephone rang. Her heart jumped. Who would be calling so late?

"David," she said a moment later, her hand clenching the phone. "The police! They've been calling everywhere for you."

As he took the phone and nodded in response to whatever the man was saying, she watched his face grow pale. "It's Maura," he said grimly as he hung up. "She . . . there's been an accident. I've got to get down to the hospital."

"I'll come with you."

"No."

Angie went out with him to his car, almost having to run to keep up with his long-legged stride. "David, call me as soon as you know anything."

He nodded absently as he slid behind the wheel.

What aren't you telling me? she longed to ask. What has Maura done? Angie stood shivering beneath the cold night sky, watching his car disappear around the bend in the driveway.

The detective was terse and to the point. "Her car went into the Allegheny down off River Avenue. Made to look like an accident."

David stared past him at the blanket-shrouded corpse in the hospital morgue. "What do you mean—'look like' an accident?" he said.

"The examining physician thinks she was unconscious even before the crash." The detective paused. "Mr. O'Rourke, did your wife have any enemies that you know of, someone who might have wanted to harm her?"

David walked past him into the bare, antiseptic room. He folded back the sheet and stared down at her. A slight frown of perplexity furrowed her brow, but her parted lips bore a faint, secret smile. What shocked him was not her stillness—the marble pallor of death—but her look of almost childlike innocence.

He thought about the bruises she had begun coming home with the past year, her boasting that she finally knew what a real man was like and his shock when the private eye he had hired to tail her reported that Maura's latest lover was Malfatti. He tried to blot out the logical extension of that fact—that it was Maura who had led the man to Angie's son.

"Mr. O'Rourke?" the police detective persisted. "You didn't answer my question."

David hesitated. He knew firsthand the extent of Malfatti's vengeful nature. Pitted against such a predatory evil, David knew he would be helpless to defend either himself or Angie.

Still staring down at Maura, he shook his head. "I don't know," he said.

Nickie sat propped up in bed with a cashmere shawl draped around her shoulders. The top of the green brocade bedspread resembled her desk at work: Piles of accounting sheets were arranged in neat stacks around her. She didn't dare post Tony's deposits in the office, so every night she brought them home with her: twenty accounts funneling $17,000 a month in untaxed income. She had set them up under various assumed personal and corporate names, careful not to deposit like amounts on the same day. She knew that the first tip-off to the bank's internal auditors would be any such tell-tale pattern. Yet for all her caution, Nickie knew that discovery was inevitable. Day in and day out for two and a half years, she had lived with the realization. The constant tension had resulted in a bleeding ulcer.

All at once she dropped her pen and rubbed her stomach. The pain was getting unbearable. Lately all she could choke down was milk and baby food, which she ate straight out of a jar. Business lunches had become a nightmare; she made a game of moving the food around on her plate and lifting the fork to her lips without actually eating: a technique she'd perfected as a kid with Pap's horrendous gruel of Roman beans and rice. Twenty years later and she was back where she started from—eating tasteless muck and living in fear under the thumb of a man she hated. "Powerless to do a goddamn thing about it," she muttered.

A soft knock sounded at the door. Burning spasms radiated through her belly as she frantically picked up the scattered piles of papers and slipped them beneath the sheet.

"Who is it?" she called, feigning sleepiness.

"It's me," Louis said through the door.

She saw at once that he had been drinking. He was not quite drunk, but she recognized the glaze on his eyes, the relaxed droop of his shoulders. A sudden burst of anger pulsed through her. Here she was endangering her security, her future, and for what? For him?

"What do you want?" she said coldly.

He sat on the edge of the bed. "Nickie," he said in a dull voice, "Mother's on to you."

Her pulse leaped. "I . . . I don't understand."

"I think you do. She's brought in an outside auditor. He uncovered your scam." Louis looked at her reproachfully. "Why did you do it, Nick? Just tell me that. Why?"

She slumped back against the pillows. Here it was,

doomsday. What was she supposed to do—lie to him? She tried an offhand shrug. "Ten percent right off the top for me was simply too tempting, I suppose."

"You're lying. You never took a penny for yourself," he said, slurring the words. "You're ambitious, not greedy. I know you, Nick. What you truly love is the game, the wheeling and dealing, the sense of power and control that comes from your position. I know damn well you'd never risk that for mere money." He forced his glazed eyes to focus on her. "I want the truth."

"No, you don't, Louis." She shook her head ruefully. "You really don't."

"Damn it, stop treating me like an idiot child who has to be protected." His fist pounded the bed. "For God's sake, let me try to help you for a change. Let me have that smidgen of self-respect."

She averted her gaze, unable to bear the sight of this weak, sensitive man trying so valiantly to be her protector, to suddenly reverse the roles that they had occupied for so long. "Louis," she whispered in a barely audible voice, "I had no choice."

He stared at her for a long time. "What do you mean, 'no choice'?"

"Tony knew some things."

"What things?" he asked mechanically, although she could tell from his expression that he had guessed.

"He threatened me. He said if I didn't work with him, he'd tell the world what you are. He had pictures," she said, her expression full of pain. "I couldn't let that happen."

Tears started in his eyes. "I thought I was safe—a married man with a beautiful daughter. If I could only have . . . controlled my impulses." He looked pleadingly at her. "But you know I needed that escape valve. I'd have gone crazy."

"There's no point in torturing yourself with recriminations," she said, forcing herself to speak with a brisk authority she no longer felt. "We have to treat this like any other crisis. We have to decide how to minimize the damage."

"There is no way, Nickie. What are the options—admit that the bank has Mob ties, or admit that its president is a faggot?" Self-loathing tinged the ugly word.

She leaned forward to grasp his hands. "Listen to me, Louis, there is a way, but it won't be easy."

"What?"

"You have to tell your mother the truth. She has to know!"

He shook his head and started to tremble. "I can't do that."

"Louis!" She shook him. "She loves you more than anything. She's not like your father. She won't judge you."

"It would kill her," he said, starting to cry.

"She loves you," Nickie insisted. "She'll do anything to protect you, you know that. We both will. With her on our side, we can keep Tony's involvement to a minimum while still protecting you," she said, not believing it herself. Yet she had to say something. She could see him crumbling before her eyes. "Will you promise to sleep on it? Things always look better in the morning, you know that."

He stood up stiffly. "You're right. I'm going on like an idiot."

"Would you like to sleep with me tonight?" She ventured a shaky smile. "No strings attached."

"I love you, Nickie, you know that, don't you?" he said with an air of strange calm that made her uneasy. "In my own way, I've loved you."

"Louis—"

"Good night," he said from the door. "I'll look in on RJ before I turn in."

She lay back against the pillows as he quietly shut her door. She heard the muffled tread of his footsteps across the hall, then the soft creak of RJ's door. Minimize the damage, she had told him, as if it were a business deal gone sour rather than the very fabric of their lives that they were fighting to keep intact. Minimize the damage, she repeated as she drifted into a light, restless sleep. The words echoed through her half-conscious mind in a feverish refrain.

55

Nickie had tossed and turned all night. Just before dawn she had finally fallen into a dreamless, almost drugged-like sleep.

Distantly she heard pounding. Against her will, she swam up through the tranquil darkness toward consciousness. The pounding grew more urgent. Her mother-in-law called frantically through the door, "Nickie!"

She jumped out of bed and grabbed her robe. "Josephine, what's wrong?"

"Jake's down in the kitchen. He says Louis . . . Louis . . ."

Nickie didn't wait to hear the rest. She raced down the stairs. The old gardener stood just inside the back door, twisting his battered felt hat between his hands. His eyes darted from the housekeeper's face to Nickie's.

"Where is he, Jake?" Nickie said, fighting to keep the hysteria out of her voice.

"In the garage, ma'am," he said softly. "But I believe he's dead."

Dead. Nickie rushed out across the back lawn, barely aware of the frost-hardened grass cutting into her bare feet, and ran through the open side door which led into the old carriage house. The dark garage reeked of exhaust fumes. Covering her mouth with one hand, she ran to push open the big doors. Then she turned back and saw him slumped over the wheel of his low-slung coupe. "O God, Louis!"

She flung open the car door and frantically pulled him out onto the garage floor. Kneeling over him, she put her mouth over his. But his lips had long since grown cold, their slack corners tinged a bright cherry red from the carbon monoxide.

"Louis," she mourned, tears filling her eyes, "you didn't have to do this."

Josephine ran up, muffling a scream. "Dear God, no!" She too knelt down, lifting her son's head into her lap. "No, no, no."

Nickie wiped her tears away. She had to get control. Gently she placed her hands on her mother-in-law's shoulders and spoke in a soothing voice, "Josephine, I want you to go up to the house and call an ambulance. Close the doors of the garage on your way out, and send Jake in here." The softness of Nickie's voice seemed to calm the woman as she rose like a sleepwalker to carry out the instructions.

The old man hung back in the doorway. Nickie beckoned to him urgently. "Please, you have to help me, Jake. I can't do this by myself."

Struggling under Louis's weight, they half carried, half dragged him out into the garden. When they got to the pool, Nickie gestured for the gardener to lower the body. Then ever so gently Nickie rolled it into the cold, murky water. She turned to the frightened gardener. "Neither you nor Berthe are to say anything to anyone about what you've seen," she said sternly. "The manner of my husband's death is no one's business but his own, do you understand me?"

"Yes, ma'am."

Nickie nodded, satisfied that he would keep their secret. Even in death, she vowed, Louis's reputation—and hers—would be protected.

Perfect day for a funeral, Nickie thought, standing at the library window and regarding the sodden brown leaves on the flagstone terrace. Cold rain had fallen steadily all day. How quiet the house was! she thought, listening to the rhythmic ticking of the old mantel clock. Such a lonely sound. Suddenly she wished she hadn't bundled RJ off to Angie's.

Hearing the library door open, she stiffened, knowing it was Louis's mother. Nickie had thought that she would have been grateful for the way she had handled everything. Instead, the long-festering animosity between them had intensified in the three days since Louis's death. A showdown was inevitable, but please not now. She wasn't ready for it now.

Josephine pulled off her gloves and dropped them on the desk. "I've invited Monsignor Carrick for dinner to thank him for the funeral mass and his beautiful eulogy. I would appreciate it if you would absent yourself."

"I see," Nickie said levelly. "You found it acceptable that I lied to the police, to the priests, to the reporters. But now that the dirty work is done, I'm supposed to conveniently disappear?"

"That's how criminals work, isn't it?"

"How dare you! What I did, I did to protect your son, Josephine."

"I'm sick to death of your lying and manipulating," Josephine said wearily. "My son didn't believe what I was telling him until it was too late. Poor Louis never understood what kind of woman you are." The older woman turned to the mantel, where her son's college golf trophies were proudly arrayed. "He was too innocent to see it. Having the truth foisted on him was too much," she murmured, her voice breaking. "You destroyed him."

"Louis was not innocent, Josephine," Nickie said coldly. "His suicide had nothing to do with me."

"What do you mean it had nothing to do with you?"

"There are things about your son which . . . which he never told you."

"How typical of you to try to put the blame on someone who is dead and can't defend himself," she cried angrily.

"You think I wanted to get involved in that laundering scam? Damn it, I was blackmailed. I had to do it to protect Louis."

"That's outrageous. Louis had nothing to hide. You were always the one with the sordid little secrets."

Nickie flushed. God, how she despised this woman. She wanted more than anything to hurt her. Before she could stop herself, the words spilled out. "Louis was homosexual, Josephine. Ours was a marriage in name only."

Josephine laughed sharply. "And my granddaughter?"

"As I said, Louis was not sexually aroused by women," Nickie said implacably. "I had to go to great lengths to appeal to him in that way. RJ was conceived the night of the opera gala. If you'd like the details of that 'sordid little secret,' I'll—"

"You're a liar! I have never heard more disgusting, filthy lies!" Josephine shouted, enraged. "I want you out of my home, out of my life! I never want to see you again."

"You can kick me out of your house, but you can't throw me out of your life. I've seen Louis's will—his bank shares are mine. We're equals now, Josephine. I'm as much an Urbano as you are."

"As long as I live, you will never be that."

Nickie appeared at work Monday morning, wearing the same black silk shantung suit that she had worn to Louis's funeral. A subtle reminder of her ties, both personal and professional, to Urbano Bank. She was not simply the owner's widow but his heir to fifty percent of the institution's privately held stock.

Heads swiveled at the characteristic quick tap of her heels across the marble lobby, then turned away as if afraid to meet her eyes. Outside her suite of offices she bumped into a man in a mover's uniform carrying out boxes.

"Madge, what the hell is going on?" she said, storming into her secretary's alcove as more movers edged past carrying furnishings out of her office.

Madge looked at her shamefacedly. "You'd better check with the board," the woman murmured. "They . . . they're waiting for you upstairs."

Too agitated to wait for an elevator, Nickie raced up the three flights of stairs and stormed into the conference room without knocking. "I demand to know what's going on here." The six men sitting around the table shifted uneasily.

Arnold Smithton stood up and looked at her, his pouchy hang-dog face without expression. "I'm afraid you've placed us in an untenable position, Mrs. Urbano." His fingers fiddled with the closed file on the tabletop in front of him. "It has come to our attention that you have used this bank for purposes that are proscribed by law," he said in his dry, shaky voice. "You have endangered the stability of this institution and the hard-earned deposits of its customers. You have, in fact, committed a federal crime, evidence of which"—he indicated the file beneath his fingertips—"has just come into our possession."

Nickie's heart pounded.

Smithton went on: "If such information were to be made public, this institution as well as its clientele would suffer. Naturally, we do not wish that to occur. Therefore," he droned on, "we, the board, are prepared to issue an ultimatum." He paused. "You will sign over your recently inherited holdings into a trust for your daughter—to be administered by her grandmother, Josephine Urbano. If you refuse to do so, you will be turned over to the proper authorities for criminal indictment. Do you understand what I have just said? If not, I will re—"

"Yes," she said sharply. "Yes, I understand."

He opened a second file before him and reached for his fountain pen. The silence in the room was so complete that the slight click of metal against metal as he removed the pen's top sounded deafening. Nickie stepped forward, her features clenched to prevent any display of emotion. She took the pen and signed the papers, relinquishing control of the institution she had transformed with such single-minded tenacity into a financial powerhouse. As she scratched her name across the pages, she felt as though she were signing away every last drop of self-worth.

56

Nickie didn't like coming out to the country. Without the solidity of concrete beneath her heels, the hubbub of traffic and bright lights and action, she felt too vulnerable. But then, what choice do I have now? she thought bitterly.

She missed her life; she missed Louis more than she wanted to admit. A cold, hard feeling of vengefulness settled around her heart, but she knew she had to bide her time.

She felt the eyes of Tony's henchmen watching her from the stable yard—round-the-clock goons whose only function was to keep Angie from her son. The bastard had covered every angle.

Nickie shook off her bitterness. She had to be an actress now, a damn good one, she reminded herself.

Her narrow eyes took stock of the surroundings, seeing not the verdant, peaceful landscape but the money and power represented by the miles of picturesque white fencing.

The sound of hooves galloping across the meadow toward her caught her attention. She waved and hailed Marshall. He was fourteen now, handsome as a prince as he cantered over to her on the gleaming chestnut mare that Tony had boasted cost him ten thousand bucks.

"Aunt Nickie," he greeted her neutrally, his voice deepened almost fully into manhood now. The boy's expression was cool and watchful. Although his eyes were like his father's, they seemed different somehow, softer. Or maybe that's just what she wanted to see, Nickie thought, for Angie's sake.

"How's life treating you, Marsh?"

"About as well as I deserve." She heard the subtle undercurrent of irony in his tone and it cheered her. Marsh had spirit and intelligence; he was a boy who wouldn't easily be cowed by Tony.

Nickie smiled. "Your mother sends her love."

A flicker of emotion played over his face before his features tightened. "How is she?"

"How is any mother without her kid? She's lonely, Marsh. She misses you."

Their conversation was interrupted by the sound of an approaching automobile. Nickie turned to see Tony's gleaming Chrysler draw to a stop in front of the barn.

Tony climbed out of the car and headed toward them. When he looked at his son, he always had the same strange, mixed emotions. He couldn't admit to himself that more often than not he felt uneasy around the boy—

never knowing what went on behind that closed face of his. Whether he tried to speak to him in Italian or English, it didn't matter; it was like trying to talk to a stone wall. They could find no common ground.

Tony frowned when he recognized Nickie. Broad thought she was so fucking smart, he thought, couldn't even keep from getting her ass kicked out of the bank. Another year and I'd a been funneling fifty grand a month through her—all cream off the top. He watched her stroll over, still managing to look like a million bucks despite the world falling on her like a ton of bricks. He had to give her that—little smart-mouth Nicoletta had guts. And class.

"Hiya, Tony, *come stai*?" She greeted him in that husky voice of hers.

"Not too bad. You?"

She shrugged and turned to watch Marshall gallop away across the field. She laughed. "Your kid looks like an aristocrat, Tony," she said. "Must have come from your side. Maybe your mother did it with some dissolute Calabrian duke before you were born. A noble in the woodpile." Tony didn't know whether to haul off and belt her or what.

Nickie grinned, unabashed. "Don't look so pissed off. It's a compliment."

He turned his back on her and started back to the barn, leaving her no choice but to follow. "What the hell you doing out here anyway?" he asked over his shoulder.

"Girl gets down on her luck, she goes to people who can help. Maybe she's thinking about hooking up with a winner for a change, instead of a loser."

Tony stopped, waiting for her to catch up. He smiled and gave her a light, friendly knuckle under her chin. "Didn't I always try to tell you, Nick? You should a never went downtown where a woman don't belong."

He started walking again, and she fell in step beside him, a rueful smile playing around her lips. "What can I say? You were right, Tony, the way you were right about the bank scam. We had a good thing going." She stopped beside her car.

"But you blew it."

"Not me, Tony. Louis blew it for us." She smiled again. "But the son of a bitch got his, didn't he?"

"So now what?"

She shrugged. "I'm free as a bird. If you and I decided to put our heads together, I think we could do business."

Tony stared at her hard. He was no fool. He knew she despised him, but so what? He knew how to handle women. Besides, Nickie had business smarts like no one he'd ever seen.

"Why don't you come out to the house?" he said offhandedly. "We'll eat a little pasta, talk . . ."

"Sounds good."

"I just got one thing to make clear, Nickie," he said, grabbing her roughly by the arm. "You work for me, you're loyal to me, understand? We don't got that *lealta*, we don't got shit. I find a Judas in my operation, he don't last two minutes. He's dead."

"Hey, Tony, what do you take me for?" She laughed huskily as she opened her car door and slid in. "If I say I'm yours, then I'm yours."

Driving back down toward the highway, Nickie clutched the steering wheel. You'll have my loyalty all right, Tony, she thought bitterly. For as long as it takes to get you.

Two guards stood beneath a matched pair of heraldic lions, watchdogs of stone and flesh impassively observing the stream of cars passing between the high gates. Tony was one of the last to arrive, his white Chrysler whispering up the drive that led to DiPiano's hilltop mansion. The big conclave was an inevitability that Tony had primed himself for. Still he felt edgy, taut, like a fighter before he steps into the ring.

Thick cigar smoke swirled around the dining-room chandelier, dimming the brilliance of its myriad crystal facets. The long, carved refectory table that had once graced the castle of an Austrian archduke was littered with dribbles of ash. The men greeted one another with coarse laughter —all peasants at heart despite the elegant surroundings.

Tony took the seat opposite Rocco seconds before Carlo made his entrance. The old man clung to vestiges of his dapper youth, but his skin was stretched tautly around his skull, giving him a skeletal look that was not without a certain grim strength. At seventy-five he was still a power to be reckoned with.

As he stood at the head of the table, his hazel eyes gazed leisurely yet with a penetrating directness around the assemblage of men. "I look at you," he spoke finally, his distinctively smooth voice only slightly roughened by age, "my family in spirit if not in blood, and I see that the last twenty-five years have been good to all of us. But a new era's coming. We gotta make room for new ideas, for the new generation."

Tony stiffened as he watched Carlo clamp his hand on his son's shoulder—like God the Father with Christ at his right-hand side, he thought contemptuously.

Carlo looked over at Tony. "Like all a you, I learned from the school of hard knocks. It made us tough. Now with this new generation, we're gonna make a stronger bond, like this." He linked his two forefingers together. "The young ones, they got education, they're smooth. They know how to deal with the politicians, with the money guys on the outside. They speak their language." Carlo's soft, insistent voice was like a wave beating against a stony cliff. "We gotta follow their lead. The world's too complicated. We can't afford to be peasants no more."

Tony felt every word like a slap in the face. How come I don't get no credit? he asked himself. Me who was hand-in-glove with the banks all this time. The old fart meant to keep him in his place, kowtowing to Joe College, who'd probably piss in his pants if someone handed him a loaded gun. Although Tony burned inside, he was careful to keep his face a stony mask.

All around him men were passing a whiskey bottle, lifting their glasses in a toast to Rocco—to the new generation. Tony tossed back his drink and slammed the glass down. Rocco met his eyes across the table. That's right, look me in the eye, Tony thought. Read the future there, you smartass fucker. Power could be forged only one way: through bloodshed.

57

Pebbles tumbled downstream by rushing waters lent their name to the beautiful countryside around Rolling Rock, 18,000 acres of field, forest, hills and trout-filled streams. Dotting the lush spring landscape were the summer manors of Pittsburgh's old guard, who turned up their noses at the nouveau riche attempting entree into their exclusive domain, except for one weekend each year when the high suffered to mingle with the low in the name of charity.

By Saturday thousands of spectators would come to watch the afternoon horse races and glimpse the rich presiding in their private boxes well above the crowd. The O'Rourkes, of impeccable Scots-Irish Pittsburgh lineage dating back to the nineteenth century, were solid old guard. The Urbanos fell in between old and new, sufficiently rich enough to be deferred to now that their immigrant roots were well buried in the past. But the DiPianos and their ilk were definitely new money and unsavory nouveau riches at that. Angie and Nickie Branzino were considered little better—upstarts who had brazenly married old money without severing their ties to their lower-class immigrant roots.

These social distinctions crystallized at the elegant Friday evening Pool Dinner in the Rolling Rock Club dining room. Old families had tables reserved up front near the dais, from which the charity auction would be called, while the upstarts were clustered at the back—their money welcome even if they themselves weren't.

David, in true renegade fashion, had spurned the O'Rourke and Donahue tables. He and Katie sat with Angie and Phil. Angie's heart constricted when she looked at David, for the past few months had been hellish for him. Despite an investigation, nothing conclusive had been determined regarding Maura's "accident." Yet Angie was aware that David knew more than he let on, that whatever Maura had done before her death had filled him with loathing, not only for his wife but for himself. Feeling her eyes on him, David looked up. His eyes glinted momentarily with their old warmth. Buoyed, Angie smiled back. She needed him now more than ever.

Her gaze moved yearningly to her son, sitting with Tony and Rocco and his family. Tony had been watching her and he caught her eye. She looked down, sickened by his smirk, and tried to concentrate on the list of horses before her on the table. Her perusal stopped at the name of Marsh's horse: MacHeath. The name tugged hazily at her memory. Then it came to her—the hood in *The Threepenny Opera*. Marshall had taken the name from the avant-garde musical he had loved as a boy in Paris. The opera featured MacHeath—"Mack the Knife"—a ruthless gangster who always managed to cover his traces. Angie couldn't help but smile at the private joke aimed at Tony.

Buzzing voices caught her attention. She noticed disapproving faces turned toward the entrance, and without even looking she guessed who had caused the sotto voce uproar.

Nickie swept in, her shadow fox fur dropped over her shoulders to reveal a scarlet dress fashioned from two huge triangles of silk tied at the neck, front and back. Simple, stylish, outrageous. "I figure they already branded me," Nickie said to Angie as she ostentatiously blew a kiss toward the DiPiano table before sitting down next to her sister. "Might as well dress the part." She looked her sister up and down. "You look gorgeous tonight." Nickie reached out to touch the sparkle of sequins on Angie's dazzling Norell sheath. "Like a mermaid."

"Mm, I figured I'd be the one upstaging you tonight," Angie teased. "Naturally I was wrong."

Nickie laughed as she scanned the bejeweled crowd. "They can't stand it that I actually show my face, can they? I should really give them a show and go over and kiss my dear mother-in-law. Wouldn't they love that— the excommunicant appealing for forgiveness to the dowager queen?"

Bitterness bled through her irreverent badinage, and Angie gave her sister a troubled look. Ever since Louis's death and her subsequent banishment from the Urbanos' world, Nickie had become very close-mouthed about her activities. Angie knew that she was working with Tony. Disturbing as the situation was, Angie never confronted her: She was selfish enough to want to maintain that additional connection to Marshall.

Midway through the evening, a pack of hounds bounded through the dining-room doors, followed by the huntsman. Nickie leaned over to Angie as the man piped his animals into parade order. "Who'd believe it—for the privilege of hobnobbing with these snobs, we have to let their damn dogs slobber all over us."

"It's a proven fact," Angie joked back. "The Johnny Bulls love their animals more than each other."

A few of the hounds wandered off from the pack, whining excitedly as guests lured them with tidbits from their plates. Angie watched Katie lift her head with delight when one of the animals leaned his shoulder against her lap. She groped to pet the dog, while with her free hand she daintily felt about her plate until she located a piece of steak. But before she could feed it, the dog had wandered off toward the DiPianos.

Angie realized Marshall must have noticed the look of disappointment on Katie's face because he collared the dog and led it back to her. She fed it and gently stroked its head. A moment later the huntsman sounded his horn, and the stray hound returned to its master. Marshall, however, lingered at the girl's side. Angie drank in the nearness of him. This was the first time she had even seen him in eighteen months. He looked fit, handsome, his beautiful eyes bright in his youthful tanned face. His eyes met hers briefly, full of hurt that vanished almost as quickly as it had appeared. She desperately wanted to talk to him alone.

Lovely Katie, oblivious to the tension, invited Marshall to join them. "I'd better get back," he said, although he seemed reluctant to leave. His voice softened as he went on: "I remember how we went after those lambs in Paris when we were kids. You . . . you still seem to like animals." She nodded eagerly. "If you want to come down to the stables sometime, I'll show you my horse."

Angie watched him return to Tony, her throat tight. As Z'Maria had promised, Marshall had not become a monster. Her sensitive, gentle boy had grown into a wonderfully sensitive teenager. Angie was so caught up by him that she barely noticed the bidding had begun.

"Going once . . . twice . . ." The auctioneer banged his gavel down. "Sold for one thousand dollars to the lovely lady in green." Flushed with pleasure, the woman at a front-row table stood up to take the parchment that entitled her to "ownership" for the weekend and the right to stand in the winner's circle if the mare won.

Angie shifted in her seat as the auctioneer announced MacHeath. Impulsively she raised her hand and bid five thousand dollars. A low murmur swept through the crowd, and necks craned to see who had started the bidding so high.

"Five thousand. Wonderful start," the auctioneer crooned. "Do I hear five thousand five hundred to beat this beautiful lady's magnificent offer? Do I—"

"Ten thousand!" Tony shouted, and the crowd's buzz grew to a loud, speculative murmur.

"Fift—"

"Twenty."

The bidding spiraled higher. Every time Tony's bark overrode Angie's warm musical voice so that before her bid was even out of her mouth he was arrogantly topping it. Hypnotized by the game, Angie kept raising the stakes— determined to show up Tony and to win back a piece of her son. She would bid all night if she had to. The crowd, delighted by the thousands being racked up for the coffers of Children's Hospital, started to applaud. But Angie barely heard them. Nothing else existed but this deadly serious contest of wills. Back and forth it went, neither even acknowledging the other's presence, except by their bids.

"The gentleman's bid fifty. Do I hear sixty?"

Angie pushed her chair back and stood up, enunciating with a stark clarity that was pure drama: "One hundred thousand."

Someone gasped, then the room hushed to a tense, expectant silence. No one so much as breathed.

Tony's defiant "Hundred and fifty!" broke the spell.

Angie was about to bid again when out of the corner of her eye she saw Marshall throw down his napkin in disgust.

"One hundred fifty thousand . . . going once . . ." Angie watched Marsh stalk out. "Going twice . . ." She sat down, shaking. "Sold! To the wonderfully generous and obstinate gentleman at the rear table. Will you please come forward, sir, and claim your prize," the auctioneer said with rising glee as the audience broke into thunderous applause.

Angie stared at her hands, ignoring Nickie, who was trying to say something over the tumult. God, how she despised what she had become. It didn't matter that she had made a fool of herself by playing out the idiotic little drama. What mattered was that out of pride and stubbornness she had allowed herself to be dragged into Tony's game, using their son to get back at each other. Once again, without meaning to, she had hurt Marshall.

After the noise, heat and claustrophobic closeness of the dining room, the brisk night air felt wonderful on Angie's flushed face. She looked up at the high, ragged clouds scudding past the moon. Against the remote clarity of the night sky, she felt small and powerless—like a character in Thomas Hardy's bleak Wessex world. Tony had defeated her again.

A light winked on in the ivy-covered stone barn at the base of the hill. She glimpsed her son in silhouette against the open door, and something inside her urged her forward. Slowly she started down the gravel path to the stables.

She stopped just inside the big doors, careful not to make a sound. Marshall had slung his dinner jacket over a hook and was pitching forkfuls of fresh hay into MacHeath's stall, his movements marked by the grace and ease of a male comfortable with his own physicality. A gift from Tony perhaps, Angie acknowledged reluctantly. She took pleasure simply in watching him, though the pleasure was bittersweet. So many years of his life have been lost to me! she thought.

An inadvertent movement on her part caught his eye

and he glanced up. Without acknowledging her presence, he continued his work. Angie gathered up her courage and advanced toward him.

"Marshall. Can you ever forgive me?" The words were an apology not only for her behavior that evening but for all the times that she had let him down. "I never intended for you to be a pawn."

"Just go away and leave me alone." He wielded the fork with quick ferocity, his knuckles white where he gripped the handle. "Haven't the two of you done enough for one night?"

"Marshall, please don't turn your back on me," she begged. "You can't let Tony keep poisoning your—"

"Yeah, use him as an excuse," he cried, his breath escaping in short, hard gasps. He loosened his shirt collar with an angry tug. "You abandoned me long before he came along."

The bald truth of his words smote her. "Listen to me, I beg you," she whispered in Italian, her voice full of pain. "I only meant to protect you."

"You lied to me." His long-festering bitterness made each word as sharp as glass. 'My whole life has been a lie."

"No! The only thing I ever kept from you was the truth about . . . about him. For God sake, you've lived with the man. You must know him by now."

"I don't care what he is. You had no right to deprive me of my father."

Watching as he drove the fork deep into the hay, Angie caught a glint of gold at his throat. A tremor of shock jolted her. He still wore the small cross that she had given him five years before—another tenuous link binding them despite the chain of broken promises and deceit that had been her legacy to him. In some hidden corner of his heart, his love for her—or at least a memory of it—surely lingered. Despite her fading courage, Angie knew she had to try to reach through the bristling defenses he had erected against her.

"I've made terrible mistakes, I know that," she began urgently. "But all the decisions I made were out of my love for you. From the moment you were born you were central to my life." Her voice choked up, but she forced herself to go on. "You always have been, you always will be—no matter what the distances between us. You must believe me."

When he lifted his eyes to her face, she read the depths of his pain and wanted only to hold and comfort him as she had when he was small.

The sound of clapping hands, sharp and ironic, shattered the moment. "*Brava!*" Tony called out mockingly from the open doorway. "Another fine performance."

Ignoring the interruption, Angie rushed on in a low, taut voice, "He's had his say for the past year. Now it's my turn. Did he ever tell you why I married him in the first place, how my mother, your *nonna* Rosa, died? Ask him about the house he burned. Ask him! And ask him, too, about our life together—the insults, the beatings. And of how he married me knowing he already had another wife—"

"Enough!" Tony grabbed her arm and whirled her around. "Shut up," he uttered menacingly.

"No, I won't. Marshall's almost a man now. He has a right to the truth—all of it!"

"He'll know what I choose for him to know."

"What makes you think you'll be able to control him the way you tried to control me?" she challenged him. "He's my son, too. He's seen me struggle to get what I want. I taught him what it takes to be a survivor. He's not going to tolerate you or anyone else trying to control him."

"Shuddup!" he roared. "Filling the kid's head with your crap . . ."

Tony lifted his fist, but Angie didn't even flinch. "You haven't learned a thing in all these years, have you, Tony? Sure, you can beat a person down with those fists, but you can't get to them inside!" She shook her head. "You know nothing about character, about the resilience of spirit. You're blind to everything except what you want. You were blind to me, you're blind to your own son. You're blind to yourself." As the words spilled out, she could no more stop them than she could stop the rain. "Fifteen years haven't changed you. All the fancy cars and clothes, the money, the big house—they don't mean anything. If you think they do, you're only kidding yourself. It's all a deception, Tony, it's all surface. Because underneath you are what you always were—a weak, bullying criminal."

The words were like slivers of ice hissing against the volcanic rage building inside him. Lying bitch didn't know what the fuck she was talking about, he told himself. Trying to make me look like an asshole in front of the kid. She was lying, lying, and yet every nerve in his body, every instinct, was screaming at him to shut her up, to go for the songbird's throat—to kill the very thing that had given her the power to defy him.

He lunged and his fingers dug into the soft white flesh of her throat. She clawed his hands, fighting for breath. Screaming, Marshall grabbed Tony's arms. "No! You'll kill her."

Infuriated by his interference, Tony lashed out with a stinging backhand that caught Marshall's face with whipsaw force. The boy staggered backward, bleeding. Breathing hard, Tony pulled out his handkerchief and shoved it at him. But Marshall angrily flung his hand away. His eyes, filled with pain, shifted between his parents. Then he turned and ran, nearly knocking over Rocco and Nickie, who had come looking for them.

"What the hell's going on?" Rocco demanded.

Tony wrapped the handkerchief around the bloodied scratches on his hands. Without saying a word he stalked out.

Nickie rushed to Angie's side. "What happened?"

"Nothing," Angie whispered. Then she laid her head on her sister's shoulder and wept.

By midmorning Saturday, colorful sun umbrellas and striped awnings had mushroomed in the fields surrounding the racetrack. Silver candelabras and china, magnums of champagne and tins of caviar issued forth from Rolls-Royce trunks in preparation for elegant tailgate parties. Diminutive jockeys in bright racing silks crossed the course toward the central paddocks, where the horses pranced and snorted in anticipation of the upcoming race. An antique stagecoach stood at the finish line—already the Mellon family and their guests were climbing inside.

Numb to the festive preparations, Angie paced anxiously in the Branzino-O'Rourke box. She waved away the glass of champagne which the caterer tried to hand her. Her eyes were fixed on the paddocks, scanning the area for Marsh's horse and his jockey's distinctive black-and-pink silks. Absentmindedly she caressed her throat, the bruises hidden by the high neck of her dolman-sleeved dress. As soon as Nickie came into the box, Angie pounced. "Have you seen them?"

"They're bringing MacHeath up now." Nickie perched on the rail, her eyes surveying Angie critically. "Look, you've got to relax. Kids are resilient at that age. Marsh is okay."

"I was little older than 'that age' when I married Tony," Angie retorted. "I know what that bastard is capable of."

A few rows over, Rocco and his entourage arrived. Marsh, looking sullen and withdrawn, came into the box with Tony.

Lost in the confused turmoil of her own thoughts, Angie didn't even notice the horses thundering forward past the roaring spectators. Her mind played back a jumbled stream of memories: Marsh's face after Tony had backhanded him, splattered blood on the broken window in Giulia Francini's ransacked apartment; her own battered face in the mirror of the farmhouse bedroom. Violence upon violence upon violence. Angie shivered.

Vaguely she heard the track announcer shouting, "MacHeath! It's MacHeath by a neck!"

Katie jumped up and down, hugging Angie excitedly. "He won! Marsh's horse won!"

Tony grabbed Marsh by the arm and pulled him out of the box. Angie had to steel herself not to interfere. My son is strong, he's resilient, he'll survive, she whispered inwardly, the words like a litany offered up to heaven. She looked up at David as he put his hand on her shoulder. How much more can we bear? her eyes asked.

58

Angie leaned her cheek against the cold glass of her library window. She watched the city lights wink on in the unseasonably cold May dusk. Pittsburgh sparkled like a newly cut gem. Across the river, she saw the partially erected steel framework of Renaissance Hall silhouetted against the evening sky. In her mind's eye she tried to envision the new performing arts center rising out of the landscape like a sleekly sculpted bird poised for flight. But for the first time the vision that had sustained her all these long, lonely months failed her. She could think only of her son. . . .

Violence upon violence. History repeating itself. Nervously she caressed the bruises on her throat that Tony had inflicted. Nickie had tried to console her. *Kids are resilient at that age. Marsh will be okay.* But Angie couldn't accept that. She alone truly knew what Tony was capable of.

Dispiritedly she turned away from the window and slipped a recording of *Tosca* onto the hi-fi. Closing her eyes, she let the aria "Vissi d'arte" wash over her: Love and music, these I have lived for. Suddenly she longed to sing the role on stage. She hungered for that moment of cathartic release when she could feel her own helplessness subsumed in Floria Tosca's. The brutal impulses of Puccini's music uncannily echoed the violent events in her own life.

She went over to the doll theater that the carpentry shop had built to her specifications. On that miniature stage she manipulated her nine toy actors, blocking out their dramatic actions within the framework of the music—in this way anticipating the problems she would face with real-life performers once she started directing them.

Scarpia's evilly triumphant voice welled up: "Tosca, finalmente mia." Angie moved the doll figure of Floria toward him, miming the plunge of her knife into his heart. Then she slowly laid the Scarpia figure down on stage, choreographing his death to reflect the ebbing of his once powerful and menacing three-chord motive, now in minor key. The force of the music was such that she trembled as the toy tenor lay dying at Tosca's feet.

The record jumped scratchily and went dead. Her heart thumping, Angie whirled. "Nickie! What are you doing here?"

Nickie closed the hi-fi lid and came over to examine the tiny theater. "No wonder you bury yourself in this place. You get to play queen to all these pawns. Must be great." Her wry smile faded as she looked into Angie's face. "What did I say?"

"Nothing." Angie turned away. "What do you want, Nickie?"

"How about a hint?" She started to hum "Happy Birthday." "Get it—Z'Maria's big day coming up?"

"Oh, no." Angie glanced at her watch. "I totally forgot about the meeting. I'm sorry."

"Forget it." Nickie shrugged. "Planning a birthday bash is right up Pete's alley, anyway. The rest of us just sort of rubberstamped his ideas."

"Good." Angie slumped in the chair behind her desk. "I don't have room for any more guilt right at the moment." She watched her sister reach into the theater to manipulate the dolls, obviously intrigued by them. "Nickie, you were right what you said a minute ago."

"About what?"

Angie sighed. "That little world is about the only thing I have any control over right now. If I didn't have that, I think I'd lose my sanity completely." She put her elbows on the desk and propped her forehead against her hands. "My mind's been going around and around. I keep wishing I could get to Marshall. But Tony guards him so closely."

"That's Tony's style, all right," Nickie said grimly. "He protects himself from every angle. Believe me, I know. I've been watching him for the past few months."

"Nickie," Angie began, choosing her words carefully, "how far have you had to compromise yourself?"

"You can be sure about one thing—I haven't had to have sex with the s.o.b."

"For God's sake," Angie said in disgust. "Can't you allow me to worry about you a little?"

"You can never stop being the big sister, can you?"

"Nor mother, either." Angie leaned forward and picked up the photo of Marsh as a toddler that she kept on her desk. "Nickie, I'm so afraid Tony's going to punish Marsh for the things I said."

"Listen to me, you've got to stop trying to put Marsh into the same situation you were in. Tony's devoted to the kid, he really is."

Angie sighed. "I know that kind of devotion and love. It's synonymous with control."

Nickie said nothing to that. "Look, I've got to run," she said, moving toward the door. "You *will* leave your dolls long enough to come to Z's party, I hope?"

Angie smiled ruefully. "Get out of here."

Long after Nickie had left, Angie sat alone in the darkness. She didn't have to put the record back on. The well-remembered music soared through her mind, providing the solace and the escape she so desperately needed.

The cable-car station on Carson Street at the foot of Mount Washington was ablaze in colorful lights. Even the cable cars moving up and down the steep slope, ferrying party guests to Pietro's Restaurant at the top, had been festooned with crepe paper. Huge banners wishing Z'Maria HAPPY BIRTHDAY and BUON COMPLEANNO extended the length of the red-brick station house. The Branzinos had spared no expense in making the evening an extravaganza.

The seventy-year-old birthday girl beamed to all and sundry, preening in a new mink stole that she wore over a navy dinner dress Bathsheba had made especially for the occasion. "You look beautiful, Z'," Angie said, brushing a piece of lint from the smooth dark fur.

"*Ma certo.*" Z'Maria grinned slyly. "Just like Grazia Kelly."

"Let's not get carried away, huh, Z'?" Nickie teased her. "Who you expecting at the top—Cary Grant?"

"*Ma quello e un uomo, eh*?" Z' lifted her joined fingers in an appreciative gesture. "Now, that's a man."

Laughing, Angie and Nickie ushered her into the waiting cable-car.

Tony's driver eased the white Chrysler into the church lot on Mt. Washington, parking so that they had a clear view of Pietro's and the station at the summit of Grandview Avenue. In the passenger seat was the specialist Tony had brought in for this job. Tony sat alone in the back seat, staring expressionlessly straight ahead.

Carlo and Marshall exited the station together, flanked by the DiPiano bodyguards. As they walked toward the restaurant, Tony leaned forward and pointed with his leather-gloved hand. "There's your target."

Pete had outdone himself: great antipasto platters of roasted eggplants and peppers, lemon chicken salad in radicchio leaves, green beans and porcini mushrooms, followed by straciatella soup and veal alla genovese sauteed with olive oil and sage. Z'Maria's Dago Hill cronies clucked in wonderment over the feast. "*Como le nozze all'antica*," they exclaimed. "Just like an old-time wedding."

Z'Maria retorted crustily, "With my oldest niece still a *zitella*, I guess this is the closest to a wedding I'm going to get, eh?"

"Hey, Z', I heard that," Nickie called from the other end of the table, laughing. "You better not let Angie hear you call her an old maid."

At the end of the meal, as the coffee was being served, Nickie stood up. "I was elected tonight to make the introductory remarks, but what the hell, most of you have known Maria Branzino longer than I have. If my language offends you, talk to Z'Maria, not me. I got my mouth from her." She paused. "Not to mention these crooked earlobes from when she twisted them because I was being a little *pistad*." The crowd laughed appreciatively.

After Nickie had sat down, Angie stood up. "As Nickie said, I don't think we need a lot of words to express what Z'Maria has meant to the lives of her nieces and nephews. You were all there; you saw what she did for us, what she was. When our mother, Rosa, got so sick she couldn't leave her bed, Z' pinch hit for her. She loved us, she disciplined us, she ran interference for us with Pap, God rest his soul." A murmur ran through the crowd at the mention of the cruel Branzino patriarch. "Z'Maria was a second mother to us. She was always ready with advice"—Angie smiled— "sometimes advice we didn't want to hear. After Mama died, she somehow kept our family together. Then we grew up and went our own ways. Thank God we each found some success, but always . . . always we have had her to come back to. She was our anchor, our link to the past generations. Her optimism, her liveliness and courage embraced us and gave us the will to go on. For all this and more, we thank her now. We take this opportunity to tell her in front of the whole world how very much we love and cherish her."

As she spoke, her gaze moved around the room to touch Nickie, Phil, Pete, Freddie. Tears starting in her eyes, she looked from Z'Maria to Marshall, sitting with Carlo DiPiano. Her gaze lingered longest on her son. This is what I was trying to express to you all those years when we were alone in Europe, she wanted to tell him. This is your family, too. This is what I so deeply want you to be part of.

The double doors from the kitchen banged open, and everyone craned their necks, oohing and aahing over the magnificent cake blazing with candles that Pete wheeled in. Angie lifted her wine glass and gestured for everyone else to do the same. "Please join with me in saluting this very, very special woman."

Joey, Tony's driver, blew into his hands. The night was cold, but Tony had forbidden him to turn on the engine to warm the car. He didn't want to attract any attention. Despite the chill, Tony sat as motionless as a spider in its web. He had planned this moment down to the last detail. The hit man was already in place outside. Tony was not impatient; he knew that the killer would not fail him.

The party broke up just before midnight. Through

half-closed eyes, Tony watched the departing guests gather at the station, laughing and talking as they waited for the next cable car. As he had expected, DiPiano was one of the last to leave. Carlo and Z'Maria strolled arm in arm down the street, followed by Marshall, Nickie and Angie. Tony touched the driver's shoulder. "Go ahead, Joey."

"Did you have a good time tonight?" Angie asked Marsh as they approached the station.

He shrugged. "It was okay."

Her troubled eyes sought his. "How about you—everything okay there, too?"

He didn't answer her.

Tony's car drew up to the curb, and he climbed out. Angie watched him make a big show of kissing Z'Maria on both cheeks and wishing her long life and health, before he turned to Carlo and thanked him deferentially for taking care of his son that night. Tony looked at Marshall. "Get in the car," he said curtly. "I told Carlo I'd save him the trip."

"Tony, what's this?" Z'Maria chided. "You gonna let him kiss his *zia* good night?"

As Marshall bent his head to her, Z'Maria caught his face between her hands and held him tight. "You a good boy," she told him gruffly. "We all love you."

Angie's Brownie camera flashed as she took a picture of them. Z'Maria started into the funicular with Carlo, while Marshall turned to climb into Tony's car, but Angie couldn't bear to see him go quite yet. "Wait!" she said urgently. "Please, Marshall, just a few more pictures with Z'Maria and Aunt Nickie?"

Before Tony could say anything, Carlo lightly pushed Z'Maria back toward her family. "Go ahead, take your pictures. Me and my boys, we'll go down to get the car and come pick you up. *Va bene*, Maria?"

He turned and walked into the waiting cable car.

"Can't you hurry with those goddamn pictures?" Tony said, pacing like a nervous cat as Angie gestured for Nickie and Z'Maria to draw in closer to Marshall. Behind them the funicular began its descent down the steep cable track, its chains clanking and groaning. Angie put a new bulb in the round flash unit, then lifted the viewfinder to her eye. The bulb flashed.

An instant later a thunderous explosion rent the air. They all turned, transfixed with horror as a great fireball shot skyward from the exploding cable car, sending shards of wood and metal flying around their heads.

"Christ Almighty, get down!" Tony screamed. Lunging, he knocked Marshall to the ground and threw his body over him.

Reacting simultaneously, Nickie and Angie pulled Z'Maria down and covered their heads. "Madonn'," the old woman murmured brokenly, her eyes glazed. "Carlo!"

Angie put her arms around Z's shoulders, realizing for the first time how thin and frail her aunt had become. "It's all right, Z', everything's going to be okay."

"Why?" Z' murmured in shock. "Why?"

Angie's eyes met Nickie's, reflecting back the same horror mixed with rage, the same intuitive knowing. They could all have died on that incline with Carlo. They knew, too, that there was no turning back now. Ultimately, they would have to confront Tony in the nightmarish world he had dragged them into so long before.

59

Beyond Angie's bedroom windows, moonlight bathed the landscape in a cool luminescence that was at once beautiful and piercingly lonely. Despite the solid, comforting heat of David's arm around her waist, Angie felt cold.

She closed her eyes, focusing on the more recondite warmth of her satiated loins glowing pleasurably in the aftermath of sex. Their lovemaking had deepened into a realm of need neither had experienced before. A new passion had emerged. A fragile tenderness borne from a love that had survived separation, violence and even death. The kind of love that bound two people forever.

The innocence of their idyll in Bedford Springs, before the world had come crashing down around them, seemed so far distant that it might have been another lifetime. Now she and David were like grains of sand on a wind-etched shore, the patterns constantly shifting, leaving them in a dangerous state of flux. Robbed of Paradise, they had to search for a new sense of wholeness.

Angie eased out from beneath the weight of David's arm. She slipped a robe over her nakedness and went to rekindle the fire. Yesterday's newspaper lay on the hearth. As she picked it up, the headlines screamed out at her again: MAFIA DON DIES IN SPECTACULAR MT. WASHINGTON EXPLOSION:

POWER STRUGGLE OR GANGLAND RETRIBUTION?

Her stomach twisted in a knot of fear as she focused on the word "retribution."

David stirred sleepily. "You okay?"

She nodded without turning around. "I'll be there in a minute."

She crept downstairs to her study. Switching on the desk lamp, she dialed Nickie's number.

"Nickie? Sorry to wake you, but I've been up—thinking."

"Angie?" Nickie's voice was thick with sleep. "You know what time it is?"

"Listen to me, Nickie, you've got to get out while you still can."

"Stop worrying," Nickie chided her. "I know what I'm doing. Besides, I have protection."

"Protection? Now who's being naive? You're in there alone. Whatever you and Rocco have arranged, it's not enough," she whispered. "Nickie, I'm terrified that you're going to be caught in the middle of their war."

Angie heard a thud on the other end of the phone. She imagined Nickie reaching for her cigarettes and lighting one up. "Do you want to see Marshall again?"

"You know I do, but not at your expense. I can't lose anyone else."

Angie listened to her sister's slow, thoughtful breathing. Finally Nickie said in a husky whisper, "It's the only way."

"No!"

"Do you want to see Tony destroyed or don't you?"

"Not this way."

"Angie—"

"Talk to Rocco. Tell him you want out," Angie insisted. "He's always been in love with you."

Nickie laughed softly. "Go back to bed, big sister."

"First promise me you'll talk to Rocco."

"I'll be careful. That's all I can promise," Nickie said. "Now, good night."

Angie hung up. She heard the branches of the newly budding sycamore scratching against the window as a gust of wind caught it. The sound reminded her of the way the wind had creaked through the cornstalks on the desolate Ohio farm where she had lived with Tony so long ago.

Mist rose up from the Allegheny River and wreathed the steep hillside on the far bank. Nickie paced back and forth on the dock of the Fox Chapel Yacht Club, her heels echoing hollowly against the wooden planks. You would think that after all these months, she told herself, I would be used to these clandestine meetings. But the nervousness was always there. It'll be over soon, she thought, burying her neck deeper inside the collar of her jacket. She heard a soft splash and turned.

A scull emerged out of the early morning mist. She shivered involuntarily. Then she saw the hooded oarsmen bent low as they rowed with a swift, even rhythm toward the dock. The men clambered onto the dock, barely giving her a second glance as they hurried toward the locker room—latter-day warriors off to do battle at their desks downtown.

Rocco, in no hurry, was the last guy up. His gray sweats clung to his well-defined shoulders and thighs, the thick cotton damp with perspiration despite the freezing air. As he walked toward her, she looked into his eyes and read the new grimness etched there. What a serious mistake Tony had made in underrating Rocco, in equating his easygoing, articulate charm with weakness.

"Nickie, how's tricks?"

472 • *June Triglia*

"Not bad, considering the ungodly hour," she joked softly. "We really do have to stop meeting like this."

He touched her cheek. "You know, I'm going to miss our early morning trysts."

She got serious at once. "Does that mean we're close—it's almost over?"

"The next few days are going to be critical. That's all I'm going to say." Seeing the look on her face, he added, "It's safer for you if you don't know the details."

"I think I have a right to know."

He shook his head impatiently. "All I'll tell you is that we figured out a way to reel him in nice and quietly."

She smiled. "No gunning him down in his favorite restaurant, like they do in Brooklyn?"

A hint of amusement glinted behind his eyes and then just as quickly died. "Nickie, before you leave, I want you to promise me one thing." He put his hands on her shoulders. "No matter what happens, you have to remember that whatever I do, I'm doing as much for your family as for my own."

Nickie's eyes flickered over his face.

"You promise?" he insisted.

She nodded finally, wondering what the hell she was tacitly agreeing to.

60

A drizzle had begun to fall, hastening the evening into darkness. Angie and Nickie sat curled up on opposite ends of the sofa, watching television. When the news came on, Angie jumped up and turned the volume louder. Even a week later, Carlo DiPiano's murder still dominated the local news.

Angie had finally sought refuge in Nickie's high-rise apartment after reporters had staked out her home and her office, badgering her for a statement regarding DiPiano's death. Nickie had sent RJ to stay with Freddie and his wife in the North Hills, outside the ugly glare of publicity. Now the two sisters sat holed up, like hunted foxes run to ground. Nickie's housekeeper, Arabel, a sturdy black woman with limitless patience, had taken it upon herself to buffer them from the outside world, answering the phone each time it rang and turning the more persistent news hounds away from the front door with threats to have them arrested for trespassing.

The doorbell chimed. Angie walked from the television set and glanced out into the foyer. She saw Arabel shaking her head decisively at someone outside. Suddenly the housekeeper was shoved violently aside and Tony burst into the apartment. Angie's heart leaped with fear when she saw his face contorted with rage. But he swept past as if he hadn't even seen her.

Nickie, smoking a cigarette, looked up at him expressionlessly. "What are you doing here?"

"Rocco's got my kid."

Angie looked toward Nickie in disbelieving anger. "What? What's he talking about?"

"Stay outta this," Tony barked. "It's none of your business."

"He's my son, too! I—"

"Shut up!" he roared, turning on her with volcanic fury.

"Are you sure, Tony?" Nickie said with an almost preternatural calm.

"I just got the call." He started to pace like a caged bull. Only Nickie's eyes, tracking him the way she had once tracked Pap to gauge his murderous moods, hinted at her taut nerves. "There's no way the asshole coulda known the kid's schedule. Someone had to tip him off. When I find out who it is, I'm gonna rip his tongue out." In a gust of fury he grabbed a lamp off a table and flung it against the wall.

Angie and Arabel flinched, but Nickie looked unfazed.

"Rocco won't hurt Marshall," Nickie said into the tense silence. "He's not that kind of man."

Her sister's coolness enraged Angie. "They're all alike—

all animals!" she shouted. "How could you allow this to happen? What have you done with my son?"

"Angie," Nickie said warningly.

But Tony wasn't paying attention to either of them. He had begun pacing again, his fists clenching and unclenching. "Rocco knows who's king of the mountain," he said half to himself. "The kid's just a lever to get me to sit down and talk. Rocco's scared, he's desperate."

Nickie's eyes had not left him for an instant. "So what are you going to do, Tony?"

Angie watched her take her time in stubbing out her cigarette, too wily a player to show surprise at anything. Yet maybe she hadn't been surprised at all. The ugly thought ran through Angie's head that Nickie was the one who had tipped Rocco off as to Marshall's whereabouts. She felt hatred and fury at her sister's betrayal building up inside her.

Tony stopped pacing. "What am I gonna do? I'm gonna get my kid back." All his murderous vitality was concentrated in his cruelly gleaming eyes. The eyes of a raging bull. "Then all hell's gonna break loose."

"Tony—"

"Now get up!" he said. "I've seen how Rocco looks at you—his old flame from the Hill. You're coming with me as insurance."

"Where to?" The barest tremor shook Nickie's cool voice.

His mouth stretched in an ugly smile. "Hot date at the mill."

Following Tony's white Chrysler, Angie watched it merge into the busy traffic on Route 51, then she pulled onto the highway behind it, careful to keep several cars between them.

They drove for miles in the cold drizzle. Traffic thinned as Angie followed the Chrysler down old Coalport Road, a narrow lane curving between dark woods. She dropped back farther, her headlights picking out bare-limbed trees and an occasional tar-paper shanty in a clearing.

Rounding a curve, she saw his car brake and turn into the American Steel rolling-mill plant. Turning off her headlights, she followed the Chrysler into the plant.

Set alongside a railroad siding, the mill looked like an immense, ramshackle warehouse. She watched Tony's car draw to a stop at the far end. Then she switched off her ignition and climbed out of her car. Two figures materialized out of the darkness with guns drawn. "You got no business here, lady."

Tony made Nickie get out first. She realized the crafty bastard intended to use her as a shield. He and his driver, Joey, had their pistols drawn, their backs almost touching as they covered each other toward the entrance.

Inside, the deafening cacophony hit them full force. The machinery screeched and clanked at full tilt, even though there was nothing but a skeleton crew moving around at the periphery of the mill. Glancing up, Nickie saw the foreman in the central control room—his face blank. Nickie had no doubt Rocco had paid his union cronies well to keep their mouths shut about whatever happened here tonight.

Off to their right lay a monstrous furnace. Its gaping maw swallowed ten-ton slabs of cold steel and then spat out molten, red-hot masses onto a massive conveyor. Overhead pipes ran the length of the conveyer, sending jets of cooling water onto the incandescent metal as it was flattened between a series of rollers. Despite the intense heat, Nickie shivered. Dante must have seen a vision of a Pittsburgh mill when he conceived his epic journey through hell.

Just as her ears were adjusting to the pounding punishment of the machinery, the millworks shut down, creaking and grinding into a silence broken only by the eerie drip of water. Nickie glanced around anxiously, wondering what the hell Rocco was up to.

Then they heard footsteps clanging sharply on metal. Rocco stepped out onto the catwalk above the flame-spurting furnace. Two of his men followed him, dragging a squirming Marshall with them.

Nickie saw Tony flinch when he saw his son. "You son of a bitch!" Tony bellowed, lifting his gun to take aim. But he couldn't shoot without endangering Marshall. "The kid ain't got nothing to do with this. It's between you and me."

"Drop the pistol, Tony," Rocco commanded him coolly. When Tony hesitated, he snapped, "Now!"

As soon as his pistol struck the floor, Joey swooped it up and pointed it at his boss. As Tony stared at him in disbelief, the pistol wavered in Joey's hands. Nickie could see the tears in his eyes. "I'm real sorry, Tony. They gave me no choice."

"Back away, Joey," Rocco snapped. "You too, Nickie."

In another moment Tony stood alone. Rocco gestured for his boys to bring Marshall closer to the edge of the catwalk, so that they stood directly over the furnace.

"You got me where you want me!" Tony said furiously. "What the hell more you want? Let my kid go!"

Rocco smiled, a slow, cold smile that chilled Nickie. "You a Bible-reading man, Tony?"

"Stop with your fucking games!" Tony cried, spittle gathering in the corners of his mouth.

Rocco continued to smile as if Tony hadn't spoken. "You know the verse I mean, don't you, Tony?" He leaned forward on the narrow rail, pulling Marshall down along beside him. " 'Life for life, eye for eye, tooth for tooth, hand for hand . . .' " The flames made Rocco's eyes gleam redly. " 'Burning for burning . . .' "

A shiver snaked up Nickie's spine. Enough, Rocco, she breathed. You've had your fun. Now stop!

Rocco stared down at Tony. "I may be the new generation, Tony, but I'm still a believer in the old ways. I adhere to the time-honored code—life for a life." Rocco straightened up. "You owe me, Tony. Your son for my father."

"Bastard!" Tony cried, lunging forward.

Suddenly the vast labyrinth of machinery—as if propelled by a mysterious, dark life force of its own—reawakened. Tony raced up the narrow metal stairway to the catwalk. At the top he looked around wildly. Rocco and Marshall had disappeared.

The two henchmen materialized from the shadows behind the furnace and leaped upon Tony, their shadows cast in weirdly gigantic silhouettes by the licking flames. Dazed, Nickie watched the mammoth red-hot slabs slide out of the furnace down onto the conveyer toward the

rollers—the unremitting impulse of the machinery an eerie counterpoint to the chaotic human drama being played
out above it. Marshall broke free from Rocco and rushed
out onto the floor, watching his father grapple and claw
against his attackers. Tony fought like a man possessed,
but the thugs overpowered him and with a final heave
hurled him over the rail. He landed sprawling on a molten slab. His agonized screams rose above the roar of the
machinery as his clothing burst into flames. His writhing
tortured body danced on the fiery slab like a drop of
water in a hot skillet. Sickened by the sight, Nickie tried
to pull Marshall away but the boy stood transfixed with
sheer horror as he watched his father's features contort in
pain and terror. Nickie knew that she would see both
their faces in nightmares for the rest of her life. Marshall
continued to stare, hypnotized, until the slab and its
writhing mass of burning flesh slid into oblivion between
the crushing pressures of the mammoth roller.

The clanking machinery ground down into silence.

Up on the catwalk, Rocco's boys were in high fettle,
puffed up with pride at a job well done. "Tony always
was a Chrysler man," one of them said with mock solem-
nity. "He'll make a nice hood."

"Shut up!" Rocco growled. "I don't care what kind of
scum he was. This is a man's life we're talking about."

Marshall had sunk to his knees on the grease-stained
concrete. Reaching out to comfort him, Nickie was shocked
at how badly her hands were shaking. She heard light,
quick footsteps and turned. Angie looked like an aveng-
ing angel as she rushed toward them.

"O God, no," Nickie breathed, seeing the look of
mingled terror and fury in her sister's eyes. "Angie!"

Ignoring her, Angie rushed to Marshall. She knelt
down and wrapped her arms around him. "Pigs!" she
screamed, tears streaming down her face as she looked
from Nickie to Rocco. "How could you do this?"

"You shouldn't have come here, Angie," Rocco said
quietly. "I'm truly sorry you had to witness this."

"Sorry? You're sorry!" Angie's powerful voice erupted
with contemptuous fury. "You commit murder, you ter-
rorize my son, but all you're concerned about is that I

had to see it?" Crying, she tenderly stroked Marshall's face. She gasped as she noticed his eyes had glazed over with shock. "You're filth, all of you!"

Rocco said sharply, "Get up, Angie. He's okay. My boys will take him out for air."

"I'll take care of my own."

"He's one of ours, too." Rocco gestured for his men to pick up the boy and carry him out.

Too exhausted to fight him, Angie stood and slowly turned to face Nickie. "So what do you have to say to me, little sister?" Her face was a grieving mask, ravaged by Nickie's betrayal. "That you're sorry, too?"

Nickie forced herself to meet Angie's eyes. "I didn't know! You've got to believe me. Ange, I'm so sorry."

Angie shook her head. "Sorry? You're just like them!" Her condemning gaze moved to Rocco as he walked away.

"That's right, Angie, just keep on pretending. Pretend you're so far above the shit that it couldn't possibly stick to your shoes," Nickie flung back. "You're nothing but a lousy hypocrite. You said yourself you wished you'd killed him when you had the chance. Rocco simply did what you lacked the courage to do. Tony had to be destroyed. This was the only way."

Infuriated, Angie slapped her hard across the face. "How dare you try to drag me down to your level?"

Nickie flinched from the pain. "You just dragged yourself down," she whispered, tears in her eyes as she reached up to cradle her burning cheek.

As Angie turned on her heel and started to walk away, Nickie screamed after her, "You're no different from me! You're as much Pap's child as I am! He planted the violent seeds. But we're the ones who have to reap them. We're the ones still paying for his sins. You, me, our kids, maybe their kids, too." Sobbing, Nickie sank to the floor. "You say I've become like them—like Pap and Tony and Rocco. But what goddamn choice did I ever have? What choice did any of us ever have?"

Angie stopped. The impact of Nickie's words cut through her. Angie knew that she bore an equal weight of guilt and responsibility. Slowly she turned and walked back.

"Come on, Nick," she whispered. Kneeling down beside her, she stroked her bent head. "The violence is done. It's over. Let's go home."

The next morning Angie sat anxiously beside Marsh's hospital bed. He had been admitted in a state of shock. Outwardly he seemed fine. But it was his emotional state she feared for.

He lay with his head turned away from her, staring expressionlessly at a pair of bluejays outside the patio doors. The birds squabbled noisily over the crumbs of toast that the morning-shift nurse had tossed out onto the grass.

Watching the scrappy birds peck each other, Angie realized it was all the same—life was a violent, unceasing struggle to overcome or not to be overcome. Nickie's response to the struggle had been to distrust love as a form of weakness, while Angie's response had been to love too much—to shield Marsh from the truth of who he was, of what they all were. She stared at him, trying to fathom what lay in the remote depths in his eyes. She sensed that she might lose him again. But she could no longer hold him back. Marshall belonged to himself, not to her.

When she reached out to smooth a stray hair from his forehead, he turned to look at her. "I just wanted to say . . . I understand why you thought you had to protect me from . . . from him."

Angie nodded.

Marshall looked out the window again. "I resented you for so long. When he showed up, I wanted to believe I had this wonderful father. But . . . but by the time I figured out the truth, it was too late." He bit his lip to keep it from trembling. "Still, for him to have to die the way he did . . ."

Angie stood and gently brushed her lips across his. "Sshh, *mi figlio*. Forget that. We have to put the past and all its ugliness behind us. We're going to start over again. A clean slate."

He looked up at her with those brilliant blue eyes that were so dark in their depths. "I want to go back to

Switzerland," he said quietly, as if he were already speaking from a great distance. "To finish school there."

Her heart constricted. "If that's what you want."

"I . . ." He hesitated. "I don't know if I'll want to come back."

She took his hand and managed through sheer force of will to smile. "Just remember," she murmured softly. "There will always be a place for you here. *Ti amo*, Marshallino. I love you."

Tentatively—so tentatively that Angie had to convince herself that she hadn't imagined it—he squeezed her fingers.

Encore

October 1953

Golden light poured through Angie's open bedroom windows, bathing the three women in the glow of Indian summer. Angie stood on a chair in front of the cheval mirror while Z'Maria took a last-minute stitch in the hem of her simple ivory sheath.

"What kinda wedding this, I don't know," Z'Maria groused, biting off the thread.

"Hey, Z', she's no blushing bride." Nickie looked up from the white orchids she was fastening to Angie's headpiece, which had been fashioned from a fragment of hand-tatted lace their mother had sewn for her trousseau almost a half-century earlier. "A quick 'I do' and a champagne toast is perfectly appropriate."

"Bull-a shit." The old woman straightened up and glared at her. "The 'mericans, they put stupid ideas in your head. You've forgotten the old ways—church in the morning, then the wedding breakfast, the supper, the music, the dancing . . ." Z'Maria lifted the hem of her dress and did a mincing waltz. "Those were weddings, eh?"

Nickie laughed. "I do remember, Z'. I can still see the old *gumbaris* tossing sandwiches from a bushel basket at the receptions. Remember, Ange? And I'd eat so many wedding cookies I'd make myself sick."

Angie stepped down from the chair, smiling to herself as the memories and their voices eddied around her, a soft swirling wave that was part of the day's surging joy. She touched her face where the sun caught the soft down on her cheek, like the fuzz on a baby's head. Never again would she be innocent, and yet today she was renewed, reborn, virginal in spirit.

In the mirror she caught the soft gleam of love reflected back from her eyes—body and soul on the brink of unfolding. She lifted her hand, imagining the weight of the carved band that she and David had chosen: an encircling ring of continuity. And she dreamed of a child rippling outward from the circle of their love. All her life she had been fragmented; she had struggled to hold the fragments together. Now, at last on the brink of wholeness, of union, she felt an inner serenity. The experiences she had lived through had been a baptism by fire. While a part of her had died in the flames, the deeper part had been tempered. Tenderness and vulnerability had resurfaced in her spirit, a reflection of the strength that was so quintessentially female. The smiling woman in the mirror shone back at her, illuminated less by the sunlight than by this new sense of peace radiating from within.

Little Rosa Josephine burst into the room, the dainty feminine appeal of her pink dress and ribbon-tied curls offset by the crumbs rimming her mouth. She held a big waffle cookie in each hand. "Come on!" she squeaked, jumping onto the bed beside her mother. "We're all getting tired of waiting."

Unperturbed, Nickie replied, "What'd you do with your gloves—eat them, too?"

"Mom," RJ said chidingly through a mouthful of cookie.

"You're going to make yourself sick eating all those *pizzelles*."

"I only had four."

"Piglet." Nickie dropped the headpiece in her lap and retied one of her daughter's ribbons.

Watching them in the mirror, Angie's smile deepened. The best thing Nickie could have done was move away from Pittsburgh, from all that was ugly in her past. She had gotten a position with an Italian merchant bank in New York and seemed content. The new job, the new life had meant a fresh start for both her and her daughter. RJ seemed to thrive on it all—music and ballet lessons, business trips to Rome with Nickie. The lively, beautiful six year old was a born cosmopolitan.

Angie watched RJ wriggle off the bed and wander over to the dressing table, where she amused herself opening and experimentally dabbing at the contents of the crystal jars. Then Angie's eyes moved up to the mirror above the table, where she had tucked Marshall's letters. She missed him terribly. Yet through her pain she felt linked again to her own mother. For the first time she truly understood what Rosa must have felt—that terrible sorrow mixed with joy—in sending her firstborn from her.

"Rosa Giuseppina!" Z'Maria barked at her little grandniece. "You gonna smell like a bordello."

"What's that, Z'?"

"Never you mind!" The old woman took her firmly by the hnd. "*Veni, bambina.*"

As they left, Nickie came over to Angie with the headpiece. "This is the best I can do."

"Looks perfect to me. You're a pretty mean seamstress."

"Shh, that's our little secret," Nickie joked. "If it ever got out, my reputation as a ruthless banking tycoon would be shot to hell." She finished pinning the flower-wreathed lace cap onto Angie's hair and stepped back. "That should do it. Are you ready?"

"Mm. But I'd like a minute to myself, if you don't mind."

Nickie nodded, then briefly touched her sister's cheek. "You're beautiful." A yearning wistfulness breathed through her husky voice. "I hope David realizes what a lucky man he is."

Smiling, Angie called out to her sister as she walked

toward the door, "It's a wonderful feeling, marrying for love. You really ought to try it."

Nickie turned and shot her a crooked grin. "Who, me?"

Alone again, Angie went to the dressing table and opened the small jewel case that held the antique sapphire earrings David had given her as a wedding present. Angie put them on, holding her hair back to admire the exquisitely hued stones that were the "something blue" of her wedding outfit. The "something old" was Mama's lace, the "something new" her gown. All that she lacked was "something borrowed." She should have borrowed one of the ribbons from RJ's hair, she thought with a smile. The child would have been delighted to oblige.

A light knock sounded on the bedroom door. Angie, still looking into the mirror, watched it open. Her heart leaped with mingled shock and joy as Marshall peeked inside. "Z'Maria told me to come up. Hope it's okay."

She nodded, not trusting herself to speak as she drank in her fill of him. He had grown taller in the past nine months. He looked lean and fit, somehow more self-possessed, though he still had that wary aura, like a wild animal that had only been half tamed.

She stood watching him in the mirror, almost afraid that if she turned around to face him he might disappear. "Come in."

He brushed his hair back selfconsciously. "I'm glad you're finally marrying David."

"I'm glad you're here," she said, her voice tight with emotion. "I couldn't have asked for a more perfect wedding gift."

A hint of a smile touched his face. "Actually, I did bring you a gift. It's . . . it's something someone gave me once. I guess you could call it sort of magical." Intrigued and charmed, Angie watched as he lifted the fragile chain and cross from around his neck.

He came toward her and slipped it over her head. With trembling fingers, she clasped the tiny gold cross with its four arms blossoming in graceful trefoils. The familiar precious emblem had gone from her to him and now from him back to her, love flowing uninterruptedly in both directions. Beautiful, precious magic indeed.

Angie met his eyes in the mirror, and she smiled.

He kissed her cheek. "I want to walk you down, Mammina. Would that be okay?"

Her heart filled to bursting, Angie turned and linked her arm through his.

The bride appeared at the top of the wide staircase on her son's arm, and the musicians in the foyer burst into Veracini's "Sonata in E Minor." Buoyed along by the wonderfully shifting modulations of the Italian Baroque composition, Angie and Marshall entered the light-filled drawing room, where the handful of guests clustered around David and the minister, Dr. Cowan.

Angie smiled radiantly as her eyes met David's. Then her gaze swept around to encompass her brothers and their wives, to Katie and RJ standing hand in hand, to Z'Maria nodding her head with a wise knowingness.

Angie and Marshall came forward to join their waiting family.

"We have gathered here to celebrate the union of David O'Rourke and Angelina Branzino Fredricks in holy wedlock," the minister began. "The blossoming of love into the solemn sacrament of matrimony is a reflection of the radiance engendered by the divine spirit. While love is ultimately the domain of God, we his creatures have sought down through the centuries to capture and express its essence. None perhaps have done so more beautifully and compellingly than the poets."

Saying this, Dr. Cowan nodded to David, whose deep, warm voice stirred with emotion as he recited the simple yet powerful poetry of Robert Herrick. "Thou art my life, my love, my heart, the very eyes of me: And hast command of every part, to live and die for thee."

Brimming with joy as she basked in the adoration from her beloved's eyes, Angie took the small volume of John Donne which Dr. Cowan handed her. But she had no need to refer to the lovely words, which she had committed to memory. Softly she recited, "All other things to their destruction draw, only our love hath no decay; this, no tomorrow hath, nor yesterday."

Angie's heart lifted. This man whom she cherished,

this family that had nurtured her, this day that had brought blessings too great to number were intertwining harmonies—intricate and inseparable parts of the perfect melody singing through her veins. Bound by blood, Angie was home at last.

About the Author

June Triglia is the pen name for June Triglia Casey and Joan Triglia, cousins who grew up in the midst of a large, close-knit Italian-American family in Pittsburgh.

Joan, an avid reader and theater buff, has taught junior high school for 17 years in Pittsburgh's North Hills. American history is her area of expertise. June, a former journalist, travels extensively with her husband Douglas. They have lived in Mexico, Spain, and Italy, and now make southern California their home.